Praise for CAROLYN HART

and her spectral-tacular new mystery series featuring the incomparable

BAILEY RUTH RAEBURN

"Nobody does it better than Hart, whose plotting skills rival those of Britain's Agatha Christie."
Cleveland Plain Dealer

"Bailey Ruth is a lively, original heroine and a pleasure to read."
The Oklahoman (Oklahoma City)

"Delightful. . . . Bailey Ruth's pleasure in her earthly wardrobe, her keen observations of the other characters, and her unorthodox but expert sleuthing will engage readers from start to finish."
Publishers Weekly

"It doesn't matter what a reader believes about an afterlife. Religious persuasion is irrelevant to the enjoyment of what is becoming one of the most heartwarming and charming of mystery series. . . . Hart's writing is as bright and cheerful as Bailey Ruth's red hair."
Deseret Morning News (Salt Lake City)

"Heavenly emissaries have certain rules they must follow when on earth, and Bailey Ruth continually and amusingly breaks them all."
Tulsa World

"If I were teaching a course on how to write a mystery, I'd make Carolyn Hart required reading."
Los Angeles Times

By Carolyn Hart

Death on Demand

DEATH ON DEMAND • DESIGN FOR MURDER
SOMETHING WICKED • HONEYMOON WITH MURDER
A LITTLE CLASS ON MURDER • DEADLY VALENTINE
THE CHRISTIE CAPER • SOUTHERN GHOST
MINT JULEP MURDER • YANKEE DOODLE DEAD
WHITE ELEPHANT DEAD • SUGARPLUM DEAD
APRIL FOOL DEAD • ENGAGED TO DIE
MURDER WALKS THE PLANK
DEATH OF THE PARTY • DEAD DAYS OF SUMMER
DEATH WALKED IN • DARE TO DIE
LAUGHED 'TIL HE DIED

Henrie O

DEAD MAN'S ISLAND • SCANDAL IN FAIR HAVEN
DEATH IN LOVER'S LANE • DEATH IN PARADISE
DEATH ON THE RIVER WALK • RESORT TO MURDER
SET SAIL FOR MURDER

Bailey Ruth

GHOST AT WORK
MERRY, MERRY GHOST
GHOST IN TROUBLE

merry, merry GHOST

A BAILEY RUTH MYSTERY

CAROLYN HART

AVON

An Imprint of HarperCollins*Publishers*

This book is a work of fiction. The characters, incidents, and dialogue are drawn from the author's imagination and are not to be construed as real. Any resemblance to actual events or persons, living or dead, is entirely coincidental.

AVON BOOKS
An Imprint of HarperCollins*Publishers*
10 East 53rd Street
New York, New York 10022-5299

ISBN 978-0-06-196292-9
www.avonmystery.com

First Avon Books paperback printing: November 2010
First William Morrow hardcover printing: November 2009

Printed in the U.S.A.

10 9 8 7 6 5 4 3 2 1

To Dan Mayer, who knows and loves mysteries.
This one's for you.

merry, merry GHOST

CHAPTER 1

"*Bailey Ruth, honey, always wait to be invited.*"

I edged a little nearer an arch of clouds suffused with gold and rose. Once around that cumulus corner, I knew what awaited, softly rolling hills, a redbrick train station, and shining silver rails stretching to the horizon.

I wanted to break into a run, yet I couldn't quite dismiss the memory of my mother's caution when I was a child. Certainly, I didn't want to impose myself upon anyone even though in Heaven I'd always found welcome everywhere.

Heaven?

Do I detect skepticism?

That's fine. Avert your eyes from beauty. Ignore love. Yawn at the splendor of the universe. Insist that the world is nothing more than rollicking atoms. Someday you'll see.

I always knew there was a Heaven, even before Bobby Mac and I met our demise when our cabin cruiser went down in the Gulf of Mexico as Bobby Mac pursued a tarpon on a fatefully stormy day. There's nothing like going out with a big splash. I recalled with pleasure the Adelaide, Oklahoma, *Gazette* and the front-page story with a picture:

OIL WILDCATTER, MAYOR'S SECRETARY PERISH IN GULF STORM

Robert MacNeill (Bobby Mac) Raeburn II, 54, and his wife Bailey Ruth Raeburn, 52, of Adelaide were presumed lost at sea following a storm in the Gulf of Mexico. Their capsized cabin cruiser *Serendipity* was discovered yesterday off the coast of Texas. Despite a massive sea-air search, no trace has been found of the Adelaide natives and well-known civic leaders.

Raeburn was a successful oilman . . .

The photograph on the *Serendipity* had been taken in sunshine, unlike the lowering black clouds and driving rain we faced that final day. It was an especially fine picture of Bobby Mac with his dark hair, dark eyes, and a daredevil smile. He held a rod bent against the pull of a tarpon. I lounged against a railing, red hair tangled by the breeze, smiling freckled face lifted to the sun. I remembered that lime green blouse. The color was a nice contrast to crisp white shorts.

On impulse (I'm afraid I often succumb to impulse), I envisioned myself in an identical blouse and shiny white cotton shorts and espadrilles. I paused and took a peek at my reflection in a sheet of crystal. Of course, I abjured vanity in Heaven. I was simply enjoying a memory. There I was, a youthful and lively ethereal me with red curls bright as flame, narrow eager face spattered with freckles, and curious green eyes. I smoothed my hair, beamed at the reflection. In Heaven, no matter our age at death, we are seen at our best, whenever that was. I'd enjoyed all my days, but twenty-seven had been a very good year. Occasionally I was reflective—not, I will admit, a usual state for me—and then I might appear a confident forty, but twenty-seven was my age of choice.

The *Gazette* story told all about Bobby Mac and me and our families, and son Rob and daughter Dil and their children and spouses. I was described as "the vivacious redheaded secretary who added a lively element to the mayor's office and was known for her frankness."

Frankness.

I sighed, came to a full stop. Frankness was a nice way of saying I often spoke without thinking. That's why I was uncertain of my welcome around the cumulus corner that was now close enough to touch. I reached out, stroked the soft wall of cloud, filmy as springtime fluff from a cottonwood tree. We had lots of cottonwoods in Adelaide.

Frankness.

Okay. I'm forthright. Quick to act. Some might say hasty.

All right. All right. I spoke aloud in admission.

I wanted to go around that corner.

All right, around that corner I would go. All Wiggins could say was no.

My heart would be broken.

Before I could change my mind, I strode around the cottony column touched by streaks of pink and gold and there was the adorable old-fashioned country train station, silver tracks stretching into the blue sky. *Department of Good Intentions* was emblazoned on a golden arch. Wiggins, who ran the department, had been a station agent when on earth. Since a well-run station was his sense of Heaven, here he was, in charge again, sending out emissaries to help those in trouble. On earth I'd often felt I was the beneficiary of celestial grace. Giving back is one of earth's—and Heaven's—greatest pleasures.

This wasn't my first visit to the department. I'd been eager to return to earth to help someone in a tough spot, and truly I'd done the best I could on a previous mission. All emissaries are issued a parchment roll inscribed with the Precepts for Heavenly Visitation. I'll admit I'd run afoul of Wiggins's rules a few times.

To be accurate, I had transgressed a great many times.

I drooped. If Wiggins listed my infractions, they'd run a page or more.

Yet when I had made my final report, Wiggins had clearly said I might be used again as a Heavenly agent, though, he'd hastened to add, I would still be on probation. Had Wiggins decided I was too unsuitable? Was even probationary status not possible for me? Was that why I'd had no summons from him for another adven-mission?

Possibly he'd simply neglected to consider me for a task. Mama told us kids not to invite ourselves, but I remembered quite a few instances when being bold paid off. The squeaky wheel and all that.

In the distance, I heard the clack of wheels on the rails and the poignant wail of the train whistle. The Rescue Express was nearing the station. Clearly Wiggins would soon be dispatching earthbound travelers or welcoming home those whose journeys were done.

I was shot through with a hot flash of sheer envy.

Oh dear. How small-spirited of me. Certainly I was delighted that others had found favor in Wiggins's eyes and been dispatched for adventure . . . Scratch that thought. Adventure was never the goal of a well-behaved emissary. Certainly I wasn't seeking fun and thrills.

Well, maybe a little bit.

Okay, okay, I loved excitement, and whether Wiggins wanted to admit it or not, being dispatched to earth to help someone in dire need was a grand adventure.

If Wiggins was aware of my unworthy feelings, surely he understood I was only revealing the depths of my desire to be helpful.

I filled my mind with a vision of the parchment roll and the Precepts and mounted the station steps two at a time. It was only as I was passing into the station that I realized I was still in a blouse and shorts. Fortunately, a new wardrobe occurs in an instant of thought.

By the time Wiggins looked up from his desk, I was in a drab black jacket dress with white trim on the jacket, and plain black leather shoes. My hair was subdued in a chignon with only a few unruly red curls. I affected a reserved expression.

Wiggins rose at once, a look of surprise on his florid round face. He was just as I remembered, stiff black cap riding high on reddish-brown hair, bristly eyebrows, spaniel-sweet brown eyes, thick muttonchop sideburns, walrus mustache, crisp white shirt, suspenders, gray flannel trousers, and shiny bootblacked shoes.

"Bailey Ruth." Big hands enveloped mine in a warm grip. Suddenly he frowned. "You look different."

Was he remembering the lavender velour pantsuit I'd enjoyed on my previous earthly adven-mission? If I were fortunate enough to serve on earth again, I could find out about the latest fashions and enjoy them. I was confident that pleasure in beauty, whether of nature or couture, was God-given. At this moment, I was determined to appear studious and contemplative, a role model of an emissary, the sort who popped to earth, worked unobtrusively, and left without notice.

Unlike my previous experience in Adelaide.

I gave a cool smile. "It's the new me. I've been studying Zen."

"Oh?" He blinked in surprise.

"The better to serve as an emissary." I remembered not to even hint at the word *ghost.* Wiggins loathes the term. Although as far as I'm concerned, calling a spade a digging implement doesn't make it not a spade. If you know what I mean.

"Zen." He raised a brushy eyebrow.

"Zen." I tried to sound authoritative.

"Zen?" His tone invited elucidation.

"Zen. Meditating on paradoxes." I dredged that from a long-ago memory of my son Rob's Zen phase when he was in college.

"Indeed." His smile was kind. "Does that assist you in remaining in the moment?"

He might as well have been speaking Greek. If he had been speaking Greek, I would have understood. In Heaven we all understand each other whether we speak Cherokee, Yiddish, or Mandarin. Or Greek.

Zen in any tongue was beyond my grasp. It was manifestly unfair that Wiggins, who'd departed the earth long before I, had obviously been attending Zen classes in Heaven.

"I don't know a thing about Zen." In admitting defeat, I hoped to demonstrate my core honesty.

His smile was huge. "Oh, Bailey Ruth, you always manage to surprise me."

I blinked back a tear. "That's the problem, isn't it? I don't do things by the book." I meant "by the parchment roll," but he understood. "Is that why you haven't summoned me for a new adven-mission?"

Wiggins tugged at his mustache, then gestured to a bench beside his desk. He settled into his chair, and after a quick glance through the bay window at the tracks he faced me, his genial face perplexed. "You have been in my thoughts."

Was this good? I was determined to believe so. I beamed

at him. "I'm glad. Perhaps my coming here today was meant to be." I leaned forward. "Clearly there's a problem on earth that I can solve." That put the ball in his court. Hopefully my can-do attitude was attractive.

Instead of an answering smile, he looked thoughtful. "You do have a special qualification."

Better and better. "Whatever the project requires, I am ready."

"Undoubtedly you have a qualification." His tone was reluctant, as if an admission wrung under duress. "However, you lack the calm and reserve of a Heavenly emissary. You are"—he ticked off the offenses one by one—"inquisitive, impulsive, rash—"

I completed the litany. "—forthright and daring."

We looked at each other, I with fading hope, Wiggins sorrowfully.

I was tempted to change back into a blouse and shorts and waft to Bobby Mac and the *Serendipity,* riding in crystal clear blue waters for another eternal day. Yet Wiggins had thought of me for a mission. There had to be a reason. "My special qualification?"

His florid face relaxed into warmth and delight. "Bailey Ruth, you always loved Christmas."

Christmas . . . Oh dear Heaven, Christmas was the most special season of the year. Cold and gray outside? When I listened to the jingle of the Salvation Army kettle, I felt warm as toast. Jammed among sharp-elbowed shoppers in a suffocatingly hot store? That cashmere sweater was perfect for Aunt Mamie. A broken oven and twenty-three expected for Christmas dinner? Bobby Mac pulled out the grill, bundled up against a forty-degree north wind, and that day's rib eye steaks were ever after celebrated in family history.

My eyes sparkled as I recalled some of my favorite things:

Sugar cookies shaped like stars and iced in red.

Main Street ablaze with green and red lights and plenty of tinsel.

Strings of holly.

Carolers on a crisp starlit night.

Cutting down our very own Scotch pine out in the country.

Bobby Mac holding Rob in one arm, Dil in the other, and small hands reaching up to place a wobbly star atop the tree.

Presents wrapped in bright red and gold foil.

Crimson poinsettias massed behind the altar and on the ledges by the stained-glass windows and in the narthex.

The exquisite peace and hope of Mother and Child in the manger.

I was swept by that wonderful feeling of the season when workaday cares recede and we glimpse a world bright with love. "Ooh, Christmas." Every Christmas Eve, Bobby Mac (a robust tenor) and I (an energetic soprano) entertained Rob and Dil with our duet of "Rudolph the Red-Nosed Reindeer" as we pulled a sled laden with gifts into the living room. A two-foot-tall stuffed reindeer with a shiny red nose was harnessed to the sled.

I came to my feet, quickly attired in my best Mrs. Claus suit and floppy red Santa hat, and belted out my most spirited version of "Rudolph." Tap was popular when I was young, and the wooden floor of the station a perfect venue . . . four slap ball changes, four shuffle hop steps, a shuffle off to Buffalo . . . Sweeping off my Santa hat, I ended with a flap cramp roll and a graceful bow.

Flushed with success, I lifted my gaze to Wiggins.

He sat, brown eyes wide, expression bemused.

Had the man never seen a hoofer before? Had I blown any chance for adven—to be of service? Had my impetuous nature once again landed me in trouble?

His lips curved in a broad smile. His eyes shone. "That takes me back. Indeed it does. I saw Bojangles in Chicago in 1909. I never miss any of his shows."

I made a mental note to check the jazz schedule for Bill Robinson's next starlit performance. You haven't lived until you've seen a show with the Milky Way as spots.

"Only you, Bailey Ruth, would remember Christmas with a tap dance." Wiggins's tone was admiring.

I think.

Abruptly, he gave a decided nod. "That's why your dossier kept reappearing." He reached out, pulled a candy-cane-striped folder close to him, flipped it open.

I craned to see. There was my picture, a sea breeze stirring my flaming hair as the *Serendipity* breasted swells.

Wiggins patted the top sheet. "You have the true spirit of Christmas and that is what I need here, despite your impetuous nature." He turned and thumbed through a stack of folders in various colors. He opened a black one.

I didn't dwell on his qualifying phrase. Christmas spirit I could supply in plenty.

His face was grave when he faced me. "This situation"—he tapped the folder—"is murky. Your previous task was clear-cut: a lovely damsel visited with a body on her back porch. Of course, I didn't expect the action you took . . ." Some of his enthusiasm seemed to drain away. He gave a quick shake of his head. "I don't know if the department should take a chance again. But"—hope lifted his voice—"possibly in this instance nothing will be required of you except calm overseeing." He nodded decisively and repeated with vigor, "Calm overseeing," as if I might have trouble hearing.

I decided not to be offended.

"On balance, you might be perfect for this visit. You love

Christmas and you have a youthful heart. I was especially touched that you spun stories for Dil and Rob about Santa's workshop and who might need a particular toy. You helped them feel the spirit of giving. Whatever happens, you can beam love on a dear little boy, an orphan whose future is uncertain." Wiggins's tone fell to a puzzled mutter. "Surely Keith's protector has the best of intentions. She is kind and caring." He pulled a map close, marked a path in red, muttered, "Adelaide obviously is her goal. However, no contact has been made at the house."

"The house?" I figuratively rolled up my sleeves. This time around Wiggins could give me the background, prepare me for my task. I pushed away the uneasy sense that no matter how prepared I might have been on my previous mission, I would have been tempted to flout the Precepts if I felt the need. This time, however, I would be on my best behavior.

For starters, I would avoid appearing. The rich swirl of colors that preceded my transformation from spirit to earthbound creature had an unfortunate effect on viewers.

I would remember that carrying discrete objects while not in the flesh was equally unnerving to them.

I would be particularly careful not to speak aloud when I wasn't there.

I wasn't concerned about the Precept prohibiting consorting with another departed spirit. Whatever my mission, it couldn't possibly involve a departed spirit. It would be easy to observe this stricture.

However, I felt a qualm. Other of the Precepts could easily pose a challenge. The life of a spirit is fraught with opportunities to transgress—however unintentionally—the Precepts.

I came back to the moment—perhaps I did have a

penchant for Zen—to realize that Wiggins had been discoursing.

"... though the decorations are up, and I will admit they are spectacular, the heart of Christmas left Pritchard House when Susan Flynn received word of her son's death. So much sadness."

"Pritchard House?" I pictured a grand home high on Chickasaw Ridge. Only one house in Adelaide was redbrick with two huge bay windows on the first floor, half timbered and stuccoed and balconied in English Tudor with Gothic accents on the second story.

Wiggins tapped my folder. "I assume you know the Pritchards."

"Everyone in Adelaide knows the Pritchards." Growing up in Adelaide, I could count on these verities: My family loved me, the sun rose in the east, St. Mildred's Episcopal Church was our spiritual home, the wind blew mostly from the south, and two families served as Adelaide's small-town aristocracy, the Pritchards and the Humes.

Paul Pritchard, cool-eyed and remote, came west from Boston in 1912 to establish Adelaide's first bank. The Pritchards were formal, reserved, elegant, and supportive of the community, often hosting charity teas in their Chickasaw Ridge home. The Humes—ah well—the Humes were another story altogether, boisterous, sensation seeking, sometimes scandalous. Their drink of choice had a bit more punch than tea.

"The Pritchards did everything perfectly."

Wiggins slowly shook his head. "Dear Bailey Ruth, don't be blinded by worldly success and social position."

I flicked the fluffy ball on the tail of my Santa hat over my shoulder. Woe be to me if Wiggins decided I was naïve. I added hastily, "In their support of St. Mildred's."

Paul and his wife Jane had been founding members of St. Mildred's, and subsequent generations continued generous financial support to the church. "Hannah and Maurice Pritchard furnished the money for the chapel and cloister." I'd been in awe of Hannah on earth, but here in Heaven she was in one of my book clubs and I thoroughly enjoyed her gentle wit.

Wiggins's smile was avuncular. "How appropriate that your first thought would be of St. Mildred's. I commend you."

My face flamed. That is a redhead's hazard, scarlet cheeks when attempting a fib.

Fortunately Wiggins was looking at his folders. Again he appeared uneasy. "It's worrisome that I am not certain of Keith's arrival at Pritchard House. Yet I see no other purpose for the trip. The car appears to be en route to Adelaide. In any event, time is fleeting for Susan."

I blinked in surprise.

Wiggins is perceptive. "In the natural order, we know when to expect new arrivals. Susan suffers from congestive heart failure but she isn't due here until June 15. Yet"—his brow furrowed—"I am definitely worried. Call it a hunch." His tone suggested the word was not one he commonly used. Possibly *hunch* wasn't au courant until much after Wiggins's time on earth. Could he have picked it up from an emissary? Indeed, he looked embarrassed at his suggestion and said defensively, "I've been doing this over the course of many years as understood in earthly time—"

Time does not exist in Heaven, but I am no more able to explain this verity than to expound on Zen.

"—and sometimes I have a feeling of impending danger, almost as if a darkening cloud is blotting out the sun. That's why I think—"

A frantic *clack clack clack,* sharp as Rudolph's hooves

on a Mission-style roof, erupted from the telegraph sounder on Wiggins's desk.

Wiggins quickly removed his stiff cap, clamped on a green eyeshade, and grabbed a sheet. He wrote furiously, murmuring, "Oh dear, what can this mean? Steps must be taken!"

The clacking reached a peak, abruptly subsided.

Wiggins tapped a response and came to his feet, all in one hurried motion. He gestured to me as he grabbed a bright red ticket from a slotted rack. "No time to stamp. Red signals emergency. The conductor will understand. I'll pull down the signal arm for an unscheduled stop of the Rescue Express. Run, Bailey Ruth."

In an instant, I was racing toward the platform, ticket in hand, Wiggins pounding behind me. What a grand turn of events. I tried to hide my excitement. Wiggins would frown upon overt delight in being dispatched to earth. That might underscore his concern that I had, in my previous advenmission, found it difficult to remember that emissaries are *on* the earth but not *of* the earth. This Precept evoked an emotional response from Wiggins, who deplored the possibility of an emissary reverting to earthly attitudes instead of exhibiting Heavenly virtues. This time would be different. I would most nobly remember at all times that I was *on* but not *of*. I would make Wiggins proud.

Despite my effort to remain suitably grave—hard to do when running full tilt—I felt my lips curving in delight. I, Bailey Ruth Raeburn, was once again ticketed for the Rescue Express. Watch my dust!

As the train screeched to a stop and a porter reached out to pull me aboard, Wiggins looked unhappily at the folder he clutched. ". . . no time for you to study the reports . . . find out everything about those who surround Susan Flynn . . . won't do for you to take the folder . . . existing matter would be a burden since of course this time you will not appear. I'm sure you won't."

I thought his tone rather pitiful.

". . . shocking turn of events . . . I should have sent you sooner . . . such an unexpected act . . . protect that dear little boy . . ."

CHAPTER 2

Stars glowed against the vastness of space, witness to the majesty of the universe. A streak of red and a fading whistle signaled the departure of the Rescue Express. Close at hand, darkness pooled from huge evergreens. Icy wind chilled me to the bone. Had I had bones. I imagined a white turtleneck sweater, charcoal slacks, knee-high black boots, and a chinchilla coat and cap. I immediately felt warmer as well as stylish. A woman wants to look her best when embarking on a new adven-mission.

As I zoomed around an evergreen, I gasped aloud, "Mercy me." A cascading stream of emerald lights represented a waterfall. White lights outlined reindeer with front hooves lifted in a perpetual trot. Blue lights gleamed on a huge silver Christmas gift box with an iridescent red, blue, and green ribbon. A spotlight on the roof illuminated Santa's sleigh, piled high with big boxes wrapped in gold and red and green foil paper. Second-floor balconies were peppermint bright with red-and-white-striped ribbons wrapped around the railings. Near the front porch, a golden light illuminated a crèche with life-size wooden figures and real straw.

Long ago when Bobby Mac and I drove around Adelaide to show Rob and Dil the Christmas lights, strings of red bulbs outlined the roof and eaves of Pritchard House. We had thought the crimson bulbs glorious. But this magnificent display was beyond my experience. Faint strains rose in the frosty air. I suppose the music was somehow beamed from the house. I smiled and hummed along to "Have Yourself a Merry Little Christmas."

I wished suddenly that I could be with Rob and Dil, but Wiggins was very firm about the Precept prohibiting contact with family members. As he explained it, the living must not be preoccupied with the dead, but I wished them the merriest of Christmases from Mom and Dad. Dear Rob and Dil, it wouldn't do any harm for me simply to glimpse them for a moment on this crisp night in December.

In an instant, I hovered over a pickup truck with the lights on and the tailgate down. Light glowed from the front porch of a comfortable old house. A sailboat trimmed with blue lights was on the front lawn.

I knew them at once. Carrying an awkwardly shaped bundle wrapped in a quilt, Rob was burly in a ski jacket but hatless. That boy never would cover his head. The sharp breeze stirred his thinning red hair now frosted with silver. Dil, always stylish, watched from a top step, clutching the lapels of her black-and-red plaid jacket.

"Don't bump him, Rob. The right front leg's pretty wobbly."

Rob rested the bundle on its side in the bed of the pickup. "I'll be careful. What would Christmas be without Rudolph? I'll get him back to you in time for you to open gifts with your crew."

He secured the quilt, banged the tailgate shut, turned toward the house. "Remember how exciting it was when Mom and Dad pulled in the sleigh on Christmas Eve?"

Dil's silvery laughter rang out. "Dad was so loud. He always boomed. Oh Rob, they seem so near tonight."

I blew them each a kiss and carried the warmth of seeing them with me when I returned to Pritchard House.

The decorated house and yard crowned a ridge. Rose shrubs divided steep steps that led up to a lawn and flagstone walk. Hannah Pritchard had been famed for her Archduke Charles shrubs. In summer, there were fragrant crimson blooms with pink centers which darkened to full crimson. Now the shrub was garlanded with pink, yellow, cherry, and orange bulbs in a triple strand.

I looked past the gleaming lights at the house. Wiggins had dispatched me because he was worried about a little boy, but so far my arrival had been nothing but sheer Christmas pleasure, air with a hint of the Canadian north, amazing lights that beckoned the spirit to smile, music more warming than my chinchilla coat, the crèche with its promise of goodness evermore. Yet I felt uneasy. I had to find Keith. Was he inside the house?

Headlights from a passing car swept across the unlighted front porch. A woman bundled in a heavy jacket knelt beside a child.

At once I was beside them. I bent toward the little boy.

The woman's whisper was low and hurried. "I'm going to ring the bell, Keith. When the door opens, hand this"—paper crackled—"to whoever comes. I can't be with you."

"Mütter?" His voice was uncertain, wavering.

The woman drew her breath in sharply. "Mütter can't be here. She's thinking about you, Keith. Remember that. Every day she is thinking about you. She loves you and wants you to be safe. Remember how she told you about your daddy, how brave he was. You're his boy. You'll be fine. Here, stand right in front of the door." The woman lifted him up, placed the boy close to the screen. "I'll ring the bell and then I have to move the car."

She reached out, pressed the buzzer. From within came a faint peal. She pressed and the bell pealed again and again. For good measure, she lifted her arm and pounded. With a last look, sad yet hopeful, at Keith, she turned and hurried from the porch, running across the flagstones to the stairway. Flying steps clattered and she was lost in the shadows of the drive.

I almost swooped after her. Yet I couldn't leave a little boy by himself, waiting for the door to open. What if no one came? He was so small and so alone.

A car motor sounded, an engine roared. Tires squealed as a car jackrabbited away.

I jerked toward the street in time to see taillights disappear. I'd lost all chance of finding the car and talking to the woman.

Wall sconces on either side of the door blazed, emphasizing the darkness beyond the Christmas display on the lawn.

Keith blinked in the sudden harsh light. He was perhaps four, no more than five, a sturdy little boy with tow hair and a narrow face and eyes dark as ebony. He took a step back, bewildered and frightened. A dingy plaid suitcase was propped against the wrought-iron railing.

I wanted to scoop him up, hold him in my arms. I called softly, "Keith, I'm here, honey. I'll be with you."

He looked up. His eyes widened. He gave a tentative smile.

I wasn't here and yet he saw me. Children behold what adults rarely see. I smiled and bent to kiss the top of his head and was taken back a lifetime at the sweet scent of a little boy's fresh hair. "Don't worry. We'll take your envelope inside where it's warm. I'll bet maybe we can get you some cookies." What well-run home didn't have Christmas cookies spattered with red and green sparkles? I ended in a whisper as the door opened.

Bubbly. The young woman at the door was as bright and fresh as just-poured champagne. Curly brown hair, wide hazel eyes in a rounded kind face, lips that were made for laughter. The pleasant look on her face was replaced by puzzlement as she looked out. Her gaze was straight. She didn't see the small stiff figure standing near the screen. "Hello?" Her voice was pleasant.

Keith stood silent and afraid, still as a bent tree in a wintry landscape.

I moved past him and tapped the screen.

She looked down. "Hello there!" Astonishment lifted her voice. She looked around, seeking an adult. "Are you lost, honey?" Quickly, she opened the screen door and stepped outside. She scanned the paved terrace, seeking life and movement, someone to care for a small boy. "Hello?" she called out into the night.

An owl hooted. A car drove past. Her call seemed to hang in the frosty night.

Beyond the pool of light from the porch and the diffused colors of the Christmas lights, the shadows were deep and dark.

She looked down at Keith, her expressive face troubled. Steps sounded behind her.

"What are you doing out there, Peg? Come in and close the door. That air's cold as a freezer." A slim young woman in a creamy shaker-stitch silk sweater and black-and-white silk skirt reached the door and stopped in surprise. "Who's the kid? What's going on?"

Keith tried to pull back. I kept a firm grip and whispered, "It will be all right." I was banking on Peg.

"I don't know. Let's find out." Peg knelt in front of Keith. "Hi. I'm Peg. Is someone with you?" Her voice was soft and kind.

"Lou." His little boy voice was scarcely audible.

Peg looked relieved. "Who is Lou?"

"Mütter's friend." He watched Peg with uncertain eyes.

The screen door opened and the slender young woman stepped outside. Impatiently, she brushed back a strand of straight dark hair. Silver bracelets jangled on her arm. She stared out at the Christmas lights and the dark shadows, empty of movement. "Do you suppose somebody's dumped this kid here? Or maybe someone has car trouble and sent him up to the house. Anyway, we'd better call the police."

Keith pressed against me, and I squeezed his shoulder.

"Wait a minute, Gina." Peg turned back to Keith. "Where do you live?"

He responded to the kindness in her voice. "Mütter said we didn't have anywhere to live after Daddy died. Lou let us stay with them. But when Mütter didn't come home, Lou said she had to bring me where I had family. She said I didn't have anywhere else to go and she couldn't keep me."

"Lou left you here? By yourself?" Peg's voice rose in dismay.

"I don't know." His high voice wobbled.

Gina gestured toward the open door. "There's no point in standing out here and freezing to death. Bring him inside and let's call the police."

I bent close and whispered, "Give Peg the envelope."

He thrust out his arm, the manila envelope clutched in a red mitten. His tan corduroy jacket was too small and rode high on his wrist. He shivered from cold. The jacket was worn and thin. He should have a nice wool coat.

Peg took the envelope. She glanced at dark printing on

the outside and drew in a sharp breath. "Oh dear heaven." Her voice shook. She looked up at Gina. "This says he's Mitch's son."

Gina looked as if the ground had rocked beneath her feet. She whirled, stared at Keith. "Mitch's son?"

Keith stood straight. "My daddy was Sergeant First Class Mitchell Pritchard Flynn. My daddy was a hero." His little boy voice was thin and high.

I doubt Keith had any inkling of what "hero" meant. He was repeating what he'd been told.

"Daddy saved his men. Daddy was hurt but he kept on going. Mütter said he was a hero and that's why he couldn't come home to us."

"Oh dear God." Peg reached out and gently touched Keith's face.

Gina yanked the envelope from Peg and read aloud the inscription on the envelope. " 'I am Keith Flynn. My daddy was Sergeant First Class Mitchell Pritchard Flynn.' How could Mitch have a son and we didn't know?"

"We didn't know Mitch was still alive until the Army told us he was dead." Peg's voice was ragged.

I was startled. Peg's words made no sense to me.

Peg made a sound between a laugh and a sob. "How do we know Mitch hadn't married? For that matter, if this is Mitch's son, what difference does it make whether he was married. Let me have the envelope. It belongs to Keith."

Gina slowly handed the envelope to Peg. "This is some kind of scam."

"Maybe. But maybe not. Maybe this really is Mitch's little boy." Peg's tone was hopeful, incredulous, joyful. She reached down for Keith's mittened hand. "For now, Keith's here and he's cold and we're going inside."

Keith looked up at me. His thin face was tired, and he looked on the verge of tears.

I gave him a warm smile, turned a thumbs-up, gestured toward the house.

Gina wrapped her arms tight across her front. "Who brought him here? Someone brought him. He didn't get here on a broomstick. We have to call the police. He's an abandoned child. It's nonsense to say he's Mitch's son."

Peg ignored her and gently steered Keith into the warm and cheerful foyer. Gina followed with a frown.

An ornate oak staircase led upward. Scarlet ribbons and frosted pinecones decorated a magnificent pine garland draped on the railing. The scent of fresh pine mingled with the yeasty smell of baking and the lemon of furniture polish. Vivid red poinsettias, their containers wrapped in silver or gold foil, were bunched on the landing. Clumps of mistletoe hung above the double doors to the right and the left in the main entrance hallway.

As I recalled from long ago, the doors to the right opened into a dining room. The double doors to the left were partially open. Light streamed out into the hallway. Voices murmured. I'd attended many a Christmas tea for the Altar Guild in that ornate room with a low-beamed ceiling, gilded Louis XVI furnishings, and a hand-carved green Italian marble fireplace.

Gina moved swiftly past Peg down the central hall, heading toward an oak door. Her silk skirt swirled as she walked.

"Don't call the police." Peg's voice was low but sharp. "I'm taking him upstairs."

Gina stopped and faced Peg. "Up to see Susan? That's crazy. We don't know anything about him."

Peg held up the envelope. "It's written here. He's Mitch's son. Do you honestly think someone would drop a strange child on the front porch and make that claim? Everyone knows about DNA. No one would try to foist off a child as Mitch's. There are tests that can be done and then we'll know without a doubt. For now, if you think Susan will thank you for trying to turn away her grandson, a grandson she never knew about, even for a few minutes, you can think again."

Gina lifted her hands. "All right, maybe he's for real. I don't know and neither do you. But we do know how sick Susan is. Do you want to kill her?"

Her round face uncertain for an instant, Peg drew in a sharp breath. "Joy never killed anyone."

They stood a foot apart on the Oriental runner in the center of the main hallway, Peg's eyes determined, Gina's sharp features resistant.

One of the doors to the left squeaked as a plump woman in her fifties stepped into the hallway. "Girls, you're missing the most fascinating description of Christmas in Lapland. Did you know Santa lives on a fell called Big Ear? Harrison knows so many things." Her voice was cheerful and only slightly tongue-in-cheek.

With a sidelong glance, Peg moved a little to her left, shielding Keith from the woman's line of vision. Peg managed a bright smile. "Please tell Harrison we'll be there in a minute. I'm sure he has much more to say. I'm going to run up and see Susan for a minute. A message came for her. Gina and I will see to it and be down in a little while. Susan may want to talk to us."

"Tell Susan we are all thinking about her. It isn't the same not to have her downstairs with us. I think this is the first time she's missed Harrison's birthday celebration. She must not be feeling well. Don't stay too long and tire her." With a quick smile, she turned away. Before the door closed, her high dithery voice could be heard. "The girls will be back in a few minutes." The door squeaked shut.

Gina jerked her head toward the closed living room door. "You had your chance to tell Jake. What's the matter? Cat got your tongue?"

Jake. It was an interesting name. I wondered if the name reflected a wish to be different or a streak of boyishness not evident in the heavyset blonde's matronly appearance.

Peg looked both uneasy and defiant. "I don't want to bother her."

Gina's grin was malicious. "She'll have a fit when she finds out, cuz. Your mom fancies herself queen of the hive in this house."

Peg's hands clenched. "Mother will understand. Besides, this is Susan's house. We have no right to keep Keith's arrival from her."

Gina shrugged. "What if this is a hoax? If he's truly Mitch's son, why would he arrive like this?"

Keith pressed against me. Gina's words held little meaning for him, but he saw her frowning face. Tears glistened in his dark eyes.

I bent down and whispered, "Let's go upstairs, Keith." I realized I no longer needed the warmth of the chinchilla coat and cap and wished it away.

The two women were engrossed in their quarrel. With a quick glance over my shoulder, I lifted Keith—the steep old steps would be a stretch for his short legs—and sped up the stairs. His sweet breath tickled my cheek and he felt warm and dear in my arms. In scarcely an instant, we reached the landing and soon were out of sight from below.

I'll admit I acted on impulse. Keith was obviously tired, probably hungry, alone, and frightened. I felt that ultimately Peg would prevail but I wasn't going to chance Keith being handed over to the police. Besides, I have faith in instinct. Somewhere upstairs a woman named Susan had no inkling of the joy that was to be hers. Bringing joy is good, and as Peg insisted, joy never killed anyone.

In the upstairs hallway, twin rosewood lamps on an English Hepplewhite sideboard shed soft light through their milky bowls. The Oriental runner was old, its colors faded to a muted glow of rust and sage. I had little time. I moved swiftly along the hallway, opening doors.

The last door revealed a spacious bedroom with a fireplace. A too-thin woman sat in a Sheraton chair to one side of the fireplace with glowing fake logs. Her oval face, even though drooping with pain and illness, was lovely, a high forehead, finely arched brows, eyes dark as shadows at midnight, long narrow nose, narrow lips, a firm chin, an air of command. Silver frosted her softly waved chestnut hair. She rested against the cushion, her gaze remote, sorrow her companion. She was in the room yet she seemed distant and unapproachable. There were no garlands of evergreen, no flicker of red candles, no red-and-green taffeta bows in this room. On a cushion by her feet, a large calico cat slumbered, her patches of red-and-black fur striking against the white.

Over the fireplace hung a reproduction of Fra Angelico's *Nativity*: Mary and Joseph with their heads bowed, the infant Jesus helpless and little on a bed of straw in the manger, a mule and an ox behind them, eleven angels above. I suspected the reproduction hung there year-round and was much more than an annual holiday decoration.

She didn't turn at the sound of the opening door. "You're early, Jake." She spoke as if coming back from a far distance. "No matter. Put the tray on the table." She turned a hand toward the gleaming dark Queen Anne table next to her chair. "You can tell me about the evening tomorrow. I'll not visit tonight."

I put Keith down, once again murmured in his ear, smelled his sweet little boy scent.

He looked up at me, his eyes huge and dark.

I blew him a kiss, nodded.

He moved uncertainly forward. His sneakered feet scarcely made a sound on the wooden floor.

She heard the faint scuff. Her head turned. A hand touched her throat when she saw him. Her robe, undoubtedly made of finest Chinese silk, was brilliant red with gold piping. As quickly as sunlight slipping across summer water, her face brightened. "Hello." Her voice was low and sweet.

When young she must have been startlingly beautiful, a beauty of elegant bone structure and mesmerizing character.

She smiled, a kind and gentle smile. "I haven't had a little boy visit me in a long time." Tears filmed her eyes but she kept on smiling. "Who are you, my dear?"

"Keith."

"I'm glad you came to see me, Keith. Come closer, please."

Steps sounded on the stairs, a rapid, hurried clatter.

Still smiling, she glanced toward the open door. "It sounds as though someone's coming after you. Please, come close for a moment."

Keith moved toward her, his face grave. He stopped next to the chair.

She lightly touched his shoulder.

Keith looked back at me.

I nodded energetically.

Keith stood very straight as he must have been told. He spoke in a rush. "I'm Keith Flynn." His words were indistinct. *Keef* for Keith, *Finn* for Flynn. "My daddy was Sergeant First Class Mitchell Pritchard Flynn. My daddy was a hero." His little boy voice ended in a wobble.

Her illness-drained face was quite still. She stared into his dark eyes, so like her own. "Your daddy . . ."

Gina hurried into the bedroom. She stopped and stared at

Keith, her narrow face exasperated. She flung out an accusing hand. "How did he know where to come?"

Keith quailed at her sharp tone.

Susan Flynn curved an arm around his shoulders, pulled him near. "It's all right. Don't be frightened, sweet boy." Her voice was as soft as the sweep of a feather.

Peg pushed past Gina. "Someone left him on the front porch with a note." She hurried forward, held out the envelope, then sank to her knees beside Keith. "I promised you some hot chocolate."

Susan opened the envelope with trembling hands, lifted out a stiff sheet.

I peered over her shoulder at script in an unfamiliar language. There was an official seal near the bottom. Gold foil glinted in the flickering firelight.

"It's in German! Mitch was stationed in Germany." Quickly she emptied the envelope. "A birth certificate from the military hospital in Würzburg: Keith Mitchell Flynn, born to Sergeant First Class Mitchell Pritchard Flynn and Marlene Schmidt Flynn." With every word, her voice grew stronger. Joy lifts voices. "Mitch's medals and news clippings." Suddenly, her brows drew down. "Here is a printed notice of his mother's death from pneumonia. So that's why she didn't bring him to me." Susan's face was puzzled. "Peg, who brought him here?"

Peg gestured toward the front yard. "We don't know. The doorbell rang, and there was no one there but Keith. He said his mother's friend Lou brought him. We don't know where she is or why she left."

Susan's gaze was thoughtful. "We'll find out." Suddenly a brilliant smile lifted her lips. "It doesn't matter really. In any event, he's here where he should be." She reached out a shaking hand to smooth a blond curl, gently touched Keith's shoulder. "It's warm in here. I keep this room too hot for a little boy. Let me help you with your coat."

He lifted his arms obediently. She folded the thin little corduroy jacket. "Are you hungry?"

He nodded, his face solemn.

"Do you like roast beef, Keith?" She looked at Peg. "Will you get him some supper?"

"And some cocoa and a cookie. I promised." Peg's smile was delighted. She turned to hurry from the room.

Keith lifted rounded fists to rub at his eyes and gave a huge yawn.

Susan gestured sharply at Gina. "Open the corner bedroom. Put on fresh sheets. Make sure there are plenty of blankets."

I drifted around the room, listening to Susan's soft murmurs as she talked to Keith and looking at the panoply of photographs in a bookcase and atop a dresser. It took only a moment to realize the pictures were primarily of a boy and girl from babyhood to late teens. The dark-haired girl had irregular gamine features and an aura of energy and enthusiasm and good humor. Snapshots showed her making mud pies when she was about six with a missing tooth and a streak of dirt across one cheek. At around ten, bony and thin with sharp elbows and knees, she held aloft a tennis trophy. As a teenager in a décolleté white gown, she smiled up at an older man whose irregular features matched her own. The blond boy was cocky with a square jaw and muscular build. He stood stiff and still with a Webelos salute in his Cub Scout uniform. As a Scout, he dangled from a climbing rope over a sandstone gorge. He pinned an opponent in a wrestling match, caught a pass on a football field, strummed a guitar in a pensive mood.

Two frames held school pictures, starting with kindergarten. The last photo in the frame inscribed *Ellen's Class Photos* showed a girl with a vivid questing glance and effervescent smile. Beneath the photograph was written in now faded ink: *Ellen's junior class picture.*

There was no senior class photograph for Ellen.

I looked at the boy's framed class pictures. He was on top of the world in his senior picture, confident, cocky, charismatic.

Peg returned with a tray holding a sandwich and potato chips, a glass of milk, a sugar cookie with a Santa face, and a Spode pitcher and cup and saucer. Keith sat gingerly in his grandmother's lap. He managed half a sandwich, drank a portion of the milk, drowsily subsided against her.

Gina poked her head in the door. "The room's ready." She was subdued, still with a faint frown.

"Thank you, Gina." Susan lightly brushed back a lock of blond hair. "He's almost asleep. Peg"—Susan's face was suddenly worried—"will you stay with him tonight? He's in a strange place. I don't want him to wake up and be frightened. If he wakes up . . ." She paused, struggled for breath.

Peg took two quick steps to the chair. "I'll stay with him. Do you need oxygen?" As Peg wheeled a portable tank near, I understood why the fireplace held fake electric logs.

Susan shakily reached out for the mask and held it to her face. Slowly her breathing eased. The bluish tinge faded from her face. She put aside the mask, sank back against the chair. "I'm tired now." Her voice was faint. "Tomorrow I'll read everything." Her voice was flagging. Susan gathered up the papers, replaced them in the envelope. "Mitch's little boy . . . tomorrow . . . some toys . . . I'll talk to Wade . . . He'll take the proper steps, make everything official." Tears glistened in her eyes. "Mitch's little boy . . ." She twisted to look up at Peg. "Take good care of him."

CHAPTER 3

Light spilled from a room at the end of the hall as Peg nudged the door wider with her knee. She carried Keith to a twin bed with the sheet turned down. She eased him gently between the sheets, then lifted the cover to untie his sneakers, slip them from his feet. He sighed and turned on one side. Dark lashes fluttered on a pale cheek. He was deep sunk in sleep, the soft and yielding abandonment of a child.

Peg lifted his head, edged a corner of the pillow beneath his cheek. She drew up the sheet and a beige wool blanket and a puffy pale blue comforter. "Good night, sleep tight." She tiptoed softly from the room, joined Gina in the hallway.

I took a moment to be certain Keith was comfortably asleep, then I moved through the closed door into the hall and joined Gina and Peg at the head of the stairs. The calico cat padded from Susan's room and moved lightly down the stairway.

Gina looked bereft and forlorn. "Do you really think he's Mitch's son?"

Peg was impatient. "What are you suggesting instead? Somebody had an extra kid hanging around and they happened to know enough about Susan and the family to insinuate him here? If he isn't Mitch's son, how did someone get Mitch's medals?"

Gina gripped the newel post. "I suppose there's some reason he was left by himself on the front porch. But why didn't the person who dropped him off stay and explain?"

Peg turned her hands over in bewilderment. "I have no idea. I suppose we'll find out. There are always reasons when things happen." A sudden smile softened her face. "Susan hasn't been this happy in years and years. I wish she were stronger and could live long enough to watch him grow up. Anyway, we can be sure everything will be sorted out properly. Susan will want everything to be on a legal basis. You know how she is. She crosses every *t,* dots every *i.* She'll tell Wade tomorrow to find out everything about Keith." Peg's smile was joyful. "What a wonderful Christmas gift to have Mitch's little boy come to us."

"Mitch's little boy." Poignant sorrow made Gina look older. She drew in a sharp breath. "Well, it's time we shared the good news." Her tone was brittle, her smile brilliant. "I'll tell you what, cuz. You do the honors. Everyone will hang on each word. It's going to be a whole new world for Aunt Jake and Tucker and me and Harrison and Charlotte. I guarantee you will upstage Harrison expounding on Lapland."

At the foot of the stairs, Peg squared her shoulders, moved to the closed door to the living room.

The calico cat looked up, golden eyes gleaming, one paw lifted as if knocking on the door.

Peg reached down, patted the svelte fur. "Ready for a party, Duchess?" Peg reached for the handle.

I went ahead of them. It was nice not to have to wait for doors to be opened, and I always got a thrill out of passing through a wall. I like hovering above things as well. Weightlessness is fun. I will admit that I do like being *on* the earth, but this time I would not yield to temptation. This time I was going to stay out of public view.

In the living room, I was delighted to find the huge room much as I remembered it: dark-stained wainscot and trim, muted rose silk walls, ornate plasterwork on the ceiling and cornices. The French doors held the same copper foil leaded-glass windows that I remembered. The room was pleasantly warm from the wood fire. An intricately carved rosewood chair sat next to the grand piano. The rose of the upper walls matched the dusty rose of the Oriental rug. On a sideboard stretched an array of tantalizing holiday treats: cheese, fruit, crackers, brownies, cookies, and what might be the remnants of a birthday cake.

I was ravenously hungry. Being on the earth, even when not visible, I needed food and sleep. I found that interesting. I zoomed to the sideboard, eyeing the Brie.

". . . stayed in a glass igloo. Charlotte and I could see the Northern lights from our bed. It was my most spectacular birthday to date." The balding speaker was comfortable in corduroy trousers, a cream turtleneck, and a seasonal red vest. His ruddy complexion suggested a man who spent a great deal of time outdoors. He was muscular despite the beginnings of a middle-age paunch. Wrapping paper obviously removed from gifts was neatly folded next to a stack of diverse items: a book by Doris Kearns Goodwin, a bright Christmas tie with green wreaths against a red background, a red-and-black plaid wool hunting cap, a wall calendar for wine lovers, and a Christmas-scene paperweight.

An angular woman with frosty hair and oversize glasses observed him with a dry but fond smile. "Harrison, I doubt anyone is interested in our accommodations." Her tone was indulgent, not chiding.

Light from the fire reflecting from his bifocals, Harrison grinned. "There speaks a wife who's heard all of this before. But hey, how many people from Adelaide have spent the night in an igloo and slept on a motored bed, much less dined in an igloo restaurant with ice tables?"

"Motored bed?" A lanky young man with dark curly hair and a stubbled chin—had shaving gone out of fashion?—stretched booted feet lazily toward the fire. He looked exceedingly masculine in a fragile-appearing gilt chair. His Western-style shirt fitted him snugly and his Levi's were white with age. "Does the bed have spark plugs, Harrison? Maybe fins? A retro motored bed?"

The hall door squeaked.

The older blonde winced. "That hinge needs oil. Tucker, why don't you see about it?"

The young man's shrug was indifferent but appealing, as if he'd help if he could but that would take effort and the fire was too entrancing, the conversation too amusing. "I do enough oiling on the ranch, auntie."

The middle-aged blonde wriggled unhappily. "Don't call me auntie. It makes me sound like a hillbilly with missing teeth."

He grinned. "Sorry, Jake. Forever young, that's our revered aunt. I forgot myself in the emotion of the moment, confronting the possibility of a motored bed and the joys of staying in a glass igloo. Glass sounds more appealing than ice. Isn't that how igloos are customarily made, with big chunks of ice?" His eyes gleamed with mirth. "Who would have thought as we gathered for Harrison's birthday that he would share this amazing tidbit of knowledge with us. Obviously, Harrison, you are a connoisseur of Christmas lore. Tell us, what are the Christmas customs in Hawaii?"

Harrison grinned. "You pulled the wrong string, Tucker.

I am a walking encyclopedia of Christmas trivia. I always try to learn something new for each birthday. In Hawaii, Santa Claus arrives on a bright red outrigger."

"Man, that sounds like my idea of Christmas." Tucker looked toward the door. "Hey, Peg, Gina. What fascinating tidbits about Santa can you share? Me, I like the idea of wassail and lots of it." He reached out, gripped a poker, and jabbed at a log. Sparks whirled upward.

I am not a fan of apple cider laced with sweet juices, but I was very hungry. I hovered near the buffet. If I were adroit . . . I glanced around the room. Every eye was on Peg. Though it lacked manners, I decided to forgo a plate. I could easily carry several chunks of cheese and some strawberries and crackers in my hand. I moved fast and no one noticed the tidbits in the air. I dropped far enough behind the sofa that I could eat without notice but still see everyone.

Peg stood stiffly by the opened doors. "I have exciting news." Her voice was brisk but her face looked strained. The calico cat walked purposefully toward the fireplace and settled on a green silk cushion and began to groom.

The strawberries were succulent. I glanced toward the small bowl of sour cream on the sideboard. That would have been nice, but I wasn't trying to indulge myself. I was simply building up strength. The crackers snapped as I munched. Fortunately the fire crackled at the same time. Too soon my snack was gone. I was tempted to forage again for food, but instead settled on an empty settee.

Gina skirted around Peg, walked toward the buffet. "We have company." Her tone was neutral. She took a plate, spread pâté on several crackers.

Tucker looked eager. "A gorgeous redhead maybe?"

Startled, I looked down. Not a trace of my sweater or slacks was visible. I didn't think I'd appeared. Not, of course, that I see myself as gorgeous. Absolutely not. Truly, I was thinking only in terms of being redheaded. I am definitely redheaded. Flaming copper, to be precise. I breathed a sigh of relief and brushed back a loose curl.

"No such luck for you, bud," Gina muttered. She pulled an ottoman closer to the fire. She looked at Tucker, legs outstretched from the gilt chair. "Don't hog the warmth, bro." She balanced the plate on her lap.

Peg stood a few feet inside the door. She clasped her hands as she spoke. "A little boy arrived here tonight. There was a note with him. He's Mitch's son, Keith. Susan told us to put him in the blue room."

The hiss and crackle of the fire was loud and distinct in sudden silence. No one moved or spoke.

I looked around the room.

Jake's big blue eyes stared blankly at Peg. A shaky hand clasped at a strand of pearls. She looked like a good-natured pig confronted with an unfathomable reality, an alligator in the kitchen or a crevasse that yawned without warning.

The lanky young man still bent toward the fire, the poker gripped in his hand. The face turned toward Peg was immobile, dark eyebrows slashed over light brown eyes, bony features rigid.

Red-faced Harrison's bonhomie drained away. He stared, sandy brows drawing down in a frown.

His wife pushed dark-rimmed glasses higher on her nose, looking as alert as a prairie dog poking out of a burrow and sighting a predatory badger.

Gina stared into the fire, her narrow face somber, her gaze mournful. The crackers on her plate remained untouched.

Peg's smile was hopeful though her eyes were anxious. "Isn't this great news? Christmas will be special this year."

Jake's head jerked toward the hallway. Her face was

suddenly blanched. Her lips quivered. "Susan isn't well." Breathing heavily, she came to her feet. "I'll go and see. This is absurd. Who brought this child? He can't stay here. Whoever brought him must take him where he lives."

Peg lifted a hand. "Susan's gone to bed. She doesn't want to see anyone now. We don't know who brought him. He was left on the porch with a note that says Mitch is his father. There's a birth certificate that lists Mitch as his father."

Jake held to the back of a chair. "There has to be some mistake."

Tucker's face relaxed. He scratched at his bristly chin. "Don't get in a swivet, Jake. He's either Mitch's boy or he isn't. Susan will find out. Well"—his expression was bemused—"you can't say we aren't starting off the holidays with a bang." He glanced at Gina. "What do you think, sis?"

"We didn't know what happened to Mitch after he ran away." Her voice was low and sorrowful. "I guess now we'll find out."

Harrison looked like a man whose boat had sprung a leak and there's no land in sight. "If it's true"—his words were reluctant—"it would be a great happiness for Susan. Still, this unannounced arrival seems suspicious to me. We may have to step in and protect Susan since she isn't well."

His wife lifted a hand as if warning him. "Susan can deal with anything, sick or well. And"—her eyes were thoughtful—"she deserves some happiness." She looked around the room. "I'm sure you all agree."

"Oh, of course." "Certainly." "Hope this isn't a disappointment ultimately." "Wade Farrell will have to be very careful."

Beyond the flurry of words, I sensed shock and, more, a flash of white-hot fury.

Wiggins had been uneasy on Keith's behalf.

I looked around a room filled with people who apparently resented his arrival. I had to find out why his existence caused such shock. And dismay.

In the blue room, I tucked the wool blanket around Keith's shoulders. That should keep him toasty. I stepped to the window, eased it up a bit. Fresh air makes everyone sleep better.

The gathering downstairs had broken up. The distant sound of voices faded. Car engines murmured. The front door closed.

I didn't know who was staying in the house. I assumed Jake was a resident. She had an aura of proprietorship. I didn't know if Peg was a guest but she'd promised to stay in the room with Keith so obviously she was to be in the house overnight.

I glanced toward the ceiling. Not that Wiggins would be hovering there, but he was either at the Department of Good Intentions or possibly out checking on his emissaries. Or was I the only one who required close supervision? I preferred to think I was one among many. Certainly I'd done nothing this evening to require his counsel. Surely the brief interlude with Rob and Dil was acceptable. After all, they may have sensed my presence, but I definitely had remained unseen. Here at Pritchard House, I'd worked quietly behind the scenes. I felt a quiet pride.

I sat on the edge of the opposite twin bed. When the house settled for the night, I planned to explore the kitchen. I needed a glass of milk and a roast beef sandwich for energy. As for sleeping accommodations, the chaise longue looked inviting.

I hoped Peg wouldn't feel crowded with the three of us there. I'd do my best not only to remain silent and invisible, but to contain my natural energy. Bobby Mac claimed I carried energy with me like static electricity.

However, for now, Keith was sleeping soundly, all was well here, and the night was still young. Perhaps I could discover who lived in Pritchard House in addition to Susan, and why her grandson's arrival had caused such consternation.

Downstairs in the living room, Peg and Gina loaded trays with plates and bowls.

Jake paced nervously by the fireplace. The cat lifted her head and gazed with unblinking golden eyes. Jake flung out a hand toward her daughter. "I don't understand why you didn't call me. I should have been summoned at once. The idea of a child abandoned on the doorstep is appalling. Someone has been criminally negligent, whoever the child is."

"Mother"—Peg looked harried but determined—"he came with papers, including his birth certificate."

"Papers." Jake's voice was sharp. She waved her hand in dismissal. "Everyone knows that anything can be faked now. You can't trust pictures on the Internet. Anything can be put in a picture. Anything at all. The other day I saw a picture of the president signing a wildlife bill and there was a flamingo on one side of his desk and a wolf on the other and they looked real as could be. I mean, they were real but they weren't in the picture until someone put them there." She nodded her head for emphasis. "So you see what I mean. What's a birth certificate? We'll have to see about those papers. But when he came, you should have told me. I take care of everything about the house. Susan relies on me utterly." Her face flushed an unbecoming pink. "It was outrageous to take him upstairs to Susan without any kind of checking! Peg, what were you thinking?"

Peg turned, her hands tightly gripping the laden tray. "Mother, I did what I thought best. It happened so suddenly."

Gina's gaze was curious. "Hold up, Jake. If Peg had told you, what would you have done differently?"

"I'd have done something." Jake's face twisted in frustration. "We could have called Wade, asked him to check into everything, not troubled Susan until everything was certain."

Peg's eyes were soft. "Susan wasn't troubled. It's the first time since Mitch died that she's been truly happy. It was wonderful."

A tic pulled at Jake's left eye. "How dreadful for Susan is he isn't Mitch's son."

"He is." Peg spoke with finality. "There are too many papers, too many links to Mitch. He said he was Mitch's son. How would he know Mitch was a hero unless someone told him?"

Gina added a bowl of nuts to her tray. "Susan intends to talk to Wade tomorrow."

Jake clasped her hands together and twisted them around and around. "She's going to call Wade tomorrow? Oh dear, what do you think is going to happen?"

Peg walked to a swinging door. "If Keith is proved to be Mitch's son, a great many things will change."

As the door sighed shut behind her, Jake stared at Gina. "What does she mean?"

Gina added a teapot to a tray, gave Jake a measuring glance. "She means the gravy train's running off the rails."

"That's not nice." Jake's tone was sharp. "We haven't taken advantage of Susan. She depends on us."

Gina gazed at her aunt with a mixture of affection and pity. "You'll probably come out all right. Susan likes you and somebody has to run the house and take care of the little guy. But for Tucker and me? We're not related to her. For that matter, neither are you, dear auntie. Face it, Jake, all of our connections to Susan are through Tom. You were married to Tom's brother. Our mom was your sister. Harrison was a cousin of Tom's. Sure, Susan's been great to her husband's family, but that was when she didn't have any family of her own." Gina turned toward the swinging door.

Jake hurried after her, caught at her elbow. "We've been her family. A good family. Susan wanted to take care of us. She always said the house will be mine. This is my home."

Gina's smile was crooked. "Think about it, Jake. Susan's always made everything clear, how the property was to be divided, the estate divided equally but you were to have the house and Mitch the ranch. Maybe she'll leave each of us something and Tucker will likely still run Burnt Creek. The only difference is that it won't be his ranch. You have to remember that none of us are blood kin to Susan. If this little boy is Mitch's son, who do you think will inherit?"

A too-tight pink satin housecoat pulled across Jake's ample bosom. The bedroom was overwarm, but she placed another log on the fire burning in the fireplace. The mesh metal fire screen rattled as she yanked it shut. She stood uncertainly by the mantel, then, with sudden decisiveness, moved to a chintz-covered chair next to a small table. She perched on the cushion and picked up a cell phone.

Quickly she punched numbers. She began without preamble. "Susan's going to talk to Wade tomorrow." She twined a bristly strand of too-often-bleached hair around a finger. "That's easy for you to say." Heavily penciled brows drew down in a tight frown. "I suppose you'll get to run the ranch, no matter what happens. And you're paid a pretty handsome salary." She tapped a nervous tattoo on the table. "No." The words came slowly. "I don't suppose she'll throw us out and I know she's generous. But Tucker, we thought everything was going to be ours." Her eyes widened. "Of course I'm going to be sweet to the little boy. If he turns out to be Mitch's son, I'll be the first to be thrilled for Susan. But it all seems peculiar to me, his arriving right before Christmas with nothing but a shabby suitcase and some papers." She massaged one temple. "I know." Her voice was dull. "They'll be able to prove the truth. I suppose he must be Mitch's son. Everyone knows about DNA. But we've all stood by Susan, when there was no family for her. Tucker, maybe you could talk to Susan. She's always liked you a lot." She sat up straighter. "I'm not asking you to beg. But it never hurts to be nice." Her face looked hurt. "I've never asked any favors of you, and Gina and I made a home for you when your folks died and now if you can help me . . . Well, if that's how you feel about it."

Jake clicked off the cell, sagged against the tufted chair back. She looked around the room, cluttered with mementos ranging from a painted-face coconut shell to a replica of the Matterhorn. "It's my house. She promised." There was pathos and despair in her cry. Jake's eyes brimmed with tears.

Gina stood by an open window, blowing out a plume of cigarette smoke. She didn't turn when the door opened behind her.

"Susan hates cigarette smoke." Peg sounded irritated.

Gina took another deep drag. "A: She won't come in here. B: I have the window open. C: I am blowing the smoke outside. Give it a rest."

Peg moved to a dresser, opened the drawer. "I don't mind sharing my room when you're here between jobs, but I don't like smoke either." She pulled out a pair of yellow flannel pajamas with a prancing reindeer pattern.

Gina leaned against the wall. "Where's the problem? You're sleeping in the blue room tonight with the little guy. Lucky me, Susan obviously has never noticed my maternal charm." Her laughter was wry. "You'll probably be named nanny-in-chief when she writes a new will. You could spend a bunch before he gets to twenty-one, maybe take him to Paris over holidays."

Peg slammed the drawer shut. She quickly undressed, neatly hanging up a blue sweater and gray wool slacks. "I wish you didn't sound so bitter."

"It doesn't bother you to go from heiress to pauper in the space of one cold December night?" Gina's voice shook a little. "One minute you're looking ahead to a couple of million and maybe you get your art history degree and end up with a job in a museum that won't pay enough to keep a mouse in cheese. The next you're out in the cold world, the real cold world, like I am. It isn't easy to get jobs these days. How are you going to pay back your student loans?"

"I'll manage." Peg's gaze was thoughtful. "How are you going to pay off your credit cards? You don't even have a job."

"I'm trying to get one. I've sent in résumés and stood in lines and filled out applications online until I'm cross-eyed. There's nothing out there, and I'm down to my last fifty bucks. I got evicted from my apartment and I canceled my cell because I got so many calls from collection agencies. Nasty calls. I'm using a prepaid cell." Gina gave a last puff, snuffed the cigarette in a potted plant. She flapped a magazine to fan the air, then closed the window. "Speaking of calls, have you buzzed Dave?"

Peg paused as she buttoned the pajama top. "No."

"Don't you think he'd like to know the latest? He's really pumped that Susan's considering advancing him enough to build a clinic." Gina strolled to a love seat, dropped onto it.

Peg's voice was even. "We don't know the latest. We'll have to see what Wade says. Besides, Susan knows a good investment when she sees one. The money will be a loan."

Gina's expression was sardonic. "A loan he sure couldn't get from the bank these days. It's a big gamble to come out of vet school and waltz right into a fancy clinic of his own. Susan used to be a sharp businesswoman, always driving a hard bargain. After all, she's a Pritchard. She may start making decisions based on what would be best for Keith."

"The loan to Dave would be a sound business decision." But Peg's voice was thin.

Peg snapped off the light, after a last check of the sleeping child. She stepped softly to the other twin bed, slipped beneath the covers. Moonlight gave the room a quality of shimmering water. Peg plumped the pillow behind her. I wasn't certain but I thought she lay staring into the darkness, perhaps watching the shifting pattern of stark tree limbs against the far wall.

I sat at the end of the chaise longue. I was aware of the deepening chill of the room. Several quilts were stacked atop a wicker chest. I intended to snag one after Peg fell asleep.

She moved restlessly.

Perhaps she sensed my unseen but admittedly impatient presence. I would give her time to relax. I'd promised myself a satisfying sandwich. I decided to make sure everyone was settled for the night and I could have free use of the kitchen.

In Gina's room, she once again stood by the wide-open

window, blowing smoke into the night. Her scarlet robe would have been flattering to her gypsy dark coloring, but her sharp features were drawn in a tight frown.

Jake rested against a bolster and two large pillows. Her faded blond hair was pinned in protuberant tufts. A white mask of night cream covered her face but didn't hide the droop of her mouth. She held an open book in her hands, but she stared blankly at the page.

Susan sat in her chair by the fake fire, the manila envelope in her lap. She lifted a cup of cocoa, absently sipped. Her patrician features were alight with happiness.

Since everyone was safely upstairs, I turned on every light in the kitchen. Have I mentioned the light in Heaven? You'll be amazed, bright as gold, lustrous as pearls, clear as a limpid pool of aquamarine water. Electricity can't compete, but the bright glow in the kitchen was cheerful. I'd grown up in a similar kitchen with a wrought-iron lamp fixture, white-painted wooden cabinets, an old gas range (any cook can tell you that cooking on gas is far superior), hardwood floor, painted wooden spice rack, pots and pans hanging from hooks on one wall, a long wooden table with a half dozen chairs, lace curtains on the window, and a back door with Victorian glass.

The calico cat rose from her cushion and ambled toward me, head lifted in hope.

I dropped down and petted her. "I don't know where they keep your food but I'll share some roast beef with you."

A purr rumbled deep in her throat.

It was not only a homey kitchen, there was plenty of good food. I made a thick sandwich of roast beef on homemade wheat bread. I provided several curls of roast beef to the cat. "Here, Duchess, we'll both have a feast." I ended with a dish of chocolate ice cream, then washed up, returning everything to its place.

I was rewarded when I returned to the blue room. Peg's breathing was even and deep. As I drifted into sleep, I carried with me the memory of Susan Flynn drinking cocoa and looking ahead to happy days with a little towheaded boy.

I love waking up, grasping after the last tendrils of a pleasant dream, welcoming the first silky awareness of a new day. I rolled over on my elbow. My quilt was bunched into a soft heap at the foot of the chaise longue. Sun spilled bright as pirate's gold through the east windows. I shivered and pulled the quilt higher. The clock on the table between the twin beds read shortly after seven.

Bedsprings creaked. Chestnut brown hair tousled, yawning sleepily, Peg lifted her head from the pillow and looked toward the opposite twin bed.

Stealthily, I drew up the quilt and folded it.

Peg's gaze shifted as I placed the quilt at the foot of the chaise longue. She gave the quilt a puzzled glance, shook her head, and turned back toward Keith.

The small form beneath the covers lay unmoving, head tucked beneath the pillow.

Easing to her feet, Peg slipped into pink house slippers. She stretched, brushed a hand through her curls, then tiptoed softly toward the door.

As it closed behind her, the covers moved. Cautiously, Keith emerged. He stared at the door, his thin face anxious, his body rigid.

Poor baby. He was scared to pieces.

I darted a look at the door. Peg surely wouldn't be back immediately. Probably she'd gone to see about Keith's breakfast.

With a defiant nod Heavenward, I swirled into being. I liked being here. I wanted to see myself in a mirror, hear my footsteps on the wooden floor. The image in the mirror was satisfactory, my green eyes bright and cheerful, my red curls tidy enough. This morning's turtleneck was white, my wool slacks red, my boots white. I hurried to Keith.

He drew back as far as he could.

I gave him a sharp salute. "Good morning, Keith. I'm Jerrie." I didn't think St. Jerome Emiliani, the patron saint of orphans, would mind if I used a version of his name. "I've been waiting for you to wake up so we can play. Do you like to sing in the morning?" I didn't wait for an answer but began to sing "Jingle Bells," throwing in a few lyrics of my own devising: Keith is here, Keith is here, what fun we'll have today . . .

The rigidity eased from his small frame. He began to smile.

"Let's pick our favorite things to do. I like to giggle and I'll bet you do, too. Have you ever seen a cross-eyed frog dancing on a stage?"

A tiny smile curved his lips.

"Or an octopus with the hiccups?"

He looked at me uncertainly. "Ogpus?"

"Oh"—I threw up my arms—"you haven't seen anything funny until you've seen an octopus with the hiccups. Octopi—that's more than one octopus—live in the ocean in caves. They have big sleek heads and lots and lots of arms. An octopus with the hiccups waves his arms every which way." I flopped my arms. "If an octopus—not having the hiccups, of course—came to see you, do you know what he'd do?"

He watched me with huge eyes.

I sat down on the bed and wrapped my arms gently around him. "That octopus would give you one hug, two, three, and then he'd take his other arms—he has lots of them—and hug and hug and maybe even give a tiny tickle."

In a minute he was giggling and twisting.

When we stopped to smile at each other, his eyes were shining.

"Now, let's look in your suitcase and I'll help you get dressed. I'll bet Peg has gone to fix you some breakfast. We'll go downstairs and surprise her."

I found fresh underwear, a thin long-sleeved shirt dull from many washes, and a pair of jeans that were too short. When he was dressed, I took his hand. "Let's pretend we are on a breakfast safari. A safari is when . . ."

I remembered to disappear as we opened the door and started down the dim hallway. I'd enjoyed being there. Invisibility has its advantages but it was nicer to actually be on the ground. When I'm not here, I feel insubstantial.

At the stairs, Keith shook off my hand and started down, one steep step at a time, chubby fingers sliding from baluster to baluster. I was poised to grab him should he misjudge.

A door clicked shut.

I whirled. The hallway behind me was unrevealing, every door closed.

Someone had looked out, seen Keith walk past.

There had been no greeting.

Keith was midway down the stairs. He looked small, his short legs stretching to reach the tread. If he fell . . .

I shook away a sense of foreboding and hurried after him.

Peg turned in surprise when we reached the kitchen. There was a welcome smell of bacon and eggs. She beamed at Keith. "Aren't you the big guy to dress all by yourself."

He shook his head. "Jerrie helped me." He pointed straight at me, but of course, only he could see me.

Peg slowly nodded. "I see." Obviously she didn't. "You have an imaginary friend. That's very nice." She turned roughly in my direction and gave a formal bow. "Good morning, Jerrie. I'll set a place for you, too."

Peg dished up bacon and toast and scrambled eggs for Jerrie's plate.

She fixed French toast as well and took time to open a can of tuna fish cat food for the calico. "Here you go, Duchess." By the time she turned back, Jerrie's plate was empty.

Peg's eyes widened. "My goodness, Keith, you are really hungry this morning!"

I smiled at him.

Keith smiled back, an impish, lively, pleased grin.

Footsteps thudded from the hallway. The door burst open. "Can you set an extra place?" Tucker's grin was disarming. Today he wore a thick red cotton pullover with Levi's and boots. His cheeks still sported a fuzz of beard. "You remember I promised to pick you guys up first thing? Gina, of course, is taking forever to get dressed."

I wondered if the house was rarely locked or if he had a key.

Peg licked a smudge of powdered sugar from the back of one hand. "I'd completely forgotten. You and Gina go on without me. I need to take Keith shopping, get him a warm coat. You don't need my help to pick out the tree."

I looked from one to the other, puzzled. The Scotch pine in the living room was beautifully decorated. I am partial to taffeta bows on Christmas trees.

"Bacon, eggs, and French toast coming up." She turned back to the range.

"I'm your man." He pulled up a chair opposite Keith. "Hey, buckaroo, I brought you something special."

Keith put down his fork, his thin face eager.

Tucker made an elaborate show of reaching into his pocket and pulling out a soft leather pouch. He held it up. "Can you guess what's inside?"

His face solemn, Keith shook his head.

Tucker leaned forward, spoke in a stage whisper. "You've heard of buried treasure?"

Keith's dark eyes widened.

"Buckaroo, here is a treasure just for you and you can spend it for special things you want." Tucker loosed the drawstrings, upended the bag. Plastic gold coins tumbled free, creating a pile that looked for all the world like a pirate's hoard. "Now, here's what you do. You think about things you'd like to have—maybe a Matchbox car or a spyglass or a cowboy hat—and you tell Cousin Tuck. I'll find whatever it is or the next best thing and you can give me however many coins you think it's worth." Tucker held out a big hand. "Is that a deal, buckaroo?"

Laughing, Peg set a filled plate before Tucker. "It sounds like you're trying to turn Keith into a little trader."

Tucker finished a piece of bacon. "It's in the blood. It didn't matter what we were trading, comic books or girls' phone numbers, Mitch always won."

Duchess walked majestically to the kitchen door, meowed, lifted a paw.

Peg laughed. "Coming, Your Majesty." She hurried to the back door.

Tucker gave Keith a swift glance. "Looks like it's happened again." His voice was low. His expression as he stared at Keith was suddenly bleak.

The door creaked and Peg didn't hear his words. Cold air flowed inside.

In the imperious way of cats, Duchess remained in place, tail flicking.

"Come on, Duchess." Peg tried to shoo the calico forward.

Duchess gave her a gimlet stare, then stepped outside.

The door clicked shut.

I remembered the earlier sound of a closing door in the upper hallway. I'd watched a little boy at the top of steep stairs and felt a rush of fear. In this warm and cheerful kitchen, Keith seemed utterly safe.

It was my job to be certain he remained safe.

CHAPTER 4

Gina rushed into the kitchen. Her black cashmere turtleneck emphasized the rich plum of slacks that flared wide at the bottom.

I really liked that style, the low snug fit over the hips and a saucy front tie. I'd have to find out what the slacks were called. They were certainly distinctive enough to have a name.

Gina's gaze jerked to the counter near the stove and a tray covered with a fine damask napkin. Some of the tension eased from her thin face. "I'll take Susan's breakfast up."

Peg looked surprised. "That would be nice. I need to fix Keith more French toast."

Tucker's brows drew down in a quick frown. "Hey, let's get the show on the road. We've got to find the right tree."

Gina was already picking up the tray. "I need to talk to Susan. I'll be down as soon as I can."

As the swinging door shut behind her, Tucker looked exasperated.

"More coffee?" Peg held up the carafe.

Tucker nodded, his face drawn in a frown. "Gina's in trouble, isn't she?"

Peg looked hesitant.

Tucker gripped the mug. "So what else is new? How much does she owe?" His voice was weary.

Outside Susan's door, Gina hesitated, then gave a brisk nod. She opened the door and called out, "Breakfast." She carried the tray to the table near Susan's chair in front of the fake fire.

Susan wore no makeup, but her lovely face looked younger. She smiled at Gina. "Thank you, my dear. I suppose Peg is busy with Keith." Her smile grew wider, her eyes shone. "Oh, what a happy day. Gina, I haven't had a happy day in so long."

Gina's eyes glistened. "We're glad for you, Susan. He's a nice little boy." She removed the napkin and the cover. "Do you want coffee now?"

At Susan's nod, Gina poured from the bottle. Then she took a deep breath. "Can I talk to you for a minute?" Her voice was shaky.

Some of the light fled Susan's face. She looked up, gave a tiny sigh. "What's wrong?"

Gina stood stiff and still, her thin face twisted in despair, her shoulders hunched. "I owe almost forty thousand dollars on my credit cards."

Susan's aristocratic features stiffened. Her dark eyes gazed at Gina with a long measuring look. She didn't speak.

Gina's hands twisted together. "I know. I'm a fool. But I had that good job for a while and I got so many credit card offers and I signed up and I wasn't thinking. I was able to make the payments until I lost my job and now I can't find a job."

Susan glanced at Gina's outfit. "I saw those trousers in a Neiman catalog. They were expensive. Bedford pants. Very distinctive."

Gina stared at the floor.

"You have beautiful clothes. You've always liked fine things." Susan was more grieved than scolding. "You've always spent money you didn't have. Tucker has helped you, hasn't he? I suppose you've asked Jake, too."

Gina pulled her hands apart, turned them out in appeal. "I'm desperate. I can't get a job, and I get all these threatening phone calls."

Susan was brusque. "You were able to make the payments. Don't you understand, Gina? That's going into debt. The interest charged is huge. What will happen if I pay the debts? Will you live on what you can earn, buy things only if you have the money to pay for them? Somehow I'm afraid you'll fall back into your old ways. I don't know. Maybe this time you will have to work out your problems by yourself." She made a sudden swift gesture. "I'll think about what should be done. Let's not talk any more. I have much to do today." She turned to her breakfast, her face stern.

Susan gestured with her ebony black cane. "Look toward the back of the closet." There was a becoming pink flush in her pale cheeks. Her softly waved hair was brushed back, emphasizing her expressive face. Regal in her red silk brocade dressing gown, she was full of cheer. There was no hint of her uncomfortable morning encounter with Gina.

Jake reluctantly stepped into a long cavernous closet with a flashlight in one hand. "What if there are fiddlebacks?"

Susan laughed aloud. "Would a fiddleback dare hide in any house under your supervision?"

Jake's voice sounded hollow as she slowly moved deeper into the closet. "No one dusts in here. No one's been in here for years."

Susan's face was suddenly somber. Lines of sorrow pulled at her face. "No. Not for years." She gripped the head of the cane. "At the back, there are boxes with Ellen's name. Look for the one that reads *Carousel.*"

"Ooh. A spider." There was a sound of a stamping foot.

Susan's expression was a mixture of irritation and amusement.

"I see the box." Jake's voice lifted in triumph. "It's on top. I'm not sure . . . Yes, I can. Oh, it's not too heavy." She stepped into the hall. She held a box out in front of her, gripping it with obvious uneasiness.

Susan led the way, the cane thumping on the floor. She opened the door to the blue room.

Keith sat cross-legged on his bed, stacking his plastic gold coins, patiently picking them up when they slid and fell. Duchess rested at the foot of his bed, golden gaze fixed on the plastic coins. Keith looked up as the door opened, his expression uncertain.

Susan's face shone with delight. "Good morning, Keith."

Peg turned from the mirror, laid a hairbrush on the dresser with a smile. "Good morning, Susan. Keith ate a huge breakfast. Keith, here's your grandmother."

Susan came across the room, bent to kiss his cheek. "I'm glad I caught you before you and Keith leave." Susan was a little breathless. "I have something special for Keith."

"Tucker brought a present, too." Peg gestured at the small leather bag and Keith's pile of play gold coins. "After we go shopping, Keith's going to think the world is made up of presents. What do you have?"

Jake stepped into the room, still holding the box stiffly.

Peg hurried toward her mother. "Let me help. What is it?"

Susan smiled at her grandson. "I've brought Ellen's musical carousel for you. Every morning and every evening we can turn it on for you to listen."

Peg's face softened. "The carousel! We loved hearing it play Christmas carols. Here, I'll take it." She carried the box to the bedside table and stripped tape from the lid.

Keith slid from the bed with a thump, came nearer, his dark eyes curious.

Jake fluttered her hands. "There may be spiders."

Keith's face was serious. "Mütter says spiders are good mütters. They work hard."

Peg smiled at him. "I like spiders, too." She lifted out a lumpy shape protected by plastic wrapping. She carefully peeled back the plastic wrap and set the merry-go-round on the table between the twin beds. She bent sideways to insert the plug.

Leaning on her cane, Susan came across the room. She reached down and turned the switch.

Lights twinkled. Animals rode up and down, including a sea dragon, a rabbit, a cat with a fish in its mouth, a rooster, a stag, and a goat as the carousel went around and around. Sweet and clear came the strains of "Silent Night."

Keith walked slowly toward the turning carousel. Lips parted in a smile, he reached out to touch the light-bright top.

Susan's eyes were soft as she watched her grandson.

Faintly, the front doorbell sounded below.

Susan nodded toward Jake. "That will be Wade. Please bring him to my room."

Susan Flynn's lawyer bounced into the room. Though middle-aged, his dark hair thinning and his athletic build contending with the beginnings of a paunch, he seemed youthful with a broad, good-humored face and a hint of boyish eagerness. He beamed at Susan and held out a plate covered with pink Saran Wrap. "Cindy's famous pralines."

Susan smiled and took the plate. "It wouldn't be Christmas without the best pralines in Adelaide."

They settled near the electric fire, she in her chair. He sat opposite her in a Morris chair.

Susan peeled back the covering, offered him a piece of candy.

He grinned. "Cindy would rap my hand with a ruler, but hey, I think it's okay if I take just one." He patted a slightly bulging waistline. "You can't be married to the best holiday cook in town and not put on a few pounds. Tomorrow she's making pfeffernuesse cookies."

Susan chose one of the smaller pralines. She took a bite, nodded in appreciation. "The pecans are wonderful. Thank you and please thank Cindy. And"—her face was suddenly serious—"thank you for taking time to come to the house. I wanted to talk to you in person. As I told you when I called, everything is upside down here, but for a wonderful reason."

Wade licked one finger, his face wrinkling in concern. "It is certainly amazing news." He paused, appeared to pick his words with care. "However, don't be too hopeful, Susan. Let me check everything out."

She wasn't disturbed. "That is precisely what I want you to do. I need verification, but I have no doubt"—she held up the manila envelope—"that these papers are authentic. And these"—she touched the medals ranged on the table next to her chair—"were Mitch's. But, of course, we must prove that I am Keith's grandmother and can properly take custody of him." Her face changed from one of sharp intelligence to somber sadness. "Poor little Keith. He must scarcely remember Mitch, if at all. And then to have his mother die from pneumonia. It is very important that I gain custody of him as quickly as possible. We'll need to see about school and his vaccinations, all that kind of thing."

The lawyer's big face was anxious. "I know you are excited, Susan. Maybe everything is exactly as it appears. However, it still seems odd that the person who brought him left him alone on the porch. That worries me."

"We'll find out the reason." Her smile was confident. "That is, you, dear Wade, will find out the truth. I know I can count on you. And now, if you will please indulge me, I want to ask a great favor. I know the holidays are almost here and you and Cindy will be off to ski, but I want this settled as quickly as possible. Move quickly. Spend whatever is necessary. It is the age of the Internet. Please try to confirm Mitch's marriage and Keith's birth no later than tomorrow."

For an instant, he looked stunned, then, with a crooked smile, he nodded. "For you, Susan, I'll do whatever needs to be done."

I breathed deeply of cold air scented by burning leaves and exhaust fumes. The December sky was as clear and distinct and blue as a Delft plate. Cars circled the jampacked Wal-Mart lot seeking a newly vacated spot. Garlands of evergreens decorated light poles. Scotch pine and firs drew shoppers to a side lot. Outside the main doors, a Salvation Army lady rang her bell.

I kept sight of Peg's car as she turned into an empty space. I ached to be part of this Christmas scene, the bustle and the crowd, the jostle and the rush. What harm would it do for me to appear? No one knew me. I ducked behind a huge blocky van and swirled into being. I tried not to take too much pleasure in a sea green turtleneck and a boldly patterned plaid wool skirt with a matching block of green. Beauty is always admired in Heaven. Are you listening, Wiggins?

Knee-high saddle-toned suede boots were perfect for crunching through an icy crust left in the parking lot from an earlier storm. Wind gusted from the north. A suede jacket was just right. I reached up, caught the ends of a cashmere scarf, and tied them under my chin. I was invigorated.

I sensed a walrus mustache quivering in distress. If Wiggins appeared, I'd simply urge him to listen to the cheer of "I'll Be Home for Christmas" that echoed through a loudspeaker. Wasn't I purely and simply in the moment?

Inside, I ducked around family groups, children tugging toward the toy department and impatient women pushing carts piled high with clothes, housewares, electronics, toys, picture frames, and boxes containing furniture to be assembled.

Peg wheeled first to the children's department. It took a moment for a harried but cheerful sales associate to help her find an appropriate car seat for Keith. Peg picked a sturdy one and plumped it in the basket.

I was close behind Peg and Keith when they reached the boys' department. Women shifted piles of jeans on tables. Babies cried. A little girl stamped her foot and demanded a Barbie. I was in shopping heaven.

Peg was quick. Soon the cart contained three corduroy trousers—fire-engine red, chestnut brown, and cream—several pairs of jeans, a half dozen nice thick fresh long-sleeved cotton pullover shirts, and a nifty dark blue snow coat.

Keith glimpsed me as she turned him to see how a shirt looked. His eyes brightened and he smiled.

Peg looked at him in surprise.

He pointed and I heard his low murmur. "There's Jerrie."

Before Peg's gaze swung in my direction, I ducked behind a table piled with sweaters and crouched low, pretending to pick something up from the floor. It was fine for Peg to equably accept Keith's invisible friend, but she might be more than a little curious if Keith's redheaded friend appeared.

A little girl under the table gazed at me. Pixie glasses gave her eyes an owl-like stare. "I like caves. Do you?"

I smiled. "I love caves. Be sure to say hello to the dragon who lives in the cave." I pointed behind her. "The one with big sweet brown eyes and green scales. If you give him a hug, it will bring you good luck." I slowly rose and peered over the mound of sweaters.

Peg was absorbed in finding the right sizes. Finally, she pushed aside a stack of jeans. "These will be perfect. I think we have everything we need. Now, let's go to the toy department." She swung him up to ride in the cart.

When they reached the toy department, Keith's eyes rounded in amazement.

Peg helped him down. "Let's pick out three toys."

Overwhelmed, Keith simply stared.

Peg took him by the hand and they went up and down the toy aisles. When they finished, he clutched a Mr. Potato Head, Spider Spud box, and a LEGO building set. Peg pushed him in one cart and behind her pulled another carrying a Cozy Coupe II Car.

I was smiling as I disappeared.

What a lovely day.

A plump dark-haired woman bustled about the Pritchard kitchen. Christmas cookies cooled on racks on the countertop. Her placid face was relaxed and cheerful. "I've baked six dozen cookies. I'm making popcorn balls and candies. We're going to have the best neighborhood Christmas party ever. This tray"—and she pointed to a lacquerware tray at the end of the counter—"has treats for the house." She placed a glass of milk on another tray with cookies and a teapot and cups and added a handful of red napkins. "Miss Susan's excited as she can be. I hope she's not overdoing.

She's come to the stairs and called down a half dozen times to see if you're back. You go right up and show her everything."

Peg smiled and took the tray. "Thank you, Tess. And thanks for the loan of the car seat. I put yours back in your car. I bought a new one when we shopped."

Keith was on his knees, his eyes excited as he carefully petted Duchess.

"That car seat's been warmed by all my grandkids and I'm glad you could use it for Keith." The cook bent down. "Here, Keith, I made this especially for you."

He turned to take the small triangular-shaped piece of candy, brown with bits of pecans. "Thank you."

"Your daddy loved Aunt Bill's candy and I'll bet you will, too."

As Peg and Keith walked up the steps, Keith nibbling his candy, I checked upstairs and down. I didn't find Jake or Gina. With Peg and Keith in Susan's bedroom and Tess in the kitchen, I was free to discover what I could.

Although I had arrived only the evening before, I feared Wiggins might feel I'd not made enough progress in learning about those connected to Susan Flynn. Although I was fairly clear on their relationship to Susan, not blood kin as Gina had emphasized to Jake, I had yet to find out the full names of everyone present last night and where they lived.

I looked for an address book in the study. I checked near the telephone. I opened desk drawers. No address book. Possibly Susan kept her address book upstairs.

Photograph albums in a bookcase yielded many pictures of now familiar faces, but the inscriptions weren't helpful. Those who identify family photos expect that first names will suffice. Nor could I utilize a phone book since I didn't have surnames. In a flash, I realized the solution. The church directory. Susan Flynn was a lifelong member of St. Mildred's, as had been her family before her. As I knew from my last sojourn in Adelaide, St. Mildred's had a pictorial church directory, the better, of course, to encourage recognition and fellowship among members. Somewhere in this house there had to be a church directory. I would find plenty of names and pictures, including, I was willing to bet, the full name and address of Susan's lawyer. As a staunch supporter of the church, Susan would be very likely to choose her lawyer from among its members. His office would contain all the information about the beneficiaries of Susan's will.

The kitchen was the most likely spot for directories of all sorts. I sped to the kitchen and was immediately rewarded. A church directory hung on a silver cord from a hook below an old-fashioned wall telephone squeezed between a cabinet and the refrigerator. The directory dangled perhaps a foot from the floor, tantalizing as a tiara to a jewel thief.

Tess rolled out pastry crust on a wooden board. She whistled an off-key but energetic version of "Deck the Halls," tapping time with her right foot. She stood at the end of the counter, very near the recess that held the telephone and the directory.

I didn't have much room to maneuver. I edged sideways to reach into the narrow space between the cabinet and the refrigerator. If she didn't look down, I could filch it with no problem. As I slipped the cord over the hook, the directory swung in an arc.

Fur pressed against my leg. The directory was yanked from my hand and dragged to the ground.

I jumped and gasped.

Tess jerked at the unexpected sound. She bumped into me, felt an undeniable presence—after all, I was there even if not seen—and gave a shocked yelp.

I scrambled backward, tripped over Duchess, and crashed to the floor, making an unfortunate thudding sound.

The calico cat howled, her tail straight up.

Tess pressed a floury hand against her chest. "My goodness me my, Duchess, whatever got into you? Look at that, you knocked down the directory. Bad girl. I'd put you out in the cold but my hands are all floury. Now you get yourself back to your cushion."

Duchess's tail switched and she gave Tess a malevolent look.

Tess snagged the cord, lifted the directory, and returned it to its hook.

Unblinking golden eyes followed the progress of the directory.

I was not going to be outwitted by a cat.

It was as if Duchess heard my thoughts. That malevolent stare settled on me.

It was time to make peace. I moved close, held out an invisible hand.

Duchess sniffed. She pushed her head against my hand, clearly inviting me to pet her.

I obliged.

Duchess dropped to the floor, rolled over on her back.

Still kneading pastry, Tess looked over her shoulder. "If I didn't know better, I'd think you'd been into some catnip."

Duchess came to her feet, moved close to me, twined around my ankles.

Tess stopped kneading. "Duchess, are you all right?"

It was time for finesse. I hurried outside, then turned and rapped on the back door.

By the time Tess opened the door, I was inside the kitchen. I yanked the cord attached to the directory from its hook.

"I declare, somebody knocked on the door and ran away."

Tess stepped onto the porch. "Who'd be playing tricks on such a lovely day?"

When unencumbered by material objects, my passage through space was as lively and quick as St. Nick in his miniature sleigh. I would be in one spot, envision my destination, and there I was. However, material objects, such as the parish directory, required portage.

I was in a hurry to get the directory and flee the kitchen. I reeled the directory up.

In a bound, Duchess was across the room. She snagged the cord with a determined paw and yanked.

The directory splatted on the hardwood floor.

Tess whirled on the porch, came shivering into the kitchen. She slammed the door behind her. "My goodness, I'm going to be vexed in a minute. Somebody knocking on the door and running away and you"—she shook her head at Duchess—"trying to cause trouble the minute I turn my back. Enough of this." Tess grabbed the directory, evaded Duchess's leap, and stuffed the booklet in her apron pocket.

I took a moment in the front hallway to catch my breath. My objective had once seemed so simple. Find the church directory, discover the identity of Susan Flynn's lawyer, go to his office, and explore his files. Admittedly, nosing into files in a busy law office might be another challenge, perhaps far more difficult than the episode in the kitchen.

However, I was determined. I intended to have a parish directory. Why not go to the source?

I thought and there I was.

I know I am prejudiced but I always felt a thrill when I saw St. Mildred's. Winter-bare elms and oaks provided a frame for the small gray stone church. Stained-glass windows sparkled bright as the richest jewels, ruby red, emerald green, royal amethyst, and ocean blue.

On the front steps, after a quick glance around, I swirled into being. Invisibility had advantages, but I was ready for the open, direct, uncomplicated approach. Besides, I was tired of not being. I hadn't realized how much of a Heavenly day I'd spent in conversation. I'd never been reclusive when on earth and this was no time to start. I wanted to see people, talk, laugh, make friends. That such action was in direct contravention of Precept Four (Become visible only when absolutely essential . . .) bothered me not at all. In fact, I intended to suggest to Wiggins that, to the contrary, emissaries should appear as often as possible, the better to be part of the community.

I strode forward, invigorated, confident of my course. I didn't bother with my chinchilla coat. I was going inside. I ducked into the church proper.

A brisk woman in coveralls directed two younger women as they placed potted geraniums in stands by each pew. She smiled a welcome, her prominent blue eyes friendly. "Are you with the Standish-Ellison wedding?"

I shook my head. "I'm a long-ago member of the church back in town for a visit." I was pleased at my quick and honest response.

We discussed the floral swags and brown candles and the lovely effect when pink rose petals would be strewn in the aisle.

I pushed through the door into the main hallway. Direct and simple, that was the path to take. Soon I would have the parish directory in hand and I could obtain the information I needed. Wiggins would be proud of me.

Christmas artwork from Sunday school classes was taped to the walls of the corridor outside the parish hall: Christmas trees made of pasted strips of art paper, stained-glass windows created by pieces of colored cellophane, manger scenes, Mary cradling Baby Jesus in her arms, stars with gold glitter, red-nosed reindeer with toothy smiles and Santa Clauses with jolly smiles, bells with silver glitter.

I threw out my arms and began to sing "Silver Bells." I couldn't resist a sweeping dance with a curtsy here and a bow there. I reached the end of the hallway and the second stanza. Portraits of past directresses of the Altar Guild graced both sides of the corridor here.

It wasn't pride that made me pause in front of my portrait, assuredly not. I was paying tribute instead to time past. I'd been proud to serve and felt I'd managed my terms with a minimum of acrimony, though there had been fractious moments. Hortense Maple, for example, had been very difficult to deal with over the matter of when to replace candles. Emmaline Wooster was slapdash when it came to ironing the linens. The time she'd been absorbed in an *I Love Lucy* episode and scorched the altar linen donated by the Templeton family didn't bear thinking about. None of this long-forgotten past was apparent in my portrait. I looked gay and carefree though much older than I now appeared. I nodded in approval at the contrast between my flaming curls and a white organza hat. That frock of pale lilac eyelet lace had been one of my favorites.

Rapid footsteps clattered near.

I whirled around, possibly with a guilty start. It wouldn't do for anyone to compare me to that long-ago portrait.

The steps paused. A graying pageboy framed a long worried face. The woman glanced at me uncertainly. "Excuse me, did something startle you?"

I gave her a friendly smile. "I'm looking for the church office."

She looked reassured. “Right this way.” She hurried ahead, held the door wide. “I’m Lucy Norton.” She gestured toward a wicker chair with plump red cushions. “How may I help you?”

I looked around the familiar room, shabby and plainly furnished, but the chintz curtains at the windows were freshly ironed. As she took her place behind the desk, I settled comfortably in the chair.

The desk was neat, envelopes tidily stacked in the in and out baskets and several folders aligned with a church bulletin next to a copy of the afternoon newspaper. A church directory rested near the telephone.

“I used to live in Adelaide and was a parishioner. I’m visiting friends.” I was, after all, Keith’s friend Jerrie. “I want to pick up a copy of the parish directory so I can call old friends.”

“Call old friends,” she repeated. Her eyes fell to a story below the fold on the front page.

“You know how it is when you pack in a rush.” I invited understanding. “I didn’t bring my address book with me.”

“Are there particular families you wish to contact?” Her smile was bright, but it didn’t reach suspicious blue eyes. She folded the newspaper.

“Just old friends.” My shrug was casual. “I talked to Susan Flynn, but I didn’t want to trouble her for phone numbers.”

Her smile was swift. “Susan is a dear. I suppose she told you the sad news about the Carstairs?”

“Actually, we didn’t talk about the Carstairs.” Carstairs? That wasn’t a name I recalled.

The secretary’s eyes widened. “I would have thought that was the first thing Susan would have brought up, the dreadful accident last week.”

“We had so many old friends to remember. Now, if you

don't mind"—I glanced at my watch—"I'll take the directory and run along." I glanced pointedly at directories stacked on a shelf in the walnut bookcase on the near wall.

She popped to her feet. Without a glance at the bookcase, she pulled a key ring from the pocket of her yellow cardigan. She came around the desk, gestured toward the hall. "The new directories are in the supply closet. If you'll come with me, I'll get one for you."

I gestured toward the bookcase. "I don't need the most recent edition."

"Might as well be up to date." She led the way into the hall.

I was tempted to march to the bookcase, seize a directory, and sail past her. Instead I rose and followed her.

As we walked in silence, she darted uneasy sideways glances at me.

Had I said something amiss?

Midway down the corridor, she stopped and unlocked a door. She swung it open and stood aside for me to enter. She turned on the light, revealing a long narrow storeroom. "The new directories are on the middle shelf."

I saw the stack. Success was to be mine. I hurried forward.

The door slammed. A click. I rushed to the door and twisted the knob. Locked!

Locked doors posed no difficulty for me, but I wanted the directory. I could waft right out into the hall but I would have to open the door to take the directory and I had no key to unlock the door once I stood in the hall.

I disappeared. In a flash, I was back in the secretary's office.

Hands shaking, she punched numbers. "Police? Come at once to St. Mildred's. I've detained a suspicious woman. She came to the church and tried to get a parish directory. I saw the story in this afternoon's *Gazette*." She yanked up the newspaper, held it with a shaky hand.

I read over her shoulder.

BEWARE CHRISTMAS SCAMS

Police Chief Sam Cobb reported today that a statewide alert has been issued by the OSBI regarding fraudulent activities common during the holiday season.

Calls purporting to come from charitable groups should be checked by the recipient. Chief Cobb advises against providing any personal information, including Social Security numbers or bank account numbers, over the telephone.

A favorite scam reported in Dallas and Oklahoma City involves a well-dressed woman claiming to have monies that will be paid over as soon as the person contacted provides a checking account number.

Chief Cobb said in another ploy, a woman arrives at a home to pick up a promised donation for a church or charity. The woman exhibits familiarity with the family using information gained from newspaper society pages or church directories.

Chief Cobb . . .

The church secretary carried the phone and poked her head out in the hallway to keep an eye on the closet door. "This woman was certainly well dressed and charming, but I didn't believe a word she said. She claimed to know people in the parish, but I think she just wanted to get the directory so she'd know what people looked like and their addresses. I locked her in a storeroom. When I let her out, I'll explain the door slipped and I had to find a better key and she can't prove otherwise, and besides if there wasn't something funny about her, why hasn't she banged on the door and shouted for help? She hasn't made a sound. Please hurry. Maybe an officer can say she was observed speeding and he can ask for identification."

I gave Lucy a cool glance. At least she apparently found me charming.

Within a few minutes, a stocky, middle-aged police officer arrived. "Sergeant Linton, ma'am." He looked concerned. "You say you have a woman locked up here in the church?"

"I've got the key. I saw that story in the *Gazette* and I knew she was a fraud." She was shaking with excitement. "She hasn't even called out and asked for help." Her tone was portentous. "That's a sure sign she isn't on the up-and-up. When I open the door, I'll explain that lock slips sometimes and I'm so sorry and I went to get a key and it took a moment for me to find it."

They walked swiftly down the hall.

I picked up the directory next to the secretary's phone. At the window, I pushed up the sash and looked outside. I didn't see a soul. I unhooked the screen and tossed out the directory. I put the latches back in place and zoomed outside.

". . . no way she could have gotten out of that storeroom." The secretary hurried into the office with the policeman behind her. The icy rush of air from the window had already chilled the office. She jolted to a stop. "That window was closed. And look, my directory on my desk is gone. Somehow she got out of the closet and came in here and she's gone out the window. With my directory."

I grabbed the directory and rose in the air.

Sergeant Linton was at the window in two strides. "No one's out there. Not a soul."

The secretary joined him, peered through the screen. "Look up there." She pointed above the bare limbs of a sycamore. "There goes my directory." Her voice was a screech. "Up there. Way up there."

I shot a defiant glance Heavenward. I knew I shouldn't, but sometimes people just ask for trouble. With a cheerful smile, I made a circle eight and swooped by the office window. I flipped open the pages and flapped the directory with the vigor of a mallard duck heading for a pond. I shot upward.

Faint cries rose from below. The policeman's voice was deep and gruff. "Wind gust. Happen anytime. Downdraft. Updraft."

The secretary's voice was shrill with an undertone of panic. "How did the directory get up there? Why does it look like it's flying?"

I made one more flamboyant swoop.

CHAPTER 5

I dropped into the cemetery that adjoined St. Mildred's. I needed a moment to regain my usual calm demeanor. Perhaps Wiggins would take exception to that self-description. Possibly I am not often the epitome of calmness. But I am always upbeat. I did a couple of shuffle steps as I coasted to a stop inside the cemetery gate and sang a verse of "When the Saints Come Marching In."

In the past, I had always found respite from worldly cares among the cemetery's old granite stones and newer bronze markers. I strolled past the Hoyt family plot and stopped to admire a scroll inscribed with Spenser's poignant lines: *Sleepe after Toyle, Port after Stormie Seas, / Ease after Warre, Death after Life Doth greatly please.*

Winter-bare limbs creaked in the ever-present Oklahoma wind. Bradford pears, sweet gums, sycamores, and maples dotted the gentle landscape. In summer, the foliage added comforting swaths of shade in the blazing sunshine. I loved the cemetery equally in every season. Peace surrounded me.

I felt a twinge of remorse over my dramatic departure from the church secretary's office with the directory. I thought of Precept Five. Once again I had transgressed.

Hey, I'd do better next time.

Of course I would.

I looked down. The directory, firmly gripped in my hand, apparently moved of its own accord a few feet above the ground.

I swirled into being. My suede coat kept me warm from the chill wind. I wiggled my fingers in soft suede gloves. I felt justified in appearing. Clearly I should avoid the possibility of an airborne parish directory disturbing a visitor to the cemetery.

I walked briskly, admiring Christmas wreaths on many of the graves. The ECW hosted a wreath-making coffee the first Saturday in December in the parish hall. I always added holly berries and frosted pinecones to mine. We placed fresh, fragrant wreaths at the graves of those who no longer had family in Adelaide to remember them.

I hurried up the marble steps of the Pritchard mausoleum. Whenever I visited the cemetery, I always stepped inside to stroke the marble greyhound at the head of Maurice Pritchard's tomb and slide my fingers on the stiff whiskers of the marble Abyssinian at the head of Hannah Pritchard's tomb. Paying tribute to Maurice and Hannah's dog and cat is an old Adelaide custom purported to bring good fortune.

I loved the feel of the cold marble beneath my fingers. "Here's for luck." Repeated homage had turned the greyhound's head shiny and added a gloss to the cat's whiskers.

A deep voice boomed. "Precept Five."

Air whooshed from my lungs. "Wiggins!"

"Precept Five." In a rat-a-tat clip, Wiggins quoted: " 'Do not succumb to the earthly temptation to confound those who appear to oppose you.' " A heavy sigh. "I am exceedingly disappointed, Bailey Ruth. I overlooked your appearance in Wal-Mart. No harm done. But this latest contretemps—"

Contretemps . . . What a cosmopolitan word choice for a rural train station agent. Perhaps Wiggins might share some of the uplifting experiences he'd enjoyed as the director of the Department of Good Intentions that had no doubt expanded his vocabulary. I'll bet he'd been to Paris. I pushed away a pang of jealousy. After all, those in charge received perks not available to foot soldiers. Certainly I was happy to bloom where I'd been planted, as dear St. Thérèse of Lisieux sweetly advised. Moreover, much as I would have thrilled to be helpful in Paris, I loved returning to Adelaide.

I sensed Wiggins was quite near. Just before a summer storm, purple-black clouds banked up against the horizon. When the storm unleashed sheets of rain and the fury of the wind, thunder rattled louder than a cannon and lightning sizzled. The senses reeled from the impact.

I felt a similar explosion was imminent.

"—reveals without any doubt that you are not now and will likely never be suited to serve as an emissary from the department."

I expected any instant to have a return ticket on the Rescue Express thrust in my hand. Tears burned my eyes. My lips trembled. I'd tried my best to fulfill my duties and now I undoubtedly faced an unceremonious return to Heaven. I felt buffeted by embarrassment, discouragement, and frustration.

So I blurted out the truth.

"I don't like being invisible all the time. In Heaven, I'm me. You know me." He had a file inches thick on Bailey Ruth Raeburn. "I want to be a part of things and talk to people and laugh and have a good time. I understand that solitude is good for the soul." I'd read that somewhere. "Everyone can profit from moments spent in quiet contemplation." Contemplating what? Being in the moment? I'd better not go there. Quiet contemplation sounded as appealing as sitting on an ice floe. There was never a moment I'd spent that wasn't better if it was shared. Sailing with Bobby Mac. Laughing with family and friends. Grieving with those in trouble. Dancing cheek to cheek. "I need to be with people. When I'm not here, I feel separated from everyone."

I held the parish directory up high. I wished I knew where Wiggins lurked. Had that last sigh come from behind me? Above me? I made a full turn, waving the directory like a knight's banner. The directory was incontrovertible evidence of my transgressions against the Precepts, but if I was on the verge of dismissal, I was going out in style. "Here's the directory and I think you should be proud of the efforts I made to obtain a copy. If I don't know how to find the people around Susan Flynn, how can I discover whether they want to harm Keith?" I might as well make my attitude clear. If I stayed on the job—faint hope—I had to be out and about and discover the good and the bad about those who surrounded Susan. If I was going to be on the earth, I'd do my best not to be of the earth (a nod to Precept Eight), but if circumstances required, I fully intended to swirl into being. "I have to find out about Jake and Peg and Tucker and Gina and Harrison and Charlotte if I'm to be on guard for Keith. That means sometimes I may have to be here, just like I am in Heaven."

"Heaven"—his voice was stern and seemed to come from the foot of Maurice's tomb—"is not here. Precepts One, Three, and Four."

I stamped my foot. Wiggins was being dense. "I can't spook around never talking to anyone."

The silence was absolute. Had I crossed Wiggins's Rubicon? If he decried the term *ghost,* how did he feel about *spook*?

"Wiggins"—I talked fast as the beat of hummingbird wings—"the directory is essential." I felt my cheeks turn pink, a redhead's unmistakable response to stress. Standing in the pale warmth of afternoon sunlight shining through the mausoleum's entrance, my curls stirred by a chill wind, I opened the directory. I flipped to Susan Flynn's picture, then my eyes settled on the photograph above her. I thumped the directory. "Look at this. Now I know who Jake is. She's Jacqueline Flynn. I didn't know her last name. But that makes sense. Her husband was Susan's husband's brother. She was at the house when Keith came." And none too pleased when Gina suggested the will might be changed. "Here's the listing for her daughter, Margaret. That's Peg. So I'm making a start."

"I will admit"—his tone was grudging—"that your actions were well-intentioned."

I tried to pinpoint Wiggins's voice. Was he standing near the greyhound now? "Susan told her lawyer to get proof about Keith." I flipped to the first pages of the directory. I didn't have to go far. Wade Farrell was on the vestry. I found the *F*'s. "Wade and Cindy Farrell, 1106 Arrowhead Drive. He's Susan Flynn's lawyer." Was Wiggins listening? Was he still here? "I'm sure I can find out a huge amount from Susan Flynn's files in his office. As soon as she has proof that Keith is her grandson, she will have the lawyer draw up a new will."

"A new will?" The sharp voice was right at my shoulder.

I jumped. "Wiggins, you scare me to death. Well, of course, not actually." But my laugh was hollow. "Don't hover about and shout. Won't you please join me?"

"Appear?" His voice rose in shock.

I wasn't asking him to embrace a cobra. "For a moment. What harm can it do?"

A deep breath was drawn. "I would rather enjoy being on earth in winter." His tone was wistful. He cleared his throat. "After all, a leader must make every effort to support his representatives. I regret that I startled you when I spoke. If my appearance will make you more comfortable, why certainly it's a small sacrifice on my part."

"Thank you, Wiggins." My lips quivered in amusement, but I managed not to smile. How reassuring for a minion such as I, subject to impatience and irritation and all sorts of worldly attitudes, to see Wiggins succumb to the wiles of rationalization. I hoped he never realized he was flouting Precept Eight (Remember always that you are *on* the earth, not *of* the earth . . .) and actually reverting to earthly thinking.

Colors swirled and there he was, stiff-brimmed cap riding high on his thick thatch of reddish-brown hair, ruddy complexion, handlebar mustache, a heavy black coat open to reveal his starched high-collar shirt, suspenders, and gray flannel trousers. He definitely had the look of another century, but how reassuring to have him here in person.

"I'm glad to see you." I truly was. Wiggins might find me a challenge, but I loved his old-fashioned courtesy and serious demeanor. "Let's walk around the cemetery. It's beautiful even in winter and the Christmas wreaths are lovely." He could kick a mound of leaves with his snub-toed black shoe, draw in that dark woody scent, and remember long-ago winter walks in the woods.

We stepped out into the sunlight and followed a graveled path toward a rise. The sunlight emphasized the rich chestnut sheen of his hair and mustache. We walked in companionable silence, Wiggins smiling and breathing deeply of the frosty air.

"Ah." Abruptly, his smile fled. He tugged at his mustache, his expression concerned. "If Susan Flynn plans to redo her will, it is highly advisable to explore the reactions of those who would have been her beneficiaries."

How nice to be vindicated. However, I minded my manners. Self-satisfaction wasn't an attractive quality even though my pursuit of the parish directory now appeared to be justified.

He nodded in approval. "It is well that she intends to make proper provision for Keith. And"—his voice was kind—"his arrival has brought her happiness. She has known very little happiness these past few years."

"I'm sorry Mitchell was killed in combat." Susan Flynn had confronted the horror of knowing that her son, strong, young, and vital with many years that should have been his, instead died from wounds far away from home. "No mother ever stops grieving the loss of a child." Mitch had died a hero, his little boy said. Bravery would ever be honored, but medals are no balm to a grieving heart.

Wiggins turned to face me, his brown eyes full of sadness. "Not one child. Two."

I came to a stop, stricken by the enormity of his quiet words.

His honest, open, frank face was full of compassion. "Young people—and old—make mistakes. Mitchell was his mother's darling, handsome, vigorous, daring, brave. Unfortunately, he was equally reckless, defiant, and hot-tempered. The weather was icy that December night. Adelaide's hills began to glaze before the party was over. Mitchell and the girl he'd brought to a party quarreled. Mitchell slammed out of the house. His sister Ellen ran after him and managed to jump into the passenger seat before he gunned out of the drive. He lost control on Indian Hill Road."

I remembered a twisting road with a steep drop.

"The car made a full turn and slammed into an evergreen. Mitchell's door opened. He hadn't fastened his seat belt so he was thrown clear, landed in a snowbank. The tree splintered and the car fell."

"Ellen?"

Wiggins shook his head. "Ellen's seat belt was fastened. They found the crumpled car at the bottom of the drop. Ellen was dead from massive injuries." Wiggins reached down, picked up a clump of leaves, and the dank smell rose on the cold air. "The road was treacherous that night. The police report concluded that the wreck was a result of weather conditions."

"Was Mitchell driving too fast?" Was he too furious from the quarrel to think? Had he pushed on the gas pedal when he should have slowed? A few times I recalled being swept by such a rush of anger that later I scarcely knew what I had said or done.

Dried leaves drifted down as Wiggins opened his hand. "His father thought so. Thomas Flynn adored his daughter. He turned away from Mitchell, said he'd killed Ellen because of his damnable temper. He told Mitchell he never wanted to see him again." Wiggins brushed his fingers against his overcoat. "And he didn't. The day after Ellen's funeral, Mitch disappeared. The Flynns did everything they could. Mitchell was sought as a missing person. They hired private detectives. They found no trace. Thomas Flynn died two years ago, a broken man. I think he grieved himself to death. Susan withdrew, had less and less contact with the outside. She has congestive heart failure, the result they say of a virus. How vulnerable to illness the body becomes when there is no will to live. From the day after Ellen's funeral to the day military officers arrived to tell her that Mitchell died a hero in Ramadi, Susan Flynn had no inkling of where her son had gone and what he had done."

I flung out my hands, outraged. "How could he do that to his mother?"

Wiggins looked past me, but he wasn't seeing graves and winter-bare trees and, in the distance, the cross of St. Mildred's. He was looking into a past filled with faces I'd never seen. "Mitchell bore the heaviest burden of all, anguish that is harder to bear than sorrow. Guilt crushed him. Guilt kept him from coming home until he came home for his final rest. He could never see past the guilt to understand the heartbreak his disappearance brought."

"No wonder Keith's arrival means so much to Susan." I reached out and gripped the sleeve of Wiggins's overcoat. "Thank you for letting me help."

His genial face folded in a frown. "Bailey Ruth, I never doubt your desire to be of help." His eyes glinted. "However, maneuvering the directory back and forth by the secretary's window was reprehensible."

"Mea culpa." I tried to sound contrite. Possibly the more formal Latin assumption of responsibility would please Wiggins. I hoped my look of regret touched his heart, which apparently was feeling pretty stony right this minute. "Wiggins, I will do my best to remain in the background, but Keith might be at risk. Surely I can stay until his grandmother has made provision for him."

He put one hand in a pocket, jingled coins. Finally, he sighed. "Someone must be on the spot to look after Keith. And"—he didn't sound overwhelmed with delight—"you are here. Very well. Remain on duty." He looked at me. A tiny smile tugged at his generous mouth. "Have you sung 'Rudolph the Red-Nosed Reindeer' for Keith?"

"I will. I promise." I broke into a vigorous version.

Wiggins laughed aloud. "You do that. And keep a careful eye on him. You shouldn't have to be here much longer." That prospect seemed to bring him great cheer.

"Probably not." I tried to sound pleased as well, but I was sorry to see my hours in Adelaide dwindling. Once Keith was firmly established in Pritchard House as Susan Flynn's grandson, my task would be done. I hoped I could dawdle a bit. I wanted to hug close the sights and sounds of Christmas, smiling faces, children's awe, twinkling lights, carols rising on a frosty night. Perhaps I'd be in Adelaide long enough to attend the children's Christmas Eve service, the boys in bathrobes as shepherds, the girls with angel wings and halos.

A shadow touched Wiggins's face. "Be sure and keep guard over—" He stopped as if jolted by a shock. "Oh my goodness! I must be off." His eyes widened. "To Tumbulgum. An emissary seduced by . . . oh dear . . . never in my experience . . . shocking . . ."

Abruptly, he disappeared.

I tried to squash an uncharitable hope that the emissary was in a big fat pickle and would absorb Wiggins's attention for a good long while. I had no idea where Tumbulgum was, but hopefully it was very, very remote. If so, perhaps when Wiggins once again considered my actions, a penchant for appearing would seem rather minor in comparison. Of course, we all know that taking pride in being less sinful than another doesn't get your ticket punched. I would never do that. Certainly not. But I felt less constrained than before.

Tumbulgum. Hats off. Wherever you are. I was reprieved for yet a while. I would attend to my duties and enjoy the season. I gazed around the cemetery at the wreaths and poinsettias and caroled "It's Beginning to Look a Lot Like Christmas."

Still humming, I hurried back to the Pritchard mausoleum, tucked the precious directory behind Hannah's tomb, and disappeared.

Wade Farrell's office was old-fashioned, three windows with faded red velvet drapes pulled wide for the pale December sunlight, a cotton braided oval rug with red and beige circles, a mahogany desk with ash inlays, legal bookcases full of golden beige law books. Face folded in thought, he wrote vigorously on a legal pad. He stopped and checked his watch. He punched the intercom. "Kim, I've finished the general revisions." He clicked it off.

In a moment, his office door opened and a poised brunette with feather-cut hair stepped inside. Her oval face was remarkably pretty, but her brown eyes were cool and remote.

I nodded in approval at her zebra-striped silk chevron blouse and black pencil skirt made stylish by large black buttons on the left front.

He pushed the legal pad to the edge of the desk. "The Flynn will. I don't know when you can get to it. It's more important to pin down the facts about the little boy. Are you making any progress?"

"Faxes from all over. We have to get a money order in German." Her voice was brisk and commanding. She looked intelligent, perhaps even a little intimidating.

"Try to get confirmation of the birth certificate and the name of the hospital and when and where Mitch Flynn was married. Work all night if necessary. Susan Flynn wants to know by tomorrow."

She nodded. "I'll do my best."

Farrell tapped a pen on the bare desk. "Thanks for being a sport, Kim. I hope this isn't ruining an evening for you."

She waved a hand in dismissal. "I didn't have anything special planned." She closed his office door behind her and walked to her desk. I followed her. She slid onto her seat, muttered, "The rich get richer, the poor get poorer; he'll go home whenever he chooses, I get to work until the wee hours." She reached for the phone, tapped a number. "Hey, Sue. I can't come. I've got to spend the night trying to scare up information on an estate." She swung her chair away from her computer, stared moodily toward a window.

I perched on the corner of her desk and leaned close to the computer and keypad. I'd become somewhat familiar with computers, programs, and passwords on my previous visit to Adelaide. Obviously her computer had previously been turned on and her password used so she was able to access files.

I reached over and used the mouse to close out the program. The screen went dark.

". . . Did you ever see that old movie *Nine to Five*?"

I smothered a giggle. Dolly Parton's song and role in that film were definitely Heavenly favorites of a certain generation of women.

"I'll try to come late if I can." She clicked off the phone and swiveled her chair to face the computer. She frowned at the dark screen, puzzled.

I watched carefully as she clicked buttons, moved her mouse, waited until instructions came up to enter her password. I'd been a first-rate typist, but I wasn't quite sure I'd followed her fingers. I edged a finger under her hands and poked *d*. The message *Invalid Password* flashed.

She gave an irritated breath, typed again.

Was her password *sable* or *cable*?

Once I again I tapped *d*.

Her shoulders hunched. This time she picked each finger up and put it down with exaggerated care.

Ah, *sable*. I glanced at a short black cloth coat, much worn, that hung from the nearby coat tree. I doubted she had a sable coat at home.

She clicked *Open*, highlighted the *FlynnEstate* file. That was all I needed to know.

. . . .

Thin white clouds streaked the afternoon sky. The backhoe operator swung the boom and dumped dirt from a two-foot hole in the front yard of Pritchard House. The excavation was located about ten feet from the Christmas light displays.

On the front porch, Keith bounced in excitement, his cheeks pink from cold. "Can I help?"

Peg ruffled his blond hair. "Maybe I can get you a special ticket." She shouted over the rattle of the motor. "Leon, can Keith ride with you?"

Gina hunched her shoulders against the sharp wind. "You're going to spoil Keith big-time." But her tone was amused. "Sorry you missed going out to the ranch for the tree. You'd think it would get old, but it never does. I always feel like a kid again. Tucker's so proud of the tree, he's about to bust."

A whip-thin man with short silver hair and a weathered face twisted in the seat of the backhoe. He had the tough look of a man used to hard physical labor. He lifted a gloved hand in acknowledgment. "As soon as the tree's in place." He jumped from the cab and strode close to the hole.

Tucker watched from the driver's seat of a tan Dodge Dakota. The cargo bed held a huge bluish-green Scotch pine.

"Ready," Leon shouted.

Leaning out of the window, Tucker backed up slowly.

Leon waved him closer and closer. Just short of the excavation, he barked, "Stop."

The wind ruffling her hair, Peg picked up Keith, balanced him on the porch railing. "Watch while they put the tree in the hole. Tomorrow, you can help decorate the tree. Everybody in the neighborhood comes and all the kids get to put on an ornament, then everyone has cocoa and s'mores and we sing Christmas carols." She looked happy enough to bounce, too.

As she spoke, Leon steadied the tree as Tucker winched it over the excavation.

Excited children pressed nearer. Face stern, Leon made a chopping gesture with one gloved hand. "Back off, kids. We have to get her in place. The party's not until tomorrow."

Peg waved hello to several young mothers with children in strollers. A teenage girl held tight to a little boy's hand.

As soon as the tree trunk disappeared over the edge of the hole, Tucker joined Leon. Grunting with effort, the two men positioned the tree. Using a pole, Tucker kept the pine upright.

Leon walked to the porch. He moved at a workman's steady pace. He looked up at Keith on the railing and Peg beside him.

Peg's smile was warm. "Keith, I want you to meet Leon. He was our best buddy when we were kids. He took us on hayrides and taught us to shoot and ride. He'll build a great bonfire tomorrow and we can roast marshmallows."

Leon's tone was brusque but his eyes were soft. "Are you big enough to ride in my backhoe?"

Keith nodded, his face solemn.

Leon held up his arms. "Sure you are. You can push the dirt into the hole and make our tree steady as a rock. Tomorrow you'll put the star on the very top. I've been setting up Christmas trees for your grandmother's neighborhood party for a long time. I lifted up your daddy to top the tree when he was your age." Leon swung Keith up to ride on his shoulders.

A door clicked on a second-floor balcony.

Peg and Gina looked up as Susan Flynn stepped outside. Susan's silk robe wasn't enough protection against the chill wind that ruffled her silver-streaked curls. Jake bustled out to join her, carrying a fleecy white cashmere shawl. "You'll catch your death. Here, you'd better wrap up."

Absently Susan took the shawl and drew it around her.

She ignored Jake's continued worried murmurs. Susan watched as Keith, sitting in Leon's lap, Leon's big hand over his, maneuvered the dirt, packing and tamping it around the massive Scotch pine. Susan's eyes were shiny with tears. Peg clapped vigorously. Gina took a quick breath, turned, and stepped inside the house.

CHAPTER 6

I hovered near the ceiling of the blue room at Pritchard House. Moonlight spilled through the windows. Keith was a small snug mound in his bed. Peg lay on her side, one hand curled under her cheek, lips curved in a half smile.

Before Wiggins abruptly left the cemetery en route to Tumbulgum, he'd warned me: *Keep guard* . . . His meaning seemed clear: *Keep guard over Keith.* Wiggins could count on me. I'd been dispatched to protect Keith and I would continue to do my best.

Was Wiggins listening or was Tumbulgum out of earshot?

I had no intention of leaving Keith unsupervised. Peg clearly welcomed him. As long as he was with her, I felt he was safe. Before I went to the lawyer's office to delve into Susan Flynn's will, I would be certain all was secure at Pritchard House.

First I stopped in Gina's room. The breeze through the open window ruffled chintz curtains but had yet to dispel the lingering scent of tobacco smoke. I wondered if Gina dismissed other dangers as easily as she ignored the hazards of cigarettes. She was turned toward the wall in bed, her face in shadow, but her breathing was deep and even.

In the next room, Jake wore a padded black sleep mask. In the moonlight, she looked like a raccoon adorned with curlers. She moved restlessly, murmuring aloud.

I swooped near the bed.

". . . door locked . . . can't get in . . . not fair . . ."

Clearly her dreams were troubled.

In Susan's room, the clock on the mantel chimed, twelve soft bells announcing midnight. She sat in her chair in front of the gas fire. The china cup held a little cocoa, the remnants of her evening drink. In her lap was the manila envelope Keith had brought. She held the papers in her hand, a smile on her face.

All was well at Pritchard House. I felt free to depart.

The computer monitor glowed. I rubbed my eyes as I completed reading the exceedingly complex disposition of the estate of Susan Pritchard Flynn. Upon Susan's death, her heirs would receive the equivalent in land, stocks, bonds, mineral rights, or property of several million dollars each. Inheriting, after substantial bequests to several charities and St. Mildred's, were Jacqueline Flynn, Margaret Flynn, Tucker Satterlee, Gina Satterlee, and Harrison Hammond.

I checked the telephone book and jotted down addresses. I knew the location of Burnt Creek, one of Pontotoc County's largest and most prosperous ranches in my day. I had no reason to doubt that Burnt Creek was still a prime piece of property.

I took a last look at the electronic files and noted one entitled *FlynnEstateRecording.* I opened the file and found a brief enigmatic statement: *Recorded discussion on CD with client Re: Disposition of Flynn estate, Cabinet 3.*

Two metal filing cabinets sat behind Kim's desk. Obviously, neither would be Cabinet 3. In Wade's office, I turned on the light. I checked and the drapes were drawn. Built into the wall behind the desk were several walnut cabinets. Cabinet 3 revealed shelves with small plastic containers with what appeared to be small records. Apparently, they were called CDs. How interesting. Possibly they didn't work too differently from the old 33 rpm record players.

I spotted a device on a marble-topped table with spindly-legged chairs. The chairs didn't look especially comfortable. I snagged a squashy red cushion from the sofa and placed it on a chair. After some punching of buttons, I popped up the lid. Yes, that looked like a turntable. I placed the little record on it, experimented further, and watched with a sense of accomplishment as it began to whir.

There was a moment of silence, then a murmur. "I think that's got it. I'm all thumbs with recorders. Okay, here we go." He cleared his throat. "Wade Farrell and Susan Flynn Re: Disposition of the Susan Flynn estate." Wade's cheerful voice announced the date.

"My, aren't we formal." Susan Flynn's aristocratic voice sounded amused. "Is this necessary, Wade?"

"This is for your protection." Wade spoke with dignity. "Since your heirs have no blood ties to you, I feel that it is wise to make a record of your wishes so that there can be no doubt about the instrument reflecting your decisions. Please explain in your own words the circumstances."

"Very well. I have no family." There was a pause.

The tape whirred.

After a moment, Susan continued in a brittle tone. "It is my wish that the following persons, who are not related to me, shall share in my estate: my sister-in-law Jake Flynn, her daughter Peg Flynn, Jake's nephew and niece, Tucker and Gina Satterlee, and my late husband's cousin Harrison Hammond. I have chosen them to be my legatees because of close association over a number of years. After Jake's husband died, Jake and Peg came to live with us. At that time our family consisted of my husband Tom, our son Mitchell, and our daughter Ellen. Peg and Ellen became close friends. A few years later, Jake's sister and her husband were killed in a car wreck. Tom and I offered a home to their children, Tucker and Gina, because Jake was her sister's only relative. Harrison Hammond was my husband's first cousin. Tom was very fond of Harrison." Susan sighed. "Will that do, Wade?"

"That's perfect, Susan." Wade sounded satisfied.

"Do you know what?" She sounded distant, weary. "I don't care what happens to any of it. They might as well inherit as anyone. They've been a part of my life. If Mitch and Ellen . . . But they're gone. Mitch loved the ranch. Ellen would have created such a happy life, such a good life." Another pause. "My time is running out. I'll see them soon. And now, I'm tired. If that's all, Wade, please go." The last few words were scarcely audible.

I pictured Susan Flynn in her bed, weak and ill, turning away from the careful lawyer, her eyes seeking the photographs on her wall and the children who would never reach out again to her in this world but awaited her in the next.

I returned the CD to its container and the cushion to the sofa. Now I knew the ins and outs of Susan's estate. I felt chilled. When Susan changed her will, the current heirs would lose the prospect of certain wealth.

Could I keep Keith safe until Susan signed her new will?

Sunlight spilled into Susan's bedroom. The bed was made. Jake dusted and straightened. "It's a shame to have to deal with business matters over the holidays. You don't want to overdo. Are you sure you want to see Wade today?"

Leaning on her cane, Susan walked slowly to a tufted gold seat in front of a French provincial dresser. "Stop fussing, Jake. I feel wonderful this morning. Now, come and help me choose a necklace." Susan was elegant in a high-collared silk-blend jacket and matching slacks in a lovely shade of antique rose. Her makeup was perfectly applied and her narrow face with its fine features echoed past beauty. How lovely she must have been as a young and vibrant woman.

Jake's pudgy hand hovered over the open silver jewel case. Necklaces lay in a heap. "How about the beaded glass necklace, the one with the green and white strands? The colors are such a good contrast to the rose jacket."

"Let me see." Susan held out her hand.

Jake stepped behind Susan. "I'll fasten the clasp."

In the mirror, Susan appeared distinguished in the silk jacket and trousers, Jake frumpy in a too-tight brown angora sweater and dark brown tweed slacks.

I cautiously edged a necklace of beaten silver coins to the top of the case.

Susan's pale face had an unaccustomed blush. Her eyes sparkled. She shook her head in rejection. "The white strand disappears." She glanced again at the case. "My silver coin necklace! That will look best. Tom bought that for me in Santa Fe. Let's try that one."

I nodded in satisfaction as the loop of silver coins glittered against the rose jacket. "That's perfect." I clapped a hand to my mouth.

Susan's eyes went to the mirror, seeking the person who spoke. Jake half turned, looking puzzled. Each glanced at the other.

I held my breath. Perhaps each would conclude it was the other's voice, even though mine is far huskier than Jake's and much more vigorous than Susan's. Once again I had acted without thinking. I must remember: I am not here, I am not here, I am not . . .

A knock sounded on the bedroom door.

Susan stroked the lustrous coins and gave them a satisfied pat. She glanced at the clock on the mantel. "Wade is always punctual."

Peg held the door. She looked young and cheerful and pleased. "Good morning, Susan. Wade's here." She stood aside for the lawyer to enter.

Jake swung toward the door with a forced smile. "Good morning, Wade."

Peg darted a concerned glance at her mother.

Susan slowly rose, steadying herself with the cane. She stood stiff and straight and looked across the room. She didn't speak.

Wade Farrell's brown eyes were kind. "Keith is Mitchell's son."

Susan wavered, one hand on the cane, the other on the dresser, struggling for breath.

Jake fluttered her hands. "Susan, this is too much for you. You've had a shock. You know you mustn't be upset. Wade can leave the file with me." She looked at the lawyer. "Susan can look at the papers later, when she's rested."

Susan's smile was tremulous. "My grandson."

The lawyer glanced from Jake to Susan. "Would you like for me to leave the folder? We can talk another time."

"We will talk now." Susan's tone was sharp. She waved a hand toward Jake. "You and Peg may leave."

Jake's plump cheeks flushed. Her lips pressed together.

Peg hurried to her mother. "We'll go down and help Keith decorate the Christmas cookies."

"Certainly. If we aren't wanted here." Jake's words were clipped. She darted a resentful glance at Susan, then walked swiftly toward the door, her shoes clumping on the floor. She brushed by Wade as if he weren't there.

When the door closed behind them, Susan gripped her ebony cane and took slow steps to her chair in front of the fireplace. She gestured toward the opposite chair. "Please sit down, Wade. I appreciate the effort you made to get the facts on such short notice." She paused, struggling to breathe. "And you are wonderful to come here on a Saturday morning."

He smiled. "I will always come when you call, Susan."

"Thank you, my dear." Her breaths came in quick gasps as she lowered herself into her chair.

The lawyer looked at her in concern.

"I'm all right. I'll get my breath." Slowly, her breathing eased.

He handed her a green folder and sat down in a Morris chair. "You'll find everything documented. Mitchell joined the Army two years after he left home. We weren't able to trace his movements before then." His voice was carefully uninflected with no hint of the despair that drove Mitchell away and the lost days that now would never be accounted for. "He trained at Fort Sill. He served a three-year tour in Germany and was stationed at the U.S. Army Garrison in Schweinfurt."

I heard a tiny click. I have acute hearing.

The Morris chair creaked as Wade rose to hand several papers to Susan.

"He met Marlene Schmidt in Bad Kissingen. That's a resort spa not far from the post. She was nineteen and worked in the gift shop at the Steigenberger Hotel. Here's a picture taken by a friend. It was sent in a digital file, but I printed it out for you."

I glanced over Susan's shoulder.

"What a beautiful girl. What a kind face she had." Susan's voice was soft.

Standing amid summer greenery near a placid pond, Marlene tossed a flower into the water. Slender and blond, she was laughing as a light breeze ruffled her pink sundress.

My eyes moved to the hall door. The knob turned ever so slowly, and the door opened a tiny crack.

"Their wedding was an outdoor ceremony in Kurpark an der Saale. Keith was born a year later on June 6 at the Sixty-seventh Combat Support Hospital in Würzburg. Here is a copy of his birth certificate. He is four and a half years old."

Susan took the printout.

I breezed into the hall.

Jake pressed close to the hairline crack, one hand tight on the knob.

Wade's voice carried well, as lawyers' voices usually do. "Mitchell and his wife and son returned to the United States and to Fort Sill. He was deployed to Iraq where he was killed in an ambush in Ramadi. The notification of his death came to you because he listed you and Tom as his next of kin when he joined and never altered the information."

"Marlene and Keith?"

"They were living in an apartment in Lawton. She thought about going home to Germany, but she decided to stay in the United States for Keith's sake. She was working at a convenience store not far from the post."

"Why didn't she come here?" Susan's voice was anguished. "She knew about us, didn't she?"

Wade settled again in the chair. "My secretary spoke to one of the platoon wives who knew Marlene fairly well. She wasn't certain, but she thought Mitchell had never explained why he wouldn't go home or contact his parents and Marlene didn't feel she would be welcome. All she had was your name and the address. You know how it is in the military, Mitchell's home address was listed here in Adelaide. She approved his body being sent to Adelaide. She wanted him to be buried at home. Last month, Marlene caught a cold and was treated for bronchitis but died four days later of pneumonia. Another friend, Lou Chavez, looked after Keith while Marlene was in the hospital. When Marlene died, Lou took care of him. She decided to bring Keith here because her husband had received orders to Fort Lewis. She didn't feel she could take Keith with them."

"Thank God." Susan's voice was strong. "My grandson." She took a breath. "This changes everything."

The cushion in the Morris chair squeaked. "I assumed such would be the case. I brought a copy of your will."

Jake took a quick breath, her face strained.

Susan was brisk. "I know the provisions. They don't matter now. I want Keith to inherit the estate. He will live here. I'd intended to leave Pritchard House to Jake. Instead, I suggest she receive a life interest in the house, contingent upon the house being kept up for Keith. On her death, of course, the house would become Keith's. That seems a fair solution. I'll speak with Jake."

Jake's face twisted in a scowl.

"More important, I need to choose a guardian for Keith. Peg and Keith have fun together, but she's still in college. I could ask my friend Jane Ramsey. There is so much to think about. Perhaps Tucker will be willing to remain on the ranch as the operator. Keith may or may not have an interest in running Burnt Creek when he is grown. Oh"—Susan's tone was passionate—"I wish I could live long enough to see what he likes and what he wants to do and who he will be. Perhaps I'll get stronger. I have a reason to live now."

"What about the previous heirs? Do you wish to leave them anything?"

"Yes, of course." Susan's answer was quick and decided.

"They've been a part of my life for so long now. I know the value of the estate has fallen with the hard economic times, but oil is still selling at a fairly good rate. I want to make a difference for all of them. Each should receive a bequest of two hundred thousand dollars."

Papers rustled. "I'll put together a draft. Let me check my notes." He was quiet for a moment, then asked abruptly, "There's the matter of Dave Lewis. Is that still on the table?"

Susan's laughter was soft. "Dear Wade. You've opposed my loaning money to him from the first, haven't you?"

Jake's face folded in a frown.

Wade cleared his throat. "I think it is unwise. He still hasn't submitted a business plan to me. When I met with him, he was too vague to suit me. And too cocky. With the economy down, it doesn't seem like a good time to build a clinic that is twice as large and fancy as it needs to be. He's called me three times to ask when the money will be available."

"Indeed." Her tone was considering. "I hadn't made a final decision. Of course, I want to see Peg happily launched. She's a wonderful girl. Frankly, I've never especially cared for Dave. Sometimes too-handsome men think the world revolves around them. He can be extremely charming when he chooses and I'm afraid Peg is dazzled, but he seems very dictatorial. I'm afraid Peg was too young when her father died and she may be looking for the sense of security that comes from letting other people make decisions. But that's not my business. I suppose I listened to his plans for her sake. And"—she sounded rueful—"I didn't really care about the estate then. Now I care. However, there was no commitment. I merely said I would consider providing the money interest-free. Now, I definitely want to see a business plan and also the blueprints for the building. When he calls again"—her voice was cool—"tell him he needs to submit a formal proposal."

"I'll do that." Wade sounded satisfied.

"You give good advice, Wade. Now is no time for extravagance. There seem to be too many demands on me suddenly. Tucker recently asked about buying a new bull. Gina wants me to pay off her credit cards. I am not inclined to do that. She must learn to live within her means."

"She'll have to face financial reality sooner or later. Now, about the new will"—he was businesslike—"our office closes on Christmas Eve and we won't reopen until January second."

Susan's words tumbled out. "I hope you don't think I'm being unreasonable, but I want to sign the will as soon as possible. That will give me peace. Could you possibly have it ready for me by Monday?"

"This coming Monday?" He was clearly dismayed.

"Please, Wade. I know it's the holidays. But it will mean the world to me to be sure everything is arranged for Keith."

There was only the shortest hesitation before he answered. "I understand." His voice was kind. "I'll bring the instrument here Monday at ten o'clock."

In the shaft of light from a hall lamp, Jake's face looked pinched. She began to ease the tension on the knob.

As soon as the panel shut, Jake would hurry downstairs. Susan Flynn would never know her conversation with Wade Farrell had been overheard. I made my decision on the instant. With a firm shove, I pushed the door open. It banged against the wall.

Jake stood frozen in the doorway, a picture of guilt.

Susan turned to look. Her patrician face reflected surprise. And concern.

Wade came to his feet. His eyes narrowed in speculation though his expression was pleasant.

Jake's face flushed a deep painful red. "I came to see if I could bring some coffee. Something banged into the door." She looked over her shoulder.

The hall was empty.

"I don't know what happened." She stared at the door.

"It is thoughtful of you to ask." Susan's voice was light and even, but her eyes held a shadow. "We won't be needing anything. Thank you."

Jake turned hurriedly and bolted into the hall, slamming the door behind her.

Susan looked at Wade, started to speak, gave a slight head shake, then said briskly, "I'll keep the papers about Keith."

The lawyer nodded. "I'll get right to work."

Susan sank back in her chair, her thin face troubled.

As Peg set the table for lunch in the kitchen, Jake paced near the oven. Her face flushed, she talked rapidly. ". . . and I think it's mean as can be. Susan promised the house to me."

Peg lifted a pitcher of iced tea from the refrigerator. "Mother, what difference does it make? The house will be yours as long as you live."

Jake slapped napkins next to each plate. "I know how it will go. There will be all kinds of provisions. Everything will be his, really. What if when he"—she jerked her head toward Keith, absorbed in stacking different-sized saucepans one within another—"gets married, his wife doesn't like me, and they want to live here?" Jake's voice rose in a wail.

Peg poured tea into bright red tumblers. "Mother"—her tone was patient but exasperated—"don't borrow trouble. Let him be a little boy and grow up. That's all years away."

Gina sliced ham. "Ease up, Jake. Peg's right. A life interest sounds great. I'd be glad to have a life interest in something."

"Two hundred thousand dollars for each of us is very generous." Peg's tone was sharp.

"It isn't two million." Gina's voice was shaky.

Jake planted her hands on her hips. "Susan promised the house to me and neither of you care. But I'm not the only one who's going to pay a price. Gina, you can whistle Dixie about those credit cards. Susan's not going to give you a nickel. As for you, Peg, Susan's not about to rubber-stamp Dave's clinic. She wants a business plan and she'll consider a plain-vanilla building for the clinic, not that fancy stacked stone Dave wants. Both of you can chew that over with your lunch. I'm too upset to eat a thing." Jake whirled and slammed out of the kitchen.

The knife clattered from Gina's hand. As she bent slowly down to pick it up, Peg came close and touched her arm. "I'm sorry, Gina. You were counting on that money."

Gina rose and flung the knife into the sink. "I'm desperate. They have a judgment against me and they're going to take my car away from me." Tears welled in her eyes.

"If I can help—"

Gina's burst of laughter was harsh and ragged. "You're poor, too, honey. Nothing can help me except cash. If I could take out a loan . . . But banks won't loan money to people like me, not when they won't even loan money to somebody like Dave, a brand-new vet who can make at least seventy thousand a year once he starts his practice. What are you going to do? Isn't Dave coming right after lunch? Are you going to tell him?"

I finished a hasty lunch, pulled together in a flash when Peg went to answer the front door and Gina took a tray up to Susan.

A remarkably handsome man followed Peg into the living room. Dave Lewis had curly brown hair and film-star features, a broad forehead, straight nose, full lips, cleft chin.

Dave held up a portfolio, his face pink from the cold and excitement. He was magazine-ad attractive in a thick Shetland wool pullover sweater and dark gray slacks and black loafers. His pale brown eyes gleamed with delight. "Got a new concept. It's even better than the first one." He stopped, gazed at Keith. "Who's the kid?"

"Susan's grandson, Keith." Quickly, Peg explained.

Keith tugged at a log. He called out, "Let's make a fire, Peg."

She moved toward the fireplace.

"That can wait." Dave pointed at the wood. "Yeah, Keith, why don't you count the logs." He turned to Susan. "Look at these." He knelt to pull out the thick sheets and spread them on the floor. "It makes sense to build as large a clinic as we can. We'll have boarders, of course. See, here's the run for dogs—" He looked up, frowned. "Come on, Peg. Take a look."

Keith tugged on Peg's sweater. "Can we have a fire?"

"In a minute, sweetie. Run upstairs and get your bag of gold coins and I'll sell you some wood."

Keith grinned and pelted for the door.

Dave grinned. "Good move, Peg. Now we can look at my—"

"Dave." Peg clasped her hands tightly together. Her round expressive face was slightly pale, her eyes anxious. "You need to check with Susan's lawyer. I think Susan wants a business plan. And"—Peg's eyes fell away from him—"she may think the building should be scaled back a little. Because of the economy."

Dave let the plans roll back together. He picked up the roll, stood. "What's up? Why the roadblock? I've got a great concept and it's all pulled together."

"Susan's looking ahead to the future. For her grandson."

"How about our future? I thought she was on board." He seemed to realize he'd spoken too loudly. "Look, Peg, Susan's fond of you. Talk to her. You can smooth everything out." He walked over, pulled her close. "I'm counting on you. This is for us."

Keith pounded into the living room, holding the little leather bag. "I'll buy two logs."

Dave took an irritated breath. "I'm going out to take some pix of a good property that's selling for a song. I'll show them to you later." He glanced at Keith. "When you aren't playing nursemaid. Maybe we can get out after the tree party." He turned and strode toward the hall.

I love a good party, but I didn't feel a part of the festivities hovering above the crowd. I landed behind a huge evergreen. After looking carefully in all directions, I swirled into being. I'd noted the coats and jackets of the onlookers crowding the front lawn of Pritchard House. The styles were casual. I much preferred dressier selections, but I wanted to blend into the festive gathering. I wasn't willing to don the slick bulky coats worn by many. I decided on a double-breasted black wool cropped jacket with oversize buttons on the sleeve cuffs, a magenta blouse, black wool trousers, argyle socks, and black boots.

Earlier in the afternoon, Leon and Tucker had erected scaffolding next to the big tree and wound the light strands around and around from the top of the tree to the bottom. Promptly at four o'clock the neighbors converged. Children from toddlers to teenagers formed an orderly line at the base of the scaffolding steps. For the past hour, Leon had guided children up the steps to a platform. Each child carried a decoration large enough to be visible on the big tree.

The decorations were both everyday and extraordinary:

Red-and-white-striped candy canes.

Models of sleds, reindeer, angels, snowmen, antique cars, even a rescue helicopter.

Wooden carvings of a giraffe, elephant, seal, whale, lion, lamb, cow, horse, armadillo, dog, cat, goat, chimpanzee, polar bear, and eagle.

Bright plastic balls with painted scenes of a skating party, roasting chestnuts, a sleigh ride, carolers, presents piled beneath a tree, a family dinner, the Salvation Army kettle, lampposts decorated with strands of red and green lights.

Leon helped the last child, a little girl in a pink snowsuit, place a sparkling candy cane on a branch. As he swung her up to wave, the crowd stirred expectantly.

The woman in front of me lifted a little boy. "Look up, Bobby. Watch the balcony."

I stood on tiptoe trying to see.

She gave me a quick bright smile. "Here, you can squeeze in beside me. Isn't this wonderful. It's just like old times." Dark curls framed a cheerful face, her cheeks red with cold.

"I'm visiting around the corner." I gestured to my left. "Is this a church party?"

She shifted the child onto one hip. "A neighborhood party. It will really make you feel like Christmas." Her smile was infectious. "I'm Kay Kelly."

I hesitated only an instant. "Jerrie Emiliani."

Kay gave an expansive wave with her free hand. "I grew up in Adelaide and this has always been my very favorite Christmas celebration. It was started by the Pritchard family years and years ago. Susan Flynn, who lives here now, is the last of the Pritchards. Everyone is welcome. It started off as a little party for children who were friends of the family's children, but now people come from all over town. Mrs.

Flynn doesn't mind. The children help decorate a big Scotch pine cut fresh from the Pritchard ranch. The tree isn't like the tree at Rockefeller Center, but for Adelaide it's a big, big tree. After the decorating is done, there's a bonfire and kids roast marshmallows and there are cookies and punch and hot chocolate and every child gets a little wrapped present. One of the family members hands out gifts to each boy and girl. The gifts are assorted by age. I still have all my gifts. My favorite was a little charm bracelet with a rose rock."

I knew all about rose rocks, the official rock of Oklahoma. Barite crystals combined with Oklahoma's iron-rich sand to produce reddish rocks shaped like roses. The Cherokee believed that each rock represented the blood of those who died on the Trail of Tears when the Cherokee were forcibly removed from Georgia in 1838 to Indian Territory.

"Mrs. Flynn"—my new friend nodded toward the house—"has been ill the last few years and hasn't come out on the balcony with the rest of the family to welcome everyone. One child will be picked to place the star at the very top of the tree and switch on the tree lights. Every year the lights are a different color. Last year they were all blue. Oh look, here comes the family."

Twin lanterns flashed on, illuminating the now shadowy balcony in a golden glow, making it a bright stage in the deepening dusk. Susan Flynn stepped outside. She was elegant in a full-length black mink coat with a wing collar and turned-back cuffs. A crimson turtleneck emphasized the dark sheen of the mink. A matching fur fedora was tilted at a jaunty angle.

A cheer rose.

My new friend was joyful. "How wonderful. That's Mrs. Flynn. She must be feeling better, though her face is awfully thin."

Susan held up both hands, smiling and blinking back tears, touched by the exuberant welcome.

I sorted them out as they stepped onto the balcony.

Plump Jake Flynn nodded this way and that as if the welcome was for her, not Susan. Jake looked like a plump robin in a red quilted vest.

A wide-eyed Keith clutched Peg Flynn's hand. Dave stood on Peg's other side. He held possessively to her elbow. His camel-hair coat looked new and was undoubtedly expensive.

Gina Satterlee drew some admiring glances for her silver fur and stylish red-and-black-plaid slacks.

An ebullient smile was bright as a Christmas wreath on Harrison Hammond's florid face. His wife Charlotte shivered and tied a red wool scarf beneath her chin. She moved toward a remaining sunny spot on the balcony.

Tucker Satterlee sauntered out last. Unlike the other men, he had a rugged outdoor appearance in his tan shearling coat and snug jeans. Tucker pulled the hall door shut and joined his sister. He leaned against the railing and folded his arms.

Gina gave Tucker a quick, unreadable glance.

Susan moved to the railing. "Merry Christmas." Her voice rang clear and true.

"Merry Christmas." The shouts rose on the clear cold air.

"Thank you for coming to our tree party." The breeze ruffled the lustrous fur of her coat. She took a quick breath. "Every year a child is invited to put the Star of Bethlehem atop the tree when the other decorations are in place." Susan gripped the railing with both hands, steadied herself. "This year, the child is special to me and this Christmas will be one of the most joyous of my life. My grandson Keith has come to live with me. Keith will crown our tree."

Murmurs rose and the crowd pressed forward.

Peg picked up Keith, held him high. "Wave, honey," she whispered.

Keith's face was solemn, but he lifted a hand and waved.

"We'll be right down." Peg swung Keith to the balcony floor.

Tucker pushed away from the railing. "Hey, buckaroo. How about a Tarzan swing?" He held out his arms for Keith, shouted to Leon, who stood by the steps to the scaffolding. "Want to catch him, Leon? Here he comes." Tucker picked up Keith and swung him out over the balcony.

Gasps and cries rose.

Susan lifted a hand in protest. "Tucker, no."

Leon hurried forward, his weathered face drawn in a frown. "Wait up, Tucker. I can't reach him."

"Uh-one. Uh-two." Tucker swung Keith from side to side. In mid-swing, he let go. "Here he comes."

Leon shifted a foot or so to one side as he held up his arms.

Keith's laughter was a gurgle of delight.

Leon staggered a bit as he caught Keith.

"Tucker, that was dangerous." Susan's voice was sharp.

He looked around, grinned. "Keith's having a blast."

Leon looked up. "I've got him all right."

Susan took a deep breath, but her eyes were still angry.

Tucker spread his hands in a charming plea for approval. "Hey, Susan, guys have to be guys. Now you wait and see if Keith doesn't remember next Christmas and insist we do it again."

"Next Christmas . . ." There was an odd note in Susan's voice.

Keith looked up from below. He wriggled in Leon's grasp. "Swing me again."

Tucker laughed out loud. "Keith's got the right idea. How about it, Susan?"

"Once is enough." She came to the railing. "Hold tight to Leon, Keith. He's taking you up to the top of the tree."

Leon wrapped an arm around Keith. At a card table at the base of the scaffolding, Leon picked up a huge white star. "Here we go." He mounted two steps at a time, carrying Keith to the top platform. Leon steadied Keith on the metal railing and, bending forward, reaching out to the tip-top of the pine, Leon's big hand over Keith's small one, they put the star in place.

Another cheer rose.

Susan watched Keith, her face shining with delight.

I looked at those around Susan.

Jake's lips compressed into a tight hard line. Peg took a step toward her mother, stopped. A frown marred Dave Lewis's handsome features. Gina hunched her shoulders and jammed her hands into the pockets of her coat. Harrison looked worried. His wife put a hand on his sleeve. Tucker gave a dismissive shrug and turned toward the hall door.

Susan lifted her hands in a gesture of hospitality. "It's time for cookies and cocoa."

In an instant, Susan would turn. Though she was caught up in the moment, thrilled with Keith and with the tree, she would surely see the closed faces of those who surrounded her, closed against Keith, closed against her.

My voice rose clear and distinct. Soon voices joined me, one after another, until everyone sang the light and lilting "It's the Most Wonderful Time of the Year."

Susan moved back to the railing, eyes shining. She turned toward those behind her and gestured like a conductor. One by one they joined in.

I nodded in satisfaction. It is difficult to frown and sing at the same time.

As the song ended, Susan beamed. "We're coming down and we'll sing more songs." She turned and walked to the balcony door and those around her followed.

By the time they came out onto the porch, Susan had to stop and grip a pillar. Peg took her arm and after a moment they came down the front steps.

I launched into "Santa Claus Is Coming to Town."

Voices rose enthusiastically around me.

Despite the upbeat music, I felt a chill as I recalled the stony faces on the balcony before I started to sing.

CHAPTER 7

Tucker poked at the fire. Flames danced and crackled, flickering blue and red. The living room drapes were drawn against the winter night. The room was cozy and warm, yet there was no aura of holiday cheer.

Susan sat in a wingback chair near the fire. She looked frail and worn, her face paper white. She nodded toward Jake. "If you'll pour the coffee . . ."

Jake bustled to the sideboard. "Of course, Susan. Will you have coffee or sherry tonight?"

"Sherry, please." Susan smiled.

Gina rose to help her aunt. Spoons tinkled against cups. Plates with slices of peach pie were offered. It might have been any family gathering after dinner for coffee and dessert in a room bright with Christmas decorations, a sprig of mistletoe dangling from the chandelier, silver bells strung along the windowsills, a lovely tree with taffeta bows and Wedgwood blue ornaments, but there was a definite sense of strain.

Tucker lifted a bronze statue of a mare running with her foal from the mantel and turned it over to look at the sculptor. "Looks like Tramp Lady, my chestnut mare." As he returned the piece, his elbow caught a green velvet stocking hanging from the mantel. As the stocking fell, he lunged to save it from the fire. "Hey, a near thing." He held the stocking up.

Keith's name straggled in uneven green sparkles on the white cuff above an embroidery of Santa studying a Christmas letter. "Nifty." He looked around with a quizzical expression. "Quick work to already have his own stocking here."

Gina shrugged. "Peg helped Keith with the stocking this afternoon. Peg's having a lot of fun with him." There might have been a faint note of envy in her voice.

Tucker carefully rehung the stocking. "Keith's too little to write a letter to Santa, but I guess he'll get whatever he wants."

Harrison put his cup and saucer on a marble table. "It's always a pleasure to be part of the holiday celebration here. The tree party this afternoon was a great success." He nodded toward Susan. "Thank you for including us, Susan. I expect it's time Charlotte and I were on our way." He stood and tried for a cheerful smile.

Susan held up a hand. "Please stay for a few more minutes, Harrison. I have something I wish to discuss with everyone. We'll wait for Peg. She and Dave are putting Keith to bed."

She'd no more than spoken when the door opened and Dave walked in. His light blue sweater accented the sheen of his carefully cut hair. He spoke to Susan. "Peg almost has him asleep." He sounded impatient. "She'll be here soon."

Harrison sat down and folded his arms across his chest. He darted an occasional uneasy glance at Susan.

Charlotte poked her glasses higher on her thin nose and smiled at Susan. "This afternoon's tree party was perfect. The songs added such a happy note."

I immediately felt much warmer toward Charlotte.

Susan was animated. "I saw the woman who started the singing. A lovely redhead. She was standing in a pool of light from the lamppost. I'm sure I know her. Her face was very familiar."

That gave me pause. Susan was a young woman when Bobby Mac and I took our last fishing trip into the Gulf. In fact, she was a new addition to the Altar Guild and I was then in my third term as directress. Moreover, Susan would have passed my portrait in the parish hall many times.

Susan's face crinkled as she tried to recall me.

The hall door opened and Peg slipped in, her face flushed. "I hope I haven't been too long. Keith was too excited to relax so we sang songs. Someone had taught him 'Rudolph the Red-Nosed Reindeer,' and he insisted on singing it twice."

I took a bow though no one saw me.

Peg dropped onto a sofa next to her young man. "He's fast asleep now."

"Thank you, Peg." Susan flashed her a grateful look. "Did he have a good time this afternoon?"

Peg's smile was quick. "He talked and talked about the *'tar.* He can't manage the *s.* He said he put the *'tar* on the tree and his eyes were as big as saucers. Oh, Susan, he is such a love."

I glanced around the room. Tucker jabbed the poker into the log and sparks whirled up in a fiery rush. Gina turned a silver bracelet on her wrist around and around. Jake placed her fork on the dessert plate with a ping. Harrison's face had an empty look. Charlotte's glance at her husband was anxious. Dave folded his arms, his mouth in a tight, straight line.

With a deep breath as if drawing on inner reserve, Susan slowly stood, using her cane for support. She placed the cane in front of her, leaned upon the curved handle with both hands. "I received confirmation this morning from Wade Farrell that Keith is Mitch's son. Today has been one of the happiest days of my life." She stood straighter, a faint flush turning her cheeks pink, bringing back a bloom that had long been gone. "For Mitch's son to be here is joy beyond belief. I pray that all of you will share in my happiness."

Peg jumped up and hurried across the room to slip an arm around Susan's thin shoulders. "Dearest Susan. No one deserves happiness more than you."

Peg's quick and sweet response almost bridged the awkward silence before the others spoke. Almost.

Tucker gave a thumbs-up. "He's a chip off the old block. He laughed when I swung him over the railing. That would have been Mitch all the way."

Gina brushed back a dark curl. "Of course we want you to be happy, Susan."

Jake came to her feet, began to collect plates. Her smile was starched. "He's a very nice little boy." Her hands were unsteady and the plates wobbled as she stacked them.

Harrison cleared his throat. "In a world where there is so much dishonesty, I wonder if Farrell has been quite careful. As a man of the world, I'd recommend that you make a thorough check of all claims."

Susan's quick glance at Harrison was cool, her voice crisp. "The matter is settled." Her look of command faded, replaced by uncertainty. She looked appealing, her classic features drawn in concern, her frail health evident. "Until Keith came, I had no direct family. I have, through the years, felt close to each of you. I appreciated your support for me. I made no secret that I had divided my estate among you. Now everything has changed. I realize"—she did not look toward Jake—"that quite reasonably each of you wonders how this will affect you."

Tucker flashed a boyish smile. "Hey, Susan, we understand. Keith's the man. None of us has a claim on you. You don't owe anybody any explanations."

Susan's smile was grateful. "In my mind and heart each of you does have a claim and I want to be clear. No one will be forgotten. Tucker, you have been the best manager the ranch has ever had. I hope you'll want to stay on. I'll make certain that you receive an excellent salary. In fact, each of you will receive a substantial bequest." She looked at Jake, a hopeful tentative look. "I'll arrange that you have a life interest in the house. I won't forget anyone."

Harrison cleared his throat. "Susan, as always, you are a gracious and generous woman. Certainly all of us are proud to be a part of your unofficial family and join in wishing you happiness. I propose a toast." He nodded at Jake. "See that everyone has a glass of wine."

Jake frowned at his commanding tone, but moved to the sideboard. She lifted a decanter and filled eight glasses.

When everyone was served, Harrison lifted his glass. "To Susan, wishing you sunny days—and years—with your grandson." His smile was wide, but his eyes were frightened.

In the entryway as coats were brought out of the closet, Dave reached out and pulled loose a short charcoal gray wool jacket. He handed it to Peg. "Let's drive around and see the lights." He was smiling but his gaze was steely.

Peg took a quick breath and swung toward Gina. "Won't you come with us?"

Gina carefully did not look toward Dave. She smothered an unconvincing yawn. "I'm early to bed tonight. Have fun." She glanced at Jake, bidding Tucker and Harrison and Charlotte good night. "Hey, Jake, after you make the cocoa, do you want me to take Susan's tray up?"

Dave took Peg's elbow, urged her toward the door. "I can show you the property while we're out."

Jake massaged one temple. "Thank you, Gina. I'm awfully tired. Everything's ready. I'll take care of making it right now. She likes her cocoa very hot to start with, though sometimes she lets it sit forever and drinks it stone cold . . ."

Jake's querulous voice was cut off as the door closed.

Neither Dave nor Peg spoke until they were in his car, a two-seater sports car. He turned on the motor. "Did you talk to Susan this afternoon?"

"There wasn't time." Peg stared straight ahead.

"Look, Peg. You have to make an effort." His tone was curt. "I'm making an effort. It's critical that I get this loan. I've got everything lined up."

Peg lifted a shaky hand, clung to the lapel of her coat. "Let's not talk about it now."

The car picked up speed. His profile in the wash of a streetlamp was set and cold. "Now is when you have to do something. She's about ready to give all the money to that brat."

"He isn't a brat. He's a sweet, dear little boy."

Dave's voice was measured. "Okay, he's the world's greatest kid. Tell her you think he's wonderful. Lay it on thick. Then explain to her that I was going to give you an engagement ring for your birthday, but everything may have to go on hold. I can't get engaged and think about a wedding when I'm trying to start up a new practice unless I've got some backing. For God's sake, she's taking away everything you've counted on. The least she can do is come through on the loan."

The car pulled up at a stop sign perhaps three blocks from Pritchard House.

"Do you know, I think I'm too tired to take a drive." Her voice was thin. She unclicked her seat belt, opened the door.

"I'll walk back. I have a headache and maybe the night air will make me feel better."

"Peg . . ."

The door slammed shut.

In an instant, the car jolted forward, tires squealing.

The occupants of the house settled for the night. Peg had turned toward the wall as if shutting out the world. A night-light glowed not far from Keith's bed. Keith was curled against an oversize teddy bear almost as big as he. Charlotte Hammond had presented the jumbo brown plush bear to him after the tree-trimming party. The bear, promptly named Big Bob by Tucker, sported a Santa hat and a red muffler decorated with candy canes.

I glided past the sleeping child and patted Big Bob's soft plush fur as I set out to make my rounds.

Gina held a book. Her irregular features were drawn in a worried frown. She stared without seeing at the printed lines.

Jake's plump face was puckered with unhappiness. She tossed and turned, misery evident even in her sleep.

Everyone was in their place. I smothered a yawn. As soon as I checked on Susan, I would settle on the chaise longue, ready to drift into sleep, remembering the friendly welcome from a stranger at the Christmas party and Keith's excitement as he and Leon placed the star on the tip-top of the tree. I suspected memories of the afternoon would weave happy dreams as well for Susan Flynn tonight. However, I feared that the dreams of those to whom she had spoken after dinner would not be so sweet. I would be glad when Susan had signed the new will. Until then, I could not assume Keith was safe.

I entered Susan's bedroom. A soft golden light spread

near one corner of the ceiling. I was puzzled. The chandelier was dark. The only other light came from the Tiffany lamp on the nightstand. That was a small pool of white light . . .

A cold hand seemed to squeeze my heart.

The light from the Tiffany lamp illuminated the still figure lying on her left side in the bed.

Forever still.

"Oh," I spoke aloud, a soft cry filled with sadness.

Suddenly, the limp right arm jerked upward and flopped.

Perhaps I was wrong. Perhaps Susan lived. I zoomed to the bed. I bumped into someone and stepped on something. "Oh!"

"Ouch." Susan Flynn's voice was sharp and vigorous. "You're standing on my foot."

I jumped to one side.

"You kicked me." The cultivated voice was aggrieved. "I don't see anyone. Where are you? What's happening? Why am I standing here and yet there I am on the bed? What's wrong with me?" The arm was yanked this way and that. "Wake up." Again the arm rose and fell.

"Susan, I'm here, but you can't see me. If I can't see you . . ." My words trailed away.

Susan was struggling against death, but there was nothing she could do.

I took a shaky breath. I'd signed up at the Department of Good Intentions to return to earth to help the living. I was, in fact, prohibited from contact with departed spirits (Precept Two). I'd dismissed that instruction from my mind. The idea that I would consort with a departed spirit was laughable.

I wasn't laughing.

The golden glow near the ceiling shone with a compelling radiance.

"That light up there, it's warm and beckoning." Susan sounded farther away. The golden glow was pulling at her, urging her to come. "I must wake up. I have to take care of Keith."

I should keep quiet, yet I felt compelled to console Susan. "Susan, I'm terribly sorry." Was Wiggins frowning mightily in Tumbulgum? But I had to speak out. She was struggling to stay in the world, a struggle doomed to failure. I could help her realize that her time on earth was done.

Everything seemed out of order. Why did Susan have to die this night of all nights? "Susan, you're dead."

"Dead?" Her clear, resonant voice was stricken.

The side of the bed dipped and I knew she sat beside that still figure. A hand was lifted and held.

I reached out, found her arm. "I wish it weren't so, I truly do. I hate for you to be dead." That didn't sound right. I didn't want to discourage Susan. As soon as she let go of the world, she would find herself in a much better place, as Sydney Carton remarked so long ago.

She pulled away and scrambled to her feet. "I am *not* dead. I can see everything. I can talk and move about and I feel wonderful. Except I'm standing here"—she stamped a foot not far from the bed—"and I can't make myself get out of bed. Besides"—her tone was reasonable as if making a rational point to herself—"I can't be talking to someone who isn't here."

"I'm here." At least I was present until orders were issued in Tumbulgum.

"Where are you? Who are you?" Her voice was thin and frightened.

For once I wished that Wiggins would arrive, gruff and irritable, fuming at my mistakes. He could tell me what to do. If I followed the rules (Precept Two), I would maintain silence, leave Susan to face eternity on her own.

I would not!

I cut my eyes around the room, quailing at my audacity.

However, that bodacious thought should assure Wiggins's arrival.

Not a sound. Not a sign.

Wiggins had always been quick to arrive when I departed from an emissary's approved role. Of course, Tumbulgum was far distant and I supposed he couldn't be in two places at once. Time zones and all that. He might find them confusing since there was no time in Heaven.

Whatever the reason, I faced up to a daunting truth: Wiggins wasn't coming.

I was on my own.

I'd never felt so alone.

"I don't understand." Susan was frantic. The limp arm was shaken harder. "Wake up, wake up!"

I couldn't stand by and do nothing. For good or ill, I refused to abandon Susan now. I swirled into being.

A gasp sounded.

I saw my reflection in the mirror of Susan's dresser: flame-bright curls, hopeful freckled face, anxious green eyes. I hoped I appeared suitably subdued, a black cashmere sweater, single-strand pearl necklace, gray slacks, and black boots. Nothing flashy. Of course, redheads always look good in black, but that is simply a fact, nothing I'd taken into consideration.

"What are you doing here? Who are you?" Susan's voice was frantic.

If I revealed the truth, she would be startled, but we had to deal with the facts. "I'm a ghost." To heck with Wiggins's preference for *emissary.* Facts are facts. "I was dispatched to keep watch over Keith. I arrived on the front porch just as Peg opened the door . . ." I talked fast, concluding with a description of the after-dinner gathering this evening in the living room.

There was no response.

I took a deep breath, brushed back a vagrant curl. The easy part was over, if announcing one's arrival in a ghostly state can be considered easy. Now for the hard part. "You see"—and my voice was gentle—"you died tonight. Now it's time for you to leave."

"I can't." Yet her voice was fainter. Was she slipping away?

"You must." I wanted to reassure her. "I'll be here to guard Keith."

"I don't believe this. You aren't here. I'm not sitting here on the bed beside me. None of this is happening. It's a dream."

"You aren't dreaming." I spoke with finality, then rushed ahead. "Don't be frightened. Heaven is waiting for you. You'll be with Mitch and Ellen and Tom."

"Oh." Her voice was soft. "That will be wonderful." There was longing and hope in her voice. Then, sharp and decisive, she announced, "Not yet. Not until I take care of Keith."

A sharp pinch stung my arm. "Ouch." I stepped farther from the bed.

"You weren't here. Now you are." Her voice wobbled. "I'm here, but I can't see me, and I'm floating and on the bed—" She broke off.

"Susan, don't be upset." How useless bromides are when someone is caught up in intense emotion. Of course she was upset, and an unknown redhead appearing next to the bed where her body lay was surely not calming. How could I reassure her? I tried again. "Look at it this way. Dying changes everything." In fact, I was puzzled. Clearly Susan was dead. She shouldn't be tethered to earth. "I don't know why you're still here. It's time for you to leave." I gestured toward the golden glow above us.

"No." The word was abrupt and determined.

"No?" Oh dear. If ever I needed a helping hand, it was now. Where was Wiggins? Oh, of course. Tumbulgum.

"I haven't made provision for Keith. If I die now, he will receive nothing. There will be no one to care for him. I must take care of Keith." She stifled a sob.

Abruptly I understood what was happening. Sometimes a spirit in great travail is bound to earth in mourning until past wrongs are righted, grievances settled. "I see." I began to pace.

A dead hand was lifted, shaken. "Wake up!"

"Susan, there's no going back." I was firm.

The bed creaked as she rose. "Then how can you be here?"

We were getting into dangerous territory. "I'm here on temporary duty." After all, I was an official emissary.

Strong fingers gripped my arm. "I'm not asking to stay long. Just long enough to take care of Keith. If you can be here, why can't I?"

Oh. And oh. And oh. "I suppose . . ." I broke off. Wiggins would forever bar me from future missions. I would be regarded as the Benedict Arnold of the Department of Good Intentions.

"Is there a way?" Her grip tightened. "If there is, I beg you to tell me." The pressure of her fingers made clear her urgency and despair and determination.

Down the hallway, a dear little boy slept cuddled next to his bear. Peg would take care of him, but he should receive his heritage and his grandmother should have peace.

I pushed away all thoughts of Precept Two and Wiggins. If this were to be my last adven-mission, I would do what I felt should be done, no matter what. "We can try." I was in uncharted territory. "I'm not sure if it will work." I pointed at myself. "Watch. If I decide to disappear . . ." My reflection in the mirror vanished. "Now, I'm going to become visible." Once again, I swirled into being. "*Think* yourself visible."

The pressure on my arm ceased.

"Picture yourself in an emerald green turtleneck and cream slacks and green boots." I held my breath.

Suddenly Susan was there, staring at the mirror in astonishment. She touched her cheek. "I look young. I feel wonderful. I could dance or run. My chest doesn't ache. Oh my." A lovely smile curved her lips. The skin of her oval face was unwrinkled, her complexion soft as magnolia petals, her hair glossy as ebony. Decisive dark brows arched over intelligent dark eyes. Her lips were a bright coral. She was beautiful, the beauty of classic features joined with good character.

I'd not been certain Susan would be able to appear. I *was* certain that I was in big trouble. I was not only consorting with a departed spirit, I was, in effect, encouraging mutiny. I looked Heavenward and murmured, "Only a slight detour."

She turned and gazed at me in awe. "Who are you?"

I explained the Department of Good Intentions as well as I could. I didn't get into the Precepts. ". . . and I used to live in Adelaide. I'm Bailey Ruth Raeburn."

She laughed, a quick, gay, lilting laugh. "Oh, of course. I thought you looked familiar. I saw you this afternoon at our tree party and that's why I thought I knew you. You were directress of the Altar Guild the year I joined. Your portrait is in the hall outside the parish hall. You were famous."

"Famous?" Was that in my dossier at the department?

Her appealing laugh sounded again. "Definitely. Every time a new directress of the Altar Guild was installed, this mantra was passed along: Remember Bailey Ruth and Proverbs. Whenever you encountered resistance, whether over linens or candles or service assignments, you smiled and exclaimed, 'Sweetie, you are an angel to think of that, but we all must remember Proverbs 15:18.' Since no one wanted to admit they had no idea what Proverbs 15:18 was, you swept right on with whatever you wished to do. Oh yes, Proverbs 15:18 rules the Altar Guild to this day: *The hotheaded provoke disputes, the equable allay dissension.*"

"And"—I tried not to sound smug—"if anyone looked it up, she certainly wanted to be considered equable, not hotheaded."

We looked at each other and laughed, laughter based on mutual experience and understanding.

Susan's laughter stopped. She was abruptly somber. She glanced at the still form on the bed and flung out a hand. "All right, I'm dead. And I'm here. What do I do now?"

"You want to make provision for Keith. Well, that's easy. Write out a will." I glanced toward a rolltop desk in one corner. "You'll need paper and a pen and an envelope."

Susan's eyes gleamed. "Of course. That's all I need to do. A holographic will. Keith will be taken care of." Susan whirled and walked briskly to the worn oak desk. She pushed up the lid and settled in the wooden chair. She found notepaper embossed with her initials and began to write, her face furrowed in thought. Occasionally she paused, scratched out a sentence, began again. Finally, she nodded in satisfaction. She handed me the sheet. "What do you think?"

I scanned the document, one page front and back. "Clear as can be." Susan's first concern had been a guardian for Keith. She instructed the court to ask Peg Flynn to serve. If Peg could not do so, Jane Ramsey was named. "I'm sure Peg will want to take care of him, but it's good to have an alternative." The major portion of the estate was left to Keith. Susan also made specific lump-sum bequests of two hundred thousand dollars to each of the previous heirs—Jake

Flynn, Peg Flynn, Gina Satterlee, Tucker Satterlee, and Harrison Hammond—and ten thousand each to the cook and yardman.

I looked at Susan with approval. "Those are generous bequests for the previous heirs."

Susan's expression was rueful. "I hope they agree. They thought they would share in a much greater inheritance." Susan glanced toward the door.

I wondered if she was remembering Jake's awkward appearance in the doorway that morning.

Susan addressed an envelope to Wade Farrell.

As she added a stamp, I held out my hand. "I'll mail it for you." Late at night, I should have no difficulty carrying a truly airborne letter. Or I might remain visible and enjoy a crisp winter night walk. "Is the post office still at Cherokee and Chouteau?"

"Yes. But I haven't signed the will yet. I want my signature witnessed." Her glance at me was cool and intelligent. "A holographic will doesn't need a witness, but I want one." She carefully folded the sheet, slipped it into the envelope.

I looked at her in surprise.

Her smile was quick. "Tom was a lawyer. Wills and trusts and probate." She gestured toward the bed. "I'll be found in the morning. I want someone to be able to say they saw the will—and me—tonight and watched me sign it. I need someone I trust, someone who knows me well." She ran an impatient hand through her hair. "Jane Ramsey is spending Christmas in London with her daughter's family. Let me think . . . Missy Burnett has been sick and she would be too shocked to see me. I haven't left the house much this past year. There has to be someone." She stood and paced back and forth, murmuring names, each followed by a shake of her head.

"Someone who works for you?"

Susan's eyes widened. She swung toward me. "Of course. Leon! He doesn't work for us any longer, but he was foreman of the ranch for many years. He was one of the few people Mitch tried to please." Her smile was a mixture of pride and regret. "Mitch was a handful, but he loved the ranch. Leon never had children and he treated Mitch like his son. After Mitch left, Leon kept everything going but I felt the joy had gone out of Burnt Creek for him. When Tucker finished school and took over at the ranch, Leon quit. But he's been good to come every year to get the Christmas tree in place and put up the scaffolding. I talked to him this afternoon. I told him I hoped Keith would love Burnt Creek the way Mitch did. Leon will help me." She started toward the hall door.

Under no circumstances did we want anyone in the household to awaken until we returned. I held out a restraining hand. "Let's disappear." I did.

Susan looked a trifle panicked. "Where'd you go?"

I gave her a reassuring pat on her shoulder. "I'm here."

She jumped. "How do you do that?"

I tried to remember exactly what I did to disappear. "Think: Gone."

"Gone," she muttered. She faded away. "Oh, what fun."

"Think: Here."

"Here." She swirled into being. "Gone." She went.

I pushed away all thought of Precept Two. "Very good. Now, think where we want to go and we'll be there. I need to know more than Leon's house. What's his last name?" I could immediately go from here to anywhere but I needed a specific location. Main and Cherokee. Perkins Drugstore downtown.

"Butler."

"Good. Think Leon Butler's house and there we'll be. Since you are carrying the letter, we'll zoom rather than pop from here to there." Material objects had to travel through space in real time.

She shook her head. "Leon lives out in the country. He never misses anything. He'd know he hadn't heard a car, and how would we explain showing up on his front porch? We have to drive." She frowned. "I haven't driven in a long time. Can you drive?"

If Susan had thought, she would have realized that driving a car was much farther distant in my past. However, I always enjoyed driving. How much fun to be behind the wheel again. "Of course." I supposed it was like a bicycle. I might wobble a bit at first, but how different could it be?

"I'll get the keys." Susan's voice was eager with no trace of worry or concern. "We'll take Jake's car. Her purse will be on the hall table downstairs."

"All right." I opened the bedroom door, whispered, "You are carrying the letter so float downstairs."

I followed the envelope over the stair rail. I heard a soft gurgle of laughter. Susan was enjoying weightlessness. When the letter was a few inches from the hall table, the brown alligator handbag on the table apparently opened of its own accord. A handkerchief was briefly lifted and replaced. A change purse jingled. "Here they are." A black plastic oblong with several keys attached dangled in the air.

"Excellent."

She tossed the keys in the direction of my voice and I caught them.

With objects to carry, Susan with the letter and I with the keys, it was necessary to open the back door. I waited until I saw the letter on the porch and shut the door.

"Oh, it's so cold." Susan sounded shivery.

"Wear that gorgeous mink."

"It's in the house."

"Think: Mink."

"Mmmm. Thank you."

I decided to think mink as well. Much warmer than suede. I followed the letter through the shadows to the garage.

Susan opened the side door into the garage and turned on a light. She punched a plastic oblong on the wall and the garage door lifted with a whir. "The blue Ford," Susan instructed.

I slipped behind the wheel and Susan settled in the passenger seat. I turned the key, pumped the accelerator. I put the car in reverse. Metal scraped against brick. In my defense, I hadn't realized the wheel wasn't quite straight when I started. I jammed on the brakes, inched forward, straightened, backed up again.

I put the car in park and reached for the handle. "I'll see about the door."

"No need. Push the remote."

"Remote from what?"

Susan cleared her throat. "It's not remote from anything. It's up there on the windshield to your left."

I glanced at another plastic oblong attached to the interior of the windshield. How complex earthly life had become. However, I appreciated not having to leap from the car to lower the garage door. "Certainly. The remote." I didn't want Susan to lose confidence in me. I pushed the button. The door slid down. At the end of the drive, I waited for directions.

"Leon lives on Shanty Road about eight miles east of Oil City."

In the early oil days, a makeshift camp had grown up on the outskirts of Adelaide when oil was discovered. Shanty Road ran between Oil City and the smaller town of Briarwood.

As I drove, Susan was curious. "Do you like coming back to earth?"

"This is only my second time to return. I love being in Adelaide. I was happy here." We passed an elementary school. "Rob and Dil went to Sequoyah." I reminisced about the harried years when Rob and Dil were little and there never seemed to be enough hours in the day and Bobby Mac was getting started as a wildcatter and twice we had to mortgage the house, the exciting years when oil gushed and we traveled to Europe and Rob was an Eagle Scout and Dil the prettiest girl in her class, and the too-short years, when I was the mayor's secretary and knew everything going on in town and Bobby Mac was at his peak. That ended with our last trip on the *Serendipity.*

Near the edge of town, I roared up a hill.

"The speed limit is sixty." Susan's tone was mild and only slightly nervous.

I glanced at the lighted display. Oh my. I slowed.

A siren sounded behind us.

CHAPTER 8

"What will we do?" Susan was distraught. "You don't have a license."

It was a statement, not a question. I'd not detailed the activities of the Department of Good Intentions, but Susan was correct in assuming an earthly driver's license wasn't standard issue.

I eased to a stop. "This is no time for a police chase. I'll think of something." I rolled down the window.

The cruiser pulled up behind us, its headlights illuminating our car.

"Change places with me. Quick. We can pass through anything. Go out the window and in the other." There was no time for explanations. Fortunately, Susan followed directions. Susan held the letter with the will and it floated through space. I zoomed out the driver's window and over the top of the car and back inside to settle in the passenger seat.

The police car door slammed. Footsteps sounded. A flashlight swept the interior of the car. The light stopped, as did the steps. The front seats were empty. The letter appeared to hang near the steering wheel.

"Uh-oh. We need to appear. Quick, Susan." I kept my voice low.

"Are you sure?"

The light continued to sweep the car interior.

"Trust me."

Susan swirled into place. She looked at the letter and placed it on the console between the seats.

The officer slowly approached. The flashlight beam settled on Susan. The mink coat looked splendid.

Susan turned a contrite face toward the window.

The officer bent down and his face was caught in full in the lights from his cruiser. He was what I thought of as Irish handsome, coal black hair, deep-set brilliant blue eyes, a broad mouth that looked as though a smile was always ready. He blinked in recognition. "Mrs. Flynn? I thought you didn't drive anymore."

Susan's smile was quick and joyous. "Johnny Cain, how are you? Your mother told me you'd come back to Adelaide. We're all proud of how well you did at the police academy."

"I wouldn't live anywhere else, Mrs. Flynn." He cleared his throat, looked uncomfortable and as appealing as Rory Calhoun in *How to Marry a Millionaire*. "I'm afraid the car was going a little fast."

"Johnny, I'm sorry. I didn't mean to go so fast. I was talking—"

Johnny looked past Susan at the empty passenger seat.

There was an awkward pause.

"Do you know"—Susan pointed toward the road—"I believe I saw a fox. Oh, that's exciting."

Johnny obediently looked forward. In profile, he was even more handsome.

I swirled into being. "Where did you put your purse, Susan?" I emphasized *purse* in a cheerful but urgent tone.

Johnny jerked back toward the window. He saw me. His rugged face was an interesting study in disbelief, shock, uneasiness, and amazement.

"Your purse." I spoke as if she might be hard of hearing.

She stared at me.

"You need your purse." I bent forward as if to pat her encouragingly on her arm and hissed, "Think: Purse."

"What did you say, ma'am?" Cain stared at me with rapt attention. It would have been flattering had I thought the gaze inspired by admiration.

A black Coach bag materialized on the floor.

"Your purse will have your driver's license." Was it possible to imagine the contents of a purse, down to a valid driver's license?

"My driver's license." Susan's voice was faint. "Johnny, I may have forgotten to put my billfold in my purse. I was so upset when we left." She picked up the leather bag. "We hurried to an old friend's house. She's very ill. Nothing serious but miserable. You know how stomach flu is. We've spent hours cleaning up."

Johnny stepped back a pace, stood straight. "That's all right, Mrs. Flynn. I'll give you a warning ticket this time." He pulled a pad from his pocket and wrote busily. "My little sister was really looking forward to coming to your tree trimming this afternoon." He finished writing, handed the slip to Susan. "You'll want to watch your speed, especially on the asphalt roads. You never know when you might hit a patch of black ice." He backed away, turned, and walked hurriedly to the cruiser.

When he climbed into the cruiser, I gave Susan a thumbs-up. "How did you think of that?" I was filled with admiration.

"No one wants to be sick at Christmas. Johnny is such a nice boy. He grew up around the corner from us in a little blue frame house—really a kind of turquoise—his mother is an artist. He cut our grass for years. Peg and Ellen and Gina always managed to be home when Johnny did the yard. When he was done, they'd bring out lemonade and cookies." Susan lifted the flap of the purse and pulled out a tan leather billfold. "I had a billfold just like this. I bought it in San Antonio." She unsnapped one side, triumphantly held up a driver's license. She returned the billfold and placed the letter in the purse.

I didn't ask if the license was current. Heaven is always in the details.

I felt our passage was charmed. We changed places, disappearing, then reappearing.

I drove very carefully.

The sky was brilliant with stars, but on the country road to Leon's house overlocking limbs, even though bare, made a dark tunnel. The twin beams of the headlights only seemed to emphasize the inky night. As we came around a final turn, our lights swept the front porch of a small two-story frame house. A battered old pickup was parked near the front steps.

As we stopped, the porch light flashed on and the door opened, our arrival announced by the headlights. I was thankful Susan had realized the necessity of a car. It would have been odd indeed if we'd arrived on Leon's front porch apparently on foot.

Susan walked swiftly to the wooden steps.

After a moment's thought, I swirled away and joined her, unseen.

Leon shaded his eyes from the porch light. He peered at Susan in astonishment. "Miz Flynn?"

Susan's smile was brilliant. "I hope I'm not too late for a visit with you."

"You can come visit me anytime." He was clearly surprised, but I thought he was also pleased. "Come right in." He held the door wide.

"I want you to meet my friend who brought me tonight." Susan half turned.

I wasn't there.

"Bailey Ruth?"

Leon looked past her at the empty car.

"Oh, she's here. She'll be back in a moment. Perhaps she took a walk."

Leon looked perplexed. The night was cold and damp, the woods dark and forbidding.

Susan briefly pressed her lips together. "She probably heard an owl. It's easy to lose her when she hears an owl."

At that moment, an owl hooted.

"Owls." He nodded in agreement. "Lots of owls in December."

"She has good hearing." Susan turned and called out. "Bailey Ruth, come in and meet Leon." For good measure, unseen by Leon, she added an imperative jerk of her thumb.

Susan meant well, but I regretted that she was bandying my name about. If anyone cared enough, my name could be found in the family plot along with Bobby Mac's on a column dedicated to our memory. Bobby Mac loved the inscription: *Forever Fishing.*

I whispered in her ear. "Not Bailey Ruth. When I come in, introduce me as Ms. Loy." I'd appropriated Myrna Loy's name when I made cameo appearances as a policewoman during my previous adven-mission in Adelaide. What harm could it do to recall her once again? I'd be sure and tell her the next time I saw her. She and William Powell have continued to star on the truly Great White Way as Nick and Nora Charles. With Asta, of course.

I waited until the door closed behind Leon and Susan. I

swirled into being and opened the door. My smile was apologetic. "Sorry," I called. "A great horned owl. Those distinctive low hoos, six of them and the last two louder. I couldn't resist looking for him."

Leon's look was thoughtful. "Mighty dark in the woods."

I patted the pocket of the mink coat. "I never go out without my flashlight."

Susan was all charm. "Leon, this is Ms. Loy, a dear friend"—she gave me a quick wink of one eye—"who's visiting over Christmas."

"Pleased to meet you, Miz Loy." Leon ducked his head in my direction. He took our coats and hung them from a wooden coat tree near the door.

A yellow-and-blue macaw in a bronze cage next to a worn leather couch spoke in a cracked falsetto. "Christmas is the merriest time of the year." He whistled a bar of "Jingle Bells."

"Oh, you're a handsome fellow." Susan was admiring.

"Ladies, this is Archibald. You hush now, Archie."

The macaw lifted his wings. "Speak when spoken to."

Leon spread an apologetic hand. "I'm afraid Archie's manners are rusty. We're two old bachelors together."

Archie chattered while Leon brought coffee in ceramic mugs and a plate of homemade peanut butter cookies. He served one to Archie, who munched in satisfaction.

Susan and I sat on the couch and Leon sat in an old and obviously comfortable easy chair with its back to the stairs.

Susan put down the coffee mug. "I came tonight"—her tone was sober, her look questioning—"to ask for your help."

Leon leaned forward, planted gnarled hands on the knees of his faded Levi's. "You tell me what you want, Miz Flynn. It's as good as done."

The parrot watched us with bright dark eyes. Leon's

living room was small but neat as a workman's toolbox, magazines in a red wooden rack, the maple side table by the leather couch empty except for a branding-iron lamp. A worn Bible lay open on a shiny maple table next to Leon's chair. A pair of glasses rested on the pages.

Susan opened her purse and retrieved the letter. She pulled out the sheet and handed it to Leon. "Please read this."

Leon picked up the glasses from atop the Bible. He adjusted them on his beaked nose and painstakingly read, his lips silently forming the words. He looked at Susan and tapped the top of the sheet. "This here says it's your will."

Susan nodded. "I wrote it tonight and I want you to witness it for me when I sign it. Will you do that?"

"Sure enough." But his face was puzzled. "You always handled everything right well, Miz Flynn. The ranch and the oil leases and the bank. I've heard people can write out what they want done with their things and the court will see to it. But Miz Welch, who lives over Tecumseh way, got crossways with her daughter and wrote out a paper leaving her place to a slick-talking lease broker and the judge he said there was undue influence and her daughter got everything. Seems like in today's world"—he picked his words carefully—"everybody's mighty big on doing things by the book. I'll be glad to sign whatever you want, but I'm thinking you maybe ought to get a lawyer to fix it up right. Put it into one of those computers."

Susan reached out and squeezed his arm. "Don't worry, Leon. My lawyer will see to everything. And besides," she laughed, "I'm not disinheriting family like Mrs. Welch. Instead, everything will go to my grandson."

"Yes'm." He nodded in approval. "That's the way it should be. Let me see." He placed the sheet on the table and patted the pocket of his flannel shirt. "I got a pen somewhere."

Susan opened her purse. She pulled out a gold-plated pen. She cut her eyes toward me in amused acknowledgment and murmured, "Everything as needed." She came to her feet, lithe and youthful, and moved to the little maple side table. She bent down to sign and date the will, then pushed the paper to Leon. Susan watched as he carefully wrote his name. "Please put the date, too."

As Leon finished, tension drained from Susan. "Thank you, Leon." When she held the precious paper, her smile was tremulous. "We have to go now, but I will always be grateful for your help."

He looked embarrassed. "Anytime I can help, Miz Flynn, you just tell me." He brought our coats and once again we were at his front door. He held it open.

I stepped outside first. Susan followed, then turned. "Merry Christmas, Leon."

"Merry Christmas, Miz Flynn."

Archibald chimed in. "And a Merry Christmas was had by all."

Susan hesitated, then spoke in a rush. "Leon, please teach Keith how to ride and fish for crappie and hunt deer. Show him all the places we love on the ranch. Take him out to the tanks and let him smell oil."

Nothing smells finer to an Oklahoman than sweet crude.

Susan's eyes were shiny. "Tell Wade Farrell I asked you."

There was longing and sadness in Leon's voice. "I wish I could, Miz Flynn. That'll be up to Tucker, I guess."

Susan looked away. Her voice was uncertain. "Tucker may not want to stay on Burnt Creek."

Leon's face folded into a frown. He started to speak, stopped, cleared his throat. "If Tucker leaves the ranch, I'll be there for Mitch's boy."

She didn't look up as she swung to give him a quick hug. She ducked her head and hurried from the porch.

I knew she ran because she didn't want Leon to see her tears. This was her final farewell, farewell to a life she had loved.

Leon lifted a hand, took a step after her, then stopped. His mouth opened. Closed. He shook his head. He turned and opened the screen door. "Burnt Creek . . ." His voice was gruff with an undertone of anger. The door closed behind him.

As I walked to the car, I carried a clear picture of his face, an honest face, grieved and forlorn.

I opened the driver's seat. The interior light flashed on. Lying in the driver's seat was Susan's letter. I picked up the envelope, saw that it was sealed now as well as stamped.

The passenger seat was empty.

"Susan?"

Suddenly I knew I was alone. Susan's task was done. *Death after Life doth greatly please.* She was free now, no longer tethered to earth. Before too long I would be home in Heaven and Susan would be there, vigorous and happy, reunited with those she had loved.

I tucked the letter in the pocket of my coat and slid behind the wheel. I didn't glance again at the passenger seat. I would never again while on earth hear Susan's light, clear voice or see her kind eyes and quick smile.

"Godspeed." I turned the key and moved the gear to *D.* I drove down the dark road and, to be honest, heaved a sigh of relief. I'd embarked on a perilous and forbidden path and was exceedingly fortunate that my gamble had succeeded. Perhaps Wiggins, occupied in Tumbulgum, would never know that I'd once again succumbed to impulse. Certainly I had the greatest respect for Precept Two and had ignored its stricture only because I felt I had no choice.

I turned onto the main road.

Ends justifying means rarely received plaudits, but in this

instance everything had worked out well and surely that was a mitigating circumstance. However, I suspected I would be climbing aboard the Rescue Express as soon as I returned Jake's car. Perhaps she'd never notice that scrape on the left rear fender. I'd hoped to stay through Christmas—was there anything lovelier than the peal of bells at the midnight service?—but it looked as though my work was done. Keith was authenticated as Mitch's son and was now officially Susan's heir. I would go by the post office and drop the letter in the slot.

I reached the top of Persimmon Hill. Here the road ran straight and true, swooping down at a steep angle. Adelaide teenagers, not to mention some adults, were sometimes tempted to put the pedal to the metal.

I rolled down the windows, felt the flood of cold air. Why not?

"Yee-hah!" The wind blew my hair, rushing past loud as the wings of a Mississippi kite. I felt as one with the bucketing car, exhilarated, adrenaline rushing, the headlights' twin beams flashing through the night, fast as a black skimmer snatching fish from a Gulf wave.

"Bailey Ruth!" Wiggins's stentorian shout shook me.

I flinched. The wheel swerved under my hands. The car whipped from one side of the road to the other, zigging and zagging down the sharp incline. I fought to keep the front end from careening into the bridge at the bottom of the hill.

A siren shrilled.

The Ford shuddered as I brought it to a stop on the shoulder just past the bridge.

"Worst ride . . . since that night . . . the Lady Luck's brakes went out." Wiggins spoke in strangled gasps.

I clutched the steering wheel and struggled for breath, but Wiggins's uneven bleats moved me. "Are you all right?"

"All right?" There was an edge of despair in his voice.

"How can I be all right? Transgression piled upon transgression. Consorting with a departed spirit. Encouraging defiance of a Heavenly summons. Appearing here, there, and everywhere. Alarming that officer."

Footsteps approached.

I twisted to look. Oh dear Heaven, here came Officer Cain, clearly revealed in the wash of lights from his car. I had a dreadful premonition. Officer Cain had no doubt marked down the license plate of the blue Ford he had stopped earlier. My mink coat gleamed a soft caramel in the sweep of his flashlight. I'd not bothered to disappear when I left Leon's house. The passenger seat, of course, was empty. Perhaps I, too, could wish a purse and driver's license, but Susan was forever beyond my call. Officer Cain might reasonably wonder what had happened to her and where she was.

I swirled away. As the coat and I dissolved, Susan's letter tumbled to the seat. I grabbed the envelope and floated out of the car.

The beam of Officer Cain's flashlight rose, following the letter into the darkness of the night until I'd gone higher than the light reached.

"Stop right there." But the shouted command came from Wiggins, not the young policeman.

This was not the time to defy Wiggins. I stopped and hovered. "Shh. He'll hear you." I glanced down.

Officer Cain's head went back at an awkward angle. He stared upward, seeking the source of the voices. He looked to be in a fearful strain. I feared tomorrow he might have a painful crick.

"I don't care who hears me," Wiggins roared. "I would have come sooner except events in Tumbulgum were out of control."

"Wiggins," I whispered, "Precept Six. Look at poor Officer Cain."

The young policeman rubbed his ears. He took a deep breath.

Now the only sounds were the urgent hoos of a courting owl, the rustle of hackberry branches in the wind, and the rumble of a passing truck.

The beam of the flashlight wobbled. Officer Cain swept the light back and forth against unrevealing darkness.

Far away a train whistle sounded.

Cain slowly, as if forcing himself, turned toward the car. Light danced across the hood, illuminated the empty seats. He plunged to the driver's window, poked the flashlight inside. In a frenzy, he opened the front and back doors all the way around the car. He lifted the trunk, slammed the lid down again.

He backed away from the car, the flashlight beam playing this way and that, up and down, and all around. After a final illumination of the clearly empty seats, he turned and ran for his patrol car.

"'Make every effort not to alarm earthly creatures.'" Wiggins sounded morose.

I didn't know what to say. Was an apology in order? For which offense? I sighed.

"Clearly there has been a failure of leadership." His deep voice was subdued.

"Wiggins, don't blame yourself." He made no response. I tried to be upbeat. "These things happen."

"Only in Tumbulgum and Adelaide." There was a wealth of despair in his tone.

"Oh. A real problem in Tumbulgum?" Possibly we could ponder some other emissary's foibles.

"Nothing similar." He spoke hastily. "Your actions are

always well meant. If only you tempered enthusiasm with restraint. If you were less inquisitive. Less impulsive. Less rash. Less forthright." A heavy sigh. "And much less daring."

I had no answer. No doubt Wiggins was ready to hand me my return ticket on the Rescue Express. I consoled myself that I had reached the goal of my stay, even if in a slapdash fashion. Keith was established as Susan's grandson and—surely this was a bonus that Wiggins should applaud—was now assured his proper inheritance.

I looked down. Officer Cain hunched in the seat of his patrol car, his lips moving rapidly. I assumed he was reporting the abandoned Ford at the foot of Persimmon Hill.

Such a nice and remarkably attractive young man. I hoped this evening's experiences didn't haunt him. That, too, could be chalked up in my debit column. Did the credit and debit columns balance out? "I did my best."

"Except for Susan." His tone was sad rather than accusatory.

"Susan?" Assuredly, my decision to aid Susan in her effort to provide for Keith might be criticized, yet his voice was somber, not angry.

"I warned you to keep an eye on her. I was afraid there might be trouble."

Fair was fair. I would certainly take responsibility for derelictions of duty re the Precepts, but at no time had I been charged with overseeing Susan Flynn. "I beg your pardon." My tone was sharp. "I was sent here to look out for Keith, not Susan." I can sound steely. It harks back to my days as a high school English teacher before I flunked the principal's son and kept Bubba out of the championship football game and had to find a new career in the mayor's office. "As for Susan, I don't know what more I could have done."

"Before I was summoned to Tumbulgum, I warned you."

A pause. "Oh. Perhaps I wasn't clear. When Susan decided to change her will, I became uneasy. I wanted you to guard her against danger. Bailey Ruth, forgive me." He spoke with chagrin, his deep voice carrying. "Likely even if you had been with her every moment, you wouldn't have made a difference."

"Difference about what?" My voice remained steely. If he meant the sojourn to get the will signed, I had been with Susan every moment, either seen or unseen.

"Her murder." He was lugubrious.

"Murder?" My voice rose in shock. "Murder? What do you mean? Susan died."

"I know she died." He sounded testy. "Of course she died. But she didn't die in the natural order. Don't you remember? When I briefed you at the department, I told you. Susan was scheduled to arrive June 15."

"Murder." I heard my cry, forlorn as the call of a loon.

The frenzied crisscross of the flashlight beam startled me. Officer Cain stood rigidly next to his cruiser, seeking to find the voices that volleyed above him in the night sky.

I whispered. "That poor young man. He heard us. Look, he's getting back into the cruiser, talking on his radio again. I'd better go down and see. Wiggins, hold the letter."

I dropped into the cruiser.

Sweat beaded Johnny's handsome face. "Two-adam-five."

"Two-adam-five go ahead."

"No trace Ford driver, redheaded woman in her late twenties in a light brown mink coat. Apparently accompanied by unknown male. Loud voices heard, cannot locate. Woman shouted, 'Murder.' Missing redheaded driver originally seen in same car with Susan Flynn. Mrs. Flynn wasn't in the car. Possibly a search should be made. Send backup."

I zoomed up until I spotted the white envelope. "Wiggins, I'd hoped to return Jake's car to Pritchard House, but there's no chance." We both knew (at least I knew) whose fault this was, but laying blame never warms relationships. "Officer Cain's calling for help. The police will contact Susan's house." I reached out, grabbed the envelope. "I'll take the will to the post office." I'd promised Susan.

He held on to the will for a moment, then relinquished the envelope. "I suppose," it was as if he spoke to himself, "that you might as well see the will on its way since the document now exists, even though I'm sure Susan's delayed arrival in Heaven caused consternation. Very well." He cleared his throat. "Deposit the envelope. I'll alert the Rescue Express to pick you up at the post office."

My return ticket was all but in my hand. I'd seen Keith safely through and helped Susan provide for his future and his rightful place as his father's son, but I was miserable.

Susan had been murdered. I'd not understood that she was in my care, but nonetheless I felt responsible now. Abruptly, I quivered with anger. I'd wondered why Susan had to die tonight when happy days with Keith lay ahead of her. "Murder! That makes me furious. Worst of all, no one will suspect a thing. She looks so peaceful lying there. They'll think she overdid today and simply died. That isn't right." I glared down at the police car. "I'd almost go down there and tell that young officer. But he'd try to take me into custody and when I disappeared that would put them off on the wrong—"

I felt a rush of excitement. "Wrong track!" I gave a whoop and I didn't care how Officer Cain reacted. "Wiggins, there's no time to lose. The police will be on their way to Pritchard House. I may only have minutes. I'll dash by the post office." Zooming through the night air above the lights of Adelaide was an experience to be savored, especially with all of the glorious Christmas decorations. "As soon as I drop the envelope in a letter box, I'll pop immediately to Susan's bedroom. I know how to make sure the police investigate her death." I took a deep hopeful breath. "Please signal the Rescue Express that my assignment has been extended. We can't let Susan's murderer get away with a perfect crime."

I waited. Time on earth can seem eons long. My chest ached as I held my breath. Would Wiggins approve? Wiggins followed the rules. I often didn't, and I had no doubt my plan would shock his conservative soul.

"Do you believe you can make a difference?" He didn't wait for an answer. "Of course you can make a difference. You always do."

I chose not to focus on the faintly bitter tone of his voice.

"Do whatever you need to do." He was gruff and determined. "Susan should have had those happy days with Keith. I'll send the signal now. Assignment extended."

CHAPTER 9

The Meissen clock on the mantel chimed a quarter after one. A little more than an hour had elapsed since Susan and I had departed, Susan laughing with pleasure as she floated through space to the hall below.

I hovered above the bed. She still rested on her side. In profile, her face looked peaceful. Yes, now she was at peace. I gently edged the pillow from beneath her head, carried it to the dresser. I opened the drawer, found a makeup kit, smudged lipstick on the pillowcase.

The phone shrilled. It rang a second time, a third, stopped in mid-peal.

I felt like a horse flicked by a crop. I moved fast, throwing back the bedcovers and tumbling Susan's body onto the floor. Quickly, I placed her on her back. I bent her arms at the elbow, placed her hands palm up, and covered her face and hands with the pillow.

I'd no more than finished when a rattling knock sounded on the bedroom door. The door swung wide. "Susan, the police just called." Jake's voice was breathless. "They said you—Susan? Susan?" The light flicked on.

Jake Flynn stepped inside, struggling to pull on a pink

chenille robe. Curlers held wisps of hair, exposing pink patches of scalp. She stared and her puffy, sleep-raddled face froze in horror. Unsteadily, as if the floor rocked beneath her feet, one hand pressed against her lips, Jake crossed the room, dropped to her knees beside Susan. Jake pulled Susan's right arm from beneath the pillow and pressed her fingertips against the wrist.

Downstairs, the doorbell pealed. Authoritative raps sounded.

Jake came to her feet, breathing in short, quick gasps. She looked toward the hall, then once again turned to that still figure. Face quivering in distaste, she bent over, reaching toward the pillow.

"Mother!" Peg's cry was stricken.

Jake whirled to face the door, clutched her chest.

"What's happened?" Peg hurried to Susan's body, stared down. "Why is that pillow over Susan's face?"

"I don't know." Jake's voice shook. "I just found her. I didn't find any pulse. And you can tell she isn't breathing. The police called and asked to speak to Susan. I told them she was sick and they said they had to talk to her and I came and found her."

The doorbell rang without pause.

"She's dead." Peg's voice was dull, leaden. Her hand hovered above the pillow. She shuddered and drew back. "We mustn't touch anything."

The doorbell continued to peal.

"Wait just a minute. I'm coming." Gina's call on the stairwell was loud and irritated. "Jake? Peg? Where is everybody?"

Jake trembled. "That must be the police downstairs. They called about my car. Someone's stolen it. The police found it. They asked to speak to Susan. I don't know why they wanted to talk to her. I don't understand. Nothing makes sense." She stepped reluctantly toward Susan's body. "Quick. We have to get Susan back on the bed."

A deep voice sounded below. Gina's reply was indistinguishable. There was the muffled sound of steps and the door closing and more voices.

Peg caught her mother's arm. "What do you mean?"

Jake tried to pull away. "Hurry. She mustn't be found like this. It doesn't look right."

Steps sounded in the hall. "Is Susan sick?" Gina called out. "Where is everyone?"

Peg held tight to Jake. "Look right?" Her young voice rose with a tinge of hysteria. "No. It doesn't look right. That pillow—oh God, someone's killed Susan."

"Susan's dead?" Gina's voice was sharp and high. She stood in the doorway. When she saw Susan's body and the pillow, Gina reached out, gripped the lintel, held tight.

Jake's gaze was desperate. "There's some explanation. Susan felt sick. She got up. She fell and maybe she was carrying the pillow. You girls have to help me. We can put her on the bed." Jake's tone was feverish. "We have to hurry. Susan would hate for anyone to see her like this."

"Mrs. Flynn?" The deep voice was loud, demanding. "Police."

Gina made a helpless gesture with her hands. "The doorbell rang and rang. I went down. The police are here to talk to Susan."

The three women stood frozen for an instant, each staring at the still figure. Jake's eyes were wide and staring, her breathing irregular. Gina's thin face was slack with shock and disbelief. Peg shuddered. Her eyes filled with tears.

"Hello?" The stern voice called again from downstairs.

Peg, her face ashen, dropped her mother's arm. She

walked stiffly past Gina into the hallway. "Police? Come help us." Her call was stricken. "Someone has killed Susan."

I sat on the chaise longue near Keith's bed. I heard noise, deep voices, the thud of feet on the stairway even though the door to Keith's room was firmly shut. I'd gained some knowledge of police procedures on my previous mission. The medical examiner would be summoned. Susan wouldn't be touched until the examiner affirmed death. Because of the circumstances in which she was found, an autopsy would be ordered. I felt no need to be present for the early moments of the investigation. I wouldn't miss anything of importance. Especially since I'd created the crime scene. Peg had taken time to check on Keith before the women were asked to go downstairs, but I was afraid the movement up and down the stairs and the brusque exchanges of conversation would awaken him. I didn't want Keith to stumble out into the hallway. Not this night.

Keith stirred. His eyes fluttered open.

I reached over and turned on the lamp, tilted the shade to keep the glare away from his eyes. He blinked sleepily, then stiffened as a loud thump sounded in the hallway. He clutched Big Bob's brown paw and looked about fearfully.

I brushed back a tangle of blond curls, bent near. "Go back to sleep, Keith. Think about bump-a-thumps, bump-a-thumps, the Christmas march of the elephants. When it's Christmastime, elephants gather to serenade good boys and girls. They wave their trunks and stamp their feet and each and every elephant has a Christmas muffler, red and white and green just like Big Bob's." The oversize bear almost crowded Keith from the bed. I smoothed the end of Big Bob's muffler.

A bang and a thump sounded in the hall. Men's voices were loud in the hallway.

"The elephants are very big"—I dropped my voice—"and they have deep, rumbly voices. When you hear them coming, you know that Christmas morning will be special." I softly sang the refrain, "Bump-a-thumps, bump-a-thumps . . ."

Keith relaxed against the pillow, the occasional thud and banging in the hallway accounted for. I sang until he slipped into sleep, his lips curved in a smile, one small hand wrapped in the end of Big Bob's muffler. In his dreams, I hoped he watched beautiful, big-hoofed, dusky gray pachyderms marching upstairs and down, striped scarves swinging, singing for a good little boy.

At the foot of the stairs, Jake drew her chenille robe tighter and glared at Johnny Cain and a tall angular policewoman standing in the foyer. "What are you doing down here? The rest of them are upstairs."

The policewoman looked at her politely. "I'm here to answer the door, ma'am."

"Are there more coming?" Jake sounded close to hysteria.

"Officers and technicians will be in and out." Her voice had the familiar Adelaide twang, her serious gaze was watchful.

Johnny stepped forward. His handsome face was grave. "Mrs. Flynn, detectives are on the way." He looked past Jake, saw Peg. His blue eyes were suddenly warm and kind. "Hi, Peg."

Peg looked young and vulnerable, shivering in her yellow flannel pajamas. Her brown hair was ruffled, her round face bare of makeup. "Oh, Johnny, I'm glad you're here. You can tell us what we are supposed to do."

Johnny gestured toward the dark living room. "Maybe you might like to wait in there. Everyone at a crime scene is asked to remain together until the detective in charge can speak with them."

Jake reached up as if to brush back her hair. A red stain flushed her cheeks. Fingers moving rapidly, she removed the curlers, stuffed them in a pocket of her robe, fluffed her hair until it looked like faded sprigs of yellow yarn. She opened the door to the living room, switched on the light. "I'll turn up the heat. We can stay in here if that's what we have to do. I don't see why we have stay in one room, but I don't want to be alone."

Johnny looked out of place in his French blue uniform as he stood beneath the cranberry and pine cone decorated doorway. "Is there anyone else in the house?"

Peg rubbed reddened eyes. "Mrs. Flynn's grandson Keith. He's just a little boy." Her voice wobbled. "He's asleep."

Johnny looked uncertain. "Everybody's supposed to be together."

Gina stood with her hands on her hips. "Johnny, you don't want to wake up a four-year-old and tell him his grandmother's been killed so he has to come downstairs."

Johnny turned his hands up in defeat. "I guess not."

Jake bristled with anger. "Somebody needs to tell us what's going on. The phone rang and I was told my car had been stolen and then the police banged on the door and wanted to talk to Susan and we found her on the floor. I want to know if somebody called the police. Did somebody know what happened to her? We ought to be told. We were all asleep and Susan was fine when we went to bed. And I don't understand about my car. Where is it? Who took it? Wait a minute." She turned and hurried out to the hall, returned with her purse. She opened it, rummaged, finally upended the bag and let the contents slide onto the top of the piano. "My keys are gone." Her voice shook. "How did someone get into the house and take my keys?"

Johnny was clearly uncomfortable. "Mrs. Flynn, an investigation is under way. Your car was found"—he hesitated—"abandoned at the foot of Persimmon Hill about a quarter to one."

"Someone stole my car. And someone killed Susan. It has to be the same person." Jake's eyes were huge. "Who was driving my car?"

Johnny cleared his throat. "When the investigating officer speaks to you, perhaps he can answer your questions."

Jake lowered herself like an old woman into an easy chair. Peg and Gina settled on the sofa. Johnny stood stiffly in front of the fireplace.

Jake fingered a lace ruffle at her throat. "Johnny, you can sit down."

He looked stiffer than ever. "Thank you, Mrs. Flynn. I'll stand."

The front doorbell pealed, and the policewoman opened the door.

Everyone stared through the open door at the foyer.

A tousle-haired young man, bristly cheeks red from the cold, strode inside, shrugging out of a ski jacket. "Can't you people find bodies in the daytime? The last three have been post midnight. How's a man to get his beauty sleep?"

"Comes with the territory, Doc. They're upstairs." She jerked a thumb toward the steps.

Jake frowned. "Who is that?"

Johnny's face looked older than his years. "The medical examiner."

Peg's gaze lifted to a painting of Susan over the mantel,

young and lovely, hopeful and eager. "Are they going to . . ." She broke off, pressed fingers against trembling lips.

Gina came to her feet, began to pace. "This is hideous." She looked at Jake. "We have to call Tucker. He should come."

Jake's tone was hollow. "What can he do? What can any of us do?"

"I'm going to call him. I'll get my cell." Gina swung toward the hall.

Johnny stepped forward. "Please, Gi—Miss Satterlee. No calls are permitted."

Gina stood very still. "No calls?" Her tone was thin.

The young policeman squared his shoulders. "It's customary procedure when police investigate a homicide. Someone will be down when they finish upstairs. You can explain there are calls you'd like to make."

I popped upstairs.

The bedroom was crowded, Susan's body, the M.E., several crime lab techs, and a man I knew at once from my last sojourn in Adelaide. I felt a tiny leap of my heart. Detective Sergeant Hal Price was tall, lean, and well-built—very well-built—with white blond hair and a quizzical expression. This early morning hour, he was unshaven, but the blond stubble was scarcely visible. When the late call came, he'd obviously swiped unruly hair with a quick brush and dressed hurriedly, an orange-and-black Oklahoma State sweatshirt, Levi's, and well-worn cowboy boots. I remembered him with pleasure. And some regret. If I'd been of the earth and not the Bailey Ruth who never seriously considered another man after she met black-haired Bobby Mac in high school, this lean blond man would have interested me. I still recalled with pleasure a moment during my previous efforts in Adelaide when Detective Sergeant

Price had looked at me in admiration. I regretted that later his look had been suspicious and wary.

Now his slate blue eyes watched the doctor. "Suffocation?"

The M.E. gazed at Susan's body, his face furrowed. "You got a funny one here. Body on the floor, pillow mashed on her face, traces of makeup on the pillow, hands apparently in defensive posture. But I don't see any facial bruising and I didn't see any hemorrhages and tears of the mucosa. I'll take a close look during the autopsy." He glanced at the chair and table near the fireplace. A small china pot sat next to a cup and saucer and dessert plate. "Have the crime lab check to see if there are drugs in the residue. It's easier to suffocate people if they're drugged." He moved quickly toward a bedside table and containers of pills. He crouched to see the labels without touching the vials. "Susan Flynn." He jerked his head at the body. "You got ID?"

"Susan Pritchard Flynn." Price's voice was weary.

The young doctor raised an eyebrow. "Even I know that name and I've only been in Adelaide a few years. The rich one?"

"Maybe the richest woman in town. Give or take a few million." Price's face was carefully expressionless. "One of the nicest. Big giver. Helped people a lot of folks forget about."

The medical examiner stood and pulled plastic gloves from a pocket, slipped them on, picked up the containers, checked the contents. "Digitalis, Lasix, potassium, Prinivil, Coreg." He nodded. "Heart patient. Wouldn't take much to suffocate her if she had CHF."

Price looked attentive. "CHF?"

"Congestive heart failure. I'll do a thorough autopsy, including tox testing."

The detective glanced at his watch. "On time of death, she was last seen alive about nine o'clock. That's a help, isn't it?"

The M.E. nodded. "I'll make a note." He replaced the pill bottles, returned to the body, and picked up his bag. "I'll do the autopsy Monday."

Price folded his arms. "How about Sunday?"

The doctor glanced at his watch. "In case you can't tell time, we are now in the wee hours of Sunday morning."

"You preaching somewhere?" Price's tone was bland.

"I got tickets to Gallagher Arena tonight, the Cowboys versus Texas at Arlington. Tickets as in two and my date's a babe. We're going over to Stillwater early, drop by her sorority house."

Price shrugged. "The chief said to ask you special. We're coming up on Christmas. Susan Flynn was a fine lady, and if we get the report Monday morning, the family can plan a service for Tuesday, not drag things out over the holiday."

"How come the chief's got a soft spot for the family? Odds are one of them killed her, right? All that money." The M.E. tucked his bag under his arm. "Looking at her medicines, I'd say the murderer must have been in a hurry. I doubt she had more than six months to live. Her doctor can probably give you an estimate."

Price's eyes gleamed. "Maybe somebody was in a hurry. We'll check that out. Can we count on the report Monday morning?"

The M.E.'s frown was ferocious, then he grinned. "All right already. I'll move fast. I'm not going to miss the game." He headed for the door. "The only reason I'm doing this is because I'm curious now. A dying woman. A lipstick-smeared pillow. No obvious traces of smothering. I'll arrange for the body to be picked up." He paused in the door, looked back. "I don't know if you're a married man, but I was once. Good-looking, high-class women don't go to bed—to sleep—with makeup on."

In the living room, no one moved or spoke. Officer Cain stood in front of the fireplace, his face thoughtful. Jake moved restively in the easy chair as if she couldn't find a comfortable posture. Peg lifted a hand to wipe away the tears that slipped down her cheeks. Gina huddled against the sofa arm. She stared at the cold fireplace, her dark hair screening her face.

The women appeared shocked, troubled, grieved. But did one of them wonder wildly with a touch of gnawing panic what had happened to derail a perfect murder? Did one of them know that Susan died this night from some other means? Her death should have been accepted as natural. Now, for reasons unknown, a murder investigation had begun. Did one of them wonder who had moved the body and who had arranged the pillow?

Footsteps sounded heavily on the stairway. "Careful. Steady. Ease around that post."

Jake's fingers plucked at the edge of a beige-and-blue shawl. Peg pressed a hand against her lips. Gina stared at the floor, her hands opening and closing over and over again.

Peg sank against the sofa as she watched the sheet-shrouded gurney pushed out into the cold night.

As the front door closed, Detective Sergeant Price walked quietly into the living room. He reached into his back pocket, pulled out a billfold, flipped it open to reveal a badge. "Detective Sergeant Harold Price. Mrs. Flynn's room has been sealed. It is officially a crime scene and not to be disturbed. I realize it is very late so I won't keep you long."

The clock read sixteen minutes after two.

Jake struggled forward in the chair, her robe gaping. "What happened to Susan?"

"The medical examiner will perform an autopsy. At the moment, her death is listed as suspected homicide. Tomorrow Police Chief Sam Cobb will interview everyone who was in the house when she died. I'd like to get some information for him."

Gina's eyes flashed. "Are you saying we are suspects?"

Price flicked her an appraising glance, but his voice was pleasant. "Anyone who was in contact with Mrs. Flynn this evening may be able to provide information that will be helpful to Chief Cobb." He looked at Jake. "May I have the names of all staying in the house tonight?" He glanced at each of them as he wrote their names.

Peg crumpled a Kleenex in her hand. "And Keith. Keith Flynn, Susan's grandson."

"Is he visiting by himself?"

Peg glanced at her mother, then said carefully, "He isn't visiting. He lives here."

Price looked puzzled. "Where are his parents?"

"His father was killed in Iraq. His mother died recently from pneumonia." Peg spoke rapidly.

Even an imperceptive man would have picked up on the tension in the room. Hal Price wasn't unimaginative. "How long has he been here?"

Jake bridled. "I don't see what any of this has to do with Susan."

"If you'll be patient with me, Mrs. Flynn, I'm new to your household. I need to provide Chief Cobb with information about everyone here at the time of the suspected homicide."

Peg hurried to speak before Jake. "Keith arrived Thursday evening. There were four of us in the house tonight: my mother"—she nodded toward Jake—"Gina, Keith, and I."

"What relationship are each of you to the deceased?" He listened carefully. "Let's see if I've got it right. The little boy is her grandson. Mrs. Jake Flynn was married to Susan Flynn's late husband's brother. Miss Flynn is Mrs. Jake Flynn's daughter. Miss Satterlee is Mrs. Jake Flynn's niece. So"—his eyes ran over his notes—"the only blood relative is Keith Flynn."

"What difference does any of that make?" Jake was querulous. "Why aren't you searching for whoever came in the house and killed Susan?" Her eyes popped wide. "Someone came in and killed Susan and got my car keys and stole my car. Where is my car now?"

"The Ford is in police custody and is being searched and fingerprinted."

Jake looked excited. "If you get fingerprints, can you find out who was driving it?"

"We are making every effort to discover the identity of the driver."

Jake frowned. "How did the police find my car?"

Price spoke without emphasis. "Mrs. Flynn was driving the car when it was stopped for speeding at approximately twelve-fifteen A.M. on State Highway 3 West on the outskirts of Adelaide."

If the detective had announced that a spaceship was ready to board on the front lawn, the effect on his listeners would not have been more pronounced.

Jake's lips parted in soundless shock.

Peg's round face was blank with astonishment.

Gina shook her head in derision. "That's impossible."

Jake lifted her hands in a flutter of rejection. "Susan hadn't left the house for months. Today—I guess yesterday now—was the first time she'd gone outside since September. I thought at the time she was overdoing. I worried that it might be too much for her heart. The driver absolutely could not have been Susan."

Price nodded at Johnny. "Officer."

Johnny spoke emphatically, his expression determined. "I was on patrol in Car 5 at a quarter after midnight. That's the first time I stopped a blue Ford." He rattled off the license number. "This was on the edge of town where the road curves into 3 West. Radar clocked the car going seventy-eight miles an hour in a sixty-mile-an-hour zone. When I approached the vehicle"—there was an odd look of discomfort on his face, perhaps reflecting a memory that the front seat had at first appeared to be unoccupied—"the driver rolled down the window. When I looked inside, I saw Mrs. Flynn."

Peg's voice was gentle. "Johnny, it simply can't be. She's been so ill and weak. It was a struggle for her to go up and down the stairs."

Johnny's face set in stubborn lines. "She knew me. She called me Johnny and she said she was glad I'd done well at the police academy. She knew my mom. She had on this black mink coat. And she didn't look a bit sick. She looked the way she did when we were kids. Anyway, the lady who was with her will confirm that it was Mrs. Flynn. She and the lady had been to a sick friend's house. The other lady was young and real pretty."

I smiled at Johnny. What a sweetheart.

"The other lady had red hair, really bright red. Mrs. Flynn said she was visiting over Christmas."

Detective Sergeant Price drew a small notebook from his back pocket, flipped it open. He looked at Jake. "I'd appreciate the name of Mrs. Flynn's friend. It will help sort out what happened this evening with the car."

Jake fumbled with her shawl. "Susan didn't have a friend with red hair."

Peg's eyes squinted in thought. "There's Midge Baker."

Jake sniffed. "Midge isn't a real redhead. Auburn and plenty of gray." She turned toward Johnny. "Was this a real redhead?"

"Yes, ma'am." His reply was swift. "Curls red as fire and green eyes and she had a friendly smile."

Honestly, what a sweetheart.

Peg turned her hands up. "I can't imagine who it could be. No one has been to see Susan over the holidays. Several people called and Susan said to tell them she wasn't feeling up to visitors. Anyway, none of them are redheads."

Price closed the notebook. "That's interesting. We'll have a sketch made, try to identify her."

Gina twirled a long strand of dark hair between a thumb and forefinger. "Maybe I'm not quick, but I think there's a disconnect here. Johnny"—she nodded toward Officer Cain—"told us what happened the first time he stopped Jake's car. Does that mean he stopped her car a second time?"

"The first time Mrs. Flynn said she was sorry about going too fast and I gave her a warning ticket. The car went on." Johnny's face was strained. "About forty minutes later I was parked on the shoulder of Persimmon Hill with my lights off, the motor idling. You know how kids go flat out down the hill because it's the steepest one in the county. A car came over the rise and took off hell-for-leather down the slope. I turned on my lights and gunned the cruiser. The car swerved big-time, like somebody had jerked the wheel. I thought there was going to be a crash. The car whipped back and forth across the road but somehow it didn't go into a full spin—"

No thanks to Wiggins. I felt I'd managed a nice piece of driving.

"—and slid to a stop just past the bridge."

Gina leaned forward, intent. "Now we're getting somewhere. You stopped the car and it turned out to be Jake's Ford. Who was driving?"

Johnny moved uncomfortably. "The redheaded woman was at the wheel. I caught a glimpse of her hair and her fur coat, kind of a light golden brown one. I didn't see anybody else." He licked his lips, swallowed. "By the time I got to the car window, she was gone. I looked everywhere. I didn't find a trace of her. I searched the car and there wasn't anybody in it, not in front or back or in the trunk."

"That's crazy," Jake exclaimed. "You must have been awfully slow getting there."

Johnny flushed. "I got there quick. I don't know where she went or how she got out of the car. The door never opened." He looked haunted.

As well he might, poor sweetie. But I didn't see what other choice I could have made.

Peg looked troubled. "The redhead must have already brought Susan home."

Gina's brows drew down in a questioning frown. "That doesn't make sense. Why would this woman still have the car?"

Jake was aggrieved. "Susan certainly was welcome to drive my car, though I don't believe the driver the first time was Susan. She was too sick. Besides, Susan wouldn't let some stranger take my car without even a word to me."

Price gave her a level look. "We have a great deal to find out, including where Mrs. Flynn was going when she was first stopped and the identity of the red-haired woman who apparently was alone in the car on Persimmon Hill. We'll hope to make progress tomorrow. If it is agreeable"—he spoke with a calm assumption of acceptance—"Chief Cobb will meet with you here at two o'clock this afternoon. Are there any others who were in contact with Mrs. Flynn yesterday?"

After a moment's silence, Peg said abruptly, "We had a family dinner last night. My cousin Tucker Satterlee was here and Susan's husband's cousin Harrison Hammond and his wife Charlotte." She looked bleak. "And a friend of mine, Dave Lewis. He's staying at his brother's house. Everett Lewis on Peace Pipe Lane."

Price quickly obtained addresses and phone numbers. "We'll be in touch with them and"—he glanced at Jake—"with your permission we will include them in the meeting with Chief Price."

"None of them were here after midnight"—Jake looked puzzled—"but ask them if you want to."

Gina looked thoughtful. "Detective Price, you said Jake's car is being fingerprinted and searched. Was that ordered before you came here and discovered Susan's body?"

"Yes."

"Is that routine procedure for an abandoned car?"

Price's cool blue eyes accorded her a quick respect. "Only because of attendant circumstances."

"Attendant circumstances?" she pressed.

"During Officer Cain's search for the driver, loud voices were heard, a shouted conversation between a man and a woman. At one point the woman cried, 'Murder.' Officer Cain mounted a search, but he was only one man. There are woods and ravines along the road. When reinforcements arrived, the decision was made to speak with Mrs. Flynn since she was earlier seen with the redheaded woman." He gave a short nod. "Chief Cobb will bring you up to date on the investigation when he meets with you." He turned to go.

Johnny moved forward. "Sir, Miss Satterlee earlier asked to make a telephone call. Is it all right for her to do so now?"

Price turned toward Gina. "Miss Satterlee, thank you for helping us follow procedure. Certainly at this time you are free to make any calls you wish." He looked at Johnny. "I'd like a word with you, Officer." Price jerked his head toward the hall.

The two men stepped into the foyer, moved out of vision of the living room. A low murmur sounded.

I moved to the foyer and hovered above Detective Sergeant Price and Johnny Cain.

Price spoke softly to Johnny. "Keep talking. Repeat the story about stopping the car." Price edged nearer the doorway, head cocked, listening.

I, too, was curious about Gina's call. I returned to the living room.

"Throw me your cell, Jake." Gina held out her hand.

Jake fished in her purse. "Should you call Tucker this late?" She tossed the phone.

Gina caught the small pink plastic oblong. She didn't answer. She flipped up the lid, punched a number.

"I suppose I'd better call Harrison when you finish." Jake sounded desperately weary.

I perched on the broad arm of the sofa quite close to Gina, close enough to see the dark shadows beneath her eyes, the stiffness of her face, the tight set of her shoulders. She took a deep breath. "Tucker . . ."

I popped to Burnt Creek.

CHAPTER 10

A dim glow marked a second-story window in the frame Victorian ranch house.

Tucker Satterlee, groggy with sleep, held a portable phone as he swung over the edge of the bed. His dark curls were tangled. He blinked sleepily. The low-wattage light from the lamp on the bedside table was flattering to the slender young woman clutching a sheet to her bare shoulders. "Who's calling? What's happened?" Her voice was shrill.

Tucker waved her to be quiet. He reached for a wool robe, stood and pulled it on. "Susan? . . . Yeah. Oh, hey." He looked somber. "I'm sorry . . ." His face changed, brown eyes narrowing, bony features taut. "Smothered? That's crazy . . ."

The woman gave a tiny gasp.

A wary look crossed his face. He spoke slowly. "I picked up Lorraine around ten. We went over to Firelake Casino to play the slots and have a couple of drinks. Then we came out here." A muscle twitched in one jaw. "Lorraine can vouch for me if somebody saw Susan at midnight. But I can't believe she was out chasing around Pontotoc County with some unknown redhead. Why do you want to know where I was?"

His tone was sardonic. “Oh, sure. You called to ask where I was when somebody smothered Susan. Always nice when your sister asks you for an alibi. Anyway, you can cross me off any list of suspects.” His eyes narrowed. “Who the hell are the suspects? . . . Yeah. I guess so. All right. Two o’clock. Yeah. I’ll be there.” He clicked off the phone, turned to Lorraine, his face grim. “A bad deal. Susan’s dead. They found her tonight lying on the floor of her bedroom, a pillow over her face. The cops say it’s murder.” His face was abruptly hard. ”I don’t know what will happen now.”

Nor did I. I was only sure—and pleased—that a stealthy killer’s plans had been disrupted and there would be more shocks to come.

Downstairs in the kitchen, I closed the swinging door before I turned on a light. Although the appliances had been updated, the big room was unmistakably early nineteenth-century with cupboards and a white wooden breakfast table and wood floors that dipped a little in one corner. I moved fast, keeping an ear cocked for footsteps. I found a directory in the drawer near the old-fashioned wall-mounted phone and flipped to the H’s. I ran my finger down the listings to Harrison Hammond, 903 Osage.

I felt intrusive poking into bedrooms, but I would go wherever necessary to find out how the news of Susan’s death affected the heirs.

Harrison sat on the edge of the bed, holding a telephone receiver. “I’m shocked, Jake. Do you want me to come there? . . . No, I guess there isn’t anything I can do at this hour of the morning . . . All right. We’ll be there at two.” He replaced the receiver and turned to Charlotte, who sat bolt upright, a pillow clutched in her hands.

His face was drawn. "You heard. Susan's dead. They think it's murder."

Charlotte stared at him, her eyes wide. "That's dreadful."

Harrison sat unmoving, his hands folded into tight fists.

Charlotte reached out, touched his pajama sleeve. "I'm sorry."

He didn't answer as he lowered himself onto his pillow.

Charlotte's face filled with foreboding. "It's dreadful that Susan was murdered tonight of all nights."

Hammond looked at her sharply. "What do you mean?"

Charlotte fingered the ruching at the throat of her green silk nightgown. "Susan announced plans to change her will. That same night she is murdered. What if the police"—her voice was scarcely audible—"find out you owe a lot of money?"

He rubbed at one temple. "It won't matter." His voice sounded hollow. "I was with you tonight."

She looked at him. Without her glasses her eyes looked fuzzy, but the intensity of her gaze was unmistakable.

"I only went to the office for a little while." He avoided looking at her. "I can't believe any of this. Susan dead. My God, I'm sorry."

Charlotte's voice shook. "She's dead. And she didn't change her will."

Harrison started to speak, stopped. He reached for the switch on the bedside lamp.

They lay on the bed, close yet separated by an incalculable distance.

In the faint glow through the windows from a streetlamp, the bedroom was a hodgepodge of shadows.

"I didn't hear you come in tonight." Her voice was a whisper.

He came up on one elbow. "Listen to me, Charlotte. I

went to my office because I was trying to figure out a way to keep out of bankruptcy. I was there all evening. I never left until I came home at midnight."

Keith was curled on one side, his fingers crooked around one of Big Bob's paws. Across the room, Peg's breathing was deep and even. I foresaw no danger for Keith now. No one knew the old will was to be set aside so Keith was safe. As soon as the holographic will was proved, Keith would also be safe because his death would accomplish nothing.

Reassured, I moved to the kitchen. I carefully shut the door into the hallway before turning on the light, although sheer exhaustion made it unlikely that anyone would wander downstairs now.

The refrigerator was well stocked. I cut several slices of rare roast beef. Oklahoma was beef country and there was none better in all the world, though of course, Kansas and Texas made similar claims. Sooners smiled kindly, having no doubt as to which state actually had the best beef. I spread two thick slices of fresh white country bread with Hellmann's mayonnaise, added bread-and-butter pickles and a curl of horseradish. I found potato chips in a cabinet, poured a glass of whole milk, and settled at the kitchen table.

With a thump, Duchess landed on the table, gleaming eyes fixed on my sandwich, nose sniffing.

I cut a thin slice of beef, placed it in Duchess's bowl.

The discovery of Susan, apparently dead from suffocation, was shocking to everyone connected to her. To her murderer, who alone at this point knew how her death had been achieved, that discovery was not only shocking but inexplicable.

I munched the sandwich and tried to put myself in the skin of Susan's killer.

The murderer must be wondering and worrying. Who wanted Susan's death to be investigated as murder? Why? Was the real murderer's role known? How could that be? How could Susan have taken Jake's car? Who was the redheaded woman? What were the police going to do?

The murderer had to be anxious, fearful, shocked, and, beneath the face presented to the world, suffused with rage.

As I took the last bite of sandwich, I was sure of that fury. To commit a perfect crime and see that undone had to have a cataclysmic effect on the killer. Yet, though I'd watched each of them carefully—befuddled Jake, grieving Peg, observant Gina, sleep-dazed Tucker, stricken Harrison, worried Charlotte—I had no inkling who was guilty.

Breakfast Sunday morning was subdued. Jake sat hunched over her coffee. She waved away food. Gina toyed with a sweet roll, crumbling it into pieces. Peg dished up Keith's breakfast, put it at his place. "Gina, will you help Keith? I'd better call Dave." She didn't sound eager.

Gina tried for a smile. "Hey, Keith, let me cut your waffle. Do you want syrup or jelly?"

Keith leaned to one side, offered a piece of waffle to Duchess.

Jake managed a smile. "That cat likes caviar, but not waffles."

Peg hurried from the kitchen. She was already dressed in a pullover sweater and jeans. She pulled a cell phone from her pocket. She carefully shut the living room door after her and stood by the cold fire. She pushed a button.

I arrived at a rambling ranch house on Peace Pipe Lane, the home of Everett Lewis, and found Dave in tartan plaid boxers, shaving. He heard the phone, grabbed a towel, and wiped his hands. His face still lathered, he walked into the bedroom to scoop up a cell phone from the nightstand. "Hey, Peg." He listened and looked astonished. "Smothered?"

His shock was evident. Unfortunately, I had no way of knowing whether the shock came from the event or from the news that a death that should have been accepted as accidental was now deemed a homicide.

"That's crazy. Did somebody break in?" His eyes narrowed as he listened. "Oh . . . Well, that's tough. I know you were really close to her . . . This afternoon? . . . Right. I'll be there. And hey, Peg, God knows this is pretty grim, but she wouldn't have lived long anyway. Everybody knows that, and the truth of the matter is that the timing is good for us . . . Don't take my head off. I'm just facing facts. She'd always promised the money to all of you and now it looks like it will all work out, and hey, we can take good care of the kid." His tone was magnanimous.

Obviously the prospect of marrying a woman with a substantial inheritance was pleasing to him.

"Do you want me to come over now? . . . Oh. Okay then. I'll see you this afternoon."

I wasn't surprised to find Police Chief Sam Cobb in his office on Sunday. His suit coat hung from the back of his office chair so I judged he'd been to church. He was as big as I remembered, a stocky man, grizzled dark hair receding from a domed forehead. His face was heavy, his jaw blunt. He'd known unhappy times. Even though only a short span of earthly time had passed, he looked older than when we'd last met, if one could describe our fleeting encounters as meeting. It had been my pleasure on my previous visit to Adelaide to assist the police in the guise of Officer M. Loy.

His oak desk was as battered and stained as I remembered. His computer screen was on. He turned from the computer to pick up a legal pad. He began to write:

Susan Pritchard Flynn stopped for speeding by Officer Johnny Cain at 12:14 A.M. Sunday in a blue Ford belonging to her sister-in-law Jacqueline Flynn. Car taken without permission. Mrs. Flynn accompanied by unidentified young woman described as very attractive redhead.

The chief paused, a frown tugging at his iron gray brows. I hoped he wasn't recalling the occasional presence of red-headed Officer Loy.

With a brief headshake, he resumed writing:

At shortly before 1 A.M., Officer Cain observed the Ford driven recklessly down Persimmon Hill. Officer Cain gave chase. The car stopped at the base of the hill. Officer briefly glimpsed driver, the redheaded woman previously seen with Mrs. Flynn. Mrs. Flynn was not in the car. Driver was not apprehended. Officer Cain overheard a man and woman quarreling but never saw them. A woman cried, "Murder." Woman may or may not have been driver.

The reason for Mrs. Flynn's midnight trip is unknown. According to family, she was too ill to be out. Officer Cain knew Mrs. Flynn personally, had known her for years, and insists that he saw and spoke with her.

The identity of redheaded woman is unknown. Family claims they know of no one—

The phone rang. Chief Cobb glanced at the caller ID, punched the button for the speakerphone. "Hey, Doc. Hope you aren't calling to say the autopsy's on hold."

"Man, I'm done. Started the autopsy at three A.M., got a pitiful nap, ran the tox test this morning. Major fact: The dig level was out of sight, 6.0. Normal is 1 to 2. The digitalis vial on the nightstand only had a couple of tabs. I didn't notice the fill date. Better check. My guess is it was a fresh prescription and Mrs. Flynn ingested most of the tablets."

The chief rustled through some papers. "Got a report here that digitalis was found in the dregs of the pot that had held cocoa as well as the cup. How did the medicine get in the cocoa?"

"I'm no fortune-teller, Chief, and that's what you're going to need here. Maybe the tablets fell in her cup by accident. That's unlikely but things happen. Maybe she tossed the tablets in the cocoa in an absentminded moment, one tablet two, three tablet four, who knows how many more, you get the picture. Maybe she dropped them into the cup on purpose. Maybe somebody brought her cocoa laced with enough digitalis to drop a horse. It's your pick: accident, suicide, murder."

I don't know when I've been more distressed. I'd assumed the medical examiner would find the cause of death, but I hadn't considered the possibility that Susan's death might not be deemed homicide. After all, I knew she had been murdered. I had it on excellent authority. Wiggins said so. Besides, Susan would never have committed suicide. I'd not known her long, but I had no doubt. She knew she had to finish the course, no matter how difficult the path. Susan Flynn had understood and accepted that the road wound uphill all the way.

Chief Cobb didn't know Susan. I watched as he wrote:

Accident? Suicide? Murder?

"But," boomed the voice on the speakerphone—for a man who'd likely been up most of the night, the medical examiner was ebullient—"I got more interesting news for you."

Cobb's eyes narrowed. "I don't like the sound of your voice. May you too live in interesting times."

The bark of laughter was satisfied. "You got yourself a muddy sandpile to play in, Chief.

"One: Except for the circumstances of her discovery, i.e., on the floor with a pillow on her face, the death would have passed as natural. She had severe congestive heart failure and coronary artery disease. No attending physician would have suggested an autopsy.

"Two: She didn't pop down on the floor of her own accord. She was placed there after death. Lividity indicates she died while resting on her left side. Now this is interesting. There were some traces of lividity on her back but the major lividity was on her left side. That's consistent with the body being moved less than six hours after her death. If more than six hours had passed, the lividity wouldn't have been changed by movement. Instead, from the amount of lividity on her side, I'd guess—and this has to be a guess—that the body was moved about three hours after she died.

"Three: Time of death is tricky, but I would have estimated around nine P.M. based on temp, lividity, stomach contents. However, Price said she was last seen about twelve-fifteen."

Chief Cobb's face corrugated in a heavy frown. "If you had to testify at a trial, when would you put the outer limits on time of death?"

"If it will help you sleep any better at night, I can equivocate like a politician. On the one hand, on the other hand . . . The defense expert medical witness could read the report and say in the range of his experience with the facts as presented, the outer limit is ten o'clock. My gut feeling? She was probably dead an hour earlier. But, on the other hand . . ."

Chief Cobb looked morose. "I got to deal with facts, Doc. She was seen around twelve-fifteen by an officer who positively ID'd her."

"Hallucination?"

Cobb returned to the open file on his desk.

I bent nearer his shoulder.

As he scanned Johnny Cain's report, he highlighted in canary yellow:

> *. . . light must have been funny in the car. When I first approached no one seemed to be in the front seat. By the time I got to the door, Mrs. Flynn was there in a black fur coat. She said she was sorry she'd driven so fast and she said, "We got to talking." I looked in the passenger seat and it was empty and then Mrs. Flynn said she saw a fox and pointed at the road. I turned that way. When I looked back there was a redheaded woman in the passenger seat in a brown fur coat. I don't see how I could have missed seeing her the first time, but I did. She told Mrs. Flynn to get her purse. She talked a lot.*

Was there an aura of desperation about Officer Cain's claims? I admired his painful honesty. How easy it would have been for him simply to report that Susan Flynn was the driver. Instead, he tried to be accurate as to what he saw. Or didn't see.

I wondered if Chief Cobb foresaw Officer Cain on the witness stand, describing his post-midnight encounter with Susan Flynn. Defense attorney: Officer, tell us how you approached the car? . . . You immediately saw Mrs. Flynn? . . . Oh, you didn't see Mrs. Flynn at first? . . . How many feet are there, Officer, from the back of the car to the driver's window? . . . Was your view unobstructed? . . . Can you account for your inability to see Mrs. Flynn as you first approached the car? . . . What did you see in the passenger seat? . . . I see, at first the seat was empty and then it was occupied by a redheaded woman?

"Chief, you there?"

"Yeah." Cobb rubbed at his neck as if it were stiff. "Problem is, there are some unusual aspects to the whereabouts of Mrs. Flynn after midnight. But that blue Ford's a fact. It was abandoned at the foot of Persimmon Hill. The warning ticket issued to Susan Flynn was found in the front seat."

"Yeah." There was doubt in the M.E.'s voice. "Maybe the timing works out. Although if he'd seen her at eleven, I could buy it a lot easier than after midnight."

Cobb cleared his throat. "Can digitalis in that amount be administered in hot chocolate?"

"Sure. If somebody put it in the drink, she'd never notice. If it was suicide, she probably popped them into the cup and drank it down and went off to bye-bye land. Maybe the easy answer's the best. She must have felt lousy. She knew she didn't have much time left anyway. Drop the pills into cocoa, give it a stir, no more pain."

The chief circled: *Suicide?*

The M.E. was brisk. "Check out her mental state. If she'd been depressed, talked a lot about death, you can close the investigation."

Cobb loosened his tie. "Can I? What about the fact that she was found on the floor, pillow on her face? Like you said, she didn't get there by herself."

"Looks like you have a few loose ends. Anyway"—the M.E. was blithe—"I've attached the file and emailed you. As soon as I have a double shot of espresso, I'm on my way to pick up my hot date and drive to Stillwater. Go, Cowboys."

I wafted away. I wrung my hands. Oddly enough, specters purportedly are often seen pacing and twining their hands in desperation. I hated to be a cliché but this turn of events was ghastly. I had to alert the chief that Susan's death was murder.

Cobb punched off the speakerphone. He looked like a man trying to piece together a broken vase, but several of the pieces were pulverized. He turned to his computer, opened the medical examiner's report, printed it out.

He clicked another file, opened it.

I read the title of that report on his screen: *Preliminary report homicide lab Re: cup and china pot with cocoa residue from bedroom of deceased Susan Flynn.*

He punched *Print,* gathered up both the autopsy and lab reports, and placed them on his desk. On the legal pad, he wrote:

1. What was Susan Flynn's mental state?
2. Interview persons who saw her in the last few days.
3. Who inherits?
4. Who moved the body after death and why?
5. Who prepared the cocoa that she drank shortly before death?
6. Are there fingerprints—

A perfunctory knock sounded on his office door. The door was opened and in came a heavyset blonde in a silver-gray wool-silk suit with a Peter Pan collar. The dropped bodice wasn't flattering to the age spots on her upper torso. Her short skirt revealed dimpled knees that deserved merciful covering.

I hadn't liked Mayor Neva Lumpkin on my earlier visit to Adelaide. I doubted she would charm me this time.

With an air of proprietorship, the mayor settled in a straight chair facing the chief's desk. She began without preamble. "The City of Adelaide has suffered a grievous loss with the death of Susan Pritchard Flynn, one of our most respected citizens." The mayor's voice rose with platform unctuousness. "Susan's generosity to her community, her selfless devotion to her family and her church, and her honorable character will always serve as a sterling example to those of us who remain."

"Blah. Blah. Blah." I clapped my hand over my mouth.

The mayor's face quivered. "What did you say?"

Chief Cobb's expression was peculiar. "I didn't say anything. The heating makes funny noises sometimes."

The mayor's head switched back and forth. "I heard a woman's voice."

I kept my fingers pressed to my mouth. I must not succumb to the temptation to confound her as I had on a previous occasion when she'd attempted to interfere in a murder investigation. Wiggins had scolded me for that incident.

"Some kind of high sound." Her gaze moved up to the heating register.

"I turned the thermostat up when I came in. Maintenance always lowers the heat over the weekend. Probably we heard some kind of"—he was making an effort not to smile—"funny wheeze."

It was a good thing I was pressing my fingers against my lips.

Her plump face pink, her eyes glittering, the mayor gave

a short nod. "As I was saying, we have suffered a grievous loss. However, not"—great emphasis—"*an unexpected loss.* We all knew Susan's time was short. She had been ill for several years. In fact, my dear friend Jacqueline Flynn doubted that Susan would see in the New Year. Jacqueline acquainted me with the odd circumstances in which Susan's death was discovered and I felt it incumbent upon me to offer you my assistance. We both agreed the theft of Jacqueline's car—"

I floated to the blackboard on the opposite side of the room behind the mayor. It was quite clean. The chalk lying in the tray was fresh. I picked up a piece of pristine white chalk and immediately felt as though I were back in a classroom. One of the pleasures of teaching English had been the dissection of character, Bob Cratchitt, Pip, Lady Macbeth, Holden Caulfield, Madame Bovary, Heathcliff, Huckleberry Finn, Jo March.

"—was an entirely separate matter." The mayor was brisk, a woman sure of her facts.

Behind his desk, Chief Cobb looked immovable as a mountain, a big, solid man. He listened, his blunt face expressionless.

I rolled the chalk in my fingers, such a familiar sensation. My hand rose. I printed, the slight scratch of the chalk lost in the mayor's volume:

Pompous

"Moreover, as we all know, at the moment of death, there will often be a magnificent, though doomed, struggle. None of us"—the mayor's tone was lugubrious, but brave—"go willingly into that dark night. Our dear Susan no doubt had some intimation, perhaps piercing pain. This would explain the posture in which she was found. Think of Susan in pain, gasping for breath—"

The chalk moved:

Phony

"—seeking ease. She must have stumbled from her bed, clutching the pillow, only to fall and embark upon that last great journey which we all shall take."

Not Eugene O'Neill

"I trust everything is clear now." She spoke with finality.

"Facts are helpful, Neva. I'm sure you will be interested to know that Susan Flynn didn't die on the floor. Someone put her there and placed the pillow over her face. A shift in the lividity of the body proved she was moved after death. That's a fact." He tapped the papers on his desk. "Susan Flynn died from an overdose of digitalis. That's a fact. My job is to figure out whether the overdose was accidental or deliberate. And, if deliberate, whether she committed suicide or was murdered. Moreover, I intend to find out who moved the body after death."

The mayor wasn't fazed. "Sometimes facts must be interpreted to be understood." She fluttered a pudgy hand in dismissal. "Could there be a reasonable explanation for the placement of the body? Of course. Who can ever know how death strikes an intimate of a family?" Her tone was kind, as if encouraging a listener who might not be attuned to human vagaries. "Reactions are often impulsive, hard to explain, hard to understand. There are many possibilities. Distraught by the finality of death, quite likely someone pulled Susan from the bed and tried to revive her. When it became heartbreakingly obvious that resuscitation wasn't possible, the pillow was blindly placed over Susan, to hide the unalterable image of death."

Cunning

"We'll do our best to find out what happened." His voice businesslike.

"It's good we had this chance to visit, Sam. It is important for me, as mayor, to be certain all of Adelaide's public servants are focused on our primary task"—great emphasis here—"*of serving our community.* Often it is necessary for public servants to be certain that we do no harm. And"—a tinkling laugh—"we must remember that truth is usually simple—"

Patronizing

"—and not twist our thoughts seeking complicated solutions. Dear Susan." Sympathy oozed from her voice. "No doubt she felt so ill she misjudged how many pills she took. Or"— she lifted her heavy shoulders, let them fall—"though there's never any need for public revelation of suicide, illness sometimes is too great a burden to be borne."

Despite her unattractive bulk and bullying nature, Neva Lumpkin was nobody's fool. Suicide was a lovely resolution.

No scruples

Chief Cobb glanced toward the blackboard as I lowered the chalk. I let the piece fall to the floor.

Frowning, Cobb pushed up from his chair and walked slowly toward the blackboard. He moved quietly for such a big man.

Mayor Lumpkin followed his progress. She sniffed as he

bent to pick up the chalk. "I believe this is the only office in City Hall with an old-fashioned chalkboard. Everyone else is up to date with dry-erase boards and colored markers. We have to keep pace with the times, Chief Cobb."

He was gruff. "Chalk was good enough for me when I was a high school math teacher. It's good enough now."

"Really! In any event," she spoke loudly, "Jacqueline will be relieved when I tell her everything will be resolved quickly and quietly."

Cobb swung toward her, his expression abstracted. "I'll bring Mrs. Flynn up to date on the investigation when I meet with the family at the house this afternoon."

The mayor's gaze was cool. "Surely that meeting is no longer necessary since it's obvious Susan's death was undoubtedly self-inflicted."

Cobb's face tightened. "I'll tell you what, Neva, you look after City Hall, I'll look after suspicious deaths."

"I am looking after City Hall." She heaved herself to her feet, face dangerously red, and strode to the door. She stopped in the doorway, head held high. A trumpet roll could not have better announced a dramatic farewell. "I expect a sensible attitude on the part of all city employees. If you refuse to accept ambiguity—and most emphatically there can be nothing certain in the circumstances of Susan's death—the council will have to consider what action to take concerning the renewal of your contract in January. It may turn out that you should consider a return to teaching." She flounced into the hall, banging the door shut behind her.

Chief Cobb's exclamation was short, explicit, and forceful.

I had to agree. She certainly was.

He shrugged. "Comes with the territory." He started for his desk, then turned back to the blackboard.

I suspected no one knew better than he that the blackboard had been quite clean.

Once again I'd intruded upon the discrete world. Despite the Precepts, it was a very good thing I had done so. The longer Chief Cobb stared at the blackboard, the more time I had. He needed help to stave off the mayor's interventions, discover the truth, and not lose his job in the process.

I looked at the legal pad on his desk. Earlier he'd written: *What was Susan Flynn's mental state?* Imitating his neat square printing, I added: *Check with Father Abbott.* The rector would know Susan Flynn well and certainly attest to her mental health.

After *Interview persons who saw her in the last few days,* I added: *Was there any disruption of the household recently?* This would catch Keith's arrival.

His third question was all-important: *Who inherits?* I added: *When did she last see her lawyer and what did they discuss?*

I studied question four: *Who moved the body after death and why?* I decided to go for broke: *Was someone aware Susan Flynn had been murdered and set up a crime scene to be sure there was an investigation?*

The pencil was yanked from my hand.

"Ooh." I swung around and my elbow jammed into Chief Cobb's side.

"Ouch." He massaged his side. "How can a pencil stand up by itself?" He looked uncertainly at his chair. "I didn't bend over. What did I bump into?"

I tried to still my quick breaths. I should have kept a closer eye on the chief. I moved well out of his way.

He stared at the pencil, small in his massive hand, then toward the blackboard. He shook his head in denial. "That woman's driving me nuts."

I was offended until I realized he was referring to Mayor Lumpkin. Perhaps he would attribute any confusion on his part to his irritation with her.

He gingerly placed the pencil on the desk, again shook his head. "Now I'm seeing things." He spoke aloud, forcefully. He flipped the legal pad shut without seeing my insertions. "I can't think straight when Neva's around." He glanced at the clock and tucked the legal pad in a folder.

CHAPTER 11

A young woman bundled in a pink jacket counted to ten. Cheeks red from the cold, Keith ran as fast as he could across the front yard of Pritchard House. He skidded around a big sycamore and pressed against the trunk.

". . . eight, nine, ten. Okay, Colin, you can look around now. See if you can find Keith."

A skinny dark-haired boy about seven years old dropped his hands from his eyes and took a half dozen steps toward a fir.

"In the freezer, Colin." She wrapped her arms tight across her front, gave a dramatic shiver.

Colin veered to his right.

"Colder. Ice on your nose."

Colin swiped his nose with a red mitten and laughed. He turned and retraced his steps.

"Warmer."

Colin trotted ahead.

"Getting hot." She clapped.

I wished I could stay outside and watch the boys play. Colin shouted as he came around the sycamore. "Got you," he shouted as he grabbed Keith, who squealed with laughter.

I dropped into the living room for a different game of gotcha!

Chief Cobb stood to one side of the fireplace. A cheerful fire crackled. The living room was warm, but there was no air of holiday cheer.

Jake's eyes were huge and strained. "I talked to Father Abbott at St. Mildred's. Do you know when Susan—when we can have her service?"

"The autopsy has been completed." The chief looked commanding, his heavy face purposeful.

Was there a greater feeling of tension among his listeners than the quiet statement should evoke? Did one of them fear what had been found?

"The body will be released this afternoon."

"I'll call Father Abbott." Jake's relief was apparent. "Tuesday morning will be good. We can announce the services in the Monday and Tuesday papers."

"I know there is much for the family to deal with." The chief gazed at his listeners. "I appreciate the opportunity to meet with those who spent time with Mrs. Flynn on her last day to live."

There was a grim finality to his words, reminding each of them of their proximity to Susan's death. He reached into his folder, pulled out the legal pad and a sheaf of printed pages. "I'd like to understand how you knew her and why you were here yesterday."

Each person in turn described their connection to Susan as Chief Cobb took notes.

Jake Flynn's face was puffy from lack of sleep. She wore a little too much makeup and her hair had untidy sprigs. Today's blue cashmere sweater and gray tweed skirt were more flattering than the brown sweater and slacks she'd worn yesterday. She sat on the sofa beside Peg, whose eyes were swollen from crying. Peg's black dress emphasized her paleness. She wore no jewelry. Even though Dave Lewis sat on the small sofa beside her, the space between them seemed huge. His face wore a conventional expression of concern. Gina Satterlee sat stiffly on a rosewood chair, twining a strand of dark hair in her fingers. She was the picture of fashion in a crimson sweater and gray worsted wool slacks and red loafers. Tucker Satterlee, his freshly shaved face brooding and still, slouched in an oversize leather chair in a rumpled plaid shirt and Levi's and boots. Harrison and Charlotte Hammond were in their Sunday best, although his charcoal gray suit was wrinkled and his tie askew. Her long-sleeved black silk blouse matched a subtle geometric square in a violet silk georgette skirt that ruffled nicely over blue leather boots.

The chief flipped back several sheets in the legal pad.

When his eyes widened in surprise, I knew he had reached the questions he'd listed in preparation for this meeting. Of course, he had no recollection of having written my additions. Understandably.

Chief Cobb's brows drew down in a line. He gave an uncertain shake of his head, cleared his throat. "In investigating a suspicious death, it is helpful to have an understanding of the circumstances surrounding the deceased. Had there been any disruption of this household in recent days?"

I would have liked to shout a loud bingo! That was the question that mattered. With backs and starts and obvious uneasiness, the story unfolded: Keith's arrival on Thursday, the summons of Susan's lawyer Friday, the confirmation of Keith's legitimacy Saturday morning.

Cobb wrote fast. I was reminded of a lion gnawing on a carcass. "Obviously Susan Flynn had an eventful weekend. Now I would appreciate your assistance in piecing together an account of her last day."

Jake sat forward in her chair, her cheeks turning a bright pink. She said breathlessly, "I spoke with my good friend Mayor Lumpkin and Neva assured me that the investigation was only a formality since no one would ever be able to determine exactly how Susan died."

I wished I could see every face at once. One listener knew exactly why Susan died.

"The mayor"—Cobb's tone was level—"misinformed you. Mrs. Flynn died from an overdose of digitalis. What remains to be determined is whether her death was self-inflicted, an accident, or murder."

Jake sagged back against her chair. Peg gave a soft cry. Dave reached for her hand, gave it a reassuring squeeze. Gina's face was abruptly an unreadable mask of emptiness. Tucker's lips formed a soundless whistle. Hammond cracked his knuckles, the sound loud in the silence. Charlotte reached over, gripped his hand, and the tiny pops ended. She didn't look at him.

Jake fluttered her hands. "It was an accident. It had to be an accident."

Cobb's gaze was demanding. "Was Susan Flynn clumsy?"

Jake's eyes fell. "No."

Cobb leaned forward. "Was she easily confused? Could she have taken anywhere from twelve to fourteen pills by accident?"

Jake reluctantly shook her head.

"Susan was compos mentis, Chief Cobb." Charlotte's tone was dry. "You will not find anyone who would describe Susan as clumsy, stupid, or easily confused. To the contrary, she was intelligent, alert, and, though weak and ill, quite capable of dealing with her medications."

Harrison said nothing, but he slowly nodded.

"Susan didn't make mistakes of that sort." Peg spoke with finality.

"Since an accidental overdose seems highly unlikely, that brings us," Cobb said smoothly, "to the question of suicide. What was Susan Flynn's mental state on her last day to live?"

A smile trembled on Peg's lips even though her eyes were shiny with tears. "She was happier than she'd been in years and years. Her last day was wonderful. She was thrilled to have Keith at the Christmas party and to introduce him to the neighbors as her grandson."

Cobb looked around. "Where is he now?"

Peg gestured toward the window. "In the front yard, playing. I asked Thea Carson who runs the children's Sunday school program to bring her son over to play. Keith's too little to understand about his grandmother's death. Although I think he knows more about death than any little boy should."

The more Peg talked, the heavier the silence.

Jake's eyes were desperate. "But Susan was ill. Very ill. I can see how she might accidentally take too much medicine. It had to be an accident."

No one else spoke.

Cobb surveyed the room. His tone was bland. "From all accounts, Mrs. Flynn was a careful and precise woman, which makes accidental ingestion unlikely. Since Mrs. Flynn was in good spirits yesterday, the hypothesis of suicide also seems unlikely."

Harrison cleared his throat. "Susan's last day was filled with great happiness and we are grateful for that. However, we all feared that she was overdoing. You have to remember that she was very ill. She hadn't attended the Pritchard House Christmas party for several years. Yesterday, she took part and even had dinner with us to celebrate Keith's arrival. How can anyone know what happened after she went to her room? She may have suffered great pain and, in a moment of despair, possibly not even reckoning the outcome, poured a handful of pills—"

"Susan would never commit suicide." Peg's eyes flashed. "Never in a million years."

Charlotte brushed back an untidy gray curl. "Susan didn't commit suicide." She spoke with utter certainty. "So"—her expression was quizzical—"I believe that leaves us with murder."

"Charlotte!" Harrison's voice was anguished.

Dave Lewis didn't look as handsome when he turned to glare at Charlotte.

Charlotte's light blue eyes watched Cobb. "You indicated Susan died from an overdose of digitalis. How was the overdose administered? Or is there any way of knowing that?"

"We can be fairly certain we know the answer." Cobb's answer was swift and emphatic. "Digitalis in a heavy concentration was found in the dregs of both a cup of cocoa and a pot of cocoa found on a table in her bedroom. Was she in the custom of drinking cocoa every evening?"

Jake looked stunned. "Every night."

Cobb held his pen over the pad. "Who prepared the cocoa Saturday night?"

Jake's fingers closed over the strand of pearls. "I did. There wasn't anything wrong with it. I fixed it like I always did, two tablespoons of cocoa, two cups of whole milk, an eighth cup of sugar, a dash of vanilla." Her breath came in irregular gasps.

Peg pulled away from Dave's grasp and leaned forward, her eyes flashing. "Mother took wonderful care of Susan. Always."

Gina stiffened. "I took the cocoa upstairs. There was a Christmas cookie on the plate as well."

Cobb swiveled toward Gina. "Where did you put the tray?"

"On the table by Susan's chair. Susan was in the bathroom. I didn't call out. I knew she'd see the tray."

"Did you pour the cocoa?"

Peg shook her head. "Susan often waited until later to have a cup. Sometimes she read late and drank the cocoa right before she went to bed."

Cobb turned back to Jake. "When you poured the cocoa from the saucepan, did you look into the china pot?"

Jake frowned at him in bewilderment. "Why would I do that? The pot was clean and waiting on the tray. I lifted the lid and poured in the cocoa." A look of horror crossed her face. "I stirred it." Her hand slid up to clutch at her throat. "Do you think there was digitalis in the pot?"

"That is a possibility. What time did you prepare the cocoa?"

"Just after everyone left. It was about eight-thirty." Her lips clamped shut.

"I'd like to see where the chocolate service was kept."

I followed Cobb and Jake to the kitchen. She pointed at the far end of one counter near the pantry. "Every morning I brought the tray down and washed everything up. I put the tray there."

He made a note. "Did anyone else ever use the service?"

"Oh no." Jake stared at him with huge eyes. "Everyone knew that was for Susan's cocoa."

Cobb glanced from the counter to the swinging door that opened into the main hall.

I timed Cobb and Jake's passage from the kitchen to the living room. It took only a matter of seconds. As they walked into the living room, I waited until the door closed behind them. I appeared. I wasn't worried about anyone coming out of the living room. Chief Cobb had much more to discuss with them. Since the hall was chilly, I changed into a pink velour blouse and slacks and pink loafers, and a wristwatch with a pink leather band. I do like pink. I checked the time down to the second. I paused in the hallway, taking a careful glance around as someone last night must have checked to be certain no one was watching. I walked up the stairs, quickly, quietly, softly. Again I looked about in the upper hallway. No one. Twenty-eight steps to Susan's room. I disappeared, slipped through the closed door, reappeared. Twelve steps to the bedside table where the pill containers had stood. They were gone, most likely removed by the crime lab. I didn't need them. I pretended to pull a tissue from a container, pick up a plastic vial, twist off the cap, empty a dozen pills into my hand, replace the cap. Twelve steps to the door. I disappeared. In the hall, I reappeared and, after a swift glance about, hurried downstairs. At the door to the living room, I looked at my watch. I had gone up and down in three minutes and forty-six seconds. I walked down the hall, entered the kitchen, pretended to drop pills into a china pot, then walked back to the front hall. I disappeared and returned to the living room.

The atmosphere was tense.

Harrison looked both upset and frightened. ". . . certainly do not appreciate the inference that I might have drugged Susan merely because I was absent from the living room for a few minutes during our after-dinner coffee Saturday evening."

Dave Lewis looked pugnacious. "I used the downstairs lavatory. I didn't go upstairs."

The Hammonds and Tucker spoke out, insisting they too had remained on the first floor.

Cobb was bland. "However, each of you was absent from this room at some point during the evening while Mrs. Flynn was still downstairs. Each of you, therefore, had equal opportunity to go upstairs to Mrs. Flynn's room, take the digitalis, and return downstairs, either to place the digitalis at that time in the china pot waiting in the kitchen or during another absence from the gathering." He gazed at Jake. "What time did you fix the cocoa?"

Jake spoke hurriedly. "I was later than usual because after dinner Susan stayed downstairs until everyone left."

Cobb's eyes were bright and alert. "Was this unusual?"

Jake moved uneasily in her chair. Her eyes darted around the room. "Oh." She looked uncomfortable. "Susan rarely came down for dinner anymore but this was special. We had the annual outdoor tree trimming in the afternoon. The whole neighborhood is invited. Susan expected us to come. Of course"—she looked at guarded faces—"we all loved the tree party. It was always a fun afternoon. Then Susan asked everyone to come back for dinner at seven because, well, I guess she wanted to see everyone again." She added hurriedly, "Christmas, you know. There's never much time to visit during the tree trimming. Anyway, Susan went off to rest. We all gathered again for dinner at seven." She concluded in a rush as if successfully completing a race.

Cobb looked at each face in turn. "Everyone in this room not only saw Susan Flynn yesterday afternoon but was present for dinner. In fact, she especially wanted each of you to return for dinner. Why?"

"Susan was terribly fond—"

"Let it go, Jake. Even if you have a guilty conscience, I don't." Tucker's expression was amused.

"Tucker, that's a terrible thing to say. Susan was very fond of all of us and that's why she wanted to talk to us."

All humor gone, he sat straighter. "Coincidences happen, Chief Cobb. Once I had a mare stolen and the next day somebody called and tried to sell me a mare that looked just like her. It turned out to be a different horse altogether. What are the odds? Anyway, last night Susan brought all of us together after dinner to talk about her will. I told her at the time she didn't owe us any explanations, but she was always direct and open. I guess you've got the drift that her grandson arrived out of the blue. Susan had her lawyer investigate and she got plenty of proof that Keith is her son Mitch's child. Susan told us she intended to change her will and leave everything to Keith though she made it clear she was providing generous bequests for all of us. She'd already worked everything out with Wade Farrell so I guess the old will is out. Now everything will go to Keith, instead of being divided among us."

Gina watched her brother. A telltale flutter moved one eyelid.

Peg's face creased into a puzzled frown.

"It's a shame she died before the new will could be drawn." Harrison shook his head as if in regret. "Barring a new will, it seems obvious to me that the old will stands. However, all of this discussion of her estate seems distasteful. There is no proof that Susan's death was anything other than an accident or possibly a result of misjudgment on her part."

Gina turned a bracelet on her arm. The gold band had a cunning inlay of diamonds in the design of tiny Christmas trees. "We can ask Wade Farrell about the will."

I felt content. Soon they would meet with Wade Farrell and they were in for a shock. Especially one of them. Tomorrow morning in the mail, Wade Farrell would receive the holographic will unmistakably written and signed by Susan and witnessed by Leon Butler.

Harrison's nod was pleased. "That's a good idea, not that there's any doubt about the current will standing. I'll call Wade and suggest we all be present for a formal announcement, possibly tomorrow afternoon. Certainly we are entitled to have an idea of what amount we will receive." For an instant there was an empty look of fear in his eyes.

Was he wondering if the inheritance was going to be enough to keep him out of bankruptcy?

"I don't like this talk about Susan's will. It's as though"—Jake glared at Cobb—"you are suggesting someone killed Susan for her money. That's horrible. Besides, the whole idea of murder is absurd. There are too many things that haven't been explained: my car being stolen and where Susan went last night, if it was Susan, and who that red-headed woman was. If Susan drove out with someone none of us knew, maybe they came back here together and that woman put digitalis in her cocoa and Susan drank it. Or Susan got confused and took too many pills. Then there's that pillow on Susan's face. Why, that's crazy enough to prove something weird was going on. And," she concluded triumphantly, "none of us know anything about any of it."

Chief Cobb closed the legal pad. He gave it a thoughtful glance, then stood. He was a big man, a powerfully built, impressive man with a face seamed by effort and intelligence and experience. He stood in that elegant living room, his gaze steady. And grave.

"All of these matters must be explained, including the fact that after death, Susan Flynn's body was moved. She died lying on her left side. Someone put her body on the floor on her back. This changed the settling of her blood. A pillow, smeared with her lipstick though she wore no makeup, was placed over her face."

Jake shuddered, shook her head in negation. She looked as if she wanted to run away.

Gina gripped her bracelet so hard her fingers showed white. She stared at the floor, her face half hidden by a swath of drooping hair.

A frowning Tucker glanced from Jake to Peg to Gina as if judging and measuring and wondering. He no longer slouched, but sat upright, slightly bent forward.

Peg pressed one hand against her lips, her round face creased in distress. Dave slipped an arm around her rigid shoulders. She seemed unaware of him.

Harrison drummed the fingers of one hand on the arm of his chair. A slight tic pulled at one eyelid. "Possibly so, possibly not. Science is often discredited these days. In any event, whatever happened, the movement of Susan's body is irrelevant to the cause of her death and the suggestion of murder has yet to be proven."

Charlotte's intelligent face looked thoughtful. "Susan on the floor and the pillow on her face made a huge difference, didn't they, Chief Cobb?"

"An enormous difference. An alarm was raised. The police were summoned. An investigation began. An autopsy was performed. That autopsy revealed death was caused by a massive overdose of digitalis, not suffocation. Let's consider what would have happened had Mrs. Flynn's body been found in her bed this morning. The doctor would have been summoned and death by heart failure recorded. There would have been no police, no investigation. Instead, I'm here today because her body was found on the floor, a lipstick-smeared pillow on her face. Someone suspected that Mrs. Flynn had been murdered and was determined to have an investigation made."

There was not a breath of sound or movement.

Chief Cobb's heavy face was somber. "Whoever set up that scene, tell me what you know. Before it's too late."

I gently pulled the soft blanket over Keith's shoulders, bent to lightly kiss his cheek. He slept with his lips curved in a smile, one arm tucked around the soft furry plush of Big Bob's arm. Was Keith remembering the thrill of setting the glistening star atop the tall tree, or the fun of hide-and-seek, or possibly, deep inside, to be held forever, the joy in his grandmother's eyes as she curved an arm around his shoulders?

Whatever the source of that faint smile, I knew that Susan was pleased that her grandson was safe and secure in Pritchard House. Tomorrow when Susan's will reached the office of Wade Farrell, Keith would be established as her heir. My task would be done and it would be time for me to board the Rescue Express.

I had one more day to enjoy Adelaide's holiday bows and bangles.

CHAPTER 12

Soft December sunlight splashed cheerfully into the living room through the east windows. Peg placed an alphabet block—letter *K*—on top of a stack of seven on the fireplace hearth. This morning's modest fire crackled cheerfully behind the black mesh screen.

Keith whooped, "Keef," and knocked over the blocks, then rolled in laughter. He looked happy and well cared for in his new red turtleneck with Santa Claus on the front and brown corduroy trousers and fancy sneakers that flashed as he walked.

Though she was pale and drawn, Peg's face lighted for an instant. "That's one more for you. You have five and I have three. This time, you build the tower and tell me which letter I can push. Let's pick out a letter. How about *C*?"

Keith nodded, his face intent beneath the tangle of blond curls. His slender fingers hovered over a mound of blocks.

I smiled though I was restive and hungry. Last night, lurking in the kitchen, I'd managed a lovely dinner, taking advantage of the generous outpouring of food from friends and church ladies. However, breakfast had been hit-or-miss, cadging tidbits while Jake, Gina, Peg, and Keith ate largely.

Keith had beamed a brilliant smile at me, but he had a mouthful of waffle and didn't say hello. My measly single slice of bacon and sparrow-sized serving of scrambled eggs hadn't satisfied. Wiggins had never explained how one was to be on the earth, thereby requiring sustenance for energy, but not of the earth with the right to sit at table for meals. Next time I traveled back to earth as an emissary, I'd have that little matter straightened out. I was confident I would be dispatched again because I'd done so well in this instance, assuming Wiggins was feeling charitable enough to overlook my encounter with the church secretary, the befuddlement of Officer Cain, and Susan's slight delay in departing.

His small fingers agile, Keith selected the block with *W* and placed it in the exact center of one of the hearth tiles. Next came *S, B*—

Jake pattered into the living room, her face worried and abstracted. "Wade's secretary called. We'll meet at two o'clock this afternoon in his office."

"Can't the vultures wait until after the funeral?" Peg's voice wavered.

Jake's face flushed in outrage. "Missy, you keep a civil tongue in your head."

"Is that horrible will more important than Susan? How can any of us go to Farrell's office and not be ashamed? Everything"—Peg waved her arm—"should belong to Keith. That's what Susan wanted. One more day and this house and the ranch and the money would be his."

Jake's hands clenched. "Susan wanted me to have this house. I'm the one who's taken care of everything and kept the house going and made it beautiful the way Susan always did. Susan appreciated me. She told me more than once that she was glad Pritchard House would be mine, that I would always love and care for it." Jake's eyes swept the ornate and elegant living room with pride and passion and possessiveness.

Peg looked at her mother with compassion, but spoke with stubborn honesty. "Pritchard House should belong to Keith."

"He can live here." Jake's cry was forlorn. "Of course we'll take care of him. But Susan promised the house to me. She promised!"

Peg's eyes brimmed with tears. "We can't pretend we don't know what Susan wanted. Instead, everyone wants to know what they'll get. Susan's dead and no one cares. She was kind and brave. The world took her heart and crushed it and she kept on going and then she had a chance to be happy, to love Mitch's little boy, and someone killed her."

Tears trickled down Jake's cheeks as well. She swiped at them with a loud snuffle. "I feel like I'm living in a nightmare and someone will wake me up and everything will be all right." Her teary eyes looked piteously at her daughter. "I loved Susan. Susan and Tom gave us a home when I didn't have anything. Your daddy was a wonderful man, but he spent his life chasing dreams. He was always sure the next big scheme would put us on easy street. When he died, we owed thousands of dollars and our house was mortgaged. Susan and Tom did everything for us and they gave a home to Tucker and Gina. No one would kill Susan, and certainly not one of us. I don't care what the police say, all of this murder talk is crazy. After all, someone took my car and nobody can explain that either. Susan wasn't well enough to go out and she didn't even know anyone with red hair. And now I've got to go to the church and talk to Father Abbott and see about the funeral." The telephone pealed in the hall. "And everybody is calling and I don't know what to say." She swung around and ran from the room.

"Mother, wait." Peg moved toward the hall.

Keith gave a little cry. He hunkered on the ground, arms wrapped around his knees, chin lowered. His thin face was frightened.

Peg turned. "Oh, Keith, honey." She moved swiftly to drop down beside him, take him in her arms. "It's all right." She swallowed, said thinly as he clung to her, "That isn't true. Nothing is right." She put a hand beneath his chin, tipped his face up. "We've lost someone we loved a lot. You know how that feels." Her voice was gentle. "But right now you and I aren't going to be sad. We're going to be glad that we have a beautiful day and Santa Claus is putting toys on the list for you right this minute and we can go to the park and climb up into the big treehouse and have fun. Then we're going to Lulu's for the best hamburger in the world." She pulled him to his feet. "Let's see who can put on their coat the fastest."

Keith jumped to his feet, eyes beginning to sparkle.

I blew him a kiss.

He stopped and looked at me. "Can Jerrie come?"

Peg didn't even pause. She made a welcoming gesture. "Join the party, Jerrie. We're on our way. Come out and play."

Why not?

I was on my way out when I paused in the entry hall. Jake clutched the phone, and if ever a woman's face looked craven, it was hers. "I don't know why the *Gazette* would be interested in the visit by the police here Saturday night. It was all about my car being stolen. Now that seems so unimportant. We've had a death in the family and even though Mrs. Flynn's death has long been expected—she had congestive heart failure—it is still such a sadness for us. The police have been so helpful. They found the car and no harm done. We aren't at all concerned with the theft now . . . Yes, I'm glad to help you . . ."

As Jake hung up, she looked both guilty and pleased. With the help of her good friend the mayor, Jake Flynn had kept the matter of a murder investigation very quiet. Until and unless Chief Cobb released information, the police arrival at Pritchard House Saturday night was now explained away.

I looked at her with some respect. Jake Flynn was more resourceful than I would have expected.

However, she was seriously underestimating Chief Cobb.

And me, though of course she had no idea I was on the case.

Instead of joining Peg and Keith in her car, I swooped in a leisurely fashion toward the park. Though only Heaven is truly carefree, I felt buoyant and relaxed. My elevated elation was not simply because I was skimming through the crisp air above holiday-bedecked Adelaide, suitably attired in an elegant jade wool pantsuit, the jacket cut in scallop fashion, a white cashmere coat, and white leather boots. Only rock stars take farewell tours, but this was my ghostly—forgive me, Wiggins—version. Everything was turning up roses. Chief Cobb was looking for Susan's murderer. At two o'clock I would attend the gathering at Wade Farrell's office and Keith would be named the rightful heir.

Until then, I could enjoy dear Adelaide and the holiday season.

Christmas lights gleamed on streetlamps. I took a moment to drop by the rectory of St. Mildred's, hoping for a glimpse of the rector's wife. Kathleen Abbott was my grandniece, and her daughter Bayroo was named after me and a bright redhead, too. My first assignment with the Department of

Good Intentions had been to assist Kathleen. I was in luck. Kathleen and Bayroo were wrapping presents on the dining room table, both smiling and happy. I was careful to stay behind Bayroo because, like Keith, she would immediately see me. I blew them kisses and whirled away.

In a strip shopping center, a young couple looked at engagement rings in a jewelry store window.

Rings. I was thoughtful. I hadn't noticed an engagement ring on Peg's finger even though Susan had considered backing Dave Lewis, thinking in terms of Peg marrying Dave.

The two supermarkets were thronged, frozen turkeys jouncing in baskets laden with produce and cans. In the crowded parking lot of Walgreen's, one fender bender was amicably resolved, another not. I skimmed above the crowds here and there. I loved the frazzled look of fatigue as well as the glimpses of joy and pleasure in the faces below. What would Christmas be without the overwhelming sense of so much to do for so many in so little time?

Autumn Heights Park was festive with tinsel-draped trees. Light strands outlined the fishing pier. A fitful breeze slapped water against the pilings. A dozen or so children braved the chilly playground, enjoying the jungle gym, swings, teeter-totters, merry-go-round, and, pièce de résistance, a treehouse with slides from several levels.

Keith headed straight for the treehouse. He swung onto the ladder and climbed, hand over hand, intent on reaching the top.

Peg moved to one side where she could watch him. Keith reached the top, edged toward the slide, looked cautiously around, then seated himself and, with a jerk, started down. He landed at the bottom, shrieking with laughter, and immediately ran back to the ladder.

As he climbed, Peg reached into her purse and pulled out

her cell phone. Her hands were bare. She wore no engagement ring. She held the cell phone, her hazel eyes troubled. She was much too young for the trouble that pulled her round, kind face into a worried frown. The breeze stirred her brown curls.

"Look at me!" Keith waved his arms.

Peg waved in return. Her smile was quick. "I see you, Keith."

I stood near the bottom of the slide.

Once again, he carefully positioned himself and down he came. He tumbled over as he landed but rolled to his feet, panting with excitement. "Did you see me, Jerrie?"

I clapped.

Keith sped toward the ladder, cheeks flaming, thin legs pumping. He climbed quickly and once again zoomed down the slide.

Peg flipped open her cell phone, punched a number. She stood stiff and straight, her expressive face apprehensive. She listened, then flipped the lid shut.

Keith ran by, almost careened into an older girl with pigtails.

Peg called out. "Slow down, Keith. Do you want to walk out on the pier?"

Keith shook his head. He was at the ladder and swarming up.

Peg started to drop the phone into her purse, then, with a determined frown, she flipped the lid, punched the number, waited a moment. "Dave, I had to call and tell you what's happening. We're meeting at the lawyer's office at two. I've been thinking everything over. Susan wanted Keith to inherit. Everyone knows that's true. I know what I have to do. I'm going to elect not to inherit in favor of Keith. I think I can do that. You remember that Susan's husband, Tom"—

she was talking fast, perhaps a little unclearly—"talked a lot about wills and estates and everything. That's the kind of lawyer he was. He had a case once where the person who was going to inherit stood aside and gave the money to someone else. I don't care what the others do. That's what I have to do." She stopped and breathed deeply, as if she'd been running. She almost spoke, hesitated, finally said quickly, "I'll talk to you later."

"Look at me, Peg. Look at me!"

Her eyes still held uncertainty, but she looked up and smiled widely at Keith. "Way to go, Keith. Five more slides and it's time for lunch."

I arrived at Main Street as Peg and Keith walked into Lulu's. It was too bad I couldn't appear and introduce myself to Peg as Keith's Jerrie. Peg would have been glad to welcome an emissary here on Keith's behalf. Wiggins was such a stickler about his don't-appear-unless-you-have-to rule.

I really wanted a Lulu's hamburger with pickles, onions, mustard, and a slice of cheddar on a bun that had been swiped across the griddle. Saturday night, I'd implored Susan to will the appearance of her purse, complete with a driver's license. I knew without doubt that envisioning a particular outfit as I appeared brought it into being. Could I wish myself present in my jade green pantsuit and white cashmere coat and white leather boots with a matching white leather shoulder bag containing a billfold with nice crisp bills to cover the cost of a magnificent Lulu's hamburger?

I plunged into the midst of the noon crowd, people laughing and chattering and intent upon their destinations. I swirled into being from the tip of my red head to the toe of my white boots and felt the delicious weight of a white shoulder bag. I opened the bag, found a billfold, saw a ten-dollar bill. I gave a chuckle of sheer delight. A tired-looking woman met my gaze. Her downturned mouth lifted. "Merry Christmas." I called back, "Merry Christmas," and darted inside the narrow café. I took a deep breath of the delicious smell of hamburgers hissing and onions browning on the griddle and hot grease bubbling with French fries.

I entered Lulu's right behind Peg and Keith. The counter to the left ran the length of the narrow café. Four booths, all full, were on the right. There were—providentially?—three unoccupied seats at the counter. We hung our coats on hooks opposite the cash register. I slid onto the seat next to Keith. An efficient waitress with a ready smile and relaxed competence took our orders and swiftly brought iced tea to Peg, cherry limeade to Keith, and coffee to me.

Keith wriggled happily on the red leatherette stool. He looked up at me and put his hand on my sleeve. "I went to the top of the big slide all by myself."

Peg turned with an apologetic look.

I smiled in reassurance and spoke to Keith in a tone of respect. "There are tall slides. And *tall* slides. Was your slide as high as a fireman's ladder?"

"Higher." His dark eyes gleamed.

"High as a tall building?"

He tilted his head as he thought. "Higher."

A muffled peal rang from Peg's purse. She reached down and brought out her cell, glanced at it. She took a deep breath. Her voice was tight as she spoke. "Dave." There was a mixture of eagerness and apprehension in her tone. "I hope—" She broke off, listened.

I held my hands far apart. "Tall as a mountain?"

Keith nodded vigorously. "Tall as a mountain."

"That makes you"—I touched his shoulder—"a mountain man."

"Mountain man." Keith giggled in delight and repeated the words again and again.

The waitress placed our orders in front of us.

Peg held the phone between her cheek and shoulder as she cut Keith's hamburger in half, squeezed a mound of ketchup near his French fries. "I don't suppose I'd have to say anything today. But Dave—"

Keith picked up a half, began to eat, absorbed in his lunch.

The waitress attended to other diners, often pausing for a cheerful though quick chat. "How's that hip doing, Rollie?" "Really like that new hairdo, Sybil." "You got a good used Camry on the lot, Milton?"

"—I know what Susan wanted. Don't you understand? I have no right to that money. None of us do."

I splashed ketchup on the French fries, added salt and pepper. My Lulu burger was as delectable as I remembered, and the French fries hot and fresh. I was careful not to let mustard drip on my jade slacks.

"Of course I care about us. But we can manage without Susan's money." Peg crushed a paper napkin in one hand. "I'm not throwing away our future. Not unless you care more about money than you do about me." Her eyes closed. When they opened, they shone with tears.

I helped Keith add more ketchup, wished there was some balm I could offer Peg.

"I'm sorry you feel that way." She shook her head. "You see, I loved Susan. I have to do what she wanted."

Peg's hamburger was untouched. She held the phone, her face etched with despair. "I won't change my mind." The words were barely audible.

I knew the moment he clicked off the phone. Peg flipped shut the lid, dropped the phone in her purse, then wiped her eyes with the crushed napkin.

"Peg." The deep voice held kindness and compassion and possibly something more.

I almost choked on my hamburger.

Johnny Cain, immaculate in his French blue uniform, dark hair neatly combed, blue eyes empathetic, stood next to Peg.

I raised my left shoulder and turned my face away from Keith, though that was no defense. If Johnny Cain glanced my way or at my very redheaded reflection in the mirror—that shade of jade was perfect—recognition would be immediate. Hopefully, I would escape his notice because of his absorption in Peg.

He bent toward Peg. "I'm sorry about your aunt. Since I was on duty, I couldn't talk to you last night like I would have. Mrs. Flynn was always great to me. I know how much she meant to you. Anyway, I saw you and the little guy at the park." He looked uncomfortable. "I was due to check in at headquarters and I happened to see you guys come in here and it's my lunch break. I usually grab a chili dog here. They're still the best in town."

I wondered if it occurred to Peg that Johnny Cain had followed her car to town and seen Peg and Keith come into Lulu's. Certainly the police station was right around the corner and I had no doubt he often ate here, but I didn't believe his arrival today was a coincidence.

"Anyway"—his ears were pink—"I wanted you to know I'm real sorry about Mrs. Flynn."

Peg swiped again at her moist eyes. Her face turned pink, too, knowing he took her tears for grief at Susan's death. "Johnny"—she reached out, touched his arm—"it meant so much to have you there Saturday night. We go back a long way."

"I wish I could have been more help. If I'd had any idea when I stopped that car that something funny was going on,

I'd have for sure tried to do something. It makes me sick to think that maybe if I'd kept following the car, I could have made a difference." His face creased in a puzzled frown.

Keith sucked noisily on his cherry limeade.

I took a last bite of my hamburger, circumspectly opened my accommodating purse, and retrieved the ten. If I quietly caught the waitress's eye and received my check, I could slip away without notice, no harm done. Johnny clearly had eyes for no one but Peg.

As the waitress neared, I quietly said, "Miss?"

She stopped. "Apple pie today?"

Lulu always melted a strip of cheddar on the flaky crust. I was tempted, but I didn't want to push my luck. "No thanks. I'm ready for my check."

She lifted the pad from her pocket. "You three together?"

I shook my head quickly. Fortunately, Johnny still talked. ". . . and the funny thing is, the car was headed out to the highway. I didn't see it come back until it came over Persimmon Hill like a bat out of hell. When it stopped, there was just the redheaded woman in the car."

The waitress slapped my check on the counter. "You got gorgeous red hair. I wish my hair was as red as yours. But yours is natural. You can always tell." She nodded sagely.

As if on a cue, Peg and Johnny turned toward me. Peg's gaze sharpened. Johnny's eyes widened. His mouth opened.

I put the ten-dollar bill on the check, twirled on the stool to step down to the old wooden floor. "Thank you." I turned away, heading straight for the door that led to a small hallway and the restrooms.

Johnny Cain called after me. "Miss, please, wait a minute. Miss . . ." He started after me.

I opened the door, stepped into the hallway, swiftly shut the door behind me, and disappeared.

The door swung in. Johnny stepped into the narrow corridor. At the far end was a door marked *Exit.* A sign warned *Alarm Sounds When Door Opened.* To the left was an unmarked closed door. Both restrooms were to his right. He should have arrived before I reached the women's restroom. Instead, the hall was empty. He shook his head, approached the restrooms. Hesitantly, he knocked on the door marked *Ladies.*

"Almost out." The voice was harried.

Johnny stepped back a few paces. He pulled a cell from his pocket, punched a number. "Detective Price. Johnny Cain . . . Sir, I've sighted the redhead who was in the car with Susan Flynn. She's in the ladies' room at Lulu's . . . I'm in the hallway . . . Right. Yes, sir."

"Reprehensible." Wiggins's roar startled both Johnny and me.

Johnny looked toward the men's room.

"Shh."

Johnny's head jerked up, seeking the source of the sibilant sound.

"Precept One." It was a piercing stage whisper.

I was astonished the hallway didn't wobble from the force of Wiggins's displeasure. He was too upset to remember his own rules.

Johnny turned the knob to the men's room. The door swung in. It was unoccupied.

The door to the women's restroom opened. A harried young mother shepherded out twin toddlers, scuffling with each other. "Stop it, Derek. Quit that, Dan." She gripped their hands, looked around. "So she was in such a hurry she didn't even wait."

Johnny leapt toward the end of the hallway, shoved open the exit. A shrill bell clanged.

Wiggins's growled "To the roof" was audible only to me.

Clumps of snow from a recent storm looked dingy against the black-tarred roof. I settled on a parapet in the sun with a nice view of the street as a police cruiser squealed to a stop, red light whirling, siren wailing. A similar wail sounded from the alley, joining the continuing clamor from Lulu's exit alarm.

Shivering, I wished for my white cashmere jacket. I felt its warm embrace. I was tempted to pop back into Lulu's and see whether the coat had disappeared. Perhaps Wiggins could enlighten me as to the properties of imagined articles. However, this might not be a propitious moment for such a discussion.

"Bailey Ruth." The voice came from across the roof near a turbine vent. Wiggins sounded cross.

"Come sit in the sun, Wiggins," I called out with cheer as if we were old friends pausing for a moment to enjoy a sparkling winter day. "I'm sitting on the parapet overlooking the street." I bent, picked up a vagrant red maple leaf, still lovely though brittle, and placed it atop the wide brick railing.

In a moment, a heavy sigh sounded beside me.

I offered the maple leaf. "Beautiful, isn't it?"

His hand brushed mine as he took the leaf. "Quite a brilliant red. Just"—he wasn't being complimentary—"like your hair."

"How is everything in Tumbulgum?" As Mother told me long ago, it's only good manners to discuss matters of interest to everyone.

"Almost"—his tone was as cold as the patches of crusted snow—"as difficult as in Adelaide."

"Where is Tumbulgum?" I truly did want to know.

"Lovely place. In New South Wales in Australia. On the Tweed River, near the junction of the Tweed and the . . . Actually, the location of Tumbulgum isn't relevant.

You do realize that your latest appearance will cause the police to focus attention on the appearances and"—great emphasis—"*disappearances* of a redheaded woman. If there is anything to be avoided, anything worse than violating Precepts One through Six, it is the prospect of creating a perception of . . ."

I waited. The term *ghost* was anathema to Wiggins, though I saw no reason to pretend that a potato wasn't a tuber.

". . . otherworldliness." The admission was grudging. "I see no way"—his voice dropped in discouragement—"to effectively combat the beginnings of what may turn out to be a legend in Adelaide."

"Wiggins"—I was firm—"I will see that this doesn't happen." Whether they realize it or not, men appreciate firmness. When a woman takes charge—graciously, of course—it offers emancipation.

"Is there something you can do?" He sounded like a man desperate to cling to a glimmer of hope.

Short of transporting Johnny Cain, Peg Flynn, the church secretary, and the always suspicious Chief Cobb and Detective Sergeant Price to a remote desert island, I rather doubted I could wipe away the collective memory of a redhead they sometimes saw and sometimes didn't. However, I am always willing to give my best effort.

"Wiggins, of course." I spoke with utter confidence. "I'll keep on top of things. You hurry right back to Tumbulgum. Everything will be fine here. I'm off to see about it."

The sirens no longer shrilled. The alarm was silent. In the street, Detective Sergeant Price stood beside a police cruiser. He gestured to the north. Peg nodded.

"Be of good cheer, Wiggins. 'Waltzing Matilda,' and all that." Too late, I clapped my hand to my lips. Possibly that wasn't the most tactful song to mention since the refrain is sung by the ghost of the swagman who haunts the billabong. Once again, I'd spoken before I thought. I didn't wait for a reply and zoomed down to join Peg and Keith.

Faintly, I heard Wiggins's plaintive cry. "Do your best. Try to remember the Precepts. Work in the background without attracting notice . . ."

Wiggins could count on me.

CHAPTER 13

Chief Cobb's moderate-sized office seemed crowded. Peg and Johnny sat at the circular table near the wall with the old-fashioned blackboard. A gawky woman with spiky violet hair and metallic gray eyes frowned in concentration at the sketch pad on the table. Her hand, the fingers long and graceful, moved with quick surety. Detective Sergeant Price stood behind her chair, his eyes thoughtful.

As red curls and a thin freckled face came clearer on the sketch pad, Chief Cobb watched with the curious expression of a man who doesn't trust what he sees.

Behind the chief's desk, Keith made whooshing noises as he pushed the swivel chair around and around.

A burly police officer with a Saint Bernard face opened the hall door. "Mrs. Norton is here. From St. Mildred's."

The church secretary bustled inside, her bony face eager. She pulled off a scarf, tucked it in the pocket of her red lamb's wool coat, handed the coat grandly to Detective Sergeant Price. Her green wool dress was as shapeless as a gunny sack. "Have you caught that woman? She was certainly up to no good."

I found her vindictive attitude hard to fathom. Did she

dislike redheads on principle? I wouldn't stoop to suggesting possible jealousy on the part of a faded brunette with sprigs of gray. After all, the hijacking of a church directory surely didn't qualify as high crime. I would have pegged it a misdemeanor.

Chief Cobb took the coat and added it to the several on the coat tree. "The artist will appreciate any help you can offer."

I looked over the artist's shoulder. Hmm. My cheekbones were perhaps a little more prominent.

Detective Sergeant Price shook his head. "She's a lot better-looking than that if she's who I think she is. Kind of a haunting beauty. Her face is thinner—"

The artist erased, reformed my cheekbones.

"—and the chin is delicate. Freckles across her nose." For an instant, he might not have been in the winter-stuffy room. His eyes had a faraway look. "I like freckles."

Johnny hunched forward. "Green eyes like a cat's, really bright."

Peg squinted in remembrance. "I wasn't paying a lot of attention. I was upset." She didn't look toward Johnny. "She had a great smile, one of those I've-just-met-you-but-I-already-like-you-and-let's-be-friends smiles."

The secretary's nose wriggled. "Really curly bright red hair. You know, the vixen-vamp kind of hair. Probably out of a bottle."

I glared at her lank graying hair and snapped, "Women with boring hair always resent natural redheads." Oh. And oh. Once again I'd spoken aloud when I shouldn't. I hoped Wiggins was safely in Tumbulgum.

The secretary's head jerked toward Peg. "I beg your pardon."

Peg clutched Johnny's arm. "I didn't say anything."

"Someone did. A woman." The church secretary glared at Peg.

Chief Cobb, Detective Sergeant Price, and Officer Cain had uncannily similar expressions of uneasiness. As if in concert, their eyes moved around the room.

Chief Cobb cleared his throat. "Mrs. Norton, the voice wasn't at all similar to Miss Flynn's voice. Much huskier. Forceful."

Certainly I have always spoken with vigor. I hadn't taught English and chaired meetings to sound meek. For an instant, I felt I heard a ghostly echo of boisterous laughter, Bobby Mac guffawing at the idea of a meek me. As he often told our kids, "You'll get the best of your mother when elephants tap-dance." Actually, there's a traveling troupe of pachyderms I caught on their last Milky Way show who did a fine shuffle hop step.

"I heard what I heard." The church secretary's voice was icy.

"We more than likely had an errant transmission in here." Chief Cobb waved a hand toward his computer. "Sometimes we get communications that we aren't expecting. Whatever we heard, the comment had no connection to you. We appreciate your contribution as a concerned citizen. Should the redheaded woman return to St. Mildred's, please call us." He retrieved the red wool coat, held it out for her. "Sergeant Mersky will take you back to the church."

As the door closed behind Mrs. Norton, Detective Sergeant Price said firmly, "I think I know who she is. Not a chance that red was out of a bottle. Her hair glistens like copper in the summer sun."

Who would have thought a homicide detective would be so poetic?

I sent a little telepathic message to Bobby Mac: *He's*

adorable, but you are my man. Not to worry. Bobby Mac always had an eye for good-looking women and understood when I admired a manly male. But we always danced the last dance together.

Cobb glanced at Price, his gaze speculative. "Right." He turned to the artist. "Okay, Tammie, print up some copies for us."

The artist made a change, smudged charcoal, added a stronger line to the jaw.

I nodded in approval. A very nice likeness indeed. However, my pleasure ebbed, it wouldn't be helpful to have this image broadcast.

The artist returned the pastel pencils to their box and slipped the sketch pad and box into a portfolio. "Major crook?" Her voice was startlingly deep.

Cobb cleared his throat. "She may have information that would be useful in an investigation."

The artist stood almost six feet tall. Although she was careless with makeup—too much eyeliner and an orange lip gloss that bordered on strange—I admired her silvery gray silk charmeuse cap-sleeve blouse and an ankle-length bias-cut jacquard skirt with swirls of raspberry, silver, and indigo and open silver sandals. I supposed she didn't mind cold toes.

She walked to the door, then turned. For an instant, her posture froze. She looked at me.

I looked back at her.

Our eyes met.

Uh-oh.

Some children see what isn't there. Rarely is that true of adults.

The artist slouched against the lintel. "Is she on the side of the angels?"

Detective Sergeant Price's generous mouth twisted in an odd, lopsided grin. "I think so. I definitely think so."

Tammie waggled her portfolio. "Who knows? She may be closer than you think." She gave a gurgle of laughter. "I have a feeling she'll be in touch."

I nodded vigorously.

Her eyes, also silvery gray, watched me. "I'll get the copies out as soon as possible."

I shook my head with equal vigor.

"Of course"—her tone was casual—"we've been having some problems with the program. Sometimes when I try to make the transfer to digital, everything gets screwed up." As she turned away, she gave me a decisive, amused wink.

The door closed behind her, and I started to breathe again.

Peg glanced at her watch. "Chief Cobb, I'd lost track of the time." Her tone was anxious. "I'm due at Susan's lawyer's office at two and I need to take Keith home."

Chief Cobb held up his hand. "If you can spare just a minute more, Miss Flynn." He was genial, but his eyes were intent. "How did you happen to have lunch with the woman Officer Cain identifies as the driver of the car the night your aunt died?"

Peg turned her hands up in amazement. "I was shocked when Johnny told me that." Her face turned pink. "I mean, when Officer Cain told me. I'd never seen her before today. She came into Lulu's behind us and sat down next to Keith. Keith spoke to her and she was very nice to him. If she knew Susan, she didn't tell me. It's so odd, all of it. But I'm sure Jo—Officer Cain isn't mistaken. He's always very precise." Her face turned even pinker. "We were lab partners in chemistry in high school. He is very methodical."

Johnny's face was pink, too. He carefully didn't look toward Peg. "Susan Flynn said the redheaded woman was a friend from out of town." He gazed earnestly at the chief. "There's no reason Peg—I mean Miss Flynn—would have known her."

Small steps sounded on the wooden floor. Keith ran toward Peg. "I found M&M's. Can I have some?" He pointed at Chief Cobb's oak desk. A side drawer had been pulled out.

"Oh, Keith." Peg came to her feet.

Cobb grinned. "That's okay. All right, Keith, it looks like you're a good M&M's detective." He strode to the desk, lifted out a big bag of the small candies. "I'll bet you count good, too. How many candies does a good detective deserve?"

Keith's eyes danced with pleasure. He held up both hands, fingers outspread.

The chief laughed aloud and measured out ten M&M's.

Peg looked at her watch. "I'm going to be late to the meeting. Leon Butler was going to show Keith some horses, but I don't have time to drive out there."

Johnny Cain stepped forward. "Sir, since Miss Flynn was helping us, perhaps I can be of assistance. Miss Flynn and I are old friends. I could take Keith out to Leon's and she'll be able to get to her meeting."

Chief Cobb looked from one to the other. "If that is agreeable to you, Miss Flynn, Officer Cain has my permission."

Johnny turned to Keith. "Would you like to ride with me in a real police car?"

Keith crunched another M&M and nodded vigorously. Peg knelt to help him into his coat. Johnny swung Keith up and onto his shoulders.

Peg squeezed Johnny's arm. "Thank you, Johnny. We can switch the car seat to the police car. Please tell Leon I'll pick Keith up . . ."

As the door closed behind them, Chief Cobb held out the M&M's bag.

Detective Sergeant Price opened his hand, popped a half dozen in his mouth.

The two men exchanged thoughtful glances.

Cobb looked dour. "Susan Flynn was last seen with this knockout redhead. Next time the redhead shows up, definitely identified by Johnny Cain, she's sitting next to Susan Flynn's grandson at Lulu's. Peg Flynn claims she never saw her before. I don't like coincidences. They stick in my craw."

Price crunched the candies. "Lots of unanswered questions on this one, Chief." He glanced at his watch. "I've got feelers out to pick up financial background on the Flynn heirs. Off the record."

I hadn't worked at the mayor's office without understanding the good old boy network in Adelaide. Someone always knew what you wanted to find out and a promise of confidentiality loosened lips faster than a shot of Jack Daniel's. If other evidence suggested the murderer's identity, a court order could be obtained to get any needed records.

Price grabbed a navy ski jacket from the coat tree. "Hey, Sam. To call a spade a spade, I'll bet this redhead is that good-looker who was mixed up in the murder at St. Mildred's, the one who talked to witnesses pretending to be Officer M. Loy. She had a way of disappearing, too. We never found a trace of her. Anywhere. She was a babe."

Cobb managed a good-humored chuckle. "You need a girlfriend, Hal. No point in holding out for somebody who clearly doesn't live in Adelaide."

"Yeah." Hal's tone was regretful. "Besides, even if she"—he didn't identify me, but that wasn't necessary—"showed up, I remember for sure she wore a wedding ring when I saw her on the back porch of the rectory. The good ones are always taken."

After the door closed, Cobb's genial expression faded. He

walked toward the blackboard. There were no marks on it. Someone had wiped away the comments I'd added yesterday.

Cobb picked up a broken piece of chalk. He muttered aloud. "Who wrote on the blackboard and every word nailed Neva. Another coincidence?" He stared down at the chalk fragment in his big fingers. "Then the chalk fell on the floor. I saw it. I think. Okay, things fall. Another coincidence? And how about my notes? That pencil sure seemed to be moving, and when I got to Pritchard House and looked at the legal pad, I found stuff I don't remember writing down. I guess I could have. And now I'm talking to myself. Out loud. Maybe it's all Neva's fault. It's hard to think straight when Neva's around." He lifted his hand to the blackboard.

I waited, wondering.

He printed in distinctive large block letters: *Officer M. Loy?* He looked hopefully around the office, then abruptly dropped the chalk in the tray, turned on his heel. "I'm sure desperate for help when I try to call on somebody who isn't here."

He folded his hands behind his back, walked to his desk with his heavy shoulders slumped. He might as well have shouted his frustration to the world. The evidence suggesting murder could be explained away, leaving the cause of Susan's death open: murder, suicide, or accident.

I'd thought I'd be off on the Rescue Express after the meeting at the lawyer's office established Keith as Susan's heir. However, that left unfinished the matter of Susan's murder. I'd believed my duty done once I'd set the stage for an investigation. Clearly the matter was not so simply resolved.

Would Wiggins let me assist Chief Cobb in catching Susan's murderer?

Wiggins had been outraged at her untimely demise. Wiggins had encouraged me to bring Susan's murderer to justice. Obviously I'd not finished my task. I had to do what I had to do.

I moved to the blackboard, picked up the chalk, wrote in a stylish hand:

Officer M. Loy reporting for duty.

Chief Cobb stood at the window, staring out. He would find my message.

Wade Farrell's conference room was shabby but reassuring, an old oak table that had seen years of use, sturdy straight chairs, faded red velvet drapes, and over the fireplace an oil portrait of a man in a judge's robe, his face both stern and thoughtful. Though Wade's face was more rounded and his hairline receding, there was a marked resemblance to the man in the portrait.

Wade waited until everyone was seated, then took his place in a chair at one end.

A dark gray folder rested at each occupied place.

Wade's face was somber. "I regret the circumstances of our gathering." He frowned and avoided looking directly at any of the heirs. He cleared his throat. "I will briefly acquaint you—"

Obviously Wade Farrell wanted to avoid any discussion of the cause of Susan's death.

"—with the provisions of the will."

Jake touched a handkerchief to reddened eyes. Tears trickled down Peg's cheeks. Tucker leaned back in the leather chair, his expression intent. Once again he was clean-shaven. Gina fingered a jade necklace that was startling in its beauty against her white silk blouse. Charlotte Hammond gazed unseeingly at the portrait of the judge. Harrison took an impatient breath.

"In the folder in front of you, you will find a copy of Susan's last will and testament. The provisions are simple. The estate is to be divided equally among Jacqueline Flynn, Peg Flynn, Tucker Satterlee, Gina Satterlee, and Harrison Hammond."

If a bucket of ice water had been upended over me, I could not have been more stunned. I leaned over Harrison's shoulder. He flipped through the pages. I recognized the document I'd found when I had explored Wade's files.

". . . would like to point out that Susan specifically indicated that Pritchard House was to be included in Mrs. Jacqueline Flynn's share and Burnt Creek in the share allotted Tucker Satterlee. Of course . . ."

I zoomed back and forth above the table, feeling frantic and helpless. Where was Susan's new will?

". . . until there is a final accounting, the amount of each bequest can only be estimated, but I feel safe in saying that the estate's current value is approximately twelve million dollars."

Jake took a quick little breath. Harrison looked like a man with a last-minute reprieve from the guillotine. He lifted a shaking hand to pull at his collar. Tucker slouched back in the leather chair. Gina clasped her hands tightly together.

Peg closed the folder with a slap, looked at Wade in dismay. "Susan wanted her estate to go to Keith. She told you to draw up a new will."

It was as if a cold wind swept the room.

Jake pressed both hands against her cheeks. Harrison folded his arms and stared down at the table. Tucker gave a slight head shake. Gina clutched at the jade beads, her face stiff. Charlotte shook her head.

Peg looked at each in turn. "You know that's true. So what are we going to do?"

Wade looked troubled. "You are correct, Peg. That was Susan's intent. The fact remains that she didn't live long enough to execute a new will. The will that exists controls disposition of her estate."

Peg's look at her fellow heirs was imploring. "We can assign our portions to Keith. All of us. That's what we should do."

Wade held up a cautioning hand. "Each of you may give your inheritance to whomever you wish. However, there will be gift taxes to consider. Or, in the event an heir elects not to receive an inheritance, that portion of the estate would then be divided among the remaining heirs, and"—he tapped the gray folder—"those heirs are Mrs. Flynn, Tucker Satterlee, Gina Satterlee, and Harrison Hammond."

"Keith is Susan's grandson." Peg's cry was impassioned.

Her mother looked away, crushing a wisp of sodden handkerchief in one hand.

Tucker shrugged. "Peg, honey, you can do what you want with what you get. Susan promised the ranch to me a long time ago. I didn't stay here to work for somebody else." His face was abruptly hard and determined. "Burnt Creek is mine."

Jake turned toward her daughter. Her eyes begged for understanding. "We'll make a wonderful home for Keith and see him through school and everything, but I don't see why Mitch's son should be dropped on us after Mitch ran away and broke his parents' hearts. Susan didn't even know about Keith until this weekend and I've spent years taking care of her and the house. Susan wanted me to have the house."

Gina said nothing, but she avoided looking toward Peg.

Harrison spoke loudly. "I agree with Jake. The boy is a latecomer and I still have doubts as to his legitimacy. Even if he is legitimate, Mitch was nothing but trouble for his parents and he killed his sister—"

Peg stood so quickly the chair tipped and crashed to the floor behind her. "That's mean, Harrison. Mitch made a terrible mistake. No one suffered more than he did. He loved Ellen. That's why he ran away. He couldn't bear what he had done."

Harrison was gruff. "Mitch disappeared and never contacted Tom or Susan. He wasn't even here for his father's funeral. You do what you wish about your share, but my share is mine."

Peg spoke to Farrell, her voice shaky. "Keith should be Susan's heir. I want my portion to be used for him. If you say there will be less if I give it to him, then I'll take the money and put it in the bank and I'll spend every penny for Keith." She whirled and hurried to the hall door. She ignored her mother's call. The door slammed behind her.

Harrison picked up the folder. "It will be helpful to have a breakdown on the estate's assets as soon as possible. Perhaps next week?"

Farrell was impassive. "My intention is to provide each of you with a definitive description of the holdings when our office reopens after the holidays."

Harrison, now a man of substance, was magnanimous. "I don't want to impinge upon your holiday. However, I'm in the midst of some financial negotiations and the figures will be useful to me."

Tucker leaned forward. "The accounts are all . . ."

As Peg predicted, the vultures had gathered, eager to tear away their succulent piece of flesh.

They had no right.

Where was Susan's holographic will?

I zoomed into Wade's private office. A memo pad on his desk listed several appointments. A stack of opened mail rested in his in-box. It took only a moment to flip through letters from other law firms and from businesses. There was no stiff square envelope addressed in Susan's distinctive handwriting and with her return address. I burrowed through the wastebasket and found no trace.

I whirled to the fireplace. Flames danced and the warmth eddied out. If the will had been burned, it was lost forever in the feathery ashes. I reached out, touched the shiny, clean poker. There was no indication the poker had been used this morning.

Why would Wade Farrell care who inherited? Was there some evidence of malfeasance that could better be hidden in an estate divided among five beneficiaries? To the contrary, wouldn't it be easier to hide theft or misuse of funds in an estate left to a child with him as the lawyer in charge?

In any event, I found nothing to indicate the will had ever reached him.

In the outer office, Wade's secretary faced her computer, her fingers resting lightly on the keyboard. She was a woman who attracted notice, deep-set eyes, long nose, full lips, firm chin. There was a toughness in her expression that suggested a focus on self. I admired the dangling silver earrings that highlighted the embroidered flower pattern on her silk jacket. Especially artful were the occasional small birds in faint pastel shades palely visible among the flowers. She gazed toward the window, her oval face confident and pleased, her lips curved in a slight smile.

I scanned her desk. Her nameplate read *Kim Weaver.*

Several folders were stacked on one side. The center portion of the desk was clear. I zoomed close to the in- and out-box. A half dozen letters and several manila envelopes, ready for mailing, were in the out-box. The in-box was empty. In Farrell's office, letters and envelopes, neatly slit and ready for his attention, awaited him. Obviously the Monday mail had been received and dealt with.

I'd dropped Susan's stamped and sealed square envelope in the main post office slot late Saturday night. It should have been delivered today.

I smiled at my reflection in the plate-glass door of the post office. When I'd cheerfully written *Officer M. Loy reporting for duty* on Chief Cobb's office blackboard, I'd had no idea how quickly she would appear on the scene. The Adelaide police uniform was quite fetching, French blue cap with a black bill, long-sleeved French blue shirt, French blue trousers with a navy stripe down each leg. French blue was a very nice color for redheads. The Adelaide police patches looked fresh and new (as surely they should) on each shoulder. The metal name tag and badge over the left breast pocket read *Officer M. Loy.* The black leather shoes were shined to a glossy sheen. I shivered and immediately welcomed the warmth of a wool-lined nylon black raid jacket inscribed *Police.*

I skirted the long line of patrons, clutching boxes from tiny to immense. I walked to the door with a bell and punched it. In a moment, a plump, cheerful woman opened the door. "You got a—oh, hello, Officer. What can I do for you?"

In less than three minutes I had the name and current location of the postman who had delivered mail to Wade Farrell's office this morning.

. . . .

The slender mailman shifted the heavy leather pouch from his shoulder to the floor of the office building. He squinted in thought, faded blue eyes vaguely resentful. "You got to remember I deliver several thousand pieces of mail every day, especially"—he sighed heavily—"during Christmas. You got any idea how much mail we handle in December?"

I beamed my most admiring smile. "Mr. Crandall, I know it's a chance in a thousand, but you look like a man who notices details. In fact, I imagine you have an unerring instinct for noting anything unusual. Our hope is that you might remember a delivery you made this morning to the law office of Wade Farrell. The particular item, Mr. Crandall, was unusual in its size, a square envelope from an expensive creamy thick stock, unlike most Christmas card envelopes. Moreover, the address was written in a distinctive script." I had a clear memory of Susan Flynn's handwriting, looping capitals and leftward slanted lowercase letters. "The *W* in Wade was quite large and the rest of his name leaned to the left, the letters very thin, almost skeletal. The engraved return address was Susan Pritchard Flynn, 19 Chickasaw Ridge."

"Oh, that envelope. Sure." His recognition was obvious and immediate. "If you'd told me right off that you meant a letter from Mrs. Flynn, I could have told you. I noticed the envelope especially. Pretty handwriting she has."

Of course, he would have no way of knowing of Susan's death. The announcement would be in tomorrow's paper. "Susan passed away last night."

"I knew she was real sick, but I'm sorry to hear that. She was a mighty fine woman. I used to deliver in her neighborhood, and every Christmas she gave me a ham." He frowned darkly. "You think any of these fancy businesses I deliver to now give me anything? They don't care if I get their mail to 'em when it's a hundred and eight degrees or when the ice is so slick the sidewalk's worse than a skating rink."

"You delivered an envelope from Mrs. Flynn to Mr. Farrell this morning?"

"Yes, ma'am. Not a doubt."

"Thank you, sir. This is a huge help to our investigation. We may be back in touch to take your formal statement."

"Be glad to oblige." His eyes gleamed. "Think I might get to testify in a court case?"

"That is always a possibility. Thank you, sir, for your cooperation."

As I turned to leave, he called after me. "If you ask me questions on direct examination on the witness stand, better not ask leading questions. You can ask me to describe the materials I delivered"—he sounded suddenly prosecutorial—"to the office of Attorney Wade Farrell on this day. I'll describe that envelope and there won't be any doubt about it."

I must have looked startled.

He nodded sagely. "I never miss *Law & Order*. That Connie Rubirosa's the gal to have in a courtroom."

As he stepped into the elevator to deliver on the next floor, I disappeared.

CHAPTER 14

The sidewalks were crowded outside Wade Farrell's office building on the corner of Calhoun and Main. Not all shoppers were at the strip shopping centers anchored by Wal-Mart and Target. Downtown boasted several dress shops, a bookstore, drugstore, and hardware store. I heard the bells of a Salvation Army kettle. The sun was slipping westward, streaking the cloudy sky with rose and gold. The shadows from the buildings deepened and darkened. A skipping wind skittered late-fallen leaves.

I landed in the entry hall. Postman Crandall was emphatic that he had delivered Susan's letter this morning. Kim Weaver had already sorted and opened mail before the heirs arrived. The will should have been deposited in Wade Farrell's in-box. If he received the will, he had chosen to secrete or destroy it. What might have prompted such an action would have to be discovered later. If he had not received the will, he had in good faith presented the earlier instrument as valid.

A woman shrugging into a car coat while talking on a cell phone hurried toward the door. I waited until the hallway was empty, then reappeared in the golden mink coat.

This time I chose a cashmere sweater and wool slacks. It was time for Susan Flynn's old friend to make inquiries.

Kim Weaver looked up from her desk as I stepped inside. There was a flicker of envy in her dark eyes as they widened in appreciation of the mink. She noted as well my white sweater, blue costume pearls, and navy slacks.

"May I help you?" Her voice was almost deferential. Not quite. Implicit in her expression was the unstated suggestion that supplicants would do well to remember that the office was hers to rule.

I nodded regally. "I'm here on behalf of Susan Flynn." My manner was somber but confident. "Her death has made it imperative that I speak with Mr. Farrell about Susan's new will." I watched her face with the attention a cat accords a mouse.

For an instant, Kim's face was devoid of response. Then she raised a sculpted eyebrow. "A new will? I'm afraid there's some confusion." She was polite but firm. "Mrs. Flynn's will has been in existence for several years."

A resonant bong tolled the half hour. An elegant early twentieth-century grandfather clock with an ornate bronze face read four-thirty.

She glanced at the clock. "I'll check with Mr. Farrell, but I believe he is on his way out. Possibly I can make an appointment for you for tomorrow afternoon."

I was imperious. "Susan drafted a new will Saturday night. I must speak with him now."

She gave me a bright smile. "I'll see what I can do. You are?"

"Jerrie Emiliani." I hoped St. Jerome Emiliani, that great benefactor of orphans, didn't mind my continued use of his name. I was trying to do my best for one particular orphan.

She pushed the intercom. "Mr. Farrell, a Ms. Jerrie—" She hesitated.

"Emiliani," I said distinctly.

"—would like to speak with you about Mrs. Flynn's estate."

There was no response.

"Mr. Farrell?"

Silence.

She flicked off the intercom. "Mr. Farrell has left the office." She turned to her computer. "Tomorrow morning is blocked out for Mrs. Flynn's funeral. I can offer you an appointment at two o'clock tomorrow afternoon."

I paused to listen in the entrance hall of Wade Farrell's house. The tile floor matched the vivid blue rim of a terra-cotta vase decorated with a charging buffalo. An eight-sided Art Deco beveled-glass mirror reflected red and white pom-pom chrysanthemums in a cut-glass vase on a pine side table. To my left a living room with comfortable sofas and chairs, not too big and not too small, looked welcoming. There was an air of come-sit-down-and-let's-share-good-times warmth. To my right in the dining room, a table looked festive with holiday decorations, a snowman centerpiece and red candles, and fine china and crystal. The stairway at the end of the hall was decorated with candy canes.

A woman's voice was cheerful but firm. "You'll ruin your dinner."

Wade's words were indistinct. "I need a pick-me-up. Mmmm. Lots of butter."

I wafted to the kitchen. Spacious and homey with savory scents rising from several pans on the range, the kitchen was obviously geared for a dinner party.

A willowy brunette in a frilly gingham apron inscribed *Cindy's Kitchen* folded dough into Parker House rolls. Her fond expression slipped into a frown. "I heard Susan may have taken an overdose of something."

Wade put down a golden brown cranberry bar. His frown was dark and angry. "Who's saying that?"

Cindy looked uncertain. "You know how rumors are. Someone heard it from somebody else and pretty soon the buzz is all over town. Liz Latham said she'd heard from her hairdresser who had it straight from somebody in the mayor's office."

"That woman's a menace."

"Liz?"

"Neva Lumpkin. How'd she ever get elected? You'd think a tarantula could beat her." He broke off another piece of the cranberry bar.

"Most tarantulas don't have husbands with enough leases in the Barnett Shale to bring in forty thousand dollars a month. Who's got the money to run against her? Anyway, you didn't come home out of sorts because of Neva Lumpkin. What's wrong, Wade?" She pushed the baking sheet with the rolls to the back of the counter. At the sink, she turned on the water, began to rinse utensils.

He pulled off his suit coat, hung it from the back of a kitchen chair, loosed his tie. "You know that trip you've been wanting to make to Tahiti? I looked at my calendar. I can get away the last two weeks of February."

She turned off the water. Her eyebrows rose. "You said we couldn't afford it."

I scarcely breathed.

His lips curved in a lopsided grin. "If I look at the books like an accountant, we can't. Right now, I don't give a hoot. Book the tickets. If there's something we want to do, something that matters to us, we need to do it now. Susan Flynn thought she had one more day. I spent Saturday at the office. I missed Billy's birthday party, but I got her new will drafted. One more day, that's all Susan needed. The will would have been signed and her grandson would have inherited her estate. Instead, she died Saturday night. I can tell you for sure she never committed suicide. Die and leave that little boy penniless? Not on your life. But maybe that's what cost Susan her life."

"Could she have accidentally taken too much medicine?" Cindy placed spoons in a draining rack.

"She would have had to be drunk or blind to have dumped that much digitalis in her hot chocolate. Sam Cobb asked me what I thought. Off the record." Wade's eyes narrowed. "I told him I think one of the heirs murdered her before she could sign the new will. Not Peg Flynn. Peg Flynn's all right. I hope our kids would be as honorable. She wants the grandson to have her share. None of the others volunteered a penny. After Peg made her announcement and walked out, the rest of them hemmed and hawed and hung around, each one waiting for the others to leave. Finally, I asked if each one would like to speak with me privately. Will it surprise you"—his tone was sarcastic—"to learn each one wanted money? Jake Flynn wants to modernize the kitchen, said Susan kept putting it off, but Jake knew that fixing everything up would be exactly what Susan would have wanted. Tucker wants to buy the Nickerson spread. That will squeeze the McKinley ranch between the Nickerson ranch and Burnt Creek. Susan was good friends with the McKinleys and knew they would be worried about access roads if Tucker bought out the Nickersons. Tucker Satterlee eats, sleeps, and breathes Burnt Creek. He wants the biggest spread in the county. Gina Satterlee's maxed out on five credit cards and she lost her job about three weeks ago and one creditor got a judgment against her. Harrison Hammond looked like a man reprieved from the gallows. He's in big trouble with the housing crisis. He hasn't been able to sell most of the homes in his new development and he's up to his ears in debt to the suppliers. Now they're all on easy street. Except Peg." His tone was admiring. "If Susan had lived one more day, they would each have had to settle for two hundred thousand."

Cindy stacked the rinsed cooking ware and utensils in a plastic dish rack. "Won't the judge make some provision for Susan's grandson?"

"She didn't sign the will." Wade looked morose.

I crossed Wade Farrell off my list. His sorrowful expression told me where I needed to go.

"So"—he came around the table and drew his wife into his arms—"make those reservations. Maybe all we've got is today, but if we make it to February, you and I are going to enjoy sea, sand, and sun. Merry Christmas, Cindy."

"Oh, Wade, that will be wonderful." Her laughter was a sweet cascade. "If you look at the books again and change your mind, that's all right, too. I'm glad you want to go, whether we can or not." She smiled and lifted her lips to his.

Christmas lights blinked on a small frosted tree. The apartment was clean and tidy, but the cheap furniture looked as if it had been there for years. Travel posters on the bland beige walls of the small living room offered brightness and a sense of dreams not bound by the confines of a rented furnished apartment. The Parthenon in its weathered glory, the Cathedral at Chartres, and Castle Hill in Nice spoke of a hunger for faraway places.

Kim Weaver sat in a maple chair with dingy green cushions. Her feathered haircut had been teased into a tousled look, as if she stood on a ship deck and the wind rushed against her. Her face was interesting, high forehead, high-bridged nose, high cheekbones. Her cold brown eyes were too calculating for beauty. The firmness of her jaw suggested a woman with a strong will.

With a dreamy smile, she leafed through an issue of *Elle,* pausing to look at fashions by Balenciaga and Prada. Her purple scoop-neck cashmere tunic fell in graceful folds onto narrow black wool trousers. Twice she glanced at her jeweled watch.

She was a woman waiting for something to happen. If she had Susan's handwritten will, as I felt sure she did, she might have interesting plans for her evening. I glanced at a black leather tote on a small table by the front door. Unfortunately, her chair faced the door. I could not explore the contents of the purse as long as she remained there.

I checked out the single bedroom. Prints by Degas and Chagall and Pollock made even these dingy walls attractive. Quickly I searched the room and closet. I lifted the mattress, ran my hand beneath it. The bathroom afforded no hiding places.

Dimly I heard the ring of a cell phone.

I returned to the living room.

Kim looked at caller ID, shrugged. "Hi, Erin . . . Thanks, but I've seen it . . . Tonight? Nothing special." Her smile was secretive, amused, pleased. "Let's catch dinner tomorrow night . . . See you then."

Several times I was tempted to leave. I was always a restless spirit. Yet I felt almost certain I wasn't imagining the aura of leashed excitement that emanated from Kim. She fixed an omelet, ate slowly, still reading the fashion magazine, but the purse was in view. After washing her dishes and straightening the kitchen, she walked to her desk and settled behind the computer. She clicked from site to site for travel to the French Riviera. The purse was now to one side, but within her peripheral vision. Besides, even if I found the will, I could scarcely float the envelope through the air. Surely at some point I would have an opportunity to explore the contents of that oh-so-tempting black leather handbag.

Time passed, but Kim made no move to prepare for bed. Every so often, she looked at her watch and frowned.

Was she waiting for someone to come? Was she waiting for the right moment to call one of the heirs?

I forced myself to be patient. Patience is a virtue. Deadly boring, perhaps, but virtuous. Wiggins would be proud of me. I wished I had a pad of paper, but I would organize in my mind. As the minutes passed, I reviewed what I knew to be true:

Susan Flynn announced after dinner Saturday evening that she would make a new will.

Susan died that night from an overdose of digitalis.

Traces of digitalis were found in the pot of cocoa and in her cup.

Susan's medicines were kept on her bedside table.

Each guest was absent from the living room at some period before Susan Flynn retired.

From these facts, I could make these suppositions:

If Susan's murder was a direct result of her announcement Saturday evening, the digitalis must have been taken from her bedroom after dinner and before she said good night to her guests.

If so, someone left the living room, hurried upstairs, filched a handful of digitalis tablets, returned downstairs. Either then or on another excursion from the living room, the murderer slipped into the kitchen and dropped the tablets into the pot which would hold Susan's cocoa.

Unless the murderer had been observed entering or leaving Susan's bedroom or dropping the tablets into the pot, there could never be proof of that person's guilt. Jake's and Gina's fingerprints would be on the pot as well as Susan's.

I didn't doubt that Chief Cobb had the results of the fingerprinting of the pot and no unexpected prints had been found.

I was daunted by the enormity of the task faced by Chief Cobb. Since he'd not been privy to Wiggins's declarative announcement of Susan's murder, the chief had to deal with the possibility of suicide or accident as well. No matter how strongly he felt that Susan's death was a result of murder, he could not prove that claim.

I had to find proof for him.

Was I wasting time here in Kim Weaver's apartment? I felt certain she had opened this morning's mail, found Susan's new will, and immediately decided to suppress the will.

However, Kim was not at Pritchard House during the critical time period when the digitalis was taken. She had no access to Susan's pot of chocolate. Kim, in fact, very likely was unaware that Susan had been murdered. So far as I knew, there had been no public announcement of a murder investigation. Chief Cobb had no duty to announce an investigation, and truth to tell, he would merely bring about increased pressure from Mayor Lumpkin if he did so. Therefore, the general public was unaware that the cause of Susan's death was in question. Apparently, rumors were swirling that she'd taken too much medicine, but so far as I knew there had been no hint of murder. Her death had come as no surprise to those who knew her. She had been gravely ill for several years.

Very likely, then, Kim's theft of the will had no direct connection to Susan's murder.

However, I was almost certain that Kim took the will. The only rational reason for Kim to suppress the will was in the belief that doing so would profit her.

I felt tantalizingly close to understanding what had unfolded that morning in the law office: Kim opened the mail, saw the new will, understood at once that the current heirs would receive a nice amount of money but nothing to compare with the several millions resulting from a division of the estate. Further, as an heiress, Peg Flynn might be even more attractive to Dave Lewis, and he was present at Pritchard House Saturday night.

Obviously, it was to the advantage of those who might benefit from the old will to be certain the new will never surfaced. It could be to Kim's advantage to have that will and keep it hidden for a share in the riches. This argued that she knew someone who benefited well enough to assume that such an offer would be welcome.

In the course of her job, she had contacted the heirs to invite them to Wade Farrell's office this afternoon. In that conversation, she could have acquainted one of them with the existence of the holographic will and offered to keep it secret in exchange for . . . something. Would it have occurred to her to make the offer to Dave Lewis? Quite possibly Kim was well aware of his connection to Peg and his interest in money from Susan.

In any event, I was seeking both the murderer and the will. I might discover one or both through Kim.

She clicked off the computer, rose, and walked restlessly around the room.

I glanced at the clock. Almost ten-thirty.

Her cell phone rang. She walked swiftly to the table, picked it up, flipped it open. "Hello." She listened, wariness replaced by pleasure. Her smile of triumph was chilling. "I was beginning to wonder if you got my message . . . Of course I called from a pay phone. You'd better be at a pay phone right now . . . We can get some of those throwaway phone cards . . . I intend for us to keep in close touch." Her tone was silky. "Very close touch. Now"—her face was set and hard—"I know what you want. You know what I want. I'm not going to budge." A taunting smile flickered for an instant. "Oh, I think the idea will grow on you." Her eyes narrowed. "I want your word in writing. We can make an exchange." A frown tugged at her face. "Why so late? . . . Sure, I understand . . . The old brick plant? Isn't it all locked up? . . . Wait a minute, let me get some paper." Kim pulled a small notepad and pen from her purse.

I looked over her shoulder as she wrote: *East entrance—half mile around pit—water tower.*

She listened a moment more, drawing a series of bells and an airplane. "I'll be there at eleven sharp." She clicked off the cell. Her face drawn in thought, she rose and walked to a worn walnut desk, opened a bottom drawer. She lifted out a twenty-two pistol, held it for a moment, gave a decisive nod.

As she walked toward the small table near the door and her purse, my view of her changed. She became more formidable. Though some Adelaidians never hunt, a good many do. From the ease with which she handled the gun, I thought it likely she was from a hunting family. That a single woman familiar with guns possessed one wasn't surprising. That she felt the need to take the gun tonight to the abandoned brick plant told me she was uneasy about the person she was meeting.

I thought of the possible suspects: Jake Flynn, Gina Satterlee, Tucker Satterlee, Harrison Hammond, Charlotte Hammond, and, possibly, Dave Lewis. Kim knew one of them well enough to feel confident in suggesting a conspiracy to suppress the new will. She also knew that person well enough to feel it would be wise to be armed when meeting late at night in an isolated setting.

As she opened her purse to slip the small gun inside, I

saw the unmistakable creamy envelope that held Susan's will.

The night shift was at work in the police department. I passed the dispatcher's office, heard laconic exchanges with patrol cars. In Chief Cobb's office on the second floor, the table was covered with open folders and stacks of paper. He absently munched on M&M's and made occasional notations on a legal pad, his heavy face molded into a frown of dissatisfaction.

The clock read thirty-six minutes after ten. I had to make up my mind quickly. Kim would likely leave her apartment in about fifteen minutes. It was approximately a five-minute drive to the abandoned brick plant on the southeast side of Adelaide near the railroad tracks. For more than a half century, red and white clay had been mined from open pits and made into bricks there, but the plant closed down not long before Bobby Mac and I set out on our last voyage on the *Serendipity.* The complex at one time included the plant, ten downdraft kilns, several smokestacks, two open pits, a boiler plant, a water tower, a filter house and pump house plant, a spur rail line, and more. I'd created many leaflets for the mayor's office celebrating highlights of Adelaide, including the brick plant, the annual August rodeo, the cement plant, and Goddard College.

I wanted to accompany Kim as she drove to the brick plant. I had no intention of permitting her to give Susan's will to anyone other than Wade Farrell. Somehow I'd intercept that exchange. But I couldn't gamble with Kim's life. If the person she had contacted turned out to be Susan's murderer, Kim could be in grave danger when she reached the water tower even though she was armed. The abandoned brick plant was a sensible place for two persons to meet who wished to do so without observation, but the remote area was also shadowy and private. Violence could flare in an instant.

The clock hand ticked as it moved. I had one minute less to decide.

There was no time for subtlety. Officer M. Loy couldn't handle this assignment on her own. Yet the Precept was unequivocal: Work behind the scenes without making your presence known. I hoped Wiggins would understand.

I picked up a piece of chalk, began to write.

Chief Cobb's hand with another half dozen M&M's stopped halfway to his mouth. His eyes, wide and shocked, watched as the words took shape:

S. Flynn wrote new will Sat night. Stolen from A.M. mail by W. Farrell's sec.

Weaver taking will to brick plant now.

I underlined *now.*

Set up immed. surveillance there. W. to enter E. gate 11 P.M., meet unknown person at water tower.

I hesitated, then added:

Trust me. Officer M. Loy

I added a quick P.S.

Leon Butler witnessed will.

Chief Cobb took a deep breath. Lines grooved on either side of his broad mouth.

He had the air of a man in a cemetery alone on a dark night who hears stealthy footsteps and rustling in the bushes and the unsettling hoo of an owl.

I understood his mental vertigo as he teetered on the edge of the unknown. I gripped the chalk:

I'll be with her. Officer Loy

Eyes fixed on the blackboard, he absently tossed the M&M's in his mouth.

I grabbed the eraser and in three sweeping movements swiped away the message, all of it, leaving only the white smudges to indicate the board had been used. I placed the eraser and chalk in the tray.

Chief Cobb pushed up from the table, rushed to his desk, punched the intercom. "Get Price . . ."

I reached Kim's apartment as she shrugged into a brown corduroy car coat and picked up her purse. She whistled cheerfully as she shut the apartment door. She hurried downstairs and out to her car.

I rode in the passenger seat. We left behind the lights of town and followed a rutted dirt road empty of cars. I bent forward, touched Kim's purse, dropped carelessly on the car floor. To be so near yet so far was frustrating. However, if all went well, the will should be in Chief Cobb's possession soon. I hoped that in the meager time at his disposal, Chief Cobb had successfully deployed his officers. I hoped they were well hidden, watching the east entrance and the water tower.

Kim's Chrysler PT Cruiser hummed as she pressed on the accelerator. The road curved and twisted as we approached the dark plant. I held to the hand grip above the door. Kim braced with an elbow. Her seat belt dangled unused. Was she simply careless or did she resent any constraint imposed by authority? She slowed as she neared the east entrance. A ramshackle gate was pulled wide.

I wondered who had opened the gate and how. As we passed into the grounds, I glimpsed a broken chain dangling from a bar.

All was dark and silent. On one side of the pockmarked road, boarded-up buildings were scarcely visible in the pale moonlight. On the other side, moonlight disappeared into the blackness of an open pit bordered by a ramshackle wire fence. Some posts sagged, pulling the wire over the lip of the excavation. An occasional red warning light gleamed on rickety wooden poles near the pit. I supposed some local ordinance required illumination of a hazard.

The Cruiser's headlights flashed over warning signs:

DANGER

OPEN PIT

NO TRESPASSING

The Cruiser neared one of the brief swaths of reddish light from a warning lamp. I felt more and more uneasy. I hoped that if the need arose, that I could move to protect her if danger threatened. Reddish light fell across the car.

A gunshot and jolt came at almost the same instant.

Despite the closed windows, the crack of a high-powered rifle was sharp and unmistakable. The Cruiser slewed to the left. Kim fought the wheel, jamming on the brakes. In the horrifying slow motion of impending disaster, it seemed forever as the car careened toward the pit, unstoppable, out of control, doomed.

The car crashed through the fence and Kim screamed. She slammed hard against the windshield. Her terrified cry ended abruptly. I reached out, tried to catch Kim's arm. The car went end over end. I whipped through the windshield and out into space.

CHAPTER 15

Flashlights beamed from every direction. Headlights cut twin swaths through darkness, illuminating running figures. Men called out as they ran, reaching the edge of the pit as a thunderous crack sounded, the impact of the car on the water.

Dazed, I hung above the pit.

Maglites swept the roiled surface, catching in their crossing beams a wavering silver plume that rose and fell. Shouts rose: "Divers, get some divers." "We need more light." "Where did that shot come from?" "Block the road." "Form search units."

Chief Cobb stood at the edge of the pit with a megaphone, directing the efforts to reach Kim's car. "How deep is the water?"

Detective Sergeant Price shrugged. "Maybe ninety feet, maybe more." He pointed a Maglite down. Ripples eddied on the dark surface. "By the time we get divers here, it will be too late to save anyone."

I'd hoped to protect Kim, envisioning a moment when I might push a hand holding a gun to one side, knowing the police would be in place and ready to pounce and make her safe. Instead, a hidden marksman shot her tire, spinning the Cruiser out of control and down to death.

I hung above the black water and called out forever too late. "I'm sorry. Kim, I'm sorry."

"Bailey Ruth." Wiggins's voice was kind and gentle. "You cannot blame yourself."

I didn't pause to wonder why he was back from Tumbulgum. I was only grateful for support when I felt such a crushing sense of failure. "I was afraid she might be meeting Susan's killer. I should have appeared and warned her."

"My dear"—his tone was emphatic—"you did everything you could to assure her safety, and I applaud your ingenuity. Forces to protect her were at hand. You could not foresee what occurred. However"—there was noticeably less warmth—"I expect you to make a strong"—he repeated the adjective with even more emphasis—"*strong* effort to remove all thoughts of *ghostly*"—the word was uttered with distaste—"intervention from Chief Cobb's mind."

As spotlights pointed down, the last ripples subsided on the surface of the black water.

"I had to intervene the best and fastest way I could." My tone was hot. "If it seemed otherworldly, well, after all, it was, and so be it." Wiggins had a talent for yanking my string. "If the police hadn't been here, thanks to me, no one would ever know what happened to Kim. She would have disappeared. Now the police know she was murdered. That proves Susan was murdered." I smacked one fist into a palm. "None of this would be known if I hadn't grabbed Chief Cobb's attention. I didn't have time to approach him any other way."

Wiggins's "Hmm" was judicious, but there might have been a hint of amusement. "Much as I admire your spirit, dear Bailey Ruth, you do not excel at logic. In fact, your conclusions rather remind me of your grasp of Zen. Imprecise. You cannot reasonably conclude that Kim was murdered by the person who murdered Susan. Kim may have been killed because an heir had no intention of being blackmailed and every intention of preventing the emergence of the new will. Her death may be quite separate from Susan's."

"The idea of two murderers is silly." How could Wiggins be so muddled? "I may not be good at logic, but I have common sense. Of course Susan's murderer killed Kim."

"I'm sure"—his voice was a bit fainter—"you will solve everything, whether there is one murderer or two. I will admit that you did a clever piece of work in arranging for the police to be here, even though your method left much to be desired. Not only did their presence make it clear that Kim was murdered"—I could scarcely hear him—"you should consider another result of their positioning tonight: the shocking effect of police intervention immediately after the shot on a murderer who assumed there was no one else within miles. Tallyho, Bailey Ruth."

More sirens sounded. The road near the broken fence where Kim's car crashed over was clogged with police cars. The sounds of a search reverberated. Flashlights swept across the plant buildings.

I lifted a hand, unseen, in farewell to Wiggins. He had come to comfort me, rebuke me, pull me from sadness to combativeness, and to point the way ahead. I mulled the meaning of his farewell.

I imagined myself cloaked in darkness, holding a rifle, watching the Cruiser swing around the curve in the road beside the pit. I would have felt, as Kim's murderer must have felt, utterly secure, the abandoned brick plant deserted, no one to see, no one to hear. The car for an instant was revealed in the red flare of a warning light. I squeezed the trigger. The tire exploded. The car jerked out of control, swung toward the pit, plummeted down, all according to plan.

Then the plan went awry. Lights flashed and shouts erupted as police raced toward the pit. There was no moment to savor success. Instead, the unimaginable, the unexpected, the unforeseen had occurred, police officers shouting, searching, seeking. The murderer most certainly was deeply shocked.

Could I take advantage of that shock?

It was hard to estimate how much time had passed since Kim's car tumbled into the pit. Fifteen minutes, perhaps? If the marksman was in a car, that was time enough in a town as small as Adelaide to leave the abandoned plant far behind.

I didn't hesitate. I intended to observe Susan's heirs as quickly as possible.

The front porch light was on at Harrison and Charlotte Hammond's house. Inside, I found the lower floor dark. Light glowed from the top of the stairs. In the master bedroom, Charlotte sat propped in bed with two pillows, reading a novel. Harrison's side of the bed was untouched. I went to Harrison Hammond's construction company. Large outdoor lighting illuminated a parking area. The supply warehouse was dark, as was the small single-story frame office. Where was Harrison Hammond?

Next I arrived at Pritchard House. A dim light glowed near a side door of the garage. Inside, I turned on the overhead light and moved from car to car, seeking telltale heat. None of the hoods was warm, but the garage was quite cold. It wouldn't take long for any heat to dissipate. As I returned to the light switch, I saw two bicycles. I was thoughtful as I stepped toward them. I moved one, swung onto the seat. The tires were firm. I squinted to remember. Though the road was hilly and winding, the brick plant was no more than a mile away.

I doubted the police had discovered how the marksman had traveled to or from the abandoned brick plant. The sounds of a departing car would easily have been lost as the police spread out to search and turned on their headlights to afford more light. But the murderer could have ridden a bicycle or approached on foot.

In the kitchen of Pritchard House, Jake Flynn closed the refrigerator door, carried the remnants of a baked ham to the counter. Her face drawn and pasty, she put together a sandwich with ham, lettuce, Swiss cheese, and mustard. She opened a Coke and sat at the white wooden table. She ate as if starved. Was food her succor when stressed? It was nearing midnight. She wore a black velour pullover and trousers and boots, a good costume to move unseen in the dark.

In Peg and Keith's room, Peg was propped up in bed with two pillows behind her, staring emptily toward the wall. She looked forlorn and depressed. I knelt for an instant by Keith's bed, lightly touched his shoulder. He was curled against Big Bob, sunk in a deep sleep.

In Peg's bedroom now turned over to Gina, the room was dark and very cold. Gina sat in a chair near the open window, smoking. In the wash of moonlight, her face was pale, her expression strained and fearful. She stared out into the night. Abruptly, she jammed the cigarette stub into an ashtray. "I'm scared. God, I'm scared . . ." Her voice was desolate, defeated, despairing.

I had no luck at the home of Dave Lewis's brother. The guest bedroom was dark and untenanted.

A Tiffany lamp on a side table glowed in the living room of the ranch house on Burnt Creek. I moved from room to room. A black Lab trotted toward me, his claws clicking on the wooden floor. I held out a hand and he sniffed. From the front hall to the back porch, there was no one in the house but me and the Lab. I dropped on one knee, gently massaged the Lab's throat. "Where is he, boy?" The Lab pushed against me. Then he lifted his head, turned, and thudded toward the front door.

I sped outside.

A horse and rider trotted down a dirt road, clearly visible in the moonlight. The rider dismounted, opened a gate, drew the horse through, closed the gate. Once again astride the horse, the rider lifted the reins and the horse headed for the barn. As the door was pulled wide and a light flicked on, Tucker Satterlee moved with easy grace, leading the horse inside.

I watched as he loosened the saddle. As I remembered my geography, Burnt Creek was a couple of miles from the brick plant. There were country roads Tucker would know well. At an easy pace, the ride could be made in a half hour. The east gate was no barrier to a man accustomed to using wire cutters.

The murderer had likely pulled the gate wide and either driven, walked, biked, or, in Tucker's case, ridden a horse to a hill overlooking the pit and waited in the shadow of the trees for Kim to arrive. As the PT Cruiser came through the gate, the rifle was lifted. When the car passed through the security light, the rifle fired. One shot and the car careened out of control.

The eruption of light, the shouts of the police, the headlights of the police cars must have shocked the murderer into immobility. But not for long. Unseen and unheard, the murderer slipped away, either to a car or bicycle hidden in shadows beyond the gate, or, if Tucker, to a tethered horse.

Inside the barn, Tucker's sheepskin jacket hung from a

hook near the door. Tucker carried the saddle and blanket to the tack room. I didn't see a rifle or a scabbard for a rifle. He returned with a bucket of water for the horse.

I felt a twinge of uncertainty. Where were the wire cutters? Where was the rifle? Where was the rifle scabbard?

The hook where his coat hung was behind him. Quickly, I checked the pockets, both exterior and interior. A ball of twine. Two oblongs of bubble gum. A crumpled map. A half-eaten energy bar.

No wire cutter.

The horse drank, then lifted her head. He gave her a pat. "Good girl," and began to walk her up and down.

I shook my head in self-irritation. The man might be a killer, but he was no fool. When pandemonium erupted as the Cruiser tumbled into the pit, the murderer knew immediately that Kim's death would clearly be recognized as murder. There were ponds, a small lake, and brush-thick gullies between the brick plant and Burnt Creek, and, of course, between the brick plant and Pritchard House or Harrison Hammond's office or home.

If Tucker Satterlee rode out tonight equipped to commit murder, he was smart enough on his return to jettison anything that could be linked to the crime. As a rancher, he would have several rifles. If he had carried a rifle tonight, I felt certain it could not be traced to him. As for wire cutters and a rifle scabbard, he likely had several of both. The lack of a firearm was no proof of his innocence.

Still, he had been out on a horse on a cold winter night. What innocent reason could there be?

If I tried to alert Chief Cobb, it would take a good while before anyone would be dispatched to question Tucker. If Tucker was the murderer, the longer time he had to relax and formulate an alibi, the less likely he was to reveal guilt when questioned.

Now was the time to ask.

Outside the stable, I swirled into being, strode quickly across the uneven ground, rapped smartly on the open barn door. "Police."

"Coming." He reached the barn entrance. His angular, attractive face held no hint of uneasiness. "Officer." He sounded puzzled. "Is there a problem?" He looked past me. No police cruiser was parked behind me. "Car trouble?"

My hope of intimidating Tucker Satterlee plummeted, like a lead sinker in a pond. I ignored his question. "Mr. Satterlee, where were you at eleven o'clock tonight?"

He looked surprised. "Eleven? Hey, that's about the time I heard a lot of noise, sirens and stuff. I wondered what was going on. Are you looking for a fugitive?" There was nothing but curious inquiry in his face and voice.

I was polite but brisk. "You are a person of interest in a murder that was committed at approximately eleven P.M."

He stiffened, his face hard, his good humor gone. "Somebody's mixed up, got some other guy in mind. Not me. Around eleven o'clock I was making sure a heifer's first delivery went okay. That's how I happened to be outside and hear the noise. If you want to ride over to the pasture with me, I'll introduce you to the calf, a pretty little black baldy heifer."

I knew the kind of calf well, all-black with a white face, a cross between a black Angus cow and a Hereford bull.

"Now, unless you need my help"—he was curt—"I need to cool down Big Sal, brush off the salt, and put her in the corral." He started to turn away, then stopped, waved his hand. "You folks can make free on Burnt Creek if it helps you in your search. And I'll let you know if I run across anything funny."

Tucker Satterlee had an answer for everything. I didn't doubt the newborn calf existed and her Angus mother. No one could prove the birth had occurred earlier than eleven o'clock. Nor could I prove his presence or, as a matter of fact, the presence of any of the heirs at the brick plant.

Chief Cobb was haggard in the slant of sunlight through his office windows. His hair was scarcely combed. He'd shaved but missed several patches. Bloodshot irises and dark pouches beneath his eyes spoke of little sleep. I empathized. I'd managed a few hours on the chaise longue in Peg and Keith's room, and I'd stoked my inner spirit with a huge country breakfast of bacon, fried eggs, grits, biscuits and cream gravy at a truck stop on the outskirts of Adelaide where a traveling redhead in a sweatshirt and jeans provoked no interest, but I too felt exhausted and weary.

Frowning, arms folded, he stared at the top of the table, which was covered by taped-down black plastic garbage bags. Displayed were Kim's open purse, the leather streaked and misshapen from immersion, and the purse's contents: twenty-two pistol, comb, lipstick, compact, Tide washout stick, nail file, cell phone, disintegrating photo folder with limp prints separated and spread out, billfold open and emptied.

Where was the will? Even though I held out little hope that the ink writing would be legible, a sodden square envelope was not among the items on the table.

Chief Cobb swung around as his door opened. His demeanor was grim and intent.

Fatigue didn't weigh as heavily on Detective Sergeant Price. He looked vigorous, his step buoyant. He was as attractive as always, white-blond hair, grayish-blue eyes, interesting and compelling face with a bold nose and chin. A folder tucked under one arm, he strode to the table with his usual energy, a man always in a hurry. "We went through Weaver's apartment like locusts. Not a trace, Sam."

The chief grimaced. He gestured wearily at the table. "The will was supposed to be in her purse."

Price slapped his folder on the table and looked quizzical. "Your source good?"

Chief Cobb glanced at the still-smudged blackboard. "Horse's mouth. I would have bet the house on it."

I wasn't sure the attribution appealed to me, but I appreciated his confidence.

Price turned his large hands palms up. "You lost."

"The same source tipped me to the brick plant." Again he gave a furtive glance at the blackboard.

Price's sandy eyebrows rose. "The source had that one right. In fact"—he pointed at a green folder—"I got confirmation from the lab. A rifle slug was in the front right tire. Too smashed to be identified. We know what happened because we were there, but if we hadn't known to look for a slug, nobody ever would have. Besides, the car would probably never have been found and she would have been tagged a missing person."

He rested one hip against the table, glanced over the exhibits. "Now we got the car, we got a body, we got proof of murder. As for the will, maybe it fell out of the purse and was thrown clear when the car went over."

Cobb was brusque. "Purse was zipped when they pulled the car out."

Price's blue eyes were sardonic. "Maybe the horse's mouth on the will was like most race tips: wishful thinking. Maybe there never was a new will."

Chief Cobb settled his shoulders like an obdurate bulldog refusing to budge from the food bowl. "There's a will. I talked to the man who signed it as a witness Saturday night. Susan Flynn brought the will to his house and signed it. She had him read it, and the terms correspond to what she'd told

Wade Farrell to draw up. Farrell's really upset by the idea that Kim Weaver intercepted the will. He said we can look anyplace we want to in his office, including Kim Weaver's desk. I don't expect to find anything. Obviously, if she kept quiet about the will, she didn't make a nice little notation recording its arrival.

"Anyway, there is—or was—a will. That's why Kim Weaver died. We may never find the will. A lot of things are possible. Maybe Weaver took the will out of her purse, laid it on the car seat. When they brought the car up, it was full of water. One of the windows broke on impact. The will could have washed right out of the car and turned into mush. Maybe she stopped on her way to the brick plant and left it somewhere and very likely we'll never find it. Right now, the will doesn't matter. We have the testimony of the witness that it existed. That's all we need to provide a motive for her murder. The existence of the previous will gives us the identities of the people who were better off, big bucks better off, if the new will wasn't produced."

The chief wriggled his shoulders as if trying to ease strained muscles. "Here's how I see it. One of Susan Flynn's original heirs or Peg Flynn's boyfriend overdosed her on digitalis Saturday night to make sure she wouldn't sign a new will Monday morning, leaving everything to her grandson. Oddly enough"—there was a strange expression on his face—"and maybe the work of providence, if your mind runs to that kind of stuff, Susan Flynn wrote the new will Saturday night, took her sister-in-law's car, and went out to get the will signed. I talked to the witness first thing this morning. I'm going to keep him under wraps. It isn't healthy to be connected to that will."

Price walked to a side table with a coffeepot, poured a mug. He held up the pot. "You want some?"

"Yeah." Cobb blinked as if trying to stay alert.

Price poured a second steaming mug, carried them across the room, handed one to the chief. "Kind of funny that Susan Flynn writes out a will when she knows her lawyer will have one ready with all the fancy language Monday morning."

Chief Cobb avoided Price's gaze. "Maybe she had a premonition. Women are funny that way. All we know for sure is that she went out that night."

"With a redheaded friend." Price's voice was carefully expressionless. He hooked his thumbs in the pockets of his gray wool slacks. "It would be helpful if we could find the friend."

Cobb paced back and forth. He didn't look toward Price when he muttered, "The witness was kind of confused about the friend's name, thought it was something like Floy."

Price tensed. "Floy? Could it have been Loy?" There was a note of excitement in Price's voice. "Last time"—he didn't elaborate on when that had occurred—"her nameplate read *M. Loy.*"

Cobb was equally expressionless. "No point in guessing about things we don't know. Let's leave it that Mrs. Flynn's friend was a redhead." Cobb glanced at the blackboard. "I've got a feeling she may get in touch. Until then, we've got other fish to fry. Susan Flynn's funeral is at ten. We'll allow time for the service and the reception. They'll all be at the house. We'll call around four o'clock, ask everybody who was at Pritchard House Saturday night to come to the station, make it clear they'll be picked up for questioning if anybody declines. If somebody wants to bring a lawyer with them, that's fine. Plus we'll have a nice invitation for Peg Flynn's boyfriend. Dave Lewis was trying to borrow from Susan to finance a vet clinic and she was having second thoughts. Lewis was there Saturday night and knew Susan intended to change her will. Maybe he decided it would be easier to marry an heiress than ask for a loan. We need to find out if he knew Kim Weaver."

Cobb moved heavily to the blackboard, weariness evident in his slumped shoulders and slow steps. He picked up a piece of chalk, gave it a bemused glance, then printed in large block letters:

Jacqueline Flynn
Peg Flynn (Dave Lewis)
Tucker Satterlee
Gina Satterlee
Harrison Hammond
Charlotte Hammond—not a direct heir, profits through husband

Cobb's face corrugated in thought. Then, with deliberation, the chalk harsh against the board, he added Kim Weaver's name to the center right of Susan's previous heirs. "There's a line from Weaver to one of them. Last night she followed it right over the edge of the clay pit. It's up to us to make the connection." He slapped the chalk into the tray. "Get Johnny Cain up here."

As soon as the door closed behind Detective Sergeant Price, I picked up a piece of chalk, stepped to one side of the chief's list of heirs. I hoped Wiggins was fully engaged in Tumbulgum.

Chief Cobb still stood within a foot of the blackboard. The movement of the chalk caught his eye. He blinked, hunched his shoulders, watched.

I couldn't convey all that I knew in the little time that I expected to have. Ever since my arrival at the chief's office, there had been a constant stream of officers in and out. Detective Sergeant Price would likely return with Officer Cain in a very few minutes. I cut to the chase.

11:30 P.M. last night:

Harrison Hammond not at home or office. Charlotte home.

Jake Flynn downstairs, dressed, appeared upset.

Peg Flynn and Gina Satterlee in bedrooms, appeared stressed.

Car hoods not warm but bikes available in Pritchard garage.

Couldn't find Dave Lewis.

Tucker Satterlee out on a horse at 11 P.M. Claims heifer in labor.

Look on hillside for shell, hoof marks, bike tread.

The door hinge squeaked. Swiftly, I wiped the eraser over what I had written. The eraser and chalk were in the tray by the time Price and Johnny Cain entered the room.

Chief Cobb stared at the smudged blackboard, frozen in shock.

Price stopped so quickly Johnny bumped into him. "Hey, Sam, you okay?"

Cobb took a step toward the door, then wavered unsteadily.

Instinctively, I grabbed his arm to provide support, though I certainly wasn't strong enough to keep him from toppling.

He jerked his arm free and reeled against the blackboard.

Price thudded across the room, reaching for the chief's elbow. "Hey, Sam, maybe you need to take a rest. Guess you didn't get much sleep last night. Why don't you take a seat?"

Cobb pushed away from the board, shook off Price's grip. "I'm okay." He slid a quick look toward the blackboard, shook his head. "No big deal. I'm short on sleep and maybe I need some breakfast."

Price jerked his head at Johnny. "Order a couple of Lulu's Early Bird Specials." His grin was quick. "For me and the chief. We've got a job for you."

Johnny stepped a few feet away, pulled out a cell phone, punched a number. "Police chief's office. Send two Lulu's Early Birds." The call ended, he looked from Price to the chief.

Cobb's color was better. "Thanks, Johnny. I'll sketch out what I want you to do in a minute." He turned toward Price. "Got a tip while you were gone. Tucker Satterlee was out on a horse—"

Price interrupted. "How'd you know? Haskins just called in. About eight-thirty this morning, he saw a horseman on a hill overlooking the pit, challenged him. Satterlee told Haskins he heard on the eight o'clock news about a car going into the pit and he rode over to take a look since the property belonged to the Flynn estate. Satterlee thought somebody from the family should check out what was happening."

A brooding expression on his heavy face, Chief Cobb folded his arms. "So we're too late."

Price looked puzzled. "Haskins told him the area was closed until further notice. Satterlee didn't get near the pit, though that wouldn't have done any harm."

"Satterlee was also out on a horse last night." Cobb's voice was grim. "Around eleven o'clock. Maybe he was out to a pasture to see about birthing a calf. Maybe he was on that hill overlooking the pit. Now we'll never be able to prove anything. All we know for sure is that if hoof marks were left last night, they can never be distinguished from the ones his horse left this morning." He stalked to his desk, picked up the phone. "Benson, get with Haskins out at the brick plant. Rope off the area where he saw a horseman this morning. Search the area for a rifle shell. Or for footprints or bike-tread prints. Search like you're hunting for a silver grain of sand." He clicked off the phone, slammed into the swivel chair behind his desk, slammed a fist on the desktop. "I don't like to be screwed over. But Satterlee's too clever by half. He drew a fat red arrow pointing to the place the shooter stood."

Price dropped into a chair in front of Cobb's desk, waved Johnny to the next seat. "Why would Satterlee take that chance? Maybe he really was out with a calf last night. Maybe he heard the news, wanted to flex a little muscle as a newly rich man."

"And St. Nick's going to bring me a winning lottery ticket." Cobb's tone was sour. "I'll lay odds that shell casing is there. If anything's found, you take me out for a steak dinner."

Price's smile was easy. "If they don't find it—and they might miss a single casing—nothing's proved. Anyway, a casing is meaningless without a rifle. Say that Satterlee or one of the others was out last night with a rifle. How many places could they have disposed of a rifle after they left the brick plant?"

"I'm not counting on linking a casing to him or to anybody. What I want is proof that he took his horse this morning to the place where the shot was fired. When I've got that, I'll know he's either the killer or he knows something we need to know." Cobb's eyes glinted. "One way or another, I'm going to find out which of them killed Kim Weaver." Cobb jerked his head at Johnny. "That's where you come in."

"Yes, sir." Johnny's handsome face also showed little effect of last night's late hours. His thick black hair, combed hard to corral the natural curl, emphasized the sea blue of his eyes. His uniform was immaculate. He looked eager, excited, and proud to be chosen by the chief for special duty.

The chief's expression was thoughtful, his face somber. "We have reason to believe Kim Weaver's murder is connected to the murder of Susan Flynn. We have a tip that Susan Flynn signed a new will and Kim Weaver intercepted it in the mail yesterday morning."

"A new will?" Johnny's face furrowed.

"A will that leaves everything to Susan Flynn's grandson. That will has disappeared." Cobb leaned forward and stared at Johnny with gimlet eyes. "Kim Weaver called each of Susan Flynn's heirs to tell them about the meeting at Farrell's office at two o'clock. I'm guessing she told one of them about the new will and together they agreed that she'd keep it quiet. For a price. Or maybe she called Peg Flynn's boyfriend Dave Lewis. Whoever she called, we know she had an appointment with someone at the old brick plant at eleven o'clock and she was to bring the will. You can help us find out which of Susan Flynn's heirs"—he ticked them off one by one—"Jacqueline Flynn, Peg Flynn, Tucker Satterlee, Gina Satterlee, and Harrison Hammond, knew Kim Weaver well enough to conspire to prevent that will from reaching Susan Flynn's lawyer. Or maybe the contact was with Dave Lewis. Peg Flynn should know whether Lewis knew Weaver."

Johnny stiffened. "What do you want me to do?"

"Talk to Peg Flynn. Find out from her how well all of them knew Kim Weaver."

Johnny looked uncomfortable. "I'm a police officer. I'll interview her as a witness."

Chief Cobb's expression didn't change. "You do that."

Johnny's face furrowed in unhappiness. "Is there anything else?"

Cobb waved a hand in dismissal.

As Johnny opened the door, Cobb spoke, his voice gruff. "Somebody's dangerous."

Johnny stood in the doorway, his shoulders tight, listening.

"I'll be straight with you, Officer. I don't think Peg Flynn's dangerous. You have a chance to take a bead on a copperhead behind the log. Copperheads don't give any warning. Peg Flynn might be the one that steps on it."

Johnny looked back, his eyes anguished. "I'll do what I can."

When the door closed, Price shrugged. "He'll do what he can. Which won't be much. You struck out, Sam. You got to remember, a good-looking woman twists a man's guts, makes him forget he's a cop." He spoke with the wry authority of a man who'd been down that road. "You heard him. He's going to tell her he's asking as a cop. That will shut her up. But we can keep looking. I've got Kim Weaver's address book. I'll talk to Weaver's friends and try to pick up a link between Weaver and one or more of the heirs or with the boyfriend."

Cobb thumped the fingers of one hand in a rapid tattoo near his phone. "We know more than these people realize. Maybe I can do a little poking. I want to catch Peg Flynn before Johnny Cain gets to her." He glanced at phone numbers next to a list of names. His eyes gleamed. "I like cell phones. Puts most folks on a short leash." He turned on the speakerphone and punched numbers.

"Hello." Peg sounded weary.

"This is Chief Cobb. If you have a minute, Miss Flynn, I have a few questions." Cobb pulled a tablet close, picked up a pen. "When did you tell Dave Lewis that Susan Flynn was unlikely to provide a loan for his new clinic?"

She drew in a sharp breath, said hurriedly, "That isn't accurate. Susan had asked for a business plan. She hadn't turned Dave down."

"When did you tell him?" Cobb was patient but inexorable.

"Saturday afternoon." Her voice was faint.

"After dinner, Lewis learned you weren't going to inherit. That night someone made sure Susan Flynn didn't sign her new will."

"Chief, that's terrible. Dave wouldn't hurt Susan. Besides"—there was a rush of relief in her voice—"he and I went for a drive after Susan went upstairs and Dave insisted I talk to her, smooth everything over, get her to agree to the loan. Don't you see? He wouldn't urge me to talk to her if she wasn't going to be all right."

Cobb looked at Price, whose expression was sardonic.

"I see. But now he won't have to worry about money, will he? Since you are going to inherit."

Price mouthed, "New will?"

The chief waved a hand in dismissal.

Peg was slow in answering. "Actually"—her tone was stiff—"Dave knows I don't intend to use any of that money for myself. I tried to give it to Keith, but Wade Farrell said I'd have to pay too much in taxes, so I'm going to set it up where every penny of my inheritance is used for Keith. I told Dave that yesterday."

"How did he respond?"

After an appreciable pause, she said reluctantly, "He doesn't approve."

"I see. Thanks very much, Miss Flynn." He clicked off the phone.

Price gave a bark of dark laughter. "If Lewis is your man, he has to be pretty frosted to know he committed a murder and the money still won't get to him."

"Maybe. Maybe not. Women change their minds. For now she looks innocent as a daisy. I'd take everything"—he spoke with emphasis—"that she says with a bucketload of salt. I'm not as impressed with her generosity as the lawyer. For sure, if she spiked the cocoa, she'd now pretend no interest in the money. So far, she hasn't signed anything. It's all words."

I heard the chief's dark analysis with a chill. I thought I'd judged Peg well. She was sweet and kind to Keith. Her response Monday afternoon when she tried to renounce her share had seemed utterly sincere.

A dark little voice whispered to me: *Someone committed murder and none of them seemed likely, not house-proud Jake, debt-laden Gina, dedicated rancher Tucker, jovial but desperate Harrison, devoted Charlotte, self-centered Dave.*

"Same thing with the boyfriend." The chief's eyes were cold. "If he doctored the cocoa, of course he'd urge Peg to talk again to Susan. Now that the old will is still in place, you can bet he'll try to persuade Peg to keep the money, which may have been her intent all along."

Price grinned. "You suspicious old man, you. In any event, Cain may get an earful from her now." Price stood with a bounce. He walked to the door, then looked back. "Hey, Sam, these tips you're getting?"

The chief leaned back in his chair, his expression abruptly remote. "Yeah?"

"Could the horse's mouth be a sorrel filly?" Price's tone was light, but his eyes were hopeful.

Chief Cobb said carefully, "I haven't seen anyone."

Price hesitated. "If you do, maybe she'll come by, say hello."

I appreciated his admiration, but his hopes were doomed to disappointment.

The door closed.

"A sorrel filly? Redder hair than that. Unless I'm totally nuts." Cobb rubbed tired eyes. "Maybe I am nuts." He reached out for his phone. His hand fell. Finally, his face folded in a tight frown and he yanked up the receiver, punched a number. "Sam Cobb. Is Doc free? . . . I'll hold." He punched the speakerphone, turned his chair to look, eyes questioning, toward the blackboard.

"Speaking." The contralto voice was brisk and firm, but genial.

"Hey, Janie. If you've got a minute, can I run something by you?"

"Sure. What's up?"

Cobb's face turned a dull reddish color. "I wanted to talk to you about one of my officers. Good guy, but I think maybe he's under a strain. Now, this is between us, but he gets these messages. It's the blackboard." Cobb ran a finger around his collar as if it were too tight. "He sees the chalk in the air and nobody's holding it, but there are words being written and in a minute there's a message and it has to do with a tough case."

"Does he hear voices?"

"Oh no. Nothing like that." He stared at the smudged blackboard. "At least, he hasn't heard voices yet. The message was on the blackboard and signed by an officer who had a previous connection to the department."

I smiled, pleased for Officer M. Loy to have even that grudging recognition.

"Would he have some special reason to remember this officer?"

"Oh yes." The chief's response was fervent. "Is it possible he's getting some tips, say over the phone, and he writes them on the blackboard and doesn't remember doing it?"

"That would be one explanation. Under great stress, the mind can deliberately shut off particular memories. The signature of the former officer could reflect appreciation for previous assistance. However, the solution may be simpler. Perhaps someone in the department wants him to have the information but doesn't want to be identified as the source. Is the officer performing rationally otherwise?"

Cobb rubbed the back of his neck. "So far as I know."

"I'd keep a close eye on the situation. I'll be glad to talk to him if you think that would help. Got to go, Sam." The line clicked off.

As the chief reached for files, a frown lingering, I vowed to avoid blackboard duty in the future. I didn't want to cause the chief further stress of mind. As his doctor said, the mind was capable of adjusting reality until it was acceptable. I'd count on time to assuage Sam Cobb's concern.

As for time, Officer Johnny Cain should arrive at Pritchard House any minute.

CHAPTER 16

The police car sat in front of Pritchard House. Johnny Cain stood next to Peg's Honda at the foot of the drive. He bent down as she opened the window. The breeze stirred his dark hair. "Hi, Peg." His face held a mixture of eagerness and apprehension.

"Johnny." Peg's wan and tired face brightened. Despite artfully applied makeup, reddened patches revealed a tearful night. She was dressed for the funeral in a black wool suit. A charcoal wool jacket was neatly folded in the front passenger seat. "I'm taking Keith to the park for a little while. I had to get out of the house. There are flowers everywhere. They're beautiful, but I feel like I'm choking."

In the backseat, Keith clicked a red toy car on the armrest of the car seat. "Va-room. Va-room." His blond hair was perfectly combed. He looked bright and fresh and happy.

I was standing a little to one side of Johnny. I blew Keith a kiss.

He looked toward me and gave a quick gurgle of laughter. His face lighted. "Can you come to the park with us?"

Johnny's face softened. "I'd like that." He looked at Peg with a question in his eyes.

"That would be very nice." Her voice was a little shaky.

With a whoop, Keith ran to the treehouse ladder.

Smiling and hurrying to keep up, Peg and Johnny stopped a few feet from the end of the slide.

"Hey, he's fast." Johnny's tone was admiring. "Maybe he'll go out for track."

Peg's smile slipped away. "I want him to grow up in a happy house and be what he wants to be. Maybe he'll love ranching like his dad. If things"—her voice shook—"hadn't gone wrong, Mitch would be at Burnt Creek right now. Maybe Keith will want to have a store or run for office or be a policeman like you. I want to do that for Susan. I tried to give him my share of the estate, but Wade said it would be better for me to keep the money and not give a bunch away in taxes and that would leave more for me to spend on Keith. I'm going to put the money in the bank for Keith."

Johnny took her hands, gripped them hard. "Keith will turn out fine. Just like you."

She clung to his hands. "I'll do my best for him. You understand that, don't you, Johnny?"

"I do." His eyes were admiring. "I want you to do that. Maybe I can help. Be like a big brother to him."

She gave his hands a squeeze, pulled free, her cheeks faintly pink. "That would be very special." Her voice was soft.

"Peg, look at me." Keith's high voice was excited.

She looked up and waved. Keith sat down and scooted to the edge of the platform and started down the slide with a shout. "Here I come."

Peg turned to Johnny. "I'm glad you came with us. " She was slightly breathless.

Johnny put a hand on her arm. "I need to talk to you for a minute." His voice was serious, his eyes anxious.

She looked at him with concern. "What's wrong?"

"I'm a cop." His handsome face was somber but determined.

Her eyes were admiring. "Of course you are. I'm proud of you. You graduated tops in your class at the police academy."

"I'm here as a cop." The words were short and hard.

The radiance in her eyes dimmed.

Johnny gazed out at the gray waters of the lake, cold and uninviting despite the vivid sunlight, then looked at her directly. "You may not have heard. It was on the radio this morning. Last night Kim Weaver was murdered."

"Kim?" Peg's face was stricken. She lifted a shaking hand. "I saw her yesterday at Wade's office. She was fine. What happened?"

Quickly Johnny described the shot and the car toppling into the pit and the desperate effort to raise the car.

Peg pressed her hands against her cheeks. "I don't understand any of this. And what does it have to do with me?"

"Chief Cobb thinks Kim was murdered because of Susan's will." Johnny talked fast. "Kim opened the mail yesterday morning at Wade Farrell's office. They're pretty sure she found a new will drawn up by Susan that left everything to her grandson."

"Oh, Johnny." Peg's eyes widened, brightened. It was as if the weight of the world slipped from her shoulders. "Everything for Keith? That's wonderful."

Johnny shook his head. "Right now that will is missing. The chief said Kim took it to the brick factory. She was meeting someone."

Peg lifted a hand to her throat. "Who?" She scarcely managed a whisper.

"We don't know. That's why I hope you will talk to me."

"Here I come, ready or not." Keith flew across the uneven ground, threw himself toward Peg.

She caught him. "Do you want to swing?"

"Way high." He darted toward the swings.

Johnny followed Peg to the swings. She settled Keith into the plastic seat. "Hold on tight."

Johnny grabbed the chains, drew the swing back, gave a mighty push.

"Hold on." Peg's cry was anxious.

Johnny was relaxed. "He's okay. Mitch's boy can handle being up high."

As Johnny pushed and the swing rose, Keith squealed in delight.

Peg looked at Johnny gravely. "Who was Kim meeting?"

He didn't answer directly. "As you know, Kim called the heirs under the other will and asked them to come to Farrell's office. Your mother, you, Tucker, Gina, and Harrison Hammond." His eyes fell. He added reluctantly, "Or the chief thought she could have called Dave."

Peg stood stiff and still. "Why would she call Dave?"

Johnny gazed toward the lake, avoiding her eyes. "The chief knows all about you and Dave and Dave wanting a loan from Susan. Kim called somebody. It had to be someone who was at Pritchard House Saturday night."

Peg nodded, her eyes filled with foreboding.

"The chief thinks Kim told somebody about the new will and agreed to keep it hidden. For a price. That's why the meeting was set up last night. Kim was supposed to bring the will." Finally, he faced her, his gaze both hopeful and uncertain. "Kim was in school with you and me and Gina and Tucker and Dave." He looked a little wry. "Between school and work, I didn't have a lot of free time to run around. She was part of the popular crowd so I don't know who she was close to."

Peg folded her arms, stared at the ground.

"Who would she tell about the new will?" Johnny gave the swing a push.

Peg's lips trembled. "I don't know. How can I know? She used to be Gina's best friend. She was at our house a lot. We hung around together, Kim and Gina and Tucker and Mitch and Dave and Ellen and me. Kim knew everyone who was supposed to inherit, one way or another. She knew us too well." Peg's voice was faint and reluctant. "She knew my mother was obsessive about Pritchard House. She knew Gina was always broke and desperate to pay her bills. She knew Tucker didn't want anybody telling him what to do with Burnt Creek. She probably knew Harrison was in financial trouble because Kim's dad had done work for Harrison. It could be any one of us, except"—she drew a deep breath—"I know it wasn't Dave."

Some of the vigor seemed to drain from Johnny's posture though he tried to look positive. "Well, sure. I mean, I know you and Dave are a couple. Obviously, Susan wouldn't have considered making a loan unless . . . Well"—he sounded uncomfortable—"I understand that you'd stick up for him."

She looked at him in surprise, flushed. "Not for the reason you think. I know he didn't because of what he said Saturday night."

Johnny looked at her sharply.

She spoke rapidly, her face forlorn. "I know he didn't harm Susan because Saturday night he demanded that I try to persuade her to make the loan. I told him I didn't want to talk about it. And"—the words came ever faster though her voice dropped almost to a whisper—"when I told him

I wasn't going to take the money, he hung up on me." Her face was white and strained, she was clearly humiliated. "But anyway he wouldn't have asked me to keep trying with Susan if he's the one who poisoned her."

"Peg"—there was anguish in his voice—"I'm sorry."

Her head jerked up. "You don't need to be sorry for me. I should have known Dave wasn't interested in me. He always dated really popular girls. He never paid any attention to me until last spring. I should have known he wanted Susan's money, not me."

He reached out, gripped her arm. "Dave's a fool."

Her eyes shiny with tears, she stood on tiptoe and kissed his cheek. "Thank you, Johnny." But the light fled from her eyes. "I wish I could believe that Kim called Dave. But I don't. That means Kim called someone I know and love."

"He's as likely as anyone." Johnny was emphatic. "Sure, he asked you to talk to Susan. Maybe that figures. Nobody said this murderer is stupid. But you're right about one thing: she called someone who was at the house Saturday night. That's why I want you to tell me what you know about Kim and the others. Who did Kim know well enough to take the chance of saying, 'I've got something here that might interest you. Susan Flynn wrote out a new will, leaving everything to Keith. It came in this morning's mail. Do you think I should put it on Wade's desk?' Whichever one she spoke to, she made a big mistake. Kim didn't know Susan had been murdered."

Peg's face was abruptly merciless. "I hated Kim."

Johnny looked at her in dismay, his open face shocked.

Peg caught the swing as it lost momentum. "Last swing today, Keith." She helped him hop to the ground. "Race from here to the slides and back and it will be time to leave. See how fast you can go."

Keith dashed away.

Peg's hands clenched into tight hard fists. "Kim was reckless and greedy and a cheat. I always thought she encouraged Gina to spend more money than she had. Maybe that's not fair. Gina still buys and buys and buys. In high school, Kim flirted with anybody, everybody. Mitch was crazy about Kim. She was the prettiest girl in the junior class. Mitch was wonderful, but having him wasn't enough. She always wanted more. She was the one who made Mitch mad that night. She was running around on him. Mitch found out and lost his temper. He stormed out. That's why Ellen died. Worst of all"—Peg's voice was flat and empty—"Kim was cheating with Tucker. We never let Susan and Tom know that it was Tucker. Tucker dropped her immediately. I wasn't sure whether he was sorry at what happened or if he had never cared about her and only used her to make a fool out of Mitch."

Out of breath, cheeks flaming, Keith ran full tilt at Peg. She caught him up and turned away, hurrying across the playground to her car.

Johnny lifted a hand, took a step after her, then stopped. With a frustrated shake of his head, he walked swiftly toward the police cruiser.

Never be late for a wedding or a funeral. I was at St. Mildred's a good fifteen minutes before the service. Unseen, I stood in the narthex near the side table with pamphlets about church teachings. The casket, covered with a cream and silver pall, waited near the central aisle. The church was filling quicky. Susan Flynn's many friends had come to bid her farewell.

I always found the order for the burial of the dead beautiful and comforting: *God is our hope and strength, a very present help in trouble.*

I saw every mourner who entered. I felt a rush of relief when Leon Butler arrived. He looked solemn and unaccustomedly formal in a old blue suit which likely hung in his closet most of the year. He sat on the Gospel side of the sanctuary near the back.

I sped outside. The parking lot was full and cars were parked on both sides of the street. I finally found Leon's battered old pickup near the entrance to the forest preserve. I flowed into the passenger seat and opened the dash compartment. It held maps, a tool kit, receipts, and a large half-eaten Hershey bar with the wrapper neatly folded back over the open end. I fished out a receipt from Hanley's Hardware. Now I needed something to write with. I had almost despaired when my fingers touched a stub of a pencil.

I placed the sheet on the dashboard and quickly wrote on the back of the receipt:

> *Mr. Butler—It is urgent that I speak with you about Susan Flynn's will. After the funeral, please meet me in the forest preserve at the end of the pier. Thanking you in advance for your cooperation—Susan's friend whom you met Saturday night.*

St. Mildred's was bounded on one side by the cemetery, on the other by the forest preserve. The entrance to the forest preserve was about twenty feet from Leon's truck. I draped the note over the bottom curve of the steering wheel. It could not be missed. I opened the latch on the passenger door. Otherwise, Leon would surely wonder how a note was placed inside his locked truck.

Everything depended upon Leon. Saturday night I'd realized there was a deep affection between Leon and Susan. I was counting on Leon to be willing to climb any mountain for Susan Flynn and her grandson.

. . . .

Mourners were still walking into the church. I entered the room where the family waited to be summoned to the front pews.

Jake Flynn nervously rolled a crumpled tissue in one hand. Her purple silk dress made her look pale. "Where's Peg? She promised to be here in plenty of time. I told her not to go to the park. It wasn't appropriate."

Charlotte Hammond smoothed her graying hair. "We have at least ten minutes."

The door opened and Peg walked in. She closed the door behind her, leaned against it. There was a desperate, intense quality to the stricken gaze that moved from face to face. "Somebody killed Kim Weaver last night."

"Kim?" Gina's voice rose in shock.

Charlotte Hammond lifted a shaking hand as if in denial.

Peg took a deep breath. "A new will leaving everything to Keith arrived at Wade Farrell's office yesterday. In the mail. Instead of giving the will to Wade, Kim Weaver kept it. She took the will to the old brick factory last night. Someone killed her."

"A new will?" Jake lifted a trembling hand. "That can't be. Susan wasn't going to sign the will until Monday morning."

Peg stared at her mother with a mixture of horror and despair.

Gina came to her feet, strode across the room, grabbed Peg's arm. "Kim can't be dead."

Tucker lounged on a small sofa. His face was calm but his eyes were alert and wary. Jake struggled to control her breathing. Harrison gripped a chair arm, as if the room had suddenly become unsteady. Charlotte watched him with concern.

"Kim is dead. She is very dead." Peg's voice wavered with hysteria. "The police think she told someone about the new will. Last night she went to the brick factory with the will and someone shot out a tire on her car and the car went into the pit."

Harrison clenched his hands. "What about this purported will? Where is it?"

"No one knows. The police can't find it. It may have been lost in the water." Her face suddenly twisted in bitterness. "Does that make all of you happy? Especially one of you?"

The door began to open, bumped against Peg.

She stepped out of the way.

A silver-haired man in a dark suit slipped inside, spoke softly. "If the family is ready . . ."

As the age-old liturgy unfolded, those who had surrounded Susan in life sat together to bid her farewell. Yet each seemed as separate from the other as figures on an Edward Hopper canvas. Plump Jake Flynn's dark purple silk dress, even though unflattering, was appropriate for a funeral. As she dabbed at her eyes, I wondered if she remembered Susan and her generosity or if she was exulting that Pritchard House was hers alone. As the haunting strains of "Amazing Grace" filled the church, Peg Flynn sang until she stopped to stifle a sob. Of them all, only Peg seemed to care about Susan's grandson. Gina Satterlee's narrow face was pale and drawn, her gaze distant. Susan's death meant she now could afford extravagant shopping. Tucker Satterlee appeared grim. Occasionally he glanced at his sister. Harrison Hammond followed the program and engaged in the proper responses, but he avoided glancing toward the pall-covered casket. If Susan had lived one more day, his financial doom would have been sealed. A teary Charlotte wiped at her eyes. With the news of Kim Weaver's murder, did she wonder where her husband was last night?

As the bells tolled, I knew the murderer must feel confident.

There might be a way to shake that confidence.

I walked to the end of the pier. The lake was a dismal gunmetal gray. Thanks to the warmth of the mink coat and a black cashmere sweater and black wool slacks and boots, I was comfortable despite the chill breeze off the lake. I turned when quick steps sounded on the wooden pier.

Leon Butler stopped in front of me, nodded gravely. "I found your note." His face was perhaps a shade thoughtful. "Guess I must have left my truck unlocked."

"That was such a bit of luck." My tone was innocent. "I hope you didn't mind my using a receipt from your dash compartment for paper. I left my purse in the trunk of my car. I didn't have anything to write on." I patted my pocket, implying a set of car keys within. "Thank you for meeting me. I don't know whether the police told you that Susan's new will is missing."

His mouth drew down in a dark frown. "No, ma'am. Sam Cobb wanted to know about me signing the will and seeing Mrs. Flynn and you, but he didn't say a word about not having the will."

Sheer fury glittered in his eyes when I told him Susan was murdered.

"Someone went upstairs and got her digitalis and placed it in the pot for her cocoa. They were all in and out of the living room at Pritchard House Saturday night: Jake, Peg, Peg's boyfriend Dave, Tucker, Gina, Harrison, and his wife Charlotte. Last night Kim Weaver went to the old brick plant and someone shot out a tire and her car went into the pit. Again, any one of them could have been at the plant."

Leon's eyes narrowed. "Tire shot out?"

I described that instant as the Cruiser swung below the pole with the red security light.

"All of the family are real good shots. Real good." Leon was emphatic. "Tom loved skeet shooting and there's a course out at Burnt Creek. Everybody competed, Tom, Susan, Jake, all the kids. Harrison's a duck hunter. Any one of them could nip a tire, even at a hundred yards. I don't know about Dave Lewis."

I was discouraged. "You've known most of them for many years. Who would poison Susan? Who would conspire with Kim Weaver to hide the will?"

"Different things matter to different folks. Pritchard House means more to Jake Flynn than any pile of bricks should. That house puffs her up. I don't know what she might do if she thought she was going to lose that house. Peg?" His face softened. "She's a sweet girl, good as they come. But"—and his eyes narrowed—"she's nobody's pushover. If she cares about something, she'll fight like a wildcat. One time we had a hired hand and Peg came around the corner and saw him beating up on a horse. She had her skeet gun in her hands and she whipped it up quick as lightning and shot around his feet and aimed the gun at him and told him to get his hide off of Burnt Creek and if she ever saw him again she wouldn't shoot at his feet. She's like the other kids, not a dime in her pocket except what Susan gave them. I heard tell that Dave Lewis wanted money for a clinic from Susan. Tucker? He and Mitch spent a lot of time together, but he didn't grieve a minute when Mitch ran away. Without Mitch around, Tucker was in line for Burnt Creek." He looked dour. "As soon as Tucker took over at Burnt Creek, he called me in, said I'd sure done a good job but he would handle everything himself now. As for Gina"—Leon hunched his shoulders against the cold breeze that tugged at his suit coat—"she's got too many fancy clothes for a gal who can't hold a job. Gina grew up without folks. It didn't seem to hurt Tucker. He loves the land. It fills him up. But Gina's empty inside. I suspect she's in a bad fix over money."

Maybe he saw my look of surprise.

He gave a little whuff of laughter. "Don't know how an old bachelor knows about buying baubles and such? I got a pretty niece, Lou Ann, a buyer for Neiman Marcus. Lou Ann comes to see me and I find out all about people who don't think the world is right unless they got the newest and the fanciest and the most expensive. That's Gina." The geniality left his face. "Maybe she felt like she had to have money. As for Harrison, everybody in town knows he's come a cropper with his latest fancy housing addition. The houses are so big the people have to go to Oklahoma City and buy outsize furniture to fill up the rooms. As for Kim Weaver, when she was in high school, she hung around the kids and spent a lot of time at the ranch. A bold piece with a gambler's eye. I'd wager she figured out which one needed money the most, made her pitch about hiding the will, and thought she was on easy street when the meeting at the brick plant was set up. I guess Kim never thought somebody would put the ace of spades on her king."

Kim had slipped a small pistol into her purse. She'd been confident she had all the cards, but the joker was out.

Leon smacked a fist into a palm. "I got to do something. I don't know what, but I got to do something." His face was burdened by grief.

I looked at him gravely. "There might be a way you could help trap Susan's killer. It would be dangerous."

He stepped toward me. "You name it." There was no mistaking his determination. "I'll do it."

. . . .

The table was laden with food. The good women of the church never fail in times of trouble. As I'd expected, Wade and Cindy Farrell were among those at the house. Cindy Farrell sat on a sofa, helping Keith pull apart and put together a Russian matryoshka doll fashioned after a penguin. The outer doll with a black head, huge eyes, yellow beak, blue bow tie, and white bottom held four smaller replicas. Cindy murmured, "One penguin, two, three penguins, four . . ."

I popped into the hallway, waited until it was empty, and swirled into being. I chose a black jacquard jacket with white floral trim and a black A-line silk skirt and black heels. In the living room, I walked to the table laden with fried chicken, casseroles, and salads. However, this was no time to overindulge. I needed to be alert. I chose chicken salad, fruit, and a croissant. I edged nearer Wade Farrell. I enjoyed my repast and waited patiently until he was free.

He nodded as a woman turned away, then looked around the room, likely seeking his wife.

I stepped up to him. "Mr. Farrell, may I speak privately with you for a moment? I was with Susan Flynn Saturday night when she signed her new will. I'm sure Chief Cobb explained the circumstances to you. If you'll come this way, we can use Susan's study."

He studied me, his eyes narrowed, his broad face wary. "The police are looking for you."

"The police station is my next stop." Telling the truth usually convinces a listener. "I fully intend to consult with Chief Cobb, but I need to speak with you first."

"In that event, I don't see any harm in talking to you." He turned and walked toward the hall.

When we stepped into Susan's study, I turned on the light and closed the door. I had a plan, but I needed help from Wade Farrell. "Mr. Farrell, Leon Butler signed Susan's new will. If he swears that he saw Susan Saturday night and she gave him her new will and he read and signed it, can the judge say the old will is invalid?"

"Absolutely not." Farrell folded his arms. "Only the production of the signed document will suffice."

I was rocked by that knowledge. I suppose my face revealed the depth of my despair.

"She signed the will." I was forceful. "I saw her sign it. Leon saw Susan sign it."

Farrell looked unhappy. "I wish it were that easy. But the judge won't set aside an existing document on the unsupported word of a witness. Don't you see? There's no proof."

I began to pace. The trap I'd hoped to set wouldn't work.

"I'm sorry." He was clearly regretful. "I can see why you thought that might be the case. I suppose it must seem simple to a nonlawyer, but I can assure you that Judge Blackburn is a stickler for procedure. If I went into his court and offered Leon Butler as a witness to a new will that can't be produced, the judge would chew on me like an old cigar."

"I don't know why people's word can't be taken. Leon Butler has an excellent reputation." I knew I sounded snappish. Wade Farrell hadn't created the laws. I couldn't blame him. I flung out my hands. "Don't you see? Susan's murderer always reacts immediately to a threat. Kim Weaver offered the new will in exchange for a reward. The murderer responded with a rifle shot. I believe the murderer will try to kill Leon Butler if you call together the heirs and tell them Leon signed the new will and his sworn testimony would be enough to declare the old will invalid. I have no doubt Leon will be attacked."

Farrell looked thoughtful. "You want to set a trap using Leon as bait. That puts Leon—"

I cut in sharply. "—in grave danger. Leon is eager to help and the police will keep him safe." And I would be there as well. "You can make this possible, Mr. Farrell, none of the prospective heirs are lawyers. They will believe what you tell them." I clapped my hands together, looked at him expectantly.

"I'd be lying." His lips pressed together. He gave a quick head shake and turned toward the door.

"Susan was your client."

He stopped, one hand on the door.

"You can do Susan one last great service."

Chief Cobb and Detective Sergeant Price were finishing a late lunch from Lulu's, the chief with a chili burger and onion rings, Price with a hickory sauce cheeseburger and French fries. I hoped they occasionally managed some grilled fish, vegetables, and fruit. They sat at the worktable near the blackboard.

Cobb dipped an onion ring in a side of horseradish sauce. He looked morose. "Like a needle to true north, I keep swinging to Tucker Satterlee. He had opportunity and motive for both murders and he's a guy used to moving fast and making quick decisions. Nobody runs a big ranch unless they've got that kind of savvy. Then maybe there's a magnetic pulse because I swing right back to Peg Flynn or Dave Lewis. It's kind of convenient the way they've presumably split. I wish I had a crystal ball and could see them a year from now. Will they be Mr. and Mrs. Newlywed with a fancy clinic under construction?"

Price finished the last of his burger. "The other heirs had equal opportunity. Jake Flynn, Gina Satterlee, or one of the Hammonds could have popped the digitalis. Johnny Cain's interview with Peg Flynn shows Kim Weaver knew all of them pretty well, so her effort to peddle the will makes sense."

Cobb rolled up greasy papers, stuffed them in a sack. "Harrison Hammond might have been the most desperate. Kim Weaver probably had a nose for desperation."

Price licked salt from his fingertips. "She'd have been around town enough to hear rumors. It wasn't any secret that Hammond's development was in big trouble. And he's a hunter. I don't see Jake Flynn shooting out a tire, but Peg and Gina grew up skeet shooting. I checked it out. Hammond's wife isn't a hunter. Opportunity and motive aren't enough, Sam. We need evidence linking one of them to one of the crimes. Fingerprints. Or someone seen in the wrong place. As for the brick plant, no shell showed up in the area where Tucker rode this morning. Sam, we don't have any cards."

The chief wiped his fingers on a paper napkin. "I'm afraid"—his voice was heavy—"we never will. My gut tells me somebody's committed two murders and left no trace."

I looked at the clock. It was half past two. To put my plan into operation required immediate action. Tomorrow was Christmas Eve. Wade Farrell's office would be closed. I had to make a move now and make it fast if a trap was to be put in place today. I'd hoped to follow Precept Three: Work behind the scenes without making your presence known. But I didn't have time to make an indirect approach to the chief.

Cobb's desk was behind him and Price. I perched in his chair, found a pen and a legal pad. I wrote quickly, then tore off the sheet very slowly to avoid any sound.

Price pushed back his chair, began to clear the table. "More coffee?"

When Price walked across the room to the trash basket and the coffee table, I put my note in front of Chief Cobb:

I can help you trap the murderer. Tell Price to bring Wade Farrell here as soon as possible.

Submitted in urgency—Officer M. Loy

"Coffee, Sam?" Price looked over his shoulder.

"Coffee." Cobb repeated the word numbly.

Price looked concerned. "Sam?"

The chief picked up my note, folded it very deliberately, put it in his pocket. "Guess I ate too fast."

Price looked relieved. "You need some bicarb."

Cobb took a moment to answer, then said gruffly, "I'll be all right." He took a deep breath. "In fact, I've got an idea." His eyes slid around the room. He shook his head, turned to Price. "Find Wade Farrell. Ask him to come here. Tell him we're up against a wall, but he can help solve two murders."

Price put down his coffee mug. "Right now?"

"Right now."

As soon as the door closed, Cobb strode to his desk, punched the intercom. "I'm in conference to everybody but Price."

"No visitors." His secretary's voice was matter-of-fact.

"Right."

"Calls?"

"I'll take calls." He switched off the intercom, looked around the room. He paced back and forth, started to speak, stopped, then blurted out, "If you've got something to say, say it. No more blackboards. No more notes."

Praying that Wiggins was utterly immersed in Tumbulgum, I swirled into being. I chose an amethyst silk shirt jacket over a black silk top and black silk trousers and classic leather pumps in matching amethyst. Amethyst is such a good color for redheads. I hoped Wiggins, if he wasn't utterly immersed in Tumbulgum, understood that a woman needs to look her best when dealing with a fractious male. To check my appearance, I imagined a black alligator handbag, plentifully filled. I retrieved the compact, flipped it open. I decided I was presentable.

Cobb sat down in his chair, rather heavily. "Officer Loy?"

In an instant, I swirled into uniform.

Cobb ground knuckles into one cheek. "I'm nuts. Totally nuts."

I swirled back into my pretty outfit, not that a woman can't look outstanding in a uniform. Still, I felt Chief Cobb might feel more comfortable with me in civilian dress. "Or," I said brightly, "sometimes I'm Susan Flynn's visiting friend Jerrie Emiliani."

"The redhead in the car." His voice sounded rusty. "The redhead who disappeared."

"Sometimes I'm here. Sometimes I'm not." I hoped my smile was reassuring. "I'll be brief. You know everything I know." This wasn't quite accurate. "Almost everything. I spoke earlier today with Leon Butler. He cared a lot about Susan Flynn. Leon's brave. He's willing to take a big chance to help us catch her murderer."

"Help *us*?" The chief's eyes were wide.

"I'm doing my best to be of assistance." I was demure. I certainly didn't want to toot my own horn, but facts were facts. "You wouldn't know nearly as much if I hadn't been on the scene with Kim Weaver."

"I guess that's right." Without looking down, he fumbled with his desk drawer, fished out the bag of M&M's, poured some in his hand, and popped them in his mouth. His eyes never left my face. "All right. What have you got?"

I strolled nearer the desk, perched upon one edge. “Sam,” I paused, “I hope you don’t mind my calling you Sam. I feel that I know you very well. You’re honest, hardworking, smart, a cop who wants to catch a murderer. Now”—I leaned forward—

He pressed against the back of his chair.

“—here’s what you can do.”

CHAPTER 17

Yellow flames danced among the logs in the living room fireplace at Pritchard House. The house was quiet now, friends departed, the table cleared of casseroles. The unmistakable reminder of death was the overpowering scent of flowers from the florists' spectacular arrangements in vases scattered atop tables, the piano, in the entry hall, curving on either side of the fireplace.

The small sofa near the rosewood piano was comfortable, but I was as tense as the mayor had been on long-ago election nights even though he'd spent plenty of walk-around money to bring friendly voters to the polls. I didn't have any walk-around money. I'd cast my one vote, and the minute hand on the big grandfather clock continued to tick, tick, tick with no sign of victory.

On the floor in front of the fire, Keith and Peg played Chutes and Ladders. Keith's face folded into an intense frown when he landed on a square that sent him sliding down.

Peg teased him. "That's what happens when someone eats too much of anything, a tummy ache and a drop back to a lower square. Don't be discouraged. You'll land on a good square and scoot right up a ladder next time."

The phone rang.

I scarcely breathed.

Peg retrieved the handset from the hall. "Hi, Johnny . . ."

I sank back in disappointment.

"It was a beautiful service. I'm glad you came." A tiny frown pulled at her face. "Oh, everything's okay. Except"—her voice was tight with misery—"sometimes I don't think anything will ever be right again. Johnny, have they found that will?"

Keith moved restively.

I dropped down beside him, pointed at the dice and Peg's hand. It was her turn.

He picked them up, tried to tuck them in her hand.

"Just a second, Johnny. I have to roll the dice." She smiled at Keith. Two and three came up. She counted five squares and ended up on a chute down to the first row. "Keith and I are playing a game. He's about to beat me . . . Yes, that would be fun. I'd love to see you. Maybe we can go to the park on Christmas afternoon and . . ."

My ESP to Peg, "Hang up. Hang up. Hang up," wasn't working.

The clock ticked. The chime sounded marking a quarter past three. Chief Cobb and I had agreed on a plan. But everything depended upon Wade Farrell. Had he changed his mind?

"Oh." Peg glanced at the caller ID window. "Johnny, I'd better take this call. Yes, thanks." She clicked. "Wade?" Peg's face drew into a frown. "This afternoon? Can't it wait until next week? . . . I see. Yes, I'll tell my mother." Suddenly her face lighted. "Is it about the new will, the one that's missing? Has it been found?" Her eagerness slipped away. "Oh, I see. All right, I'll tell Mother. Yes, I'm sure we'll be able to come."

Keith was counting and moving his marker up to the next level.

Peg clicked off the phone. "I'll be right back, Keith. I'll bring you a cookie."

I followed Peg into the kitchen. All was spick-and-span. Sparkling clean china platters and cut-glass dishes were ranged on counters, awaiting their return to cabinets.

Jake sat at the white wooden table, comfortable in a velour blouse and pants, drying silver spoons and slipping them with loving care into a felt cutlery wrap. She looked weary but at peace.

Peg stood in the doorway. "Wade Farrell called. He says we need to be at his office at four o'clock. He's calling everyone to come. He has information about Susan's new will."

The aura of contentment vanished from the kitchen. Jake's eyes flared in alarm. "Has he found that will?" Her voice was high and strained, her face suddenly gaunt and fearful.

Peg's gaze filled with uncertainty and doubt. "He doesn't have the will, but he said he felt it was his duty to inform us of new information."

The faded red velvet curtains at the windows were drawn. Despite the glow of light from the fluorescent fixtures, Wade Farrell's conference room seemed gloomy. This afternoon there were no folders on the table.

Wade waited until everyone had entered, then closed the conference room door. He walked to the chair beneath the judge's portrait. He remained standing until everyone was seated: Peg Flynn, Gina Satterlee, and Tucker Satterlee on one side of the table, Jake Flynn, Harrison and Charlotte Hammond on the other.

All eyes were on Farrell, who looked flushed and uncomfortable. I edged out the chair opposite him and slipped onto the seat. As I had hoped, all the previous heirs were here. The only absent suspect was Dave Lewis. There was no excuse for him to be present. However, if the chief's suspicions about Peg and Dave were correct, she would very likely inform him of what occurred during the coming meeting. I was sure the chief was wrong about her.

There was no police presence. That was essential to my plan.

Wade's expression was strained as he settled into his chair. He looked like a man who wished he were elsewhere. His eyes flicked uneasily from face to face. "I felt I had to speak with all of you since I have been apprised of facts that clearly impact the information I previously gave you in regard to Susan Flynn's estate. I'm leaving tomorrow for the holidays and won't be back until after the first. When we met on Monday, I had no way of knowing that Susan had written out a new will on Saturday night."

Harrison leaned forward, his worried gaze magnified by his bifocals. "Wait a minute, Wade. I don't know what Peg's told you, but if there's a new will, no one knows where it is. I asked the police about that. I don't see any point in talking about a piece of paper that may not exist."

"The police may not know where the will is"—Wade nodded in agreement—"but they know that Susan drafted a new will before she died on Saturday night. The police are interested in the will only as an apparent motive for the murder of Kim Weaver. The police believe Kim intercepted the new will when it arrived here in the Monday mail and offered it to someone." Wade's tone was grim. "I am upset that my employee apparently took advantage of her position to prevent the receipt of Susan's new will. However, Kim paid a terrible price for her decision. The police said that she planned to meet someone at the abandoned brick plant and that she apparently had the will with her when her car went into the pit. As I understand it, the police also searched her apartment. No trace of the will has been found."

The deep lines grooved in Harrison's face eased. "If that's the case, why are we here? Either there is a will or there isn't. I, for one, don't believe for a minute there was another will. There's no proof."

Charlotte's gaze was somber. Jake lifted a shaky hand to her lips. Tucker had the air of an observer at a sporting event awaiting the game's conclusion. Gina hunched in her chair as if she were cold and stared down at the bare table. Peg's face furrowed into a disappointed frown.

Wade took a deep breath. "There is definite proof that the will existed. The will was seen, read, and witnessed on Saturday night. The terms of the holographic will, written on Susan Flynn's stationery with her monogram, corresponded to the terms of the will she had instructed me to prepare for her signature on Monday morning."

Tucker's question was quick and to the point. "Even if a new will existed and someone claims to know what was in it, what difference does it make if there isn't a copy of the will?" His posture was relaxed, but his eyes never left the lawyer's face.

Wade tugged at his shirt collar as if it were too tight. "Although I can make no definitive judgment, in my considered opinion Judge Blackburn would combine the testimony of a reputable witness that a holographic will had been duly signed with the undeniable evidence that Susan intended to sign a new will with similar content on Monday. If he did so, I believe Judge Blackburn would rule that clear and convincing evidence existed that a will had been drawn up and that would effectually void the previous will."

His words came in gruff bullets which possibly made his message even more effective. Only I understood that he was making a herculean effort to lie and he hated every minute of it.

He took another deep breath. "In my considered legal opinion"—his expression was dismal. The man had no talent for subterfuge—"Judge Blackburn will rule that the estate should be apportioned on the basis of intestacy since the proven existence of a new will, notwithstanding its disappearance, effectively voided the previous document. If the estate is distributed on that basis, the heir would be the closest living relative."

"Oh, Wade"—Peg's voice rose in excitement—"does that mean Keith inherits even if they never find the new will?"

Wade flushed again.

I hoped a shot of Jack Daniel's would ease his blood pressure later. Or did whiskey raise blood pressure? I'd always preferred plain club soda.

He avoided looking at them. "That is my judgment." He spoke slowly, weighting each word evenly. "The determining factor, in my view, will be the testimony of the witness. If Judge Blackburn believes the witness to be credible, I don't see how he can rule otherwise."

"Who is this presumably credible witness?" Harrison's tone was tense. "Why, this could be a sensation-seeking, delusional person off the street."

Peg turned on Harrison. "How did some unknown person know enough to describe a will that reflects what Susan had already directed Wade to write?"

Harrison ignored her question. "If everything depends upon this unknown witness's credibility, who is this witness? We have a right to know."

Wade folded his arms. "The witness is a man you know well, a man who has the respect of Adelaide, a man who spent most of his working life protecting Susan Flynn's investment in Burnt Creek. Susan Flynn took that new will to Leon Butler's house Saturday night. Moreover, Susan asked Leon to read the will and sign it as a witness. Leon Butler will swear to the existence of the new will and he will also testify to the contents and that he watched as Susan signed the document. I have arranged for his testimony to be taken here in the morning with a notary public present. As soon as the courthouse opens after the holidays, I will present Leon's affidavit to Judge Blackburn."

Harrison pushed back his chair. "There's still no will. I'll have my lawyer get in touch. I'm going to fight this trumped-up claim." His bluster was loud and determined, but his face was slack with shock. He turned on his heel, walked blindly to the door. Charlotte hurried ahead to open it.

The other presumptive heirs filed out of the conference room. Jake moved like an old woman with hunched shoulders and slow steps. Gina burrowed her hands into the pockets of her coat, her face grim. Tucker walked swiftly, leaving the others behind.

Only Peg smiled. She looked back from the doorway. "You're doing the right thing, Wade."

He massaged one temple, clearly glad the meeting was over. "I'm doing what I can for Susan."

In the law firm parking lot, Jake tried to stifle sobs. "It isn't right. If the judge does what Wade said, I won't even be able to live in the house."

Tucker's pickup gunned out into the street. Harrison and Charlotte passed without a word of farewell.

Peg reached out a hand toward her mother. "Of course you will. We're going to take care of Keith and—"

Jake swung away, broke into a trot to follow Gina. "I'm going to drive home with Gina. Oh, it won't be my home. Not anymore."

Peg stood by her car. All traces of her elation in Farrell's office drained from her face. She slid into the driver's seat, sat there in despair. In the light from the lamppost, she looked terribly young and unhappy and alone. One hand reached for her purse. She lifted out her cell phone, held it for a moment, started to slip it into the purse, then, her eyes huge and empty, quickly punched a number.

"Dave, I wanted to let you know—"

I wasn't certain of her tone. Was she calling in hope or in dread?

"—that I don't have to decide anything about Susan's will. Leon Butler witnessed the new will Saturday night and he's going to make a sworn statement tomorrow and that means Keith will inherit."

She listened.

I wished I knew what Dave Lewis was saying.

Peg's face was abruptly resolute. "I'll call you later." She clicked off the phone.

Leon Butler's pickup was the only vehicle parked in front of his house. Light outlined closed blinds at several windows. The front porch was shadowy. The early dusk of winter turned the surrounding woods dark and menacing. The only sounds were those of the night, the rustle of leaves, the occasional hoo of an owl, the faraway whistle of a train, the falsetto yips of a coyote.

It took me ten minutes of scouting to find the silent sentinels, at least a dozen of them, dressed all in black, caps, jackets, trousers, and boots. They were stationed in various places around the house and in the woods near the road. They had blended into the night, shadows among shadows.

Relieved, I popped inside. Since the blinds were closed, no sharpshooter would spot Leon Butler through a window and fire. If an attack came, that attack would have to occur in the house.

My stomach knotted. Kim Weaver had no warning when a rifle shot punctured the front right tire and her car careened into the water-filled pit. Tonight when the doorbell rang or the knock came at the back door, I would be there first. I had no weapon, but I could move without being seen. If a hand lifted with a gun ready to fire the instant the door opened, I would push the barrel to one side, afford time for a rescue to occur. From this moment until the trap either succeeded or failed, Leon Butler was my responsibility. True, he'd agreed to provide a target for an elusive killer, but it was I who had asked him to take that chance.

Water splashed and silverware clinked in the kitchen. Leon stood at the sink, washing his supper dishes. He worked with the sleeves of his red plaid flannel shirt rolled to the elbows. His lined, weathered face was somber. He dried the dishes and silverware and returned them to their proper places. He unrolled his sleeves, buttoned the cuffs, and walked to a door near the refrigerator. He opened it, flicked on the light to reveal basement steps. He closed the door, pushed home a bolt. At the back door, he slid the bolt into the bracket.

He walked across the wooden floor, his boots clumping, into the living room.

"Who's coming?" the parrot squawked.

Leon shot a quick glance toward the cage at the blue-and-gold macaw. "Never miss a trick, do you, Archie? I don't know. We'll find out." Moving purposefully, Leon strode to a gun safe tucked in a corner near an old walnut cabinet. He twisted open the lock, lifted out a thirty-eight, closed the safe. He spun the chamber, then retrieved a box of cartridges, loaded the gun. He balanced the gun in his hand with easy familiarity. In a moment, with a decisive nod, he placed the gun on a small wicker table next to an easy chair that faced the front door. The kitchen and stairs were behind the chair. He draped a copy of *Field & Stream* over the gun. He settled into the chair with its clear view of the front door, retrieved the magazine, and began to read.

Archie muttered, "I'm a good boy, am I," and began to swing, the faint squeak a companionable sound in the quiet room.

Methodically, I checked out the rest of the house. Upstairs, there were three bedrooms and a study with a desk, bookshelves, and a computer. Downstairs, I flowed through a closed door to the left of the front door.

Three men waited in semidarkness in a small, military-neat bedroom with twin beds, a maple dresser, and a bedside table. Some illumination came from a hooded flashlight resting on the floor near Chief Cobb.

Cobb sat in a folding chair angled to the door. The door was opened a sliver, affording a narrow view of Leon in his easy chair, the stairs behind him, an old leather sofa to his left, and a portion of the parrot's cage. In the narrow shaft of light from the open door, Cobb's heavy face looked stern and determined. His gray suit was rumpled, his necktie loosened.

Detective Sergeant Price lounged in another folding chair. He was dressed in black, loose jacket, pullover sweater, slacks, tennis shoes. In a single stride, he could burst into the living room if Cobb flung the door wide. A police-issue revolver rested on one leg, his hand curved around the butt. In the dimness, his craggy face was calm, yet there was a sense of readiness and power about him despite his casual slouch.

Johnny Cain pulled a window shade back just enough to watch the front porch.

The men neither spoke nor moved. There was no sense of impatience. They were there, and there they would stay until night passed into day if necessary.

Occasionally Chief Cobb checked the luminous dial of his watch. Twilight faded to darkness.

I moved outside. Neither the house nor the woods gave any hint of watching eyes, listening ears, muscles ready for action.

Headlights abruptly swept the front porch. I blinked against the glare, trying to discern the vehicle, but I couldn't see past the lights. The motor was turned off, the headlights doused. A car door slammed.

I almost went forward to see, knew that didn't matter. What mattered was Leon. I went inside.

Leon's head raised. He looked toward the door, his eyes narrowed. He placed the magazine over the gun and came to his feet.

Quick steps sounded on the front porch. The screen door rattled as a fist pounded. "Leon? Are you home?"

Shock held me immobile. I had never expected to hear that voice at Leon Butler's house this night.

Leon's face folded in a frown. He walked to the door, turned on the porch light. He slid open the bolt and turned the knob.

Peg Flynn held the lapels of her unzipped blue jacket against the chill of the night. The breeze stirred her light brown hair. She looked desperately unhappy.

I flowed onto the porch, poised to grab Peg's arm if she held a gun. Unlike Chief Cobb, I'd been so sure of Peg's innocence. She had offered her share of the estate to Keith. Yet it was she who had recalled the discussions at the dinner table when they were young and Susan's husband Tom spoke of wills and estates. Did she know full well when she offered to stand aside in favor of Keith that Wade Farrell would explain, as he had, that her stepping aside would simply afford a greater share to the current heirs? Then she'd tried to give her share to Keith and the lawyer explained about gift taxes and the wisdom of Peg retaining the inheritance and spending it for Keith if she wished. Had all of her apparent generosity been an elaborate charade, designed to portray her as lacking any motive? And tonight, in the parking lot outside Wade Farrell's office, she'd called to tell Dave Lewis about Leon as a witness to the new will.

In the glow of the porch light, her round face was drawn and tired, her eyes strained, but both hands were empty.

The door opened. Leon looked out, his expression grave. And sad.

She spoke fast. "I can only stay for a few minutes. I had to come. Leon, I'm in trouble. I don't know what to do. And you always helped us." Her voice was shaky.

Leon stepped back, held the door for her. He gestured toward the small sofa, waited until she took her place before he settled into his easy chair. If ever a man looked as if his heart had turned to stone, it was Leon.

Archie whistled and sang the first line of "A Pretty Girl Is Like a Melody." The words were grotesque in his scratchy voice.

Peg pulled off her coat. She looked nervously toward the door.

I was inches away, alert for a gun.

She folded the coat, placed it beside her. Tears welled in her eyes. "I'm almost sure I know who killed Susan and Kim, but I don't think it would do any good for me to go to the police. I don't have any proof, at least not the kind the police need. And I'm scared for Keith. I brought him with me. He's asleep in his car seat so I've got to hurry."

My heart twisted as I pictured Keith in his pajamas and his new snow coat slumped in sleep on this dangerous night.

"Don't cry, little girl," Archie shrieked.

Peg leaned forward. "I'm sure I'm right because Gina is dreadfully frightened. And there's something that happened a long time ago. I kept quiet about it. I should have told Susan and Tom, but I promised Mitch I wouldn't." She pressed knuckles against her cheek. "I shouldn't have made that promise. Mitch could have been killed so easily. I still can't think why he wasn't crushed, the gun going off and Black Abbott rearing up above Mitch, eight hundred pounds of horse. Somehow Mitch flung himself backward and rolled away. I was up in the sycamore at the house. I could see the pasture and Mitch with his horse. Everyone knew Black Abbott could be spooked by a rabbit and the gunshot was close, so close, and Black Abbott went up—"

"We were all pretty good at climbing trees." The lazy drawl came from behind Leon. Tucker Satterlee stood just below the landing on the stairs to the second floor. He was lean and muscular and tense in a black sweater and Levi's and running shoes. He held a twenty-two pistol, aimed directly at Peg. He glanced briefly toward Leon. "That's a nice big oak tree on the west side of the house, Leon. When I saw Peg's car outside, I climbed up and pushed up a window and landed in your study. And here you are with pretty little Peggy, who's hoping you can help get me hanged." Tucker spoke without expression, his eyes empty. "Or do they punch you with a bunch of drugs these days? I don't know. That's not what I needed to know to run the ranch." His face twisted in despair. "That's all I ever wanted. I've done a good job. Everything's up to date. The herd's healthier than it's ever been. I've made Burnt Creek better and better."

Peg clutched at her throat. She was suddenly ashen. "Tucker, how you could hurt Susan? How could you?"

I hovered near the banister. If he lifted the gun suddenly, I had to move at exactly the right moment. Should I shove his hand toward the wall? From his vantage point on the stairs, Tucker looked down on Leon and Peg. Was Hal Price getting ready to make a move? For now, the police likely were waiting to see what Tucker might do, whether he would come down the stairs, be easier to reach.

Tucker hunched his shoulders. "Susan was dying. What difference did a few days or weeks make? If she'd lived another day, she was going to give the ranch to Mitch's kid. When Mitch ran away, I was the one who worked the ranch, kept everything going. Then he was killed in Iraq and I was sure Burnt Creek would be mine. Who would have thought he had a kid and the kid would come here." His eyes ached with pain. "Susan drank her cocoa and she didn't hurt anymore. And the kid didn't care. What was Burnt Creek to him? You would have taken good care of him." His face twisted in despair. "You shouldn't have brought Keith with you tonight, Peg. You really shouldn't. He's a nice little guy. He reminds me of Ellen. Not Mitch, but Ellen. Mitch killed Ellen."

"You went after Kim to make Mitch mad." Peg's voice shook. "That's why Ellen died. Because of you."

"Ellen died because of Mitch's temper." Tucker's reply was hot and angry. "I just wanted to gig him a little with Kim. How could I know he'd storm out of the party and drive like a fool? If he'd had any sense, he wouldn't have gone so fast. Ellen died because of him. Not me. I never would have done anything to hurt Ellen." Sorrow weighted his words.

"But Ellen died. And Susan. And Kim. You shot out Kim's tire." Peg's voice quivered. "Tucker, you made love to Kim."

Tucker's eyes glittered with anger. "Kim said she'd give

me the new will if I'd marry her. She wanted me and Burnt Creek and money to go to France and the Riviera. She'd already started planning a wedding trip. She deserved what she got." His face was ugly with hatred. "She didn't tell me there was a witness to the new will."

Tucker turned the gun toward Leon. "That turns out to be your bad luck, Leon. I've gone through too much to lose everything now." His gaze flicked toward Peg. "I wish you hadn't come tonight. But"—and his voice was that of a man persuading himself—"you came here to try to get me in trouble. I wish you hadn't brought the kid."

Peg lifted her hands. "Please, Tucker. He's only a little boy. Don't hurt him."

Tucker's shoulders hunched. "I can't turn back now. It's your fault." His voice was accusatory. "You brought him here."

Leon's powerful hands rested on the chair arms. With patience and care, he edged forward in his chair.

The barrel of the gun lifted. "Don't move again, Leon. I can shoot fast. Remember? I can shoot you and Peg in an instant."

Leon turned his work-worn hands over, as if in acceptance. "Tucker, you need to put that gun down. The house is surrounded by police. They'll hear shots. They'll protect Keith. You may kill me and Peg, but you won't get away tonight. You're all finished." Leon dropped his hands. His left hand was about three inches from the magazine draped over his gun.

Tucker started down the stairs, his steps heavy.

I sensed Leon's intention when his eyes flickered toward the magazine. Any instant now, he would move, grab his gun. I'd persuaded Leon to put his life on the line. It was up to me to make sure he didn't lose it.

I launched myself, grabbing Tucker's right arm and pushing the gun toward the wall. I screamed, "Help, help . . ."

The bedroom door slammed open. Detective Sergeant Price, gun level, plunged across the floor, shouting, "Police. Hands up. Drop your weapon. Police!"

I held on with all my strength, but Tucker twisted, jerked free.

I felt myself falling away. I managed a flip that would have been a ten in any diving competition and kicked his arm as he swung the gun forward. A shot rang out, thudding into the wall, splintering the plaster.

Johnny Cain, like a running back swerving around a tackle, thudded past Price. Johnny's face was convulsed with fury. He ran with his hands out, feet pounding as he hurtled up the steps. Before Tucker could aim again, Johnny slammed him down onto the treads, one hand gripping Tucker's right wrist, the other tight on Tucker's throat.

CHAPTER 18

I had one more task to accomplish if I could.

I'd last seen Susan's will on Monday night in Kim's purse, shortly before I went to the police station. When I returned to her apartment, she was leaving for the abandoned brick plant. I'd assumed the will was still in her purse. In the car the distinctive square envelope had not been in Kim's lap or loose on the front seat. But the police didn't find the will in the zipped purse retrieved from the submerged car.

Nothing in Kim's demeanor when I returned to her apartment Monday night suggested that she had—in the very short amount of time I'd been absent—taken the will and left it somewhere outside of her apartment.

I entered her apartment, drew the curtains, and turned on the lights. Detective Sergeant Price and other officers would have thoroughly searched the apartment, searched it as only police know how to search. They had found no will.

Was it possible that Kim had managed to secrete the will so well that even seasoned investigators missed the hiding place?

I settled on the sofa. When I left Monday night, Kim had

been in the living room, the will in her purse. If she decided to leave the envelope behind in her apartment, that decision had been made in the short span of time that I was in Chief Cobb's office. She must have moved quickly.

I looked slowly around the living room at the beige walls decorated by travel posters and the shabby sofa and chairs. The police search would have unearthed the envelope had it been tucked beneath a cushion or slipped into a drawer.

Travel brochures lay askew on the table next to her chair. She'd looked at them, planning a wedding trip to the Riviera. The lure of foreign lands was vividly revealed in the posters of the Parthenon, the Cathedral at Chartres, Castle Hill in Nice.

Tucker had dallied with Kim to anger Mitch. Kim had responded to Tucker's charms, chosen him over Mitch, the scion of the wealthy family. After Ellen's death, perhaps Kim blamed Tucker's defection on pressure from the family. When she offered Tucker the will, she wanted marriage in exchange.

I felt a sweep of sadness. So much sorrow and despair. Kim had likely smiled happily as she worked to frame the posters of exotic destinations. Monday night she must have felt that she was taking the first step toward the French Riviera and a new life as Mrs. Tucker Satterlee. I gazed at the travel posters. The Riviera . . .

Abruptly I was across the room. I unhooked the framed poster of Castle Hill in Nice. I turned the frame over. I moved the prongs holding the backing in place and slipped the cardboard free.

Susan Flynn's monogrammed envelope lay against the slick white back of the poster.

I opened a window, loosened a screen, and then I was out into the night, carrying the envelope. Stars spangled the cold night sky. I zoomed from the apartment house to downtown, enjoying the sounds and sights of the holidays, carolers, car motors in store parking lots as last-minute shoppers drove up and down seeking a space, Salvation Army bells, partygoers calling out cheerful farewells, and the brilliant panorama of decorated yards and strands of bright lights on lampposts and strung across downtown streets.

It was time for Officer Loy's last appearance. On the second floor of City Hall, I waited until the dispatcher turned to answer a call. ". . . please repeat the address. I can't help you unless I have an address . . ." I swirled into being. If she looked up, she would see the familiar French blue uniform with a hand raised to punch the electronic keypad at the door to the police offices. I swiftly bent down, as if tying my shoe, and placed the envelope on the floor.

I disappeared, moved through the panel, opened the door from the inside. The dispatcher was absorbed in the call. I scooped up the envelope and closed the door.

The hallway was empty, though a mutter of voices and ringing phones sounded from the squad room. I walked down the central hallway to Chief Cobb's office. As I'd expected, the frosted glass gleamed from light within. He had many tasks to accomplish with the arrest of Tucker Satterlee.

The small square envelope seemed oddly heavy in my hand. I would be relieved to deliver it to a safe haven.

Officer Loy once again disappeared. I put the envelope on the floor, slipped through the door and into the office. Chief Cobb sat behind his desk, several folders opened and spread out. His face was intent as he wrote briskly on a legal pad. His gray suit was more rumpled than ever. He'd discarded his necktie and his white shirt was open at the throat. With his left hand, he plucked M&M's from a half-emptied sack.

I eased the hall door open, retrieved the envelope, and shut the panel.

The phone rang.

Without looking up, he punched the speakerphone. "Cobb."

"Got the transcripts of the Satterlee tapes from the Butler house." Detective Sergeant Price's pleasant tenor sounded ebullient. "Do you want me to bring them to you?"

I picked up the envelope and moved close to the wall.

Cobb's mouth spread in a satisfied smile. "I can wait until tomorrow. I was there. I didn't think it would do any good to wire Leon. I thought for sure there would be a shot with no warning like the brick plant." He paused, a frown tugging at his brows. "That's probably what would have happened except for Peg Flynn showing up. My guess is that when Satterlee saw her car, he decided to come inside and see what was up. That changed everything."

"Yeah." There was an odd tone in Price's voice. "You know, that was strange at the end, when a woman shouted for help."

Cobb's expression was uneasy. "Yeah. Strange."

"Thing about it is," Price ruminated, "the shout seemed to come from the stairs, from right beside Satterlee. Peg Flynn has a high sweet voice. The voice that called out was throaty, kind of husky. Kind of . . . unforgettable."

Cobb scrambled in the M&M's bag, grabbed a bunch, tossed them in his mouth.

"In fact"—Price was emphatic—"if I hadn't seen what happened, I would have said Cain getting to Satterlee without being shot was impossible. Cain ducked past me like he was running downfield with the ball but he was a good ten feet from the stairs. How did he get there without being hit?"

"Crazy guy," Cobb muttered.

Price's laughter was wry and rueful. "Known as woman power, Chief."

"I understand. But he's a brave kid."

"Brave and lucky. Or"—Price's tone was thoughtful—"blessed. Satterlee fired into the wall. Why'd he shoot into the wall? If he'd shot straight, a slug should have caught Cain in the chest."

Cobb munched M&M's. "Cops have to work with facts." His voice was indistinct. "All we know is, Cain got there in time."

"Who was the woman who called out for help?"

"Let's keep it simple. There was a woman in the room. A woman shouted. Let's leave it there."

"Whatever you say, boss. That's not the only odd thing."

Cobb grabbed more M&M's. "Yeah?"

"Who moved Susan Flynn's body?" Price demanded. "For sure it wasn't Tucker Satterlee. Why would he? But if the body hadn't been moved, nobody would ever have suspected murder. If somebody found Mrs. Flynn dead and staged that fake crime scene, it almost has to mean someone saw Tucker on the stairs when he shouldn't have been or near the chocolate pot and was worried about murder. So there are three women in the house. Who would protect Tucker Satterlee but still want police to suspect murder? The only likely person was Gina Satterlee. Yet I don't think she would have upset the applecart or done anything to jeopardize inheriting."

Chief Cobb doodled on the legal pad, a series of question marks. "Well"—his voice was hearty—"all we have to know is that someone did us a big favor."

Price suddenly laughed. "I get you. Be grateful for favors and don't try to figure everything out. Right. But I've got some ideas about what happened and I keep thinking, one of these days I'll walk into a room and there will be a gorgeous redhead smiling at me. I'd like that, Sam."

"Next time there's a tough case, maybe she'll show up. Anyway"—Cobb was abruptly brusque—"wrap it up for tonight. Have a good holiday."

"You too, Chief."

Cobb flicked off the speakerphone.

I was standing next to the blackboard. I placed the envelope in the chalk tray, picked up a piece of chalk, wrote in looping script:

Compli—

At the first squeak of the chalk, Chief Cobb shoved back his chair and was on his feet, striding to the blackboard.

—ments of Officer M. Loy

I returned the chalk to the tray, next to the envelope.

Chief Cobb watched the chalk in its downward swoop. His eyes locked on the envelope. As he picked up the letter with Susan Flynn's monogram, I moved out of the way. He pulled out Susan Flynn's handwritten will, then looked in every direction. "Officer Loy?"

I blew him a kiss and blew another for Detective Sergeant Price, my favorite blond homicide detective. I paused at the window and called out, "Merry Christmas, Sam," then whirled into the brightly lit night.

I was alert for the whistle of the Rescue Express as I stopped at Keith's bedside where he slept curled next to Big Bob. I settled on the chaise longue, thinking I would soon be gone, but the next morning was happy to realize that I'd apparently been granted one more day on this earthly sojourn.

Either Wiggins was too occupied in Tumbulgum to arrange for my departure, or perhaps, in his kindness, he had granted me the pleasure of being in Adelaide for Christmas Eve. Surely that augured well for future adven-missions.

Late Christmas Eve afternoon, Charlotte Hammond looked across the quiet room at her husband. Her tone was gentle. "Are we going, Hammond?"

He looked worn and tired, a figure of defeat. He stared down at his hands, flexed the fingers. "My arthritis is bothering me."

She waited, but there was understanding in her gaze and love.

He lifted his eyes. "I know. We always go to the service with them." He paused, cleared his throat. "Nothing will be the same without Susan. And"—the words came slowly, reluctantly—"I shouldn't have fought against the little boy getting everything. That wasn't the right thing to do. I'm glad they found Susan's will." His look at Charlotte was rueful. "I mean it. When Peg called and told me, it was hard to talk. I hope she understands. But I know it must be hard for Jake and Gina, too. Still, what does any of it matter when you think about Susan and Tucker. But I don't know if we'll make it. Susan's bequest will be a big help, but even so we may have to file for bankruptcy."

"It will be all right, Harrison." There was quiet confidence in her voice. "Maybe the bank will help. They say credit is loosening up. Whatever happens, let's not worry about anything tonight. Let's go over to Susan's and go to the service with them. Just as we always have."

He pushed up from his easy chair. "Sure. That's what we'll do." There was some of his old bluster in his voice. "What are we waiting for? It's time to go. They'll be waiting for us."

. . . .

Keith, his blond curls freshly brushed, his brown eyes curious, stood patiently as Jake Flynn tucked up another inch of a little boy's red bathrobe, fastening it with a safety pin. A packet of pins lay on the floor beside her. She looked over her shoulder at Peg. "Is that about right?" Despite a face puffy from tears, Jake was caught up in the cheer of the moment.

Peg knelt beside Keith, too. Peg was pale, her eyes reddened from a tear-filled night, but now in the lovely old room elegantly decorated for the holidays with the cheerful crackle of a fire, she was absorbed in judging the length of the hem on the bathrobe. She finally gave a decisive nod. "That's perfect."

Jake continued to lift and pin.

Charlotte smiled, her eyes soft. Harrison nodded in approval. "Keith will be the dandiest shepherd there."

Jake glanced up at Peg. "Is Dave coming?"

Peg stiffened. Her face was carefully expressionless. "No. Not tonight. Not any night. He called, and when I told him the new will had been found he started backing away. I hung up on him."

"Well, that's good riddance." Harrison was emphatic. "We don't need anyone like him in the family."

Jake looked sorrowful. "Oh, Peg."

Peg's quick smile was light and bright and eager. "I have a better date." Then she turned to Gina, abruptly sad and uncertain. "Johnny Cain is coming. Oh, Gina, do you mind terribly?"

Sunk in a chair near the fire, pale and drawn, Gina said abruptly, "I'm glad for you, Peg."

"Please come with us." Peg reached out a hopeful hand. "It will bring back good days, Gina. Remember how Mitch used to always try to knock off my angel wings?"

Gina almost managed a smile. She said steadily, "I'll come. I can't miss seeing Keith as a shepherd."

The early evening Christmas Eve service for families with young children had always been one of my favorites. The magnificent midnight service is triumphant and glorious, an outpouring of joy, but there is something heartfelt and touching when the younger children, to the vibrant sound of "Once in Royal David's City," come down the central aisle, the little boys in bathrobes as shepherds and the little girls with wire halos and cardboard angel wings, to gather around the wooden crib and sing "Away in the Manger," their childish voices rising in the sweetest song of all.

The front doorbell rang.

Peg looked uncertainly from Gina toward the hall.

"It's all right." Gina's voice was shaky yet firm.

Peg gave Gina a swift hug, then turned and ran quickly to the hall. In a moment, she was back in the living room, Johnny Cain close behind her. He was not in uniform this night. He was resplendent in a dark blue suit, white shirt, and red tie. He smiled first at Keith. "I like your robe. Hey, you're going to have fun tonight." Then Johnny looked across the room at Gina. There was a taut silence that he finally broke. "I'm sorry about Tucker."

Gina lifted trembling fingers to flick away tears. "You were there for Peg. You saved Peg."

Peg lifted a hand to her throat, gazed at Johnny with remembered horror in her eyes. "I don't know how you managed to reach Tucker in time."

Johnny shook his head. "God knows."

And that was true.

Peg abruptly moved to Johnny. He reached out, took her in his arms, held her tight. Jake came to her feet, moved to curve her arms around her daughter and her rescuer. Charlotte and Harrison and Gina came across the room and they all held one another, moving only to make room for Keith as he joined them with a whoop, ready for a holiday scrum.

In the distance, I heard the whistle of the Rescue Express.

Outside I circled high above Adelaide, glorying one last time in the brilliance of the holiday lights. I heard clear and sweet and beautiful the strains of "It Came Upon a Midnight Clear," a midnight such as this.

I swung aboard the Express with both pleasure and trepidation. There had been some moments during my advenmission that Wiggins would likely mention without pleasure. Yet I had accomplished my primary task. Keith Flynn was safe in the arms of his family.

I popped into the first carriage and headed for a comfortable seat, ready to enjoy my farewell views of lights blazing from dear planet earth on this night when joy lifted hearts and souls. The carriage was filled with travelers of all sorts and backgrounds, some shabbily dressed, some elegant, but all with happy faces. There was an air of festivity and a sense of eagerness.

The gray-haired conductor, tall and thin with smiling eyes, gently took my elbow. "Compartment 3, please, in the next carriage."

A private compartment! Perhaps I had been promoted. As I reached the door at the end of the corridor, I looked back, wishing I could stay and meet some of my fellow travelers, perhaps exchange stories of derring-do.

Trains always afford excitement, the lurch and swing as the heavy door is pushed open. I felt the jostle and jolt of the connecting plates and lurched to the opposite door. The next carriage was very quiet, compartment doors lining either side of the corridor. I hurried to Compartment 3, tapped. The door swung open. I stepped inside.

Wiggins rose to greet me. "Bailey Ruth." There was warmth and kindness in his tone.

At his nod, I sank onto the opposite plush seat. I feared the worst. Had I been invited to a private compartment because my contraventions of the Precepts for Earthly Travel were so egregious they must be addressed before the Rescue Express reached Heaven?

Wiggins settled onto the plush seat, next to a black topcoat. He was imposing in his stiff white shirt and broad suspenders and heavy gray flannel trousers. His hair was a bright chestnut beneath the stiff, dark station agent's hat. He lifted a hand to smooth his walrus mustache. "I was pleased when I learned you would be on the Express tonight."

Pleased? I managed a stiff smile. "I'm happy to see you." Was insincerity a bar to any future adven-missions?

He suddenly boomed with laughter. "You didn't follow the Precepts. But"—he leaned forward—"I must share a truth with you."

I scarcely breathed. This was the moment when I would learn of my permanent banishment from the Department of Good Intentions, though it was rather cruel of Wiggins to find the prospect so amusing.

"In Tumbulgum"—and his brown eyes gleamed with delight—"neither did I."

Turn the page for a sneak peek at Carolyn Hart's next Bailey Ruth mystery

GHOST IN TROUBLE

Available in hardcover in October 2010 from William Morrow

I *lounged on a deck* chair, comfortable in an orange polka-dot bikini. A breeze fluttered the brim of my wide-brimmed straw hat. Unlike the sun, Heaven's golden light never burns, but a lovely white straw is always flattering to a redhead. Oh, you're wondering about Heaven. Heaven, Montana? Heaven, Florida? Not even close.

I said Heaven. I meant Heaven. Quite possibly that calm statement either amuses or offends you. The worldly dismiss Heaven as a fable. With kindly, condescending smiles or cold sneers, they refuse to face up to the Hereafter. Their choice is to whistle while Rome burns. That's fine. They can tap-dance until the curtain falls, but they mustn't expect to take any bows. However, I would be lacking in candor—never one of my failings—if I didn't frankly state that Heaven is my customary residence.

I am Bailey Ruth Raeburn, late of Adelaide, Oklahoma, population 16,234. My husband, Bobby Mac, and I were lost in a Gulf storm on *Serendipity*, our beloved cabin cruiser. Bobby Mac was—and is—a fishing fool. It was his determination to track a tarpon that led to our precipitous arrival here in the latter part of the last century, but we've never lost our love for sea, sand, and serenity.

Today the *Serendipity*, as bright and fresh as on her launch day, rocked in a swell in turquoise waters. I enjoyed happy memories and admired Bobby Mac's tanned back as he struggled against the strength of a determined tarpon.

Bobby Mac and I fell in love in high school. I was a

skinny, redheaded sophomore and he was a black-haired laughing senior. We are still in love and having fun a lifetime and beyond. He's definitely the handsomest man in Heaven, but most of all I treasure his boisterous eagerness. Bobby Mac never met a steak he couldn't eat, an oil well he wouldn't drill, or a beautiful woman he didn't notice. Of course, he always assured me I was the loveliest of all. What a guy, then and now.

I was content, drowsing in the golden light, enjoying the gentle rock of the boat, occasionally waving to friends in other boats, feeling quite sublime.

A telegram sprouted from my hand.

I knew at once the telegram must be from Wiggins. Who else still tapped a Teletype to make contact? Wiggins had sent me a telegram! Nicely enough in Heaven, there's never a need to wait. A message arrives at once. A friend remembered suddenly appears. Wherever you want to go, there you are. Solitude is yours if you wish. Companionship is available instantly. In need of spiritual rousing? Saint Teresa of Avila strides along a mountain path, smiling, talking, welcoming everyone. Ready to laugh? Lucille Ball and Desi Arnaz's new skit is as funny as their long-ago movie about the vacation trailer. Want to perfect your culinary skills? Julia Child's kitchen is simply Heavenly and her reminiscences of World War II derring-do riveting. You suddenly recall your childhood friend who helped you staff a lemonade stand on hot August days? Why, here she is, smiling, arms wide. Perhaps you always wanted to play the piano? Fingers flying, ragtime pounds.

I jumped to my feet. "Bobby Mac, a telegram!" I tore open the yellow envelope, read aloud, my voice rising in eagerness, " 'Urgent Delivery to Bailey Ruth Raeburn. Skulduggery afoot in Adelaide. Come at once if interested. Wiggins.' "

At the bottom of the telegram was Wiggins's special

stamp of a shiny silver locomotive bearing the legend: *Department of Good Intentions.*

Bobby Mac held tight to his bending rod as he looked over his shoulder. "Are you sure, sweetheart? You had quite a challenge when you helped Susan Flynn."

I flapped the telegram, dismissing the past. "Everything will go better this time." Wiggins, who can be a bit stiff, had actually unbent with an approving smile after my last adven—mission to earth.

Bobby Mac grinned. "What are the odds? You have a talent for trouble."

I blew him a kiss and zoomed away. Bobby Mac understood. He couldn't resist the lure of fishing. As for me? I was already excited.

Skulduggery.

How Heavenly.

Dashes of pink and gold highlighted the arched clouds at the entrance to the Department of Good Intentions. There was a welcoming glow, warm as a friendly smile.

As I'm sure I've explained before, the department is under the supervision of Wiggins. In the early days of the twentieth century, he was station agent at a train depot. When he came to Heaven and was given the opportunity to continue assisting travelers (and all earthly creatures, whether they know it or not, are surely travelers in the best sense of the word), he joyfully re-created a small, red-brick country train station with a wooden platform and tracks running away into the sky.

When the signal arm dropped and the Rescue Express thundered on the rails, sparks flying, dark smoke curling to infinity, my heart raced. I wanted to leap aboard immediately, a blithe spirit.

The first time I'd approached the department, I'd felt anxious. I had no idea whether I would be welcome. Happily, Wiggins had immediately made me feel at home. In fact, he'd commented that he'd been expecting me.

Wiggins obviously had been well aware that I wanted to offer my services to his department. He knew how grateful I was to the brave and generous sailor who'd saved my life when I was a girl and I fell off an excursion boat en route to Catalina. I still remembered the shocking coldness of the sea. A deckhand had jumped into the water and saved me. Thanks to him, I enjoyed a full and happy life. Ever since I'd arrived in Heaven, I'd been eager to offer help to someone in trouble.

Wiggins and the Department of Good Intentions gave me that chance, sending me to my beloved hometown in hilly, south-central Oklahoma. I knew the terrain, understood the mores.

Admittedly, there had been a few mishaps. Perhaps I'd become visible—not a desired status for a Heavenly emissary—a bit more often than the department wished. You will note that I avoid using the term *ghost.* Wiggins insisted that we consider ourselves emissaries. Ghosts, you see, have an unfortunate reputation on earth and evoke quite pitiful reactions of fear and shock. In any event, I had appeared a good deal more than Wiggins considered desirable. Moreover, he remained doubtful about the pleasure I took in the new styles. I'd pointed out that a naked emissary or, Heaven forfend, an emissary droopily draped in an ill-fitting sheet, would surely be more shocking. I'd simply taken advantage of the ease afforded me as a traveling spirit. All I had to do was envision clothing and I was clothed. I saw no reason to eschew fashion. What was the moral worth of appearing as a frumpy emissary?

He'd had no answer to that.

Now, as I hurried through the station waiting room to his office, I could scarcely contain my excitement. I passed under the lintel with the sign marked STATION AGENT. There was no door. Heaven has no need for doors. No one is shut in. Or out.

The office was just as I remembered. From his golden oak desk positioned in the big bay window, Wiggins could look out and see the platform and shining silver tracks. He sat in his desk chair, head bent, green eyeshade hiding the upper portion of his face, finger rapidly tapping the telegraph key.

I didn't want to interrupt. I edged inside, waited behind him. Was I ready? I'd dressed more formally than usual in a pale blue springlike tweed suit. Not a heavy tweed. Indeed, a rather ethereal tweed as befitted a vivacious though equally ethereal redhead. A rose floral pin added a softening note and rose leather sandals afforded a jaunty air. I felt a moment of unease. Too jaunty? Quickly the artificial flower and sandals changed into a matching blue. My nose wrinkled. Boring, but perhaps it would be best if Wiggins thought me a trifle boring.

I patted one of the jacket's patch pockets. Wiggins's telegram crinkled. In my other hand, I held a roll of parchment which contained the Precepts. Unlike my first visit to the department, I now knew the Precepts well, but I hoped bringing the parchment roll might impress Wiggins. While he was engaged, I unrolled the parchment and admired the ornate gold gothic letters:

Precepts for Earthly Visitation

1. Avoid public notice.
2. No consorting with other departed spirits.
3. Work behind the scenes without making your presence known.

4. Become visible only when absolutely essential.
5. Do not succumb to the temptation to confound those who appear to oppose you.
6. Make every effort not to alarm earthly creatures.
7. Information about Heaven is not yours to impart. Simply smile and say, "Time will tell."
8. Remember always that you are *on* the earth, not *of* the earth.

This time I would remember each and every Precept. This time . . .

"Wiggins, I'm here." I intended to sound cool and casual, but my voice—eager, bubbly, and excited—gave me away.

Wiggins's wooden chair swung about. He came to his feet, large face breaking into a warm smile. Shining chestnut curls poked from beneath the green eyeshade. His walrus mustache gleamed in Heaven's golden glow. He was unmistakably of his time, high-collared white shirt stiff with starch. Arm garters between his elbows and shoulders puffed the upper sleeves. Substantial suspenders and a wide black belt held up heavy gray wool trousers. Black leather high-top shoes glistened with polish. His golden brown eyes glowed. "Bailey Ruth. Good of you to respond. I knew you would. Your intentions are always of the best."

There was an unmistakable emphasis on *intentions*.

I dismissed a suspicion that he sounded like a man trying to convince himself.

"In any event"—he looked harried—"matters may soon be out of control. We are very concerned. I feel that a woman's delicate touch is needed. And there isn't anyone else available who knows Adelaide."

I decided to overlook the implication that he'd scraped the bottom of the volunteer barrel.

He waved me to a seat beside his desk and settled in his

chair. His face furrowed. "Before we get into the particulars, let's discuss the Precepts. The last two times you were dispatched in such a rush, you hadn't had time to study them. I'm sure that accounted for"—he cleared his throat—"a rather wholesale departure from the directives."

He opened a drawer and pulled out a thick folder. When he opened it, I recognized the untidy mass of paper that had comprised my initial report. He skimmed through it, murmuring aloud about the flying crowbar in the mausoleum, impersonation of a police officer, liberation of the tan-and-black hound . . . His face drew down in a frown as he reminded himself about my Christmas visit at a historic Adelaide home. ". . . serious breach of Precept Two . . . and Precepts Three and Four . . ." He looked discouraged. "Your efforts are well meant but"—he shook his head—"so often you don't stop and think."

Actually, I often did stop and think, but possibly I should not share that truth with Wiggins. I scooted to the edge of the hard wooden bench. "Wiggins, this time I will have everything under control." I placed one hand on my heart, looked deep into his golden brown eyes, and quoted the Precepts verbatim. From memory. In the sixth grade I'd won a prize for reciting "Thanatopsis." The Precepts were a snap in comparison. If I do say so myself, I spoke with resolution and beautifully clear diction and concluded, "Now that I am aware of my obligations, you can count on me. I shall be the most tactful, behind-the-scenes, unobtrusive emissary ever!"

A flicker of a smile touched his face. His eyes softened. "A willing heart counts for much. That's what Heaven is all about."

I maintained a look of selflessness or as near as I could manage, selflessness not being a customary attitude for an energetic, exuberant redhead who loves to tango, reel in a fish, or cherish a romantic moment in the moonlight.

Slowly, he nodded. "Very well." He slapped my folder shut, reached for a slim file on his desktop. "Kay Clark intends to stir things up. That can be dangerous." His tone was grave. "Foolhardy. She has returned to Adelaide after an absence of many years. She is still as willful and headstrong and reckless—"

I watched a flush mount in his cheeks. I'd never seen Wiggins so exercised.

"—as ever. Of course, free will complicates everything." He looked at me doubtfully.

"Free will." I gave him a bright smile.

He looked pained.

Possibly that wasn't the response he'd hoped for. Quickly, I achieved an expression of thoughtful inquiry and folded my hands prayerfully. "Free will." My tone was musing, almost rueful. I tried to imply that I spent much of my time engrossed in this fascinating topic. Actually, I'd never given free will a thought.

"Ah, well." His tone was long-suffering. "We can only work with the materials we have at hand. But there is that complicating factor . . ." He flipped through sheets, muttering to himself. "Oh, my." He shut the folder. "I'm in a quandary. Perhaps another volunteer would be a better choice."

"Wiggins, please pick me. You know how much I love Adelaide. I can handle anything. I promise."

Wiggins leaned back in his chair, stared at me. "Very well. Let me give you a brief history. The family circumstance is exceedingly complicated and the situation is exceedingly volatile. You'll be spending most of your time at The Castle."

"The Castle!" I felt a quiver of delight. The Castle was Adelaide's showplace, built by J.J. Hume, an oil baron. Bobby Mac found oil, too, but he was a wildcatter, not a multimillionaire. The Castle, a Mission-style mansion with a series of descending terraces, sat high on Spotted Owl Ridge. The spectacular centerpiece was an active pump jack in the middle of the garden. As J.J. had told his wife, "Roses are fine, but nothing smells as sweet as fresh crude."

I'd attended charity balls and civic functions there. Every small town has its aristocracy. In Adelaide, the Pritchards and the Humes fulfilled those roles in strikingly different fashion. The Pritchards were aloof, elegant, and the great patrons of St. Mildred's Episcopal Church. The Humes . . . Suffice it to say that J.J. was a hard-drinking, rabblerousing iconoclast, though his long-suffering wife, Millie, was a stalwart Baptist who loved her Sunday school class and spent much of her life murmuring, "J.J. didn't mean . . ."

I beamed at Wiggins. "The Castle is amazing. It has a ballroom and a balcony and terraces. A terrazzo-paved avenue framed by Italian cypress leads from the lower terrace to the site where the Millie number one was drilled." At Wiggins's puzzled look, I smiled. "The oil well in the garden. I think J.J. had a sense of humor. Honestly, to frame a pump jack and tank battery between rows of Italian cypress!"

Wiggins continued to look bewildered. I gave him a crash course in oil terminology, explaining how when a well was completed—and the Millie number one was a fabulous well, pumping three hundred barrels a day—the rig was replaced with a pump jack. The big silver tank held the recovered oil. "J.J. said a pump jack and tank battery were better than sculpture any day. Of course, every big windstorm knocked over the cypress, but J.J. had new ones planted the next day. Does The Castle still belong to the Humes?"

I had a vivid memory of J.J.'s darkly handsome grandson

Everett. My daddy referred to Everett as a good-for-nothing lout. But oh, how he could dance. I had once been tempted . . . But that was long ago. Bobby Mac had simply picked me up from the dance floor (actually our high school gym) and carried me out the door. What a guy. My attraction to the brooding Everett dissolved in the mists of memory, overwhelmed by images of Bobby Mac. Especially that wonderful summer we'd tramped through Europe . . . As I recalled, Everett came to no good end.

". . . and so the current family included J.J. IV, known as Jack." Suddenly I realized I'd missed a goodly portion of Wiggins's reply.

". . . and Diane, his brother's widow, is no match for Kay Clark. Diane seems to believe everything she's told. Not a sensible course in life. Diane lacks sophistication. She has a sweet nature." Wiggins sighed. "It is sad that those with kindly hearts often are vulnerable to manipulation. Although I will admit that Kay's scheme is clever. However, duplicity is reprehensible even if in a good cause." A reproving sniff. "As for the Humes . . . oh well, free will."

"Free will," I repeated with an air of complete understanding.

"But, given all of those facts, are you willing to do your best?" His gaze was searching.

"Of course." I didn't want Wiggins to know I had no idea of the facts or my duties. Once I arrived, I'd quickly discern what I needed to know. Look, listen, act—that was my motto. I shot a quick glance at Wiggins. Had he picked up on my thought? It might suggest impulsiveness. "I will proceed with caution."

Wiggins looked pleased, as well he might, since my lack of caution had always been one of his concerns.

I felt ennobled. This time I would be a model emissary. "Behind the scenes."

Wiggins's obvious relief was almost pitiable. "Bailey Ruth, I should have known I could count on you." His voice was admiring. "Such a refined spirit."

How lovely to think of myself as a refined spirit. And soon to be a traveling spirit. I was ready to go, but I didn't want to hurry Wiggins. Perhaps he would think of me as not only boring, but far above earthly temptations.

"Although an emissary such as you, endowed with both beauty and charm"—he gave me a gallant nod though his eyes were worried—"is perhaps in more danger of reverting to worldly ways. Not," he added hastily, "that I would expect you of all people to forget Heavenly attitudes." It would have been nice had his voice contained more assurance.

"Reversion." I dismissed the possibility with a casual wave of pink-tipped fingers. Wiggins worried a good deal that one of his emissaries, when on the earth, would revert to earthly attitudes, that is, succumb to anger, jealousy, suspicion, or any of the other undesirable passions. That possibility was the least of my worries. Why would I revert?

"All right." He was businesslike. "We fear for Kay Clark's safety—"

A staccato *dot dot dot* sounded from the telegraph sender on his desk.

Wiggins's eyes widened. He bent near, tapped a rapid response.

The sender's *clack clack* was frenzied.

Frowning darkly, Wiggins pulled down his eyeshade, wrote with a dark-leaded pencil on a pad. The instant he finished, he pushed back his chair, gestured to me.

"You must leave immediately. An emergency. I hope you arrive in time." He dashed to the ticket window, grabbed a white slip of cardboard, stamped it.

I took it, saw the bright red marking—ADELAIDE—and ran for the platform. The Rescue Express was thundering on the rails. I grabbed a handrail and swung aboard, eager for my journey. Over the mournful yet exuberant peal of the train whistle, I heard Wiggins shout, "Save Kay Clark if you can!"

I clung to a handrail as the express shot across the sky. I was on my way and the refrain sounded in time with the wheels.

. . . on my way . . . on my way . . . on my way . . .